# Rustication

"Palliser's hold on his narrative is enough to turn it into an exercise in pure form. As in a superior detective novel, character, scene and incidental detail fade away and all that remains is the thrill of the chase." —D. J. Taylor, *The Spectator*

"Few historical novelists weave such complexly absorbing plots as Charles Palliser and *Rustication* shows him delighting in his skill. . . . A twisting, mesmerizing story." —Nick Rennison, *The Sunday Times*

"The set-up is pure sensation novel . . . and his plotting is as tight as a Victorian corset. His nerve is admirable, too." —Michael Prodger, *The Financial Times*

"[A] delicious wicked, twisted Gothic tale that turns the cosy Victorian family drama on its head. . . . Palliser is an old hand at creating suspense and raising narrative tension, and he excels at it here in this literary page-turner." —*The Scotsman*

"A supremely confident performance." —*The Literary Review*

"When opium-addled Richard Shenstone, the 17-year-old narrator of Charles Palliser's Gothic melodrama, grabs your hand and leads you into his twisted world of sexual obsession, murder, and sadistic letters (which may or may not be Richard's doing), you won't want to let go. The newly destitute Shenstones are forced to inhabit a dilapidated old mansion where Richard's unsteady mind makes much out of rooms with beds made for people he's never met and things that go bump in the night. Though the house isn't the source of evil, it deserves lots of credit for the book's spooky atmosphere."

—Julie Buntin, *The Huffington Post*

"Readers will have as much grisly fun just sorting out the facts as they will solving the mysteries." —Nicholas Mancusi, *The Daily Beast*

"Engrossing . . . rich, dark and evocative."

—Tucker Shaw, *The Denver Post*

"Palliser has gone and done it again. . . . [H]e has created a story so engrossing that you'll be flipping the pages in desperation trying to discover the mystery surrounding the characters. . . . Those who enjoy Gothic-esque novels and historical fiction will enjoy this book, with Palliser's dark humour and graphic scenes firmly woven into the story." —Press Association (UK)

"Charles Palliser is a wonderful novelist, and *Rustication* is a wonderful novel." —Iain Pears, author of *An Instance of the Fingerpost*

"*Rustication* is an ingenious take on the traditional Victorian Gothic novel, daring us to unravel the dark and twisting tale of a murder that hasn't happened yet. Charles Palliser takes us on a harrowing journey with a questionable narrator as he desperately tries to unravel a host of shadowy movements and motivations, including his own. The gripping voice and masterful plotting swirl together in a relentless undertow of gothic intrigue and dread that's impossible to resist. Not that you'll want to. This is a brilliant read."

—Kieran Shields, author of *The Truth of All Things*

"Charles Palliser's new novel, *Rustication*, is a wonderful, sly, compelling tale of mischief, greed, and malice. His narrator, Richard Shenstone, is so marvelously and credibly naïve that I couldn't stop turning the pages, hoping he would recognize before it was too late that what he doesn't know could well be the death of him."

—Valerie Martin, author of *Property*

"Charles Palliser is one of our finest writers and a new novel from him is always cause to celebrate. *Rustication* is a book for lovers of mystery and suspense, for those who enjoy reading between the lines of the text. Palliser turns the reader into a detective as the story unfolds: who is writing these vicious letters? And what is their purpose? How much can we trust the narrator's account of events? This is an extremely clever novel in which not only is there a mystery in the invented nineteenth-century world of the story but also a mystery about the nature of the text the reader is reading. Here is a book to satisfy fans of Wilkie Collins and Vladimir Nabokov."

—Jane Harris, author of *The Observations*

*also by* CHARLES PALLISER

*The Unburied*

*Betrayals*

*The Sensationist*

*The Quincunx*

# Rustication

❧ A NOVEL ❧

## CHARLES PALLISER

W. W. NORTON & COMPANY

NEW YORK   LONDON

For information about permission to reproduce selections from this book,
write to Permissions, W. W. Norton & Company, Inc.
500 Fifth Avenue, New York, NY 10110

For information about special discounts for bulk purchases, please contact
W. W. Norton Special Sales at specialsales@wwnorton.com or 800-233-4830

Manufacturing by Courier Westford
Book design by Fearn Cutler de Vicq
Production manager: Devon Zahn

Library of Congress Cataloging-in-Publication Data

Palliser, Charles, 1947–
Rustication : a novel / Charles Palliser. — First Edition.
pages cm
ISBN 978-0-393-08872-4 (hardcover)
1. Young men—Fiction. 2. London (England)—Fiction. I. Title.
PR6066.A43R87 2014
823'.914—dc23
2013031249

ISBN 978-0-393-34981-8 pbk.

W. W. Norton & Company, Inc.
500 Fifth Avenue, New York, N.Y. 10110
www.wwnorton.com

W. W. Norton & Company Ltd.
Castle House, 75/76 Wells Street, London W1T 3QT

1 2 3 4 5 6 7 8 9 0

*For Marcus*

# Rustication

# ⅜ *Foreword* ⅝

What follows is my transcription of a document which has lain unnoticed for many years in the County Records Office in Thurchester. It is a Journal which casts light on a murder that attracted national interest at the time but which, since nobody was ever charged with the crime, was subsequently forgotten.

The book in which it is written is a leatherbound quarto volume of three hundred pages of unlined paper of which the Journal takes up two hundred and eighty. At an unknown date in the past someone had pasted into it a number of the anonymous letters relating to the case. I have reproduced them exactly as and where I found them. One of them, however, was not stuck into the Journal but came from another source and it is the last and the most revealing.

This is part of that letter:

> *You think you can fuck any girl you like and just walk away because of who you are. Well you can fuck your whores as much as you please but if you lay hands on a decent girl you must pay for it. I don't mean*

*money. I am going to make you pay with
your blood. You think you have got away
with it. But you are wrong. You won't be
able to hide behind your friends the next time
we meet. I am going to kill you but before
I do that I am going to hurt you so badly
you will scream for mercy. You are so proud
of your cock. See if it will get you an heir
when it's stuffed down your lying throat!*

That threat was executed in full.

Near the end of the Journal a police-officer reads out a section of that letter but admits that he has not been allowed to see the whole. I was intrigued by that and, wondering if something crucial had been suppressed, I decided to try to find the original. I will return to that topic in my Afterword.

CP.

## The Journal of Richard Shenstone:
### 12<sup>th</sup> of December 1863 to 13<sup>th</sup> of January 1864

*Saturday 12<sup>th</sup> of December, 10 o'clock at night.*

I'm baffled by Mother's reception of me. I'm sure she blurted out either *William* or *Willy* when I caught her by surprise. But I can't think of anyone of that name she could have taken me for and I don't see how she could have been expecting a visitor at such a late hour in this out-of-the-way place. What is even stranger is that she wasn't pleased to see me.

As for Effie! She was obviously horrified at the sight of her brother.

I wonder how long I will be able to endure this benighted backwater. When I lifted a corner of the curtain and looked out a moment ago I saw nothing but the moon shining palely across the silvery expanse of mud and waves—both so smooth that it's hard to see where the marsh ends and the sea begins. Nothing. Not a house. Not a light.

I'm astonished that the house is in this state. Almost nothing seems to have been done to make it habitable. Yet they've been here for weeks.

And I have lost my trunk! Because that wretched carter who brought me from Thurchester station was afraid of getting stuck in the mud, he forced me to deposit it at a grimy beer-shop along the way. And the brute of a landlord charged me a shilling but would not give me three minutes to unlock it and remove its precious contents. From now on I must keep an account of my expenses and not fall into the old ways. That should not be hard: there is nothing here to spend my money on.

. . .

*Memorandum:* OPENING BALANCE: *13s. 4½d.* EXPENDITURE: Carriage to Whitminster (*2s. 3d.*) and storage of trunk at 4d. per diem for three days (*1s.*) TOTAL EXP: *3s. 3d.* FINAL BALANCE: *10s. 1½d.*

. . .

Then 2 hours on foot along a winding muddy way until at last I rounded a threadbare hedgerow and before me lay an inland bay filled by a salt-marsh that spread towards the distant sea like a great black stain of ink on a blotter. In the fading twilight I could just see an ancient house with a muddle of high chimneys like an age-bent hand raised against the grey sky. This truly is the last place in England.

I opened the iron-studded door and found myself in a large hallway with an ancient oak staircase. It had black panelled walls and narrow casement windows. No fire burned in the hearth. The place was so dark and musty that I believed I must have mistaken the house.

I passed through one comfortless chamber after another, ducking my head beneath the low cornices of the doorways. Then in a cramped scullery lit by a flickering oil-lamp, I came suddenly upon a little old woman bent over a sideboard with her back to me. She turned. It was the mater! For a moment she recognised me no better than I had recognised her.

That's when she said: *Willy? I wasn't expecting you so early.*

I said: *Who is "Willy"?*

*Richard? Is that you?* Now she sounded frightened.

*Who did you think it was, Mother?*

She came towards me and I thought she was going to kiss me

but she only stretched out her hand and touched my coat as if she thought I were a phantasm.

*Who is the "Willy" you expected?*

*I did not call you "Willy". You misheard me. I cried out in astonishment because I didn't think you were coming until after Christmas.*

I said: *Why weren't you expecting me?*

*I thought you were going on a walking holiday.*

*Didn't you get my letter?*

She shook her head.

I had overtaken it!

I said: *Mother, aren't you glad I'm back?*

She came up to me at last and raising herself on tiptoes, she kissed me. Then she stood back and looked at me. *You're thin, Richard. You haven't been eating well.*

It's odd how one's mother treats one as an object. She was eyeing me as if I were an old table she was thinking of purchasing. I was almost afraid she would kick my legs to see how they sounded.

Then she said: *Stay here. Your sister should know you've come.*

I was astonished. Effie was here! How could my fastidious sister endure the darkness, the dirt, the lack of gas, of carpets?

I raised my candle. On the sideboard was a neatly folded pile of bed-linen and towels, two pillows—all starched and ironed—and two enamelled metal basins. She watched me looking at them. Was someone unwell?

*No*, she said, *it's better if I take you to your room first. Where is your trunk?*

*I had to leave it at The Black Lion. The carrier will bring it when the weather improves.*

She turned and led me through a series of dark little rooms.

*This is a strange old place*, I said as I followed her through low doors and along dark passages. *You inherited it when your father died?*

She hesitated and then said: *Yes. Herriard House is mine. It has been in my family for centuries.*

We climbed a staircase and then walked the length of a corridor whose uneven floorboards creaked like twittering birds.

She pushed open a door and showed me into a big gloomy old chamber with a four-poster bed. It smelled musty.

*I'll have the girl bring you some hot water. You'll want to wash after your long journey.*

*The girl?*

*The servant. Betsy.*

*I suppose none of the old servants could be induced to come out here?*

*Come down as soon as you're ready, Richard. We dine early here.*

She left me.

After a few minutes there was a mouselike scratching at the door and in came a little creature bent over and carrying a jug of hot water. I could not see her face clearly as she kept it averted. Just to get her to turn round I said: *Is your name Bessy?*

Without looking up, she muttered: *Betsy, sir.* Then she scuttled out.

I washed my face and changed my linen and went down the stairs.

As I reached the hall, suddenly there was Effie. She appeared as astonished to see me as I was to encounter her. And, moreover, she had obviously been out in the rain. We stood facing each other in the dim light. She looked as if she were about to attend an evening party: She wore her hair up and was in a dark green velvet gown I'm sure I had never seen before. It left her shoulders perfectly bare and was cut so low that it emphasised her bosom in the most striking manner. There were raindrops running down her naked shoulders and onto her front and into the top of her bodice. She has become a very handsome girl—tall, black hair, large grey eyes, regular features.

When I was young she had no hesitation in undressing in my presence down to her shift and even beyond that, but one day when I was about twelve she saw me looking at her and I don't know what she saw on my face but she never did it again.

Without a word she showed me her back and hurried up the stairs.

I found the mater in a large room at the back of the building. She was sitting, as I had seen her a thousand times in the other house, working at an embroidery-frame.

I said: *You didn't tell me we are dressing for dinner.*

She said: *What are you referring to, Richard?*

I told her I had just seen Effie togged up like a costermonger's wife on a Saturday night.

*Then I assume your sister has made a special effort to dress up for you.*

Then why did she respond in that way? Like a deer staring at the stalker's gun and then loping away?

Mother went on: *Your sister is a very beautiful young woman and it gives her pleasure to adorn herself. She has had few opportunities to do so since we left town.* She added, with a little fluttering smile: *She reminds me so much of myself at that age.*

As I sat down she asked: *Why are you here, Richard? I believed you were going to the Lakes.*

*As it turned out, I couldn't afford to.*

*It seems a shame you should lose that pleasure after what you've been through.*

*Mother, you're the one who has borne the brunt of it. I should have been by your side for the funeral.*

*What could* you *have done?* she said almost angrily.

*I wish you had told me at the time. You must have known it would be in the newspapers.*

She said: *I thought it was for the best. I won't discuss it now.*

(*For the best!* That meant I had the shock of reading about Father's death in a newspaper.)

I said: *Mother, I still don't know what happened. At the end, I mean.*

*We're talking about your holiday, Richard. If it's a matter of money, I can give you a little.*

*I'm very grateful, Mother, but it's too late. Unfortunately, my friend is now unable to go.*

She went on with her work and said: *It would be better if you went away now and came back when we've made the house fit for habitation.*

*I want to help you do that.*

*This is women's work, Richard. You'd be in the way. Why don't you go and visit Thomas?*

That was a surprise. *Uncle Thomas?* I said. *Are you and he in touch now?*

*I wrote to him, of course, to tell him his brother had died.*

(Yet she didn't write to me!)

*And he came to the funeral,* she added rather nervously.

*He came to the funeral,* I repeated. *Mother, you sent me that telegram telling me to stay in Cambridge and then I found I had missed the funeral!*

Without looking up she said: *I didn't invite Thomas. He came of his own accord. And there were things we had to talk about. Your Cambridge expenses, for example. He undertook to continue to pay them. And that's why you should go to him now—to thank him for all he is doing for you. And there might be more to follow.*

That was a horse I didn't want to saddle. And why was Mother suddenly favourable towards Uncle T? Even Father could never abide his own brother. Luckily fate came to my aid. *Is something burning?* I asked.

Almost without knowing it, I had become aware of a dark ancient smell as of things long decaying.

*Probably,* Mother said, rising to her feet. *I've left Betsy preparing dinner. I'd better go and try to rescue something edible.*

· · ·

She has aged so much. And she seems smaller. Seeing her like that for a few seconds when I believed she was a stranger, I realise that she is an old woman. She doesn't appear to be looking after herself as she used to. Her hair is straggling and her cheeks pale. She's wearing some faded old gown that I don't remember seeing before. What happened in November has added years to her. I wanted to tell her that I loved her but at just that instant she was less motherlike towards me than I have ever known her.

. . .

I took a candle and went to look for some of Father's wine in the dark little back-offices around the kitchen.

I struck lucky and located a dozen of Father's claret in a mouldy cupboard in the smallest scullery. I noticed that the towels and metal pans I had seen earlier had gone.

When I joined Mother in the dining-room she looked meaning-fully at the bottle but said nothing.

At last my sister deigned to descend and it was clear that she was late because she had changed out of her fine clothes. Did I get an affectionate greeting and a sisterly kiss? Far from it. She came in and sat down without even looking at me even though it was the first time we'd met since I'd gone away at the beginning of October. Not counting our strange encounter just a few minutes earlier.

*I'm very pleased to see you, Effie,* I said.

*How long, may I enquire, are we to have the pleasure of your company?* she asked.

*Until I choose to go.*

*Children,* Mother said brightly, *we must try to make the best of things.*

*Richard is doing that already,* my sister said pointedly as I raised a glass to my lips.

*What's happened to the rest of Father's cellar?* I asked them. *He had some very fine wines. And all the books?*

*Your priorities are very revealing. The books come a poor second, I see.*

*We have some of his books,* Mother said. *I've put them in one of the rooms at the back of the house.*

Just then Betsy came in to serve the soup and now at last I glimpsed her face. Pale, large brown eyes, a thin mouth compressed as if in secret resolution.

When she had gone I attempted to identify the ingredients: *Something of the leather boot has certainly gone into it. And a sprinkling of sawdust with . . .*

*You're not being funny,* Effie interrupted.

I said very forbearingly: *I'm just trying to cheer us up. I know this has been difficult for you, Effie.*

*What do you know about it?* she said. *Father's death has made no difference to your life. Your expenses are being paid at your blessed college, thanks to Uncle Thomas. You'll go back there in a few weeks, I assume, and Mother and I will still be stuck in this muddy hole. You shouldn't even be here. Why did you come back so early?*

She stopped when Betsy returned to take away the bowls.

Seizing the chance to change the subject, I asked: *Have you met any of our new neighbours?*

*Do you imagine there's anybody here I would want to know? In this windswept marshland?*

*There must be some people worth knowing,* I said. *What about the church in Stratton Peverel? In my experience, where you find a church you find a parson and most of them, whatever their intellectual deficiencies, are at least able to read.*

*Mother, how long will we have to endure this childish facetiousness? He's come back more insufferable than ever.*

*Children, children,* the mater said reproachfully.

*I'm just saying that I'm sure there must be some society in this neighbourhood to make up for the friends we've left behind in the town,* I said.

*You never even had any friends in Thurchester. Everyone found you queer and eccentric. Apart from that odious creature you befriended at school. Are you claiming him as a friend?*

I don't know how she could ask that. Bartlemew and I had nothing in common at Harrow except that we came from the same town and, since we had won Scholarships, were both despised for being clever.

I said: *Mother, why did you come to live out here?*

*Oh for goodness' sake!* Effie exclaimed.

*We're very poor now, Richard.*

*I understand that. There is no stipend and of course that makes a differ-ence. But you must have a pension from the Church?*

*I'm not receiving a pension.*

*Why on earth not? It's been two months.*

*This isn't the moment to talk about it,* Mother said and glanced towards Betsy who had just come in carrying a large dish with a lid. She removed it and scurried out as if she wanted to be clear of the room before we could hold her to account. We all stared at our dinner. Some black lumps floated in a thick slurry of grease. Mother poked the contents nervously with a big spoon and then served it. It tasted no better than it looked.

Euphemia suddenly asked: *Why aren't you in the Lake District? You weren't expected for another week.*

*Richard won't be here long,* Mother said. *He's going to visit Uncle Thomas.*

*How soon?* my sister asked.

This was alarming. I said: *Mother, I have no cash and I can't think of taking money from you now.* I added for my own amusement: *Uncle Thomas will have to be patient.*

*I'll decide what I can afford to give you, Richard,* Mother said sharply. Then, as if to soften the effect of her words, she went on: *You'll be here until Monday at least so you'll see what society this place has to offer when we go to church tomorrow.*

I must have frowned because she went on: *The Rector has two rather pretty daughters and both of them are about your age.*

*No, surely, Mother,* Effie cut in. *One is only fourteen or fifteen and the other about a year my junior.*

*As I said, my dear, they are about your brother's age.*

*Hardly, Mother,* I pointed out. *You can't imagine I'd have anything to say to a schoolgirl of fourteen.*

*And by the same token,* Effie said quickly, *the elder girl won't be inter-ested in a boy of seventeen.*

*Seventeen and a half,* I pointed out. *Will there be anyone else worth wading through the mud for?*

*There's a lady who comes to church in a veil,* Mother said. *She has one of those fine old houses on the Green. And lives alone, it seems. I mean, with just her servants.*

I said: *Well, I'm intrigued.*

*Then you can represent the family if it's raining tomorrow and you'll probably see her,* Mother said.

*I'll go whatever the weather,* my sister said.

*You want to speak to Mrs Quance?* Mother asked with a frown. *You still want those tickets?*

*Tickets?* I asked.

*There's a subscription ball that Euphemia wants to go to in town early in January.*

*What does it have to do with Mrs Quance?* I asked. *Who is she?*

*The wife of the Rector and the secretary of the committee organising the ball,* Mother explained. She turned to Effie: *However, I'm not sure that we can afford to go.*

*I've decided we can,* Euphemia said rather abruptly.

Mother said: *Then if it's wet tomorrow you and I need not go to church. Richard can ask Mrs Quance about the tickets.*

*And request one for myself,* I said.

*You will be gone by then,* Effie snapped.

*Oh will I?*

Mother said quickly: *I hope it's dry for you by Monday, Euphemia.*

*Where are you going on Monday?* I asked Effie.

When she made no response, Mother said: *To Lady Terrewest's house.*

*Who is she?*

*I knew her many years ago. She's a very old lady now. Euphemia goes to visit her.*

*Why?* I asked Effie.

My mother answered for her: *To play the pianoforte and read to her. She's housebound on account of her infirmities.*

I was surprised. It didn't sound the sort of thing Effie would choose to do.

.   .   .

When we had finished eating we removed to the best parlour at the front of the house where Betsy had lit a fire. And we needed it. The house is cold even though the weather is mild for the time of year. The pianoforte from Prebendary Street was in a corner. Effie went straight to it and launched into something loud and angry.

Mother ensconced herself on one side of the fire with some embroidery, her work-basket stacked against her arm like a mediaeval redoubt. I picked up Ovid's *Tristia* and threw myself onto the sopha.

After a while I said quietly, though it was hardly necessary to lower my voice against the noise Effie was making: *Do I have to sit here every evening and listen to that?*

*We can't afford to have a fire in another room.*

I saw an infinity of such dreary evenings stretching out ahead of me. Trapped in a dirty old house with a grieving old woman and an irritable young one. And with only the books I had brought with me, most of which were still in my trunk anyway.

After a moment Mother said: *Anyway, you must leave for London on Wednesday at the latest.*

I took her cold hand and said as gently as I could: *Mother, I still know nothing at all of how Father . . .*

She could not have looked more frightened if I had raised my fist to her. All the time Effie was crashing and banging away on the old Broadwood. Mother pulled her hand away and lowered her eyes to her work and after a few seconds said: *It's very painful to talk about, Richard. It was so sudden. His heart . . .* She stopped.

*It was heart failure?* I said gently.

*I think his heart was broken.*

He was much older than Mother, I think about sixty or sixty-one. And he suffered from palpitations and pains in the chest. I began to ask another question but she held up her hand as if to ward off a blow and said: *Wait until tomorrow evening. We'll have a Family Conclave after dinner.*

A Family Conclave. It will be strange to have one without Father presiding.

I stood up and walked up and down the room a few times. I couldn't endure the noise Euphemia was making and the heat of the fire any more. Muttering something to my mother, I fled the room and came up here—cold though it is without a fire.

*1 o'clock.*

As I write I can hear sea-birds wailing like the ghosts of drowned sailors.

I don't know why Euphemia is so keen for me to leave. She spoke of what happened to Father so bluntly it's hard to believe she was upset by it. Yet I am sure she is distraught. *The violets withered all when my father died.*

I had such a wicked thought when I heard the dreadful news: I don't have to worry any more about being forced into the Church. It's my first death. I could not have imagined what it is like. It's as if I were standing on a cliff looking out at the view when suddenly a huge piece of the ground slides into the sea. The very land has betrayed you. There is a vast gulf where once there was something solid. The sea is suddenly closer.

And what is this business about Uncle Thomas that Mother is hinting at? Does he want me in his trading-house? I have better uses for my time and energies than grubbing figures in a gloomy office.

*2 o'clock.*

The silence. I've just put down my pen and listened. Not a breath or a whisper came to me. Since it's a windless night there is no rustling of leaves from the garden. The tide is at its lowest ebb so I cannot hear the sea. I've just looked out at the faint moon shining through a gauze of clouds, its light gleaming in long streaks on the mudflats.

The candle is guttering romantically and it's time to bring this to a close. Here ends my first day in the house of my ancestors.

*½ past three.*

I suddenly woke up. I thought I heard footsteps outside the house as if someone were walking around it. I got out of bed and without lighting a candle made my way out into the passage and stood at a window. All was in darkness. I thought I heard the murmuring of voices—and one of them, strangely, seemed deeper than a woman's. I stood for a long time listening and gradually the sounds I had taken for human voices seemed to resolve themselves into the rustling of foliage and the faint hiss of the waves.

I'm writing this in the front parlour. I can hear clattering from the rear of the house where Mother and Betsy are preparing luncheon. The rain is descending with unhurried malevolence and although I'm chafing at the bit, I know I won't be able to get out of this dreary old house this afternoon. I couldn't walk an inch without getting soaked and slipping on the mud.

However, my excitement is leading me to get ahead of myself. Let me go back to this morning.

I was half-awake and it was very early when I heard voices rising and falling in animated argument. Only after a few moments did I realise the sound came from seagulls roosting on the eaves. That means there must be worse weather coming.

I found my mother and sister in the dining-room where they had just finished breakfast. The rain having held off during the night, it was decreed to be dry enough underfoot for the expedition to church.

Behold, therefore, a few minutes later one unimpeachably respectable family, the widow and children of a senior cleric, no less, in their full Sabbath regalia setting off for worship.

Seeing the house in daylight, I realise that, standing on a promontory that juts into the marshland, it is virtually on an island.

A strange thing happened as we walked. A smart carriage overtook us and its occupants were Mr and Mrs Lloyd whom Mother and Father knew in Thurchester. (They have a daughter of about my age, Lucy.) Yet neither side even acknowledged the other. I tried to find out why but Mother just shook her head.

We saw the tower of the church long before we reached Stratton

Peverel and heard the bell ringing out its steady chime. It is dedi-
cated to St James the Less—a saint for whom I've always felt a great
deal of sympathy without knowing anything more about him than
his name.

We took our places. A minute later the Rector pranced pompously
on stage in his surplice followed by his train of acolytes. He wore one
of those Tractarian ruffs which made him look like a leg of mutton.

I looked around. In the better pews I saw only the Lloyds and
another family—a couple and some young people—who Mother
whispered to me were called "Greenacre". And then a tall lady in a
veil slipped quietly in and took her place in one of the boxed pews.

It was easy to identify the parson's wife and daughters. Mrs
Quance is a large woman in a flower-sprigged gown and with a red-
dish complexion which is an infallible sign of a short temper. (I follow
the adage: *Don't cross the rubicund.*)

There was an older lady beside her of whom I took little notice
at the time. The daughters, of course, were what interested me. The
younger is a little snub-nosed creature with sparkling black eyes and
long golden hair who kept glancing around with mischievous curiosity. But she is only about fourteen or fifteen so hardly has a heart
worth breaking.

Her sister is tall and slender and when at last she looked round,
I saw a long melancholic face with large grey eyes—striking against
her alabaster complexion. Her movements are slow and languorous. I
gazed at her all during the sermon through which her father trudged
with a drayhorse tread—slow and laboured, drawing behind him a
load of clanking quotations. I thought she was never going to notice
me, but she did at last turn her head in my direction and I felt myself
blush.

As we left the church the Rector stood in the porch with his wife
beside him—an unnerving display of lace and chins and jowls—
ceremoniously shaking hands with the departing worshippers.
Quance gave me the impression of timid belligerence. He has a fierce

nose but a jaw that drops away abruptly as if taking fright at such boldness while his eyes appear to be starting as if surprised to find themselves there at all.

When Mother introduced me to them, the Rector nodded perfunctorily and turned to the next member of the congregation.

His wife, however, took my hand. She has the kind of features that would fall into a scowl if they were not held up by the invisible strings of propriety into a caricature of a smile. Her heavy jowls hang like the flaps of a fleshy helmet on either side of her face and her small eyes nestle in the folds of her eye-sockets like sharpshooters searching out targets.

She gave us a grimace of acknowledgement and said to me: *I do hope your prospects are not affected by these unhappy events. Had you been hoping to take holy orders?*

I stupidly shook my head and mumbled some inanity. Looking as if her hopes in me had been suddenly disappointed by this display of idiocy, she let go of my hand.

She smiled at Effie—a Borgiaesque rictus laced with poison—and said: *I'm sorry to have to tell you, Miss Shenstone, that your request for tickets has not been successful.*

Euphemia, plucky girl, replied: *I am surprised that all the tickets have been sold already.*

*I didn't say that, Miss Shenstone. Your application has been considered by the committee and it has found itself unable to accede to it.*

Euphemia who, knowing no Latin, is more of a Roman than I could ever be, did not even flinch at that.

Then something very rum happened. The veiled lady was now next in line. Mrs Quance looked at her with those eyes like nails and, raising her voice, said: *You may well fare better with an application to Lord Thurchester himself. Others doubtless have more influence in that quarter than a mere Rector's wife can aspire to.*

I joined my mother and sister and we slowly walked along the gravel path towards the gate like survivors limping from a battle-field. Mother had heard every word of that venomous rebuff and looked beaten and crushed.

As I passed the Rector's daughters the younger girl dropped her umbrella. I picked it up and returned it to her and she gave me a smile of thanks. An old lady who was with them said: *Thank you, young man. That will be perfectly sufficient.*

(*Literal meaning:* Loathsome male creature, how dare you besmirch the virginal modesty of my protégée.)

*I hope my son is not being a nuisance,* my mother said.

(*Literal meaning:* You must be insane to believe that my son is try-ing to scrape an acquaintance with that shameless hussy.)

The old lady turned to Mother and said in the most ingratiating manner: *I do beg your pardon. I had no idea this young gentleman was with you.*

She is a small elderly woman who wears little round pince-nez that keep falling off her nose. Her features are constantly shifting with the eagerness of some small animal that, while it is feeding, glances around the whole time in case a predator is approaching. Her head is permanently cocked to listen out for an approaching sparrow-hawk (Mrs Quance!).

Mother held out her hand with a smile and we were all intro-duced to each other. The old lady is Miss Bittlestone and the girls are Enid (the elder) and Guinevere.

Like an old gamebird waddling into flight, Miss Bittlestone, flap-ping her nearly featherless conversational wings, took off: *I was just saying to the young ladies how lovely it is to see so many new faces here.* She smiled at Euphemia. *It will be so nice for the girls to have a new friend.*

Guinevere looked up and caught my eye and smiled at that.

At that moment the sound of manly laughter came from where Mr and Mrs Lloyd were talking to the lady in the veil. Mother asked: *Who is the lady?*

*That is Mrs Paytress. She is a widow.* The old woman stepped closer to us and, lowering her voice dramatically as if to keep her next utterance from the girls' hearing, added softly: *Apparently.*

The word was delivered with the smoothness of a hired poniard sliding into a Renaissance neck.

Remembering what Mrs Quance had said, I asked: *Does Mrs Paytress know Lord Thurchester?*

The younger girl made an ill-concealed attempt to stifle a laugh. The old woman turned to me a face that was both horrified and thrilled: *What makes you ask that, Master Shenstone?*

(*Master Shenstone!* I'm not a schoolboy.)

I told her how Mrs Quance had mentioned the earl and had looked at Mrs Paytress at that moment as if there were some connection.

The old spinster said in tones of hushed awe: *Mrs Quance and the Rector, of course, know Lord Thurchester and have dined at the Castle.*

*What an honour,* my mother murmured politely.

*And Enid was one of the guests.* She simpered in the elder girl's direction and said: *She was invited because the earl's nephew was staying at the Castle. The Honourable Mr Davenant Burgoyne. Such a very charming young man.*

The young lady turned away as if to hide a blush at this tribute to her magnetic power of attraction.

*He took her down to dinner,* the old woman crowed.

*Though he couldn't hold her arm,* the younger sister put in slyly. *And he could not dance.*

*Poor young man,* the old woman agreed. *He had recently suffered a grave misfortune and as a consequence, he was limping and had his sleeve pinned to his coat. So romantic. He looked as if he had just returned like a triumphant hero from a great victory.*

Miss Bittlestone suddenly blenched. I followed her gaze and saw Mrs Quance summoning her with a menacing smile. With a quick bow in our direction, the old woman scuttled off with the girls behind her.

They were barely out of earshot when Euphemia said: *What a malevolent old gossip that woman is. What has Mrs Paytress done to her that she should blacken her name by implying that she is not really a widow and hinting at something improper involving the earl?*

*The mysterious widow,* I said.

*Why do you have to find a mystery everywhere?* she snapped. *Why does everything have to become a thrill from a railway novel for you?*

*It's clear that the Lloyds don't believe Miss Bittlestone's insinuations,* Mother said emolliently.

*Or Mrs Paytress's quarrel with Mrs Quance,* Euphemia suggested, *has earned her their friendship.*

I said: *In that case, all we have to do is to make enemies of the right people and our social success is assured. And we seem to have made a good beginning.*

Euphemia rounded on me and said: *You turn everything into a joke. One day the joke will be against you.*

. . .

I was listening for the name "Willy" or something resembling it. Nothing. And I saw no man who looked plausible as an admirer of my sister. There is no curate, for example. Though knowing my sister, I think Effie would aim rather higher than a mere curate—the protozoa of the clerical phylum!

*½ past 7 o'clock.*

Stuck inside all afternoon. I'd have been out exploring the country if it weren't for this infernal rain.

Finding mysteries everywhere. I don't have to manufacture them. They are all around me:

Nr 1.) What were the circumstances of Father's death and
why is Mother so unwilling to talk about it?

Nr 2.) Who is *Willy* or *William* and why was Mother expecting him on Saturday evening?

Nr 3.) Why was Effie dressed up and out in the rain last night?

Nr 4.) And why is she so keen to go to the ball given the distance and the expense?

Nr 5.) Why did the Quance woman refuse her a ticket? And the Lloyds pretend not to know us?

. . .

*Enid.* What an enchanting creature. The delicate features framed by her dark hair. The pale eyes with their long lashes. She exudes a sense of gentle melancholy.

. . .

Just as we were finishing dinner, I mentioned the quality of the repast and not in flattering terms, and the mater said: *I have engaged someone to take care of that.*

*A cook?* I exclaimed.

Mother nodded: *She would have arrived on Thursday but for the bad weather. I hope she'll come when the carter brings your trunk.*

*That won't be until the roads are passable again,* I said.

My tone must have betrayed me because Euphemia asked: *What is in your trunk that is so precious?*

*Just my books and my flute.*

*Is it missing your books that is making you so insupportable? If you can't be more agreeable, why don't you find somewhere else to lodge for the vacation?*

*I'm not lodging here,* I said. *I live here.*

She spoke as if I had not answered: *Did you make any friends at Cambridge? If so, then go and stay with one of them.*

*Of course I made friends*, I said. *Some close ones since I count friends by their quality and not by their number.*

She scowled and I could see that had struck home.

*You certainly had a large number in Thurchester, Euphemia*, Mother murmured in a placatory manner.

*A positive militia*, I said. *How are your senior lieutenants—Maud and Cecily and Lucinda?* I saw a warning glance from my mother. What had I said? *Haven't you seen them since you moved out here?*

*It's too far, Richard*, Mother said.

I could see that Effie was getting more and more irritated, but some spirit of devilry made me go on teasing her: *What? Not even Maud?*

She is her best friend. Or was. A handsome creature and very alluring with those darting eyes and that secretive smile. She's been spoilt by her rich father and is accustomed to getting what she wants. She must have irritated Effie by her assumption of superiority as the daughter of Archdeacon Whitaker-Smith. I went to her house with Effie a few times and all they ever talked about were dresses and suitors. And there was that little brother of hers—whose name I forget—but he was a gifted musician and came to our house to take singing lessons with Father and he joined the Cathedral choir. Then I heard that he had been sent away to public-school and I remember wondering if he was hating it as much as I had since he seemed a quiet, thoughtful boy who would be unsuited to the rough-and-tumble of a place like Harrow. *Perceval!* That's his name. Occurs to me that Maud and Effie are too alike to have stayed friends for long.

*Oh will you be quiet!* Effie cried. *Nobody wants you here. Why don't you just go?*

*Effie, Effie*, Mother said soothingly.

*It was bad enough before he came but now . . . I can't bear it. I just can't bear it. I'm stuck here and I've got nothing.*

*You've got your music*, Mother said. *You must practise diligently and it will stand you in good stead.*

*I hate music,* Effie exclaimed. *I hate it.* She got up and ran out of the room. A moment later we heard her angry footsteps going up the stairs.

I looked at my mother in amazement. *I suppose she was looking forward to the ball,* I said. *And to seeing all her friends.*

*Richard, please don't mention Maud to her again.*

*Oh,* I said. *Have they quarrelled?*

She didn't answer but that would make it all the more puzzling that Effie was so anxious to go to the ball. Those girls were always squabbling over their "beaux".

Mother and I moved into the parlour and she seated herself on the old sopha and started knitting grimly. The rain was falling. I felt frowsty, cabined, cribbed, and confined. I wanted to be striding across the fields with the clean fresh air blowing into my face. I picked up my book but after a while we began to talk.

She recounted some of her old stories about her father that I loved as a child. Having inherited a fortune from his father at an early age, he spent it with magnificent generosity. He once gave a great ball and had ordered a huge frozen cake to be made in London but by the time it arrived it had begun to melt and it covered the floor with sugary water so that the dancers skidded in all directions.

Then Mother began a story she had never told me. One of our ancestors living in this very house fell in love with a girl from a neighbouring family but her relatives refused to let them marry. So one night he spirited her back here. But her brothers burst into the house and killed him. Mother concluded: *They say the bride went mad and one day she ventured into the marsh and was swallowed up. They say she still wanders up and down the shore at night.*

*That's a fine tale, Mother. But I'm sure there's not a word of truth in it.*

*Well,* she said, *there is a red stain on the floor outside the back-parlour that is said to be the poor young man's blood.*

So of course we had to go and find it and while we were looking for it Euphemia suddenly appeared behind us: *Whatever are you doing?* she asked with a laugh that was half mocking and half conciliatory.

So she had to hear the whole story as we went back into the parlour.

Betsy brought us a pot of tea and a plate of round metallic objects that she insisted were biscuits. For the first time we seemed to be as we were in the old days.

. . .

Have just remembered that Lucy Lloyd was a pert little creature with reddish-gold hair falling in curls over her collar.

. . .

I can't help thinking of Mother's head bent over that stain studying it as intently as if she expected to find some message of encouragement from our ancestors. At that moment I saw that her hair is now almost entirely grey. The events of the last few weeks have dealt her a serious blow. The spring has gone from her step.

. . .

Three days' abstinence since I parted from my trunk. Some trouble sleeping but nothing worse.

*11 o'clock.*

At dinner Effie began talking about Father and what a loss he was not only to his family but to the Church: *He was respected by all who knew him. I would go further than that. I would say he was loved.* I looked up involuntarily. I'm sure Father was respected by his colleagues and parishioners but few of them even liked him, I fear. The Canon Precentor loathed him and I remember once hearing him almost shouting: *I will not allow that man near my choristers!*

My gaze met Mother's and it seemed to me that she was as surprised by Effie's claim as I was.

. . .

Effie seems much older than just the two and a half months I've been away can account for. She's not a girl any longer but a woman. She seems fuller of figure. And yet her features are softer. Her temper is no milder, though.

At the end of supper we stayed at the table drinking our tea and I asked Mother to tell me everything.

*It's money, Richard,* she said. *We have only a tiny income to live on now.*

*Surely you will have father's pension?*

*There will be no pension,* she said gravely. *Everything had to be sold to pay off your father's debts.*

*What do you mean?*

*Mr Boddington handled everything.*

Mother is too trusting. Boddington has screwed a fortune out of his clients.

I asked: *So what do we have to live on?*

*Nothing but my own annuity.*

A hundred pounds! About an eighth of Father's stipend! How could we live on that?

*You said that everything had to be sold,* I said. *But you kept the pianoforte.*

*I bought it at the auction,* Effie said coldly. *With my own money.*

*There was an auction?*

Unseen by Mother, Euphemia frowned at me and shook her head.

Mother said: *But I have something very exciting to tell you, Richard. Uncle Thomas gave me a strong hint that he might offer you a post when you've taken your degree.*

What a ghastly prospect. No sooner have I escaped Father's sentence of death as a clergyman than I have to deal with his brother condemning me to a life in trade! I couldn't face that topic now.

*You say we're poor and yet you're hiring a cook!* I exclaimed.

*She won't stay long,* Mother said. *She will teach Betsy to cook.*

(*And to fly at the same time,* I thought.) *Two weeks at the very most,* I said.

*Who are you to say that?* Effie demanded. *You're being very high and mighty but you're hardly more than a schoolboy. You'll be living on Uncle Thomas's charity for the next two years and long before then I'll be working and independent.*

*Euphemia is searching for a post as a governess,* Mother said.

*I should have been consulted about that,* I said. My sister a governess! What a humiliation. *I'm the head of the family now.*

Euphemia snorted.

*I don't think you can be until you're twenty-one,* Mother said. *By then you will have taken your degree and be working for Uncle Thomas. And he has no children so one day . . .*

She broke off when she saw my face. *Richard,* she said. *Your sister and I are depending on you. I want to see Euphemia make a good marriage and I want to be proud of you and know that you are settled in life. And that I will be near both of you and able to share in your happiness.*

*Mother,* I said. *I've got something important to say. Three years until I take my degree—it's a long time. I've talked to the College about my future.*

She looked so anxious that I could not bear to tell her the truth. I just said: *We've discussed my coming down sooner than expected.*

She smiled and said: *So that fits well with Thomas's offer.*

I turned away and found myself looking into Effie's face. She is like a rock-pool when the shadow falls across it: You stare into it and see nothing but the black surface and your own reflection.

. . .

Is Effie practising on the pianoforte for her own pleasure or to improve her chances of securing a post? She plays demure little "governess pieces" for the latter and thundering Beethoven with lots of fumbles for her own gratification.

*1 o'clock.*

I can't stop thinking about Enid. I keep going back to that moment when our eyes met in church and she turned her head away so shyly.

*2 o'clock.*

The wind from the west is rising and I believe it will bring rain tomorrow. I feel the black vapours coming on. *O taedium vitae!* If only my trunk were here.

*A ¼ past 3.*

As I was writing a few minutes ago I heard a sound like a cry of pain. I took the candle and went out into the passage. I heard nothing. As I crossed the corridor on the first floor, I seemed to hear voices murmuring, but I think it was the wind.

I crept up the back staircase and discovered a little room with a narrow bedstead covered by a thin blanket. Odd.

*Monday 14<sup>th</sup> of December, 2 o'clock.*

It was an oppressive cut-throat day but at least it was dry and so Euphemia set off after breakfast to walk to Lady Terrewest's house.

Mother and I were lingering over the breakfast-table when the fateful letter came.

It was brought by a female letter-carrier in a much-patched topcoat and wearing men's boots. (I later discovered she is called "Old Hannah".)

The old creature tottered off up the lane and I handed Mother the letter she had delivered.

She glanced at it and then exclaimed: *But it's from you!*

She read it and then looked up at me with such an expression that I felt a stab in my heart. She said: *What does it mean?*

*I got into a bit of a scrape at College. I failed an examination.*

*I thought your tutors had talked of your taking your degree early.*

*You misunderstood me. I meant not going back. The College hasn't made a decision yet.*

She was silent for a moment and then said: *You should go to Thomas before he hears from the College.*

*Mother, that would be the worst thing I could do. You know he despises Varsity men anyway.*

She sat twisting her hands in her lap. Then she said sadly: *You were supposed to be helping your sister toward a better situation in life. This is one more thing for her to worry about.* She hesitated and then said: *She formed an attachment a few months ago and it all ended badly.*

*What are you saying, Mother? Some man has compromised her?*

*Let me tell you in my own way, Richard. And don't leap to any conclu-*

*sions. They reached an understanding—she and the young man—but then it turned out that there were circumstances which made the match impossible.*

I began to say something but she held up her hand: *Don't ask me any questions about it. I've said as much as I intend to.*

I was going to ask if the "circumstances" were the consequence of what had happened to Father.

*6 o'clock.*

I won't have time to write all that I want to because I can hear the distant clattering of pots and pans and smell something ominously food-like.

Although the morning had seemed to promise fair, the sky grew dark at midday and there came distant rumblings like cannon fire across the marshes. The wind hit the house like a blow from a giant. Doors slammed in distant rooms and the old casements of the windows rattled as if the house were full of frightened strangers.

While Mother and I sat drinking our tea after luncheon, the rain beat against the windows and poured in floods down the panes.

*That poor girl will be soaked to the skin on her way back!* Mother exclaimed. *Be a good boy and take her an umbrella.*

I had no choice but to obey. As I was about to open the front-door and brave the blasts, Mother said: *Tell her your news about Cambridge as you walk back, Richard.*

I nodded and went out.

As I battled against the gusts, a white winding-sheet of rain seemed to be wrapping itself around me. In the distance the hills wept under their umbrella of dark mist. I had just got to the other side of Stratton Herriard, when I saw a woman standing under the shelter of an open-sided barn. She was despondently holding an umbrella that had blown itself inside out and broken its struts. It was the veiled lady I had seen at church The mysterious Mrs Paytress.

I showed her the umbrella I was carrying and said I would be more than happy to escort her into the village.

*Don't you need that for yourself?* she asked with a teasing smile for the umbrella was clearly intended for a lady. When I explained my mission and said that we would meet my sister on the way, she accepted my offer. We began to talk and how many topics we covered! Music: How much we both missed it. Books: How much pleasure they gave us.

We were almost at the church when Euphemia came in sight. I could see how surprised she was that her uncouth brother had managed to engage the attention of such a distinguished neighbour.

We met and I began to make the introductions but Mrs Paytress insisted I hold the umbrella over my sister and when we both united in refusing to do that, she said: *It's absurd to stand here while you get wet. Come inside.*

We followed her up the carriage-drive to a handsome house of mellowed red brick with a steeply pitched roof in the severe style of the Restoration. When she rang the bell, the door was instantly opened by a young servant-girl in a neat cap.

The maid took our coats and we followed Mrs Paytress into the morning-room at the front of the house. I heard her tell the girl to have a fire lit in the drawing-room. There were sophas and elegant chairs and pictures and shelves filled to overflowing with books.

We seated ourselves in front of the blazing fire and Effie and Mrs Paytress were soon chattering away: the dreadful weather, the remoteness of the place, the flatness of the countryside, etc.

Then she suddenly said: *Come and see my pianoforte. The room should be warmed by now.*

She led us across the hall and into the drawing-room—a large room that formed a capital "L" giving a view of the garden.

Even I could see that the pianoforte was a fine instrument. While Effie was admiring it, Mrs Paytress invited her to visit her one day soon and they would play duets. My sister expressed her delight at the prospect.

Mrs Paytress turned to me and asked if I were as fond of music as my sister.

I said I played the flute badly and that I mostly spent my time reading or, in fine weather, walking. I love the countryside and am fascinated by the history of buildings and the stories of the old people.

She said: *I wonder if you know an elderly gentleman in the district who is an enthusiastic antiquary. He is called "Mr Fourdrinier".*

I said I did not and would be most interested to make his acquaintance.

She and Effie talked about the ball and how Mrs Quance's enmity had prevented us from attending. Mrs Paytress told us how she had unintentionally offended that fearsome individual with an innocent remark at a dinner-party given by the Earl of Thurchester. She added: *He is the patron of the ball and Mrs Quance is on the committee because she and her husband know his lordship. Their elder daughter is believed to have an understanding with his nephew, Mr Davenant Burgoyne.*

*I know of him,* I said. *He was at Cambridge a couple of years ago.*

(He gambled away a fortune, kept a brace of whores for the use of himself and his friends and when he went down left a string of small tradesmen with debts that drove them out of business.)

Mrs Paytress said: *He will open the ball and there is much speculation about which young lady he will choose to dance with.*

Remembering what Miss Bittlestone had told us, I said: *Unless he has another accident.*

Mrs Paytress looked at me in surprise and said: *He rarely goes out at night now.*

.  .  .

Now that I write it down, that strikes me as a strange remark. Why should Davenant Burgoyne fear another accident? And why avoid going out at night?

.  .  .

I had lost the thread for a moment and then I heard Mrs Paytress say: *I know that people wonder why I've come here. The reason is very simple. I have old associations with the sea and the marshes.*

Then she asked about our mother and suddenly exclaimed: *Come to tea! Come with your mother on Wednesday.*

We accepted.

Then something very rum. The door opened and a middle-aged female looking like a housekeeper came in. She had on spectacles with small oblong lenses. Looking straight at Mrs Paytress, she said: *Will you come immediately, ma'am.*

With a quick "excuse me" her employer rose and hurried out. As she did so I thought I heard a weird moaning sound. But the door shut quickly behind the two women and there was silence. Effie and I stared at each other in astonishment. Then she stood up and hurried around the corner into the other part of the room, saying: *Stand there and speak if Mrs Paytress or anyone else comes in.*

*What shall I say?*

*Anything, you dunce. I just need you to warn me that someone is there.*

I watched as she hurried over to the writing-desk and opened the drawers. She looked at the contents of each before pulling open the next. I saw her grasp something white—a piece of paper?

*What is it?* I asked.

She made no response.

A minute later Mrs Paytress came back into the room with a distracted air. I said loudly: *I hope nothing is amiss, Mrs Paytress.*

Effie emerged slowly from around the corner as if she had merely been looking at the garden. She glanced at a painting and asked: *That's lovely. Is the subject Gloucester Cathedral?*

Mrs Paytress said: *No, it's Salisbury. I lived there for some years when I was left by circumstances to fend for myself.* She suddenly said: *My dear, if you don't think it impossibly rude of me, I must ask you who you have found in this desert to clear-starch your collars? I've been admiring them surreptitiously. I can't get my laundress to do mine properly.*

*We don't send out,* Effie said. *We have someone in the house who is very adept at that kind of work.*

Betsy? Is she adept at anything? Certainly not at cooking.

After a while Effie screamed: *Good heavens. Is that clock striking six! We can't have taken up so much of your time.*

When the maidservant opened the door we found that it was still raining. Mrs Paytress insisted that we accept the loan of a second umbrella.

Remembering my promise to Mother, I tried to bring up the subject of Cambridge as we walked home. As soon I uttered the word, however, Effie stopped and turned to me, the umbrella flapping above her head: *Mother won't say this to you because she wouldn't wish to hurt your feelings, but you should leave as soon as possible. Go back to Cambridge if you won't visit Uncle Thomas. She wants to put things right in the house and your presence is obstructing that.*

We walked the rest of the way in silence.

. . .

As we entered the hall, brushing off raindrops and shaking our umbrellas, Mother hurried out to find out why we were so late.

Interrupting each other, we told the story of our great adventure: the friendliness of Mrs Paytress, the number of books, the beautiful pianoforte, etc.

*But you'll be able to see it for yourself,* I said. *She has invited us all to tea on Wednesday.*

Mother frowned: *What? Even myself whom she has not even met! That is strange. Did she reveal anything of her past life?*

*She told us that she is a widow,* Effie replied.

*Did she?* I asked. *I didn't hear that.*

*Not in so many words,* Effie answered with a quick glance of disdain. *But it was clear when she said: "I was left by circumstances to fend for myself."*

*Were those her words?* Mother asked slowly.

*Mother, what can you be suggesting?* Euphemia exclaimed.

*We cannot risk becoming involved with someone about whom there is any scandal.*

Euphemia said: *If Mrs Paytress is good enough for the earl, she's surely good enough for us.*

Mother looked alarmed: *What do you mean: "Good enough for the earl"?*

*Simply that she seems to be on friendly terms with Lord Thurchester.*

Mother pursed her lips and changed the subject.

.  .  .

Betsy being adept at something. Now that is an interesting idea. She may not be beautiful but she is a girl and she's young. Is she too young? She has little budding breasts. She must have begun to feel the sweet pain of unsatisfied desire. How I'd love to run my fingers round the back of her neck, burrow under the hem of her little blouse.

.  .  .

What a pity Euphemia mentioned the earl and raised Mother's suspicions! If we and Mrs Paytress become friends, life in this wasteland might be bearable.

.  .  .

I was writing those words just now when there was a tap at the door and Betsy came in and said: *I need the bath for the young mistress.*

As she bent to pick up the tin bath, I said: *Betsy, do you wash her back? The young mistress?* She looked down and said nothing. I wondered if I dared to ask her if she would wash mine. I must not frighten her. I must not scare her so that she says anything to Mother.

.  .  .

It's quite obvious that Effie has fallen out with Maud and probably the rest of her friends in town. In that case, why is she so keen to buy tickets to a ball at which they will all be present? Tickets that we can't afford now.

*11 o'clock.*

As we seated ourselves for dinner, the rain was lashing at the windows and the wind was rattling the frames. I said to Betsy: *You'll have a hard time getting home in this weather.*

She stared at me as if I had spoken in Greek.

Mother said: *What are you talking about? She doesn't go anywhere. She sleeps here.*

I looked at the girl in surprise. She said: *Why, I'm in that little room on the top floor, sir. Didn't you know that?*

Did she smile as she said *that little room* as if I should know it. Is she aware that I crept up there and saw it last night? I rather think she is. The saucy little monkey.

Mother told Effie that I had some grave news and so I had to tell her about Cambridge.

*Do you mean that you have been back here for two whole days without having found the courage to confess to us?* Effie expostulated.

I said nothing and she went on: *Uncle Thomas won't go on paying now so you won't be going back to Cambridge at the start of term, will you? You've been rusticated.*

Mother jumped at the word and stared at me in alarm.

*It just means that the College won't let me go back for a while,* I said. *I told you that, Mother.*

*I suppose you've got debts?* Euphemia said.

I didn't answer.

*How much do you owe, Richard?* Mother asked.

*Not more than twenty pounds.*

"*Not more than twenty pounds,*" Euphemia repeated. *You might as* well have said "not more than twenty thousand pounds". You can't stay here. We can't afford to feed you.

Dear child, Mother protested.

Well, it's true, Mother. You and I have been scrimping and saving and counting every penny.

And hiring a cook! I just said: Mother is paying for your keep just as much as mine.

She glared at me and said: I pay my own way. It's time you started to. So what are you going to do? Anything like the law or medicine is out of the question. You'll have to find work as a private tutor or in a school.

Those don't offer decent prospects, I pointed out.

And what do you think my prospects are? she demanded. A governess! Can you imagine the humiliations I'll have to endure?

Children, children, Mother said. This is getting us nowhere.

You know what Richard's like, Mother. Unless we prod him, he'll simply sit around doing nothing. He should be looking for a way to earn a living.

I'll get my degree first, if that's all right with you.

Oh will you? Do you imagine Uncle Thomas will go on paying for you after this?

I can't bear this, Mother wailed. You're squabbling like Irish tinkers in a garret.

Betsy came in at that moment and Mother snapped: Go back to the kitchen and wait there until you're wanted.

The girl scurried away and Mother went on: I've struggled to preserve the decencies of civilised life. I've made sure we sit down to eat proper meals properly served wearing proper dress. And now you're undermining all of that by shouting and abusing each other.

She started weeping.

This is your doing, Euphemia said to me. You've shown nothing but your usual selfishness since you came back.

Don't speak to your brother like that, Mother said through her tears. You've been as bad as he has. Worse, in fact, as you very well know.

Euphemia swung round and fixed Mother with a look of fury and contempt. She seemed about to speak.

*I won't discuss it any further,* Mother said and almost ran from the room.

Euphemia and I had stood up at the same moment and now stared at each other over the remains of the meal.

*You see what you've done,* she said. *If you had any self-respect you'd leave immediately.*

I've never seen Mother behave like that. She has always been able to deal with domestic crises.

Euphemia left the room. I suddenly remembered poor Betsy who must be cowering in the kitchen. I went out to the back of the house and found her in the scullery cleaning a pan.

*So, Betsy,* I said. *Are you cosy in that little room?*

She made no response. I suddenly had a vision of her alone up there hour after hour.

*Betsy,* I said. *I want a bath tonight.*

*I'll take the tin up now, sir, and then come up with the hot water later.*

*Come as late as you can,* I said.

At that moment Euphemia came in. She told me to go back into the parlour with her and once we were there she shut the door and said: *You can fool Mama but you can't fool me. What did you really get up to in Cambridge?*

*I don't have to justify myself to you.*

She sank into a chair and to my surprise said in a mild and even affectionate tone: *Richard, I don't think you understand what Mother has been through in the last few months. You weren't here when it all happened. She wanted to protect you.*

*What was she shielding me from?* I asked. *Why didn't she let me come to the funeral?*

*She didn't want you to hear the cruel things people were saying about Father.*

*What were they saying?*

She shrugged impatiently. *You know how the other clerics envied him. You can imagine what they said. That's not the point. She lost everything within just a week or two: her husband, her household, her position in the town, and her so-called friends. I'm desperately worried about her. And I don't want you to increase her anxieties.*

I was really affected by her words and even more by her manner. I said I'd try to do nothing to make the situation worse. And we parted on good terms.

. . .

Rustication. How is it that Euphemia knows the word? (It should be called *rusty-cation*. I feel myself becoming unusable like an old lock.)

. . .

*Dear Uncle Thomas,*
*I am addressing you now in order to lay before you in a manly and frank way . . .*

. . .

It's after midnight. Betsy hasn't come up yet though she did bring up the bath earlier. She should be here very soon.

[This is the first of several passages written by Richard in English but using Greek letters—presumably on the assumption that if either his mother or sister found the Journal she would not be able to read the entries since women rarely studied the language at that period. I have simply transcribed them in Roman letters. *Note by CP*]

I wonder if she has ever seen a man's thing. I wonder if I dare offer her sixpence to put her hand on it. I'd be in the bath and she'd pour the water in and it would rear up out of the water and she couldn't help but notice it and I'd look at her and she'd blush and I'd say: *Would you touch it?* She says: *Oh sir, I couldn't do that.* I say: *I'll give you sixpence, Betsy. Just to hold it for a while.* She says:

*Sixpence, sir?* Then she reaches down and her small rough hand closes around it and . . .

Δ

[The passage in Greek letters ends here. *Note by CP.*]

½ *past 1 o'clock.*

By ½ past midnight I knew Betsy wasn't coming.

[A passage in Greek letters begins here. *Note by CP.*]

I can't stop thinking about her somewhere near me in that little room. She takes off her clothes and wriggles into a nightshift. I can see the shape of her little bubbies through it.

Δ

[The passage in Greek letters ends here. *Note by CP.*]

T hank heavens the rain has stopped today though it is still too muddy for the cart to bring my trunk.

I went into the parlour for breakfast and found Mother and Effie finishing their meal.

They had been talking about our visit to Mrs Paytress and Mother said: *We are trying to think of an explanation for that letter of Mrs Paytress.*

*What letter?*

*While she was showing you her escritoire, Euphemia noticed a letter to an individual in Salisbury that was addressed to someone else. Why would she have such a letter?*

*To whom was it addressed?* I asked.

*To "Mrs Guilfoyle",* Euphemia said.

Mother said softly: *Lord Thurchester has a house in Salisbury.*

*Mother,* I protested, *surely you're not suggesting some sort of improper relationship?*

*Well, why has she come to live here?*

Euphemia answered: *She told us it was on account of her old associations.*

Mother pursed her lips. I could see what she was thinking.

I said: *If you have any doubts, you have the opportunity to raise them with Mrs Paytress yourself on Wednesday.*

*If we go,* Mother said.

*Why shouldn't we?* I must have said quite angrily for they both looked at me in surprise.

*Mrs Quance . . .* Mother began.

*Oh well, if you're going to take her opinion into account!* I exclaimed.

*Don't interrupt me, Richard. Mrs Quance has suspicions about Mrs Paytress and to ignore that would be to fly in the face of local opinion.*

It seems extraordinary to me. The only intelligent and amiable person in the neighbourhood has sought our friendship and we are discussing whether to accept or reject it!

Euphemia said to Mother: *You do know what Mrs Quance's motive is for wanting Mrs Paytress to be ostracised?*

Mother nodded: *She hopes that one of her girls will marry the earl's nephew.*

*Which one?* I asked.

*I believe it's Enid,* Euphemia said off-handedly. *The Quances are afraid that Mrs Paytress might interfere with that.*

*I understand,* Mother said. *If she married the earl and bore him a son, the nephew would inherit neither the title nor the fortune.*

(I must say, that seems unlikely since he must be in his late fifties or even sixties.)

Euphemia rose to her feet and announced that she was going to Lady Terrewest.

I seized the opportunity of her absence to persuade Mother to defer my exile since I have to wait for my trunk to arrive and then take from it the clothes I will need while I'm away. Since the weather is turning colder the carrier might be able to bring it in the next day or two. Mother accepted that argument and gave me a reprieve until Friday.


*7 o'clock.*


As I approached the village the smoke from the chimneys hung low and there was the smell of coal-smuts mingled with fog, and even here my nostrils were filled with the odour of the marshes and the sea. The Christmas candles in the windows made me think of all the preparations and parties that must still be going on in Thurchester without us.

On the other side of the village I passed a tall stranger who was striding along with a rapid slouching gait. When I nodded a greeting, he walked on without acknowledging it.

It was getting dark so I quickened my step. I made one final circuit of the Battlefield and that was when I saw Effie. She was several hundred yards away and walking in the direction of Stratton Herriard. What was she doing there? If she had gone to Lady Terrewest she would be there by that time and it was too soon for her to be returning. And anyway, we were now more than a mile from the road.

Taking care not to let her see me, I followed her at a distance of a hundred yards or so. I dared not get too near in case she turned round but in the gathering twilight, I was able to come closer and closer to her without risking being spotted. I watched her enter the house and then I walked up and down the path for ten or fifteen minutes in order not to make it obvious that I had followed her home.

*½ past 8 o'clock.*

Ate very little at dinner. My appetite goes when I'm like this. Missing it badly. Craving it and nothing else. Mother was worried and Effie looked at me knowingly. As long as Mother doesn't suspect.

After dinner I found Effie alone and asked her what she had been doing on the Battlefield. She was very indignant. When at last she deigned to give me an answer, she insisted that I must have been mistaken because she had been home at that time. I persisted and she said: *Are you saying you followed me?*

*No, of course not,* I said.

*If you doubt me, ask Mother. Don't you spy on me and I won't ask any
questions about what you got up to in Cambridge.*

I said I had no idea what she meant.

Just at that moment Mother came back into the room and Effie
said: *Mother, Richard has the absurd idea that he saw me out on the Battlefield at about 6 o'clock but you can confirm that I arrived home before 5,
can't you?*

Mother looked from one to the other of us and then said: *You
shouldn't accuse your sister of things, Richard.*

I said: *I wasn't accusing her of anything. I merely said that I had seen
her there. But if you tell me she was at home at that time, then I can say no
more.*

Mother nodded without looking at me and sat down and pulled
her work-basket towards her.

I cannot understand why Mother lied—and over such a trivial
matter. I couldn't let it go. After a few minutes I said: *Mother, are you
suggesting that I was wrong to be concerned?*

Her hands scrabbled nervously at her work. *You have no right to
spy on your sister.*

Euphemia smiled at me in triumph. She said: *Richard is bored and
he's just trying to amuse himself by provoking me.* She turned to me: *You
appear to be restless without the contents of your trunk. What is it that you
are so habituated to?*

Mother said: *That's an odd word to use.*

I said: *I am very attached to my books, if that's what you mean.* I
walked out.

How does she know so much?

.  .  .

All evening that bitterly cold wind from the north-east buffeted the
old house so that it shook as if it were being shelled. It has at least
blown away the mist and Mother said it will bring frost and snow.
Yes, and my lovely trunk!

*½ past 9 o'clock.*

Just before I came up I ran into the girl in the passage to the stairs. *Are you cold?* I asked and put my hand on her waist. She did not flinch. I ran my hand gently around her waist lower down over the top of her thigh and then over her belly. I said: *You don't feel cold.* She stared at me boldly with a half-smile. I said: *Your arms. They're warm, too.* Her arms were bare to above the elbow and I touched them. I leant forward to kiss her but she ducked her head with a laugh and scurried out of the room.

When I got up here I found that she had already filled the bath and the water was tepid by now. I got into it anyway and the air was so cold it seemed to burn my skin.

. . .

How thin she was and poorly-clad. I could feel her ribs.

. . .

I can see how Mother lives through Euphemia. All her pleasures are experienced vicariously. She looks at her as a miser gazes at his gold.

. . .

So far I've avoided a direct lie to Mother about Cambridge—though I've certainly allowed her to draw the wrong conclusions. Effie is harder to put off—but I feel less compunction about deceiving her.

*½ past 5 o'clock.*

No sound but the scratching of my pen.

Earlier this evening: Sitting all three of us in the parlour reading, knitting, and fretting restlessly through some sheet-music (respectively) when some demon of tactlessness prompted me to muse aloud:

*Just think,* I said, *how different things were six months ago. We'd be in the drawing-room at Prebendary Street waiting for Father to come home.*

They both stopped but didn't look at me. I'm sure we were all remembering how intently we would listen for the way Father came up the steps trying to divine if he was himself or, as Mother used to say, "out of sorts". If he stumbled on the steps we would brace ourselves.

*6 o'clock in the morning.*

I'm trapped in this house and in this body. I long to float away, to hover above the fields. I haven't slept a wink since I woke up two hours ago. It's the pain I get when I haven't . . . So cold. It has frozen hard in the last few hours. My hands are numb as I write this. But at least the lanes will be iron-hard so perhaps that damned carter will decide to risk his axles. I'm sitting here wrapped up as warmly as I can with nothing to heat me but this candle, dreaming of that trunk coming towards me.

Once Edmund and I tried to stop and we lasted just two days. This has been five. Tonight it has been worse than ever. Every bone aches and I feel on the point of vomiting. The thought of food nauseates me.

*Wednesday 16<sup>th</sup> of December, 7 o'clock in the evening.*

At last, at last. As I write I have it in front of me. The crack in the prison-wall of reality through which I can escape to the superreality of the Imagination! I can only hold back by an exercise of will. Tonight, when the house is asleep I will cast off the shackles of corporality and float free.

. . .

When I awoke the light was fainter than usual and I found that there was ice on the inside of the window-panes and the glazing-bars, and it had formed thick teardrops. My first thought was that the carter will certainly bring the trunk now.

Then began a restless, fretting morning. At last I could bear it no longer and hurried out of the house and up the lane and then along the path to the Battlefield.

Strange incident. I came over the summit of a slope and saw a young labourer with a faded red neckcloth loosely wrapped around his neck. He was deep in conversation with a tall individual who looked like a gentleman though he had a raffish air and was shabbily clad. As I drew near, the latter strode away in the opposite direction so that I did not see his face. Was it the man I had seen in the half-dusk yesterday? I could not be sure.

I was so curious that I accosted the younger man and asked him the way to Brankston Hill.

He had a scowling brow and a great jutting jaw that made it seem he was gritting his teeth in irritation. His eyes were wide as if in outrage at an unspoken accusation and his gaze did not meet mine. At my question he merely pointed and turned away.

. . .

At 3 we all set off for the tea-party with Mrs Paytress. As we were passing through Stratton Peverel I saw the Quance girls coming towards us. The younger was chattering away while Enid marched ahead sweetly silent and pensive. What a really beautiful creature she is. Her eyes swept briefly over me and I think I saw a slight flush in her cheek. I could not resist turning round a few yards further on. The younger girl was looking back at us. Not Enid.

As we were welcomed into Mrs Paytress's warm house, Effie and I made the introductions and we seated ourselves.

We talked of the frost and when I mentioned that it made it easier for my sister to walk to Lady Terrewest's house, Mrs Paytress said: *I have heard of that lady as a relative of the Earl of Thurchester. Is she an old friend of yours?*

Mother replied in some embarrassment: *In fact, she is related to me.* (Strange that she has never told me that.)

Conversation turned to Mother's widowed status and Mrs Paytress said: *I can sympathise. A woman without a husband has much to endure.*

She turned her attention to the teapot and I saw my mother glance significantly at Effie. She said cautiously: *I understand you have lived in Salisbury?* When Mrs Paytress nodded with a smile, Mother said: *It's a charming city. It must have been hard to leave.*

*It was,* Mrs Paytress said. *I came here for the sake of someone who is very dear to me. I have made sacrifices for him as one does for someone one loves.*

Mother flushed and looked down and hardly spoke again. After a few minutes she stood up saying: *We should be going.*

I think we were all surprised at the abruptness of this. We had been in the house less than an hour.

As we shook hands at the door I said: *We've forgotten to bring the umbrella that we borrowed.*

*It's of no importance*, Mrs Paytress protested. But Mother said stiffly that she would send me back with it very soon.

We had only gone a few paces when Mother announced: *Our acquaintance with that lady is at an end.*

Effie and I began to protest but she said indignantly: *You heard her. "I came here for the sake of someone who is very dear to me." She even called herself "a woman without a husband".*

Effie was about to speak but Mother held up her hand: *I'm thinking only of you, Euphemia. As an unmarried girl, you cannot be associated with anyone touched by scandal.*

We walked on in a smouldering silence. As we were approaching the fork that leads to our house, we heard the sound of a horn and a few minutes later the rattle and clatter of a cart. It came up from our lane and it was, as I had hoped, the carrier who had brought me and my trunk to Whitminster. He pulled up and when we had drawn level with him he told us he had just left my trunk at the house. He said: *A devil of a job it was on that narrow track.* Then he added as Mother was handing him the money: *And that woman, good riddance to her.*

I had forgotten about the cook.

I was anxious to get home and take possession of the trunk but as the vehicle moved off Mother said: *Richard, I am inviting Miss Bittlestone to tea tomorrow. I want you to go and ask her if she is free.*

I suppose the invitation is to be an overture of peace towards the Quance camp. Now that we've rejected the friendship of the only person in the district who is worth knowing, we have to woo her persecutors!

I set off but I was soon lost. I stopped to ask an old countryman in gaiters and smock with a crushed and battered stovepipe hat on his head. He had the most magnificent side-whiskers I've seen for a long time: white as snow and curling out from either side of his face like a great cloudy ruff that had risen from around his neck. With his unlighted pipe held in front of him and his ancient blue eyes, he seemed to have been hewn from the living rock and to have been waiting there for me from the beginning of recorded time. He told me what I wanted to know and as I was about to walk on, he said: *You're a strange face. Are you from the family that's living in the old Herriard house?*

I said I was.

*A dreary old place it is, and no mistake,* he said. *You know the story they tell about it?*

*That a man was murdered there after eloping with a girl?* The old man looked at me with a smile. *He was killed by her brothers,* I added.

*Aye,* he said. *By them damned Burgoynes.*

*Is that true?* I asked in surprise.

*That's the tale right enough, but you don't know about the babby?*

I shook my head.

*The wench had just birthed a child when her brothers came to the house. After killing her man, they threw the babby into the fire and dragged her home.*

I grimaced in horror and thanked him for his ghastly information.

I found Miss Bittlestone's cottage at last. It's a tiny little hovel of a building constructed of lime-washed cobb with a thatched roof.

I tapped on the knockerless door and when I heard a frightened squawk of surprise I entered. There is just a single room with a rickety stair up to the one above. It was very cold. The only heat came from a tiny fire in the single hearth and the tenant of the cottage was standing before it holding a toasting-fork on the end of which was an unappealing lump of bacon.

*Oh, Mr Shenstone, what a surprise, I wasn't expecting anyone and you least of all!* she exclaimed.

I delivered my mother's invitation. A summons from the Queen could not have brought more pleasure.

She pressed me to seat myself in a battered but once-handsome old chair.

She simpered and said: *Mrs Quance sits in that chair when she hon-*

*ours me with a visit. It's one of the few pieces I managed to bring with me from Cheltenham.*

She confided that with such impressment that I had an involuntary image of her fleeing from a burning city with the chair strapped to her back like Aeneas in flight from Troy with his father on his shoulders.

She suddenly exclaimed: *Don't worry, Tiddles. You'll get your share.*

She was addressing a skinny black cat and now took the piece of meat off the end of the fork and held it out to the animal which gobbled it down. I suspect the creature eats better than its foolish owner.

. . .

When I entered the house I almost tripped over the trunk. My glorious bountiful treasured trunk! It was too heavy to carry up here so I removed what I most wanted and concealed it in my room. Then I unpacked the rest and conveyed the items up here.

While I was kneeling at the trunk a deep voice suddenly spoke: *You'll be young Master Richard.*

I turned. It was Mrs Yass, the cook. She is a large woman of about Mother's age. She has a big doughy face with tiny black eyes like currants in an unbaked white bun and folds of flesh hanging down like uncooked pastry over the edge of a pie-dish. Mother said she's a plain cook but she is plainer than I had expected.

I asked her where she had been in service before and she named a number of places. Seems never to have stayed long. A mixture of boldness and evasiveness in her replies. I asked her what she most liked to cook. She stared at me from that paperwhite round face and eventually said: *Paritch.* Well, even I can cook porridge!

Then Mother arrived. She said sharply: *Mrs Yass, aren't you preparing dinner?*

The woman looked at her impertinently and, turning like a great horse reaching the end of the furrow, lumbered toward the kitchen.

*I don't want you to keep her from her work, Richard,* Mother said.

(In fact, her dinner turned out to be every bit as revolting as Betsy's efforts. I don't know why the mater has hired a cook who can't cook. And frankly we couldn't afford her even if she was a female Soyer.)

*11 o'clock.*

Twenty minutes ago I went into the parlour and found Effie sitting on the sopha, her eyes brimming with tears. She turned her head away. I asked her what the matter was and she responded ferociously: *Do you think I can be happy living like this? Wearing these patched and darned old dresses. Seeing nobody from one week to the next.*

I said it was hard for me as well.

She said indignantly: *You were supposed to rescue us from this. To get your degree and start working for Uncle Thomas.*

I defended myself and at last she shouted: *Just go away, can't you.*

·  ·  ·

I wonder. Is she still nursing a broken heart?

*Midnight.*

Σ

Mother must not know about poor Edmund and his damnable family of bloodthirsty leeches. It's not the money his family is concerned with. They want revenge.

·  ·  ·

I am haunted by the image of her sweet face, her serenity, her pale silence. *Oh beautiful Enid, as lovely as your name.*

·  ·  ·

*Dear Uncle Thomas,*

*I decline your offer since I have no wish to become a supe-rior shop-keeper.*

. . .

Where does that great white slug have her quarters? That huge peeled potato in its bed of pastry.

. . .

I can hear my own blood coursing through my veins.

. . .

After so long—what is it? nearly a week?—it is almost like the first time. Everything I see has meaning even if it slips from my grasp as if I were clutching at curlicues of mist. I float among hanging shrouds of cloud looking down at houses like toys scattered on a green car-pet. I perch in a tree hundreds of feet above the ground. The startled birds fly from me. The moonlight is like cloudy milk poured into a glass bowl full of water.

. . .

Frozen grass. Tiny green pieces of ice. As my foot comes down they seem to shatter.

I raise my eyes to the vast dome above us sprinkled with white specks and I laugh at the tininess of our earthbound concerns.

The pump is frozen and covered with ice like thick ropes of dia-mond or the crystal branches of a magic tree.

. . .

The vast pat of uncooked dough has a room beside the girl's. Damn damn damn. I found that out when I crept past and heard a jarring symphony of flutings and rumblings as she breathed, shaking the house with each expansion of her diaphragm.

*Thursday 17ᵗʰ of December, ½ past 11.*

Slept late this morning and felt terrible. I will be better in the future. The cold was so fierce that I did not want to get out of my warm bed. When I came down to breakfast Euphemia stood up and walked out.

Mother shook her head at me and she was as angry as I have ever seen her. She said: *What occurred last night must not happen again.*

I had to confess that I remembered very little.

She said: *You were blundering about in the night and you went out into the yard half-dressed in the bitter cold and shouting like a madman. From now on you are permitted only one glass.*

When Euphemia had departed for Lady Terrewest's house, Mother told me there were things she wanted to say to me. I seated myself on the sopha beside her while she picked up her embroidery frame and then, her voice trembling, began: *Richard, you should be aware that my life has seldom been free of cares. Your father wasn't an easy person to live with. If he sometimes seemed harsh towards you, it was because he hoped so much that you would succeed in life. All the more because of his own disappointments.*

(I thought: *Here comes the bishopric.*)

*He never obtained his mitre, as you know. That's why it was so important to him to see you launched on a successful career in the Church. I know that was never your wish and so we'll say no more about it. But now you have to decide what you do want to do in life. You must write to Thomas and apologise for your conduct and say that if his generous offer is still open, you gratefully accept it.*

*What, Mother? Am I to grovel for favours from a man who hated his own brother and did him harm?*

*Don't say that, Richard. He has paid your Cambridge expenses. Would he have done that if he hated your father? It's a more complicated story than you've ever been told. The reason why he and your father quarrelled was because of our marriage.*

*I know he was against it but I don't understand why.*

*I'll tell you,* she said. *When your father and I became engaged, my aunts and uncles were horrified. They looked down on him and Thomas because their father had been nothing more than a lawyer's clerk.*

*But didn't your father defend you?*

She fumbled nervously at her embroidery for a moment and then said: *He was not in good health by that date.*

I began to have the strangest feeling. Mother was holding something back. Even distorting the truth.

She said: *But he gave your father and me a lease on this house for twenty-one years.*

*But you said it was yours! That your father left it to you.*

*He did but that was under the will that Cousin Sybille is disputing. Once the suit is settled, the house is mine.*

*If we win it! But what if we don't? When does the lease expire?*

Falteringly she said: *Next December.*

*Then if we lose, we will have nowhere to live. What does Boddington say?*

She looked down and mumbled: *He's worried about the costs.*

*How high are they?*

*I've paid a hundred pounds so far.*

*A hundred pounds! Mother, the suit could ruin us! I should talk to Boddington about it.*

She put down her work: *No! I forbid you. Don't meddle in it.*

*I've never understood why you had to go to court to get what was yours under your father's will.*

She didn't respond.

. . .

I'm pretty certain that the man who broke Effie's heart is the earl's nephew—no less than the heir to his title and to his whole estate. Did Effie come so close to becoming a countess?

*4 o'clock.*

It was a fine frosty morning and I had to get out into the fresh air. I passed the village and wandered on and rather to my surprise found myself in Lady Terrewest's village of Thrubwell. I thought I might as well look at where she lives, so I asked my way and was soon standing outside a tall old redbrick house. It looked joyless and grim.

Knowing that Effie would have to leave soon, I positioned myself a little way along the road behind the stout trunk of a tree. Sure enough, after half an hour she emerged from the house and, staying a long way behind her, I followed her all the way home. She went into the shop for a few minutes but apart from that she spoke to nobody.

After luncheon I decided to extend the palm of friendship. I said to her: *Shall we play a duet? I've got my flute now.*

She said: *You can't keep time.*

*8 o'clock.*

I went into the parlour just now and found Mother sitting on the sopha coughing badly. When she left the room I noticed that she had dropped a handkerchief on the floor. There were specks of blood on it. Is she seriously unwell? Is that what Euphemia was implying? If so, perhaps that is the explanation of the towels and basins that I found when I arrived and that vanished so quickly.

*9 o'clock.*

Mother and Effie had another argument—raised voices and doors slamming—but by the time Miss Bittlestone arrived they had managed to patch together at least the semblance of good relations.

Our guest—our first ever in this house!—was welcomed and I saw my mother slip into the role she had played so often in the old days when she presided around a tea-table encircled by the wives of senior clerics: charming, attentive, even amusing. Wielding her sugar-tongs like a rapier, as Father used to say.

I was delegated to open the door and lead the old woman with all proper ceremony into the parlour. It was cold even though Betsy had been instructed to build up the fire in readiness for our guest.

I had barely got the front-door open before the old biddy's tongue was rattling away. We learned that Miss Bittlestone is the only child of an impoverished clergyman who was Quance's curate in Cheltenham. When the Quances moved here about three years ago, she was "so sweetly" invited to come and live near them.

Yes, to become an unpaid nanny and chaperone!

The tea—to which I suspect she is unaccustomed—loosened her tongue and she informed us that the Rector inherited rather a lot of money recently. So Enid is an heiress and therefore has a fair chance of scooping an earl.

She hinted that Davenant Burgoyne was on the point of proposing marriage and gleefully revealed that the Lloyds were furious that their own daughter had seen the prize snatched from her grasp.

When the bones of that had been sucked dry, Mother asked: *Now Mrs Paytress is a friend of the Lloyds, is she not?*

*Ah, Mrs Paytress,* said Miss Bittlestone with the relish of a hungry diner seeing a new dish approaching. *Now there is a lady about whom there is much speculation. She has almost wilfully excited curiosity. She brought her own servants with her and none of them will reveal the smallest parcel of information about her. She positively defies her neighbours not to be suspicious. And there are many things to be curious about. Odd comings and goings in carriages late at night. Unearthly cries of rage or pain at all hours.*

We savoured this juicy mouthful together in silence. Then Mother turned to me and said: *That reminds me, Richard, that we promised to return her umbrella. Will you do it now, please?*

I pointed out that I had not finished my cup of tea and was given a reprieve.

This was my chance to find out something.

*Miss Bittlestone*, I asked, *the earl's nephew is his heir, is he not?*

*The Honourable Mr Davenant Burgoyne*, she confirmed with a sort of verbal curtsy. She strews titles and dignities like a maiden throwing blossoms round a maypole.

I went on: *Now suppose, just for the sake of the argument, that Mr Davenant Burgoyne dies without leaving an heir . . .*

The old lady gave a little scream—a stylised sketch of outraged horror which I accepted as a sacrifice to the proprieties which was the price of admission to the raree-show of speculation into which I was luring her and after a moment I carried on: *In that case, to whom would the earldom and the fortune descend?*

*Oh, Master Shenstone*, she said with her hand on her heart. *What a dreadful question. And especially after that lamentable incident in which poor Mr Davenant Burgoyne was nearly killed.*

*You mean the accident?* I asked.

She looked at me slyly. *I mean his injury, Master Shenstone. And the answer to your question is that the earl has no other legitimate nephew. So the title would go to a distant cousin.*

*And the estate—the land and money?*

Miss Bittlestone lowered her eyes. *They would pass to the nearest relative of the earl.*

*And who is that?* I asked.

Without looking up she muttered: *I understand that it is a connection of the earl's late brother.*

I made one last attempt: *I can imagine that Mr Davenant Burgoyne is considered quite a prize: a title and a fortune. The earl must be concerned about his choice of a wife.*

*Oh I could tell you a story about that,* Miss Bittlestone exclaimed. *About the way a ruthless family prevented a young man from marrying the girl he loved.* Then she flushed and said: *Oh, I shouldn't have mentioned it.*

*Oh you can't titillate us so brazenly and then disappoint us,* Effie cried.

Miss Bittlestone looked coy and apprehensive at the same time: *I shouldn't say any more. It will only get me into trouble.*

*How intriguing,* Effie said with the most seductive smile. *We're all longing to hear it.*

*Well,* Miss Bittlestone said, *you must promise solemnly never to breathe a word of it to a living soul.* Then the old creature began: *A few years ago there was a family living in . . . well, let's just say a large town in the West of England. They had a daughter of seventeen. The father was a man of the cloth—dear me! I shouldn't have said that! Anyway, he was a vicar and there was a young man who attended his church whose family was terribly grand and when he reached his majority he would inherit a vast fortune and one day become a viscount.*

*And something occurred,* Effie suggested, *between this fortunate individual and the vicar's daughter?*

*They fell madly in love,* the old lady gasped. *Isn't that romantic? But his relatives put every obstacle imaginable in their path and eventually removed him from Bath and carried him off to Brighton.*

*And did the young lady abandon herself to despair?* Euphemia asked innocently.

*As it happened,* Miss Bittlestone said, *her family took a holiday in Brighton just a week or two later and she found a means of communicating with her lover.*

*Richard,* Mother said sharply. *You've finished your tea. Take the umbrella back now.*

I had no choice.

When I knocked at the front door of Mrs Paytress's house it was opened by a man-servant whom I had not seen before. Short and stocky like a retired jockey gone to seed. I handed him the umbrella.

As I was coming out of the gateway of the drive I almost bumped into two people who were passing at that moment. They were an old man—who was carrying a huge leather bag—and a girl.

*Good day,* I said. *Are you on your way to visit Mrs Paytress?*

The old gentleman looked astonished at this greeting and professed not to know who she was so that I had to explain that I had taken him for Mr Fourdrinier.

*But that is my name!* he exclaimed.

It turned out that I had misunderstood Mrs Paytress. She must have heard of Mr Fourdrinier and his archaeological explorations, but she does not know him personally.

We both laughed once this confusion was cleared up. Then we introduced ourselves properly. I liked him immediately. His face is a type that I became used to in Cambridge among the dons. It is that of a child in a man of fifty: innocent, round-cheeked, and inquisitive. Behind his tiny round pince-nez glasses are a pair of twinkling eyes. From under his hat a few carefully-cherished locks of thin grey hair cautiously extend like tendrils feeling their way towards the light. When he is not speaking his lips are pursed with a worried frown so that he looks as if he might be wondering whether to jump across a deep chasm. His coat-pockets bulge with instruments—presumably for measuring and recording his finds—so that he looks like a professor pretending to be a naval officer.

He waved his hand at the girl and said: *This is my niece.*

I shook hands with Miss Fourdrinier. She is very pretty indeed and has a lovely modest manner. She looked down and said nothing. In fact, she did not utter a word during the entire encounter. It was hard to catch more than a glimpse of her sweet face now and then but eventually I pieced it together: delicate features like fine porcelain with the most charming little snub nose that made her look like a Meissen shepherdess.

We were going the same way for a while since they were heading for the Battlefield and we walked along together. I asked him about his interest in archaeology and in a rush of enthusiasm, he told me he was hoping to carry out an excavation on Monument Hill, the distinctive mound with the tower atop. Then he went on quickly: *What is really interesting is that the local people still call it by its old name: "Fawler Hill". Do you know Anglo-Saxon?*

*I'm afraid not.*

*Well, the word comes from " fag flor" meaning "decorated floor." And that is the name of a village where a Roman villa with a mosaic floor was recently found.*

*And so you think there is a Roman villa with such a floor near the hill?*

*I'm convinced of it. The street, the old Roman paved way, runs within a few hundred yards. Stratton is from "straet tun" meaning "the town of the street".*

He broke off suddenly and demanded: *You're not finding this tedious, I hope?*

*On the contrary. It is fascinating.*

He smiled with pleasure and said: *I'm not invited to people's houses. I am considered a bore because I talk so much about old pottery and bones. And I am happy to accept that term. In my view, a bore is a man who is keener on amusing himself than on entertaining his neighbours.*

I indicated my enthusiastic interest and he reached into a pocket and pulled out a handful of coloured stones. *And I've found these tesserae from a mosaic. They prove the existence of such a villa.*

He stopped suddenly and, glaring at the tower, exclaimed: *I hope to God that damned monument was not placed on top of it.*

*Why was it erected?*

*It commemorates the battle fought there during the Civil War,* he said. *It was put up about a century later by a member of the Burgoyne family.* He glanced at the girl and lowered his voice: *He was a notorious rakehell and furnished it for the entertaining of young women in the neighbourhood whom he lured there with trinkets.*

*I know something of the Burgoynes,* I said. *I live in Herriard House and am descended from the family of that name.*

*Indeed?* The old gentleman looked at me with interest.

I told him I had heard the story of the Herriard who had eloped with a girl from the Burgoyne family and been followed back to his house by her brothers and killed. I repeated the words of the old countryman about the fate of a newborn child.

*There are documents confirming something like that,* Mr Fourdrinier said.

We then discussed—well, Mr Fourdrinier did most of the talking—the following subjects: the controversy over the age of fossils; Paley's *Evidences* and the absurdity of his arguments in defence of Bishop Ussher's chronology of the Creation which put the date at 4004 B.C.; Ockham's razor which dispenses with irrelevancies and the consequent redundancy of any notion of a Creator (*videlicet* the recent work of Mr Darwin).

As we conversed the girl attended to us with such an intelligent expression that I was sure she was about to contribute something. I looked at her several times in order to bring her into the conversation but she always looked down demurely and uttered not a word.

When we had been talking for about a ¼ of an hour, she suddenly touched the old man on the arm. He broke off and apologised for having to curtail our discussion and he invited me to come and find him any fine afternoon.

Then he added with a smile: *You must come to tea one day and we can continue this conversation.*

*I should like that very much,* I said. *What is the address?*

He hesitated and it seemed to me that he did not like my asking that. He said: *I'll send my man over with a note in a day or two giving directions.*

*Is it the old Hall at Bickleigh Farrant? I've heard it's for sale.*

I had the idea—insane, as I now realise—of sending a poem to the girl. I really seemed to have offended him. But if I was to go to tea there, I would need to know where it was!

Very grudgingly he said: *No, it's Heyshott House in the village of that name.*

I said to the girl: *Miss Fourdrinier, I look forward to meeting you again.* She looked at the old man with a smile but did not speak.

To my surprise he frowned and said with sudden irritation: *My niece is very shy.* Then he turned and walked away with the girl scurrying along behind him.

Don't know what to make of that.

. . .

When I got home I found Mother and Euphemia in the parlour which stank horribly of coal-smoke. I said: *So Miss Bittlestone finished her story eventually, I assume?*

Mother smiled and said: *She is rather "tongue-free" as my old nurse used to say, but she had better not tell that story to too many people.*

*I think we all know who the family was who were so desperate to marry a daughter to a wealthy peer,* I said.

Effie looked at me: *You were missed after you'd gone.*

Mother explained that the chimney started smoking shortly after I'd left and they had felt the want of a masculine mind on the premises.

*It was probably the change in the direction of the wind,* I suggested. *It draws badly at the best of times.*

*I don't know if that can be right,* Mother said. *There were very strange noises coming from it. Scratchings and flutings.*

I tried to peer up the great chimney but could see nothing.

*It is puzzling,* I said. Some imp of mischief made me say: *Perhaps it's a restless spirit. I wonder how many wretched little climbing-boys have perished in that chimney. Perhaps the ghost of one of them lingers on in pain.* Mother shuddered. I said: *It puts me in mind of something I heard recently.*

I told them about my encounter with Mr Fourdrinier and the girl and said that he had confirmed the historical truth of the story Mother had told us.

Then I said: *But Mother, you left out part of the story. And it must relate to this very fireplace since it's the principal one in the house. When the brothers came here and killed our ancestor and took their sister home, they also flung her newborn baby into the fire.*

To my astonishment Euphemia uttered a harsh exclamation that seemed to come from deep within her and stood bolt upright, pale as milk. Then she ran from the room.

I was left staring at Mother in astonishment.

She shook her head: *Oh, Richard. Didn't it occur to you that that is not a story to tell so lightly? Particularly to a young woman.*

She hurried out after her.

Can Euphemia be afraid of ghosts? So solidly planted on the earth and so superior to my own flights of fancy?

Effie didn't appear for dinner and Mother sent Betsy up to her with something. While we ate I told Mother that I simply do not understand Euphemia any more—as if I ever did! What was she so upset about? Was it something Mother could tell me? Apparently not because she slipped away from that subject with all her skill in evading topics she does not want to discuss.

When she pulled the curtains back before retiring for the night, she called out to me to come and look. Snowflakes were falling gently from the dark grey sky, turning and glittering as they floated to the ground.

*11 o'clock.*

*The truth is that the debts I have incurred are greater than I have revealed to my mother. I am trying to shield her from worry. The money I owe was advanced to me by a friend called Edmund Webster whose family is now demanding its repayment and I fear they might make an approach to yourself.*

. . .

Just before dinner I was in the kitchen with Mother and I asked the cook: *What are you preparing for us, Mrs Yass?*

She said: *Well, for you, young genelman, it ain't going to be tartar and vinegar.*

Then she cackled like an old witch and Mother shooed me out.

. . .

*½ past 11 o'clock.*

Heard a scampering sound behind the wainscoting a few moments ago. Rats. They've been living here at least as long as the Herriards! And recently in considerably better style.

*Midnight.*

A few minutes ago I parted the curtains and looked out at the falling snow. I happened to notice that the curtain across one of Euphemia's windows was not properly drawn. Since there was a candle alight in the room I could see a figure moving which I was pretty sure was my sister. Then I seemed to see another person in the room but at that moment the candle was extinguished. Was it Mother?

. . .

What a sweet little face the Fourdrinier girl has. And such a beautiful slender neck. How I would love to run my hands round it. I touch it with my lips. It feels like the petals of a rose. My arms are around her.

[A passage in Greek letters begins here. *Note by CP.*]

We are in this room. I am lying with her on my bed holding her, with my mouth rubbing softly against her neck and my hands are stroking her and my hard thing is digging into her. She says *What's that?* like a child finding a new toy and she reaches round and she feels my thing and she rubs along it with her fingers and I put my hands on her . . .

Δ

[The passage in Greek letters ends here. *Note by CP.*]

*1 o'clock.*

Strange how the barking of those dogs sounds so much louder across the snow.

I'm sure the others are all asleep. I have waited long enough. I can wait no longer to transcend the limitations of our earthbound existence. The little ritual that Edmund taught me—he the officiant and I the acolyte—is a transmutation, a sacrament of the imagination. The little dark rubbery ball that I am about to melt with the flame of the candle and then drop into the bowl of my pipe, redeems the world. The first draughts seem to warm my whole body bringing a sense of peace and yet a thrilling awareness of infinite possibilities. I am not fleeing from daily reality but experiencing it more intensely.

. . .

Σ

*2 o'clock.*

I can't hear a sound now. Just the distant chafing of the waves against the shore. *The unnumbered pebbles.*

*½ past 5 o'clock.*

I've just returned from the other side of Stratton Herriard. What pleasure to steal from a slumbering house and roam the countryside unseen. I walked through the silent villages. All the windows were blank. Night and darkness belong to me. While my neighbours dream, I come and go around their houses. Peer through their windows if they have a candle still flickering.

I wandered across the unlit fields and marshes until I came to the edge of the land where the sea frets unrestingly. The moon hung like a golden ring that had been snapped in two while the ocean rippled like the back of a wrinkled old woman's hand. I made out boats near the shore with lanterns gleaming through the mist and realised that fishermen were at work.

I circled round and walked back along the muddy shore.

*Friday 18<sup>th</sup> of December, noon.*

Woke up this morning with a thumping headache and found several inches of snow had fallen since I got home. The house lies under a great feathery muff. There are Siberian drafts under the doors and the ill-fitting windows are rattling in their frames. The roads will be impassable for a couple of days so that there can be no question of my leaving. I don't know if I'm pleased about that or horrified.

.  .  .

Mother suddenly asked me: *Did I hear you coming in very late last night?*

Before I could think, I found that I had denied it.

I was weak last night and I must not give in to temptation so soon again.

### 4 in the afternoon.

After luncheon I went and looked at the Monument. It is an octagonal tower about forty feet high and surmounted by an absurd cupola held up by a ring of classical columns.

As I was crossing the path between the village and the shore, I spotted the Quance girls with their old cicerone. As we approached each other Guinevere stopped and said something. Her sister glanced in my direction and frowned. She made a *moue* of distaste. We had not been on a course to meet, but Guinevere led them towards me.

Simply don't know what to make of Enid. Was she teasing and mocking me by her silence? Does she have no idea how I feel about her?

The old woman exclaimed: *Master Shenstone and I are quite old friends.*

The girls exchanged glances. *Oh yes, the famous tea which we've heard so much about,* Guinevere said. She chattered away and gave me the chance to observe her properly for the first time. Pity she isn't a little older. Even a year or two. She might be quite a beauty by the time she's sixteen. She has a tiny dimple on her left cheek near her mouth which gives her a strange charm. She's a teasing little vixen.

She started talking about the ball: What she was going to wear. What her sister was going to wear. Then she inquired: *Are you coming, Mr Shenstone? You and your sister?* She giggled and placed her hand over her mouth in a theatrical manner.

She must know that her mother has refused Effie tickets. I can see her merry face now and I'm sure the little shrew was teasing me. Then she demanded: *Who do you intend to dance with? Mrs Paytress?*

Enid said: *Don't be a goose. You know very well that that woman is not going to be there.*

Guinevere turned to her chaperone: *Is she also on Mama's blacklist, Miss Bittlestone?*

(*Also?* So we Shenstones are on the list?)

The old woman stood in confusion.

Guinevere addressed me: *It's the earl's ball and is to be opened by his nephew, Mr Davenant Burgoyne, and there is a great deal of speculation about which young lady he intends to dance with.*

At this Enid looked conscious. Is it true? Are she and that boor destined to marry?

*He's fearfully handsome,* Guinevere said. *Isn't he, Enid?* Her sister blushed obediently. *And very tall. How tall are you, Mr Shenstone?*

*Oh, my dear girl, what an indelicate question,* Miss Bittlestone muttered. *Whatever next?*

Guinevere giggled.

I told her my height and she said: *Mr Davenant Burgoyne has the advantage of you by a good three inches.*

I instantly thought of the tall man I had encountered on Tuesday.

A moment later Guinevere started talking about her mother's criteria for selling tickets: *No governesses, Mama says.*

Enid nodded and said: *Only ladies.*

Guinevere frowned as if genuinely puzzled: *What is your view, Miss Bittlestone? Can a woman be paid money and still be a lady? Mama says not.*

*I would not dream of dissenting from your mother's view. A lady is one who behaves as a lady should.*

Guinevere screwed her pretty face into the expression of one troubled by a philosophical issue and asked: *Can an unmarried girl go about on her own and still be counted a lady, Miss Bittlestone?*

*Well*, the old lady said doubtfully. *That depends.*

*Suppose the girl were seen coming out of her friend's lodgings at ten in the evening*, Guinevere went on. *And the lodgings were in, say for example, Hill Street in town where I believe a number of young unmarried gentlemen lodge . . .*

*What!* the old woman shrieked. *You're not talking about a single man's lodgings?*

*Yes, Miss Bittlestone*, Guinevere said with an expression of irreproachable innocence.

*My dear child! No woman's character could survive such an episode.*

By now the old woman was clucking like a broody hen and urging her charges to walk forward. So we parted and I strolled on. That little chit, Guinevere, is a strange mixture of coquetry and caprice. She bids fair to becoming an outrageous flirt.

Then in the distance I saw two figures—a man and a woman. The man was very tall. And the woman, I realised as I drew nearer, was my sister. I could see that they were walking arm in arm and seemed to be laughing. At moments their heads seemed to come close together and stay there for a moment.

I could not get any closer because it was impossible to cross the open fields without being seen. And then, before I could approach them by a more circuitous route, the falling dusk hid them from my sight.

As ever, Euphemia thinks nothing of bringing dishonour on the family. She has never shown respect for the feelings of anyone else. Father allowed her to do what she chose. He beat me for minor offences and smiled at her for much more serious ones. But I suppose she doesn't realise what she is doing. A girl brought up in the cossetted, protected way that Euphemia was, knows nothing. If she had seen and heard what I've seen and heard at Cambridge she would understand the danger she is in.

*7 o'clock.*

Odd thing a couple of hours ago. I went into the kitchen to find Betsy and saw Mrs Yass laying out some herbs on the table. I asked her what they were and she said: *Tansy and pennyroyal.* I said I didn't know they were ever used in cooking and she replied: *That depends on what you're cooking, don't it?*

. . .

Earlier this evening I turned round suddenly in the parlour and saw Euphemia looking at me. An unguarded look of loathing for myself. I've never seen such open hatred. What can have provoked that?

*11 o'clock at night.*

Unpleasant scene after dinner. When we had had our coffee we repaired to the parlour and Effie began thumping away at the piano-forte—all the while complaining that her hands were too cold to play. And the instrument is out of tune. Well, we've thrown away the chance to remedy that by turning our backs on Mrs Paytress.

I sat beside Mother on the sopha and opened my book while she began her embroidery. Euphemia was playing louder and louder and at last I went over and almost had to shout in her face: *I can't read while you're making that row.*

Euphemia is so selfish. Nobody else matters when her pleasures are at issue.

*You can go and read in your room,* she said. *You spend enough time there. Heaven alone knows what you do.* With those words she shot me such a look.

*You almost read too much,* Mother murmured with threads dangling from her mouth so that I could not help thinking of a ferret with a rat in its jaws. *You're like your father who always had his nose buried in a book.*

On the rare occasions when he was at home, I thought, and sober.

Then Euphemia said: *People are more interesting than books, Richard. And you can't put them back on the shelf when you're bored with them.*

I said: *I don't ever find people uninteresting. On the contrary, I find them so fascinating and so highly-flavoured that after small helpings, I have to go away and chew them slowly and analyse the taste of them.*

Euphemia said: *Chewing and swallowing! That's a very revealing remark. You think other people are created just for your benefit!*

I said: *That's ironic. You're the one who's only interested in people for what they can do for you.*

Mother made a low noise of reproof, her mouth still full of thread.

My words had stung Euphemia: *That's a lie. People do things for me because they like me and so they want to. Who has ever wanted to do anything for you?*

*Are you suggesting that people don't like me?*

Mother said: *If you two are going to bicker I'm going to bed.*

Euphemia said: *I'm not trying to pick a quarrel, he is.*

Mother said: *That's what you used to say when you were a little girl, but I said to you then and I will repeat it now: You are older than your brother and should know better.*

Effie said: *Will you still be saying that when I'm fifty and he's forty-seven?*

Mother looked shocked: *I won't be here to say it then.*

Effie said: *You always punished me more harshly than him because I'm older.*

*That isn't so,* Mother exclaimed.

*You always wished I had been a boy because that's what Father wanted and what he wanted was always what you wanted.*

*I can't imagine why you say that,* Mother said. She was still holding a needle in one hand and her glasses had slid down her nose. *If anything, you were Father's favourite even after Richard was born.*

*And you didn't like that did you, Mother?*

Mother started and said: *Whatever can you mean?*

*You were jealous. You always wanted to come between Father and me. You begrudged every moment of his attention to me.*

Mother put her hands over her ears and, when Euphemia stopped speaking, stood up slowly, letting her work fall to the floor. She said: *I won't be spoken to like that.* She went slowly to the door and then turned: *You wouldn't dare to adopt that tone if your father were still alive.* Then she walked out of the room.

I said: *That was cruel of you. Can't you see how much pain you caused Mother?*

*You're a fine one to speak! You're causing her pain just by being here. Just as you vexed and worried Father.*

*How can you say that and at the same time claim that he preferred me to you?*

*My dear Richard, I didn't say he liked you more than me.* (I hate it when she addresses me like that. So superior. As if she were a generation older than me.) *But you were a boy. You were going to be Father's heir and bring glory on all of us. Like Jacob you took your elder sibling's blessing. And look how you've disappointed everyone. At least Father didn't live to see it, though he guessed that you were not going to be the son he'd hoped for.*

*That's a lie!*

*Not long before he died he talked of how your reports had always accused you of being dreamy and idle at Harrow. And he'd scrimped and saved to send you there. He feared you'd never make anything of yourself and his fears were confirmed when he found out that you were getting into bad company at Cambridge.* Her voice almost breaking with sudden emotion she said: *It's no coincidence that he died shortly after that.*

I said: *You must have invented something to discredit me. You always tried to turn him—him and Mother—against me. You told lies about me.*

She almost shouted: *You yourself turned them against you! It was only when you showed yourself to be idle and dissolute that they began to found their hopes on me.*

*It wasn't my fault things went badly. Father sent me away to Harrow even though I hated it and begged him to let me go to school in the town.*

*Father was determined to make a man of you. He hoped Harrow would do it and he was bitterly disappointed when it failed.*

*Father never thought that.*

*Yes he did. You don't know what really happened. You were too young. Father loved me until you came along. As soon as you were old enough to amuse him, he lost interest in me. He had his beloved son at last. I was cast aside.*

I said: *He shouted at me and beat me and he never did those things to you.*

*That's because he cared about what you would make of yourself. For years he hardly noticed me.*

*That's not true. He loved you. Look at how he played music with you. You'd inherited his aptitude for it and I hadn't. He was furious with me for that.*

She said: *Let me tell you something. From when I was nine years old Father always used to take me to choir practice but when you reached that age, he started taking you instead.*

*But you'd almost turned twelve. It wouldn't have been proper to take you to a place where there were only men and boys.*

*It wasn't that. He was so proud to have a son. And then you failed him so badly.*

That was enough. I walked out.

. . .

Can Effie really believe it was such a privilege to have been sent to Harrow? My time there still haunts my dreams. The food, the boredom, and the beatings. And the thrashings by the masters were nothing compared to what the prefects and the other fellows inflicted on us little ones in the first years. Especially on the hated scholars.

But most of all, Euphemia could not begin to imagine the things that happened in the Great Hall when we were locked in together at night—fifty boys of all ages with no master present. Many a time I fought to protect myself. Bartlemew, on the other hand, submitted without a struggle. What a sly, eye-on-the-main-chance weasel he was. Nobody trusted him and I was besmirched in the eyes of the other fellows just by dint of coming from the same town.

. . .

Euphemia was always preferred by both Father and Mother. She was the firstborn and a girl and handsomer and more charming and musically gifted than I. Father treated her much more gently than me. He liked to have her with him. He found more occasions to be alone with her than with me.

. . .

Those girls. Those lovely teasing girls. I can't get them out of my thoughts.

[A passage in Greek letters begins here. *Note by CP.*]

I am out in the fields and it begins to pour with rain. I find them sheltering under a tree. I lead them back here. They are soaked. In front of the roaring fire I encourage them to remove their dripping garments. Blushing, Enid takes off her blouse, turning away from me. She wraps herself in the towel I have given her. The younger girl is soon naked but holds her towel carelessly around her breasts and it hangs down just touching her belly. It's as if she's too young to know how much pleasure the sight of her sweet body gives a man. She says: *But you're wet too.* She runs her hand across my trousers innocently. She notices the swelling. She says: *Are you hurt there?* She starts to unbutton me.

Δ

[The passage in Greek letters ends here. *Note by CP.*]

*Saturday 19<sup>th</sup> of December, 11 o'clock.*

I came down late for breakfast and found Mother in a very strange mood. She seemed tense and was very quiet as if she had learned something ominous. I mentioned the noises we had been hearing and she said she thought they were caused by rats and asked me to buy poison today. I saw a letter on the table beside her but she made no reference to it.

*Noon.*

Reading after breakfast alone in the front parlour. Sounds of raised voices from the rear quarters. When Mother came in she explained what had occurred. Betsy had complained that she freezes all day because she has access to no heat apart from the kitchen fire and Mrs Yass sleeps in front of it, blocking it from her.

Mother said she wonders what Betsy does when she is not working. She has no friends since she is not from this part of the country.

I said: *Perhaps she reads.*

*She has never learned her letters. Euphemia promised to teach her though she seems to have forgotten.*

*2 o'clock.*

Luncheon just over. A morning of ill temper. House full of hysterical or irritable females. What is it that Mother and Effie are arguing

about? I often hear raised voices but when I enter the room they fall
silent.

*4 o'clock.*

Odd thing today in the little shop. (Mother had given me 1s. 6d. to
buy her needles, thread, and rat poison.) Mrs Darnton, the woman
who keeps it, has a gaunt, watchful, intelligent face. She is tall and
thin with a beaky nose and a mouth drawn into a grimace of disapproval. What must it be like to be born poor in this backwater
but afflicted with a keen wit, and to be denied education? Clearly
her unused intellectual capacity goes into inquisitiveness about her
neighbours for she was deep in conversation with another woman of
about the same age but her exact opposite physically: large and fat
and blowsy.

They were holding their heads together conspiratorially and
speaking quite softly and did not notice that I had come in. Keeping
far from the gaslight near the door, I lurked in a corner. At intervals
the other woman would raise her head and incline it backwards in
order to emit a harsh repetitive noise in her throat that I realised was
a chuckle.

I only heard scraps because they kept dramatically lowering their
voices at the most critical moments:

DARNTON: *Must hate the earl's dandified nephew . . .*

BLUBBER: *Many and many a time I've heerd him with my own ears when
he was in his cups a-telling of how he'd like to squeeze the last drop of
blood from his guts and then strangle him with them.*

DARNTON: *It must gall him to see everything go to his younger brother and
be pushed aside by a Johnnie-come-lately just as Esau was. He must
hate him. It stands to reason. And that's why they say that it was he
who . . . that night in Smithfield . . . fired at him . . .*

Blubber thumbed her nose with an expression of deep knowingness.

At that moment I unintentionally rustled a newspaper and alerted them to my presence.

Mrs Darnton demanded to know what I wished to purchase and when I said "rat-poison" she looked at me as if she thought I intended to murder the whole neighbourhood with it. Without taking her eyes off my face she called out: *Sukey!*

Instantly a little crushed, washed-out dishclout of a woman hurried out from the back-premises—hunched back, scared eyes darting from side to side. Mrs Darnton barked out *Rat poison!* and the creature scuttled into a dark corner of the shop and returned with a tiny jar.

I also bought a small box of honey and cinnamon sweetmeats to help me win Betsy's trust.

*Memorandum:* OPENING BAL: *10s. 1½d.* RECT: (from Mother) *1s. 6d.* EXP: Purchases for Mother: (*11d.*) and sweetmeats (*4d.*) TOTAL EXP: *1s. 3d.* FINAL GROSS BAL: *10s. 4½d.* (of which I owe Mother: *7d.*). FINAL NET BAL: 9s. 9½d.

·  ·  ·

Did I misunderstand? How can a man be disinherited by his younger brother? It makes no sense.

*½ past 5 o'clock.*

What a blind stupid fool I have been!

This afternoon I went towards Monument Hill and ran into the Quance sisters teetering along the path in their fashionable footwear.

All Guinevere wanted to talk about was dresses and parties and of course the ball. Always that ghastly ball.

Even Enid found her prattle tiresome and at last snapped: *Hold your tongue and walk on.*

Guinevere said spitefully: *You're just sulking because Willoughby hasn't called on us for ages and ages.*

*Who is "Willoughby"?* I asked.

They both turned to me in surprise.

*Mr Davenant Burgoyne, of course*, the younger girl said.

*I thought his Christian name was "Davenant"?*

Enid addressed me for the first time: *You were mistaken. His full name is "Willoughby Gerald Davenant Burgoyne".* She recited that ridiculous succession of syllables with an almost proprietorial air. Then she added: *Only his most intimate friends call him "Willoughby".*

That was the name Mother blurted out when I took her by surprise in the scullery. It is proof! The man I saw Effie with yesterday is indeed Davenant Burgoyne. Euphemia has been meeting him and that has become widely known and so her good name is in tatters. The day I came home he must have been expected as a visitor and that is why Euphemia had dressed for dinner and why she went out in the rain to warn him not to enter the house.

Guinevere was studying my face. *You look surprised, Mr Shenstone. Have you heard anyone speak of "Willoughby"? Or of his lodgings in Hill Street?*

At that point Enid uttered a sound that was so strange that it took me a moment to realise that it was a laugh.

People talk of falling suddenly in love but little is said of how you can fall just as precipitately out of it.

It was at this moment, looking at their faces brimming with gleeful malice, that I grasped the point of the story they told yesterday. The one about the young woman who was seen leaving a gentleman's lodgings late at night. I wanted to say something that would throw their spite back in their faces. I said: *I am astonished that you should pass on tittle-tattle about people's private lives.*

*It wasn't so private*, Guinevere said. *The girl intended to be seen. It was a mantrap. She had made a dead set at the gentleman and hoped to compromise him so that he would have to make a proposal of marriage.*

I said: *I grasp your meaning perfectly. She trusted to his honour and he turned out to have none.*

The girl enjoyed that but Enid said indignantly: *He refused to be blackmailed by a shameless adventuress.*

Enid is not just spiteful. She's stupid as well. Is that worse than being clever and malicious like her sister?

She turned, and without even the briefest goodbye, both girls walked away.

*6 o'clock.*

I'll probably never speak to either of them again. And I hope I never do. How could I have ever thought Enid worthy of my interest? To see her laughing at me behind her hand. How wrong I have been. What a fool. Cold, cold. Cold-hearted creature. That thin-lipped smile while she and her sister were trying to cause me pain. She's a heartless shrew.

*A ¼ past 6 o'clock.*

My heart is hardened, the blossoms of love have withered. I will never love again.

*½ past 6 o'clock.*

Found the moment to slip the little gift from the shop into Betsy's hand. She was surprised and I think pleased. I whispered: *We will talk later.*

*7 o'clock.*

Effie has just accosted me and pulled me into the damp old dining-room at the back of the house and said: *I know exactly what you get up to.*

I said: *What do you mean?*

She said: *Up in your room. It's disgusting, that foul practice of yours. And if you don't leave the house tomorrow or on Monday at the latest, I'm going to tell Mother.*

I said I had no idea what she was referring to.

She was leaning so close that I felt her breath on my cheek. She said: *You're going to hurt her horribly when she finds out but you don't care about that, do you?*

I said: *You want me to go so that you can continue your scandalous conduct.*

I just pushed past her and left the room.

*½ past 7 o'clock.*

Awful. Awful. I've never seen Mother so distraught. So unable to cope with her feelings.

About an hour ago she summoned me into the parlour where she and Euphemia were trying to keep warm in front of a miser's fire of three lumps of coal. I could see how upset she was. She showed me the letter I had seen at breakfast and said it came from Uncle Thomas this morning and that he has been informed that I have been rusticated for "gross misconduct".

Before I could open my mouth, Euphemia said: *You weren't rusticated for failing an examination. It was because of your debts, wasn't it? And they wouldn't send you down for just twenty pounds.*

I had to admit that the total was about seventy.

Mother gasped. *Oh, Richard, you lied to me!*

Euphemia said: *At every turn you have tried to hide the truth from us. First you had come home early because you had no money for your holiday. Then you had been suspended for failing an examination. Then for debts of twenty pounds. Is there some further disclosure to come?*

How like Father she sounded!

With a heavy heart I promised that this was the whole of my offences.

*What did you spend it on, Richard?* Mother asked.

Euphemia cut in: *The question is not where the money went but where it came from. How did you manage to get so deeply into debt?*

I said nothing.

She hissed: *You've brought shame on all of us.*

Her words stung me into saying: *You can't talk about shame. The whole neighbourhood is gossiping about you. I ran into the Quance girls this afternoon . . .*

*Those primped up little vixens! How dare you listen to anything they say about me. The farrow of that evil old sow.*

*They said you've compromised yourself.*

Mother started to speak but Euphemia rudely waved her to be silent: *No, Mother. I want him to go on.*

*I saw you myself.*

*Tell me what you are talking about?* she said coldly.

*I saw you with your friend, your paramour, your what-you-will, on the Battlefield yesterday afternoon.*

Mother said in terror: *What are you saying, Richard?*

I said: *I saw her with Mr Davenant Burgoyne.*

I turned back to Euphemia and saw that she was stunned. She and Mother were looking at each other in a state of amazement.

I said to my sister: *Mother has told me about your attachment to him in the autumn that was broken off by his uncle. Obviously you've continued to meet him.*

I had never seen my sister so angry. Her face was white and her lips were pressed into a thin line: *You can't imagine I care for that dissolute pampered perjurer!*

*I've seen you walking arm-in-arm with him,* I said.

*You snivelling little sneak. How dare you meddle in my business. You talk about my reputation. What about yours?* She came up to me and whispered: *I'll make sure Mother and everyone else everyone knows about your nastiness: sneaking around the countryside at night and spying on people and trying to see things that shouldn't be seen.* She turned to Mother: *He must leave the house immediately. I won't have him here any longer.*

*Leave the room, Richard,* Mother said.

I was only too pleased to oblige. From the coldness of the dining-room I heard their voices murmuring.

After a few minutes my sister came to the door and said curtly: *Mother wishes you to go to her.*

I joined her in the passage but she turned away and hurried towards the stairs. Mother was sitting where she had been. She looked small and old. I had barely seated myself when she said: *Richard, I'm asking you, no, I'm ordering you, to leave. Go away for two weeks. Don't ask me why. For my sake and for your sister's, just go.*

*What have I done?*

*This harassment of your sister.*

*Mother, people are saying she visited Mr Davenant Burgoyne at his lodgings. At night.*

Looking down at her hands folded on her lap, she said: *I don't know why you would say such a thing about your own sister.*

*Is it true, Mother?*

She looked up and said: *Of course it's not true.*

She has never been a good liar. I had a feeling she was hiding something so I persisted: *He has lodgings in the town, in Hill Street. Euphemia was seen leaving late at night.*

*Then that's nonsense! I happen to know that Mr Davenant Burgoyne lives at his uncle's.*

*The earl's house?*

*Yes. His townhouse on Castle Parade.*

So those little imps were just trying to torment me with spiteful lies. I said: *I'm sorry, Mother. I shouldn't have said that about Effie. It worried and upset you unnecessarily. Please forgive me.*

*No, Richard,* she said. *I won't forgive you. It's not just that. By incurring those debts you've sabotaged everything I managed to rescue from the wreckage. The College is angry with you, Thomas is furious. Don't you understand how vital it is that Euphemia be able to go into society and meet young men from good families? I have to see her settled and there isn't much time. Where is the money to come from? On top of that, you've annoyed Mrs Quance by your absurd attempt to befriend a woman condemned—rightly or wrongly—by Society. And you've lied to me. Your behaviour is unacceptable, Richard. You must leave immediately. You must go tomorrow morning and not return for at least a fortnight.*

*Mother, I would if I had anywhere to go.*

*I interpret this as a refusal.*

*I'm not refusing, Mother. I can't comply.*

*Very well. I have been contemplating a way to settle this and now I see no alternative. I am going to say something and then you will leave the room immediately and without speaking. You will think over what I have said and then you will come back in one hour and give me your response. Do you understand?*

I nodded.

*If at eight o'clock you tell me you will not leave, you will have to be told something so shocking and horrible that simply by hearing it, you will inflict irreparable harm on all three of us.*

*½ past 8 o'clock.*

Mother only pretends to care about me. All she really cares about is Euphemia. Well, if that's how she feels, I'll go away and I'll never come back. See how she feels about that!

Mother's revelation must be about Father. People said unkind things about him and I don't want to hear them. I might not have loved him as much as a dutiful son should, but I respected him and I don't want that to change.

I went downstairs and found Mother sitting precisely as I had left her. I said: *Mother, I will go away.*

*Thank goodness for that,* she said and turned away so that I could not see her face. She dabbed her eyes with a handkerchief and then looked at me again and said: *There will always be room for you here.*

I said: *I've thought of someone I can go to in Thurchester. I'll write now and should have a reply by Tuesday. I can leave the same day. Is that soon enough for you?*

She put her hand on mine without saying anything.

She must guess that I am referring to Bartlemew but all her objections to him are now suspended in the higher interest of getting me out of the house!

*½ past 11 o'clock.*

When all was quiet I slipped down to the kitchen and, as I had hoped, found the girl still polishing pans and putting them away. The only light came from a single oil-lamp standing on a sideboard and when she turned to me the half-light and the shadows flattered her and she was almost handsome. I asked if she had liked my little gift and she nodded and looked down.

*Are you happy here, Betsy?* I asked.

*I'm happier here than any place else I might be, Master Richard.*

I said: *I'm going away, Betsy. I'm leaving here on Tuesday and I don't know when I'll come back.*

*I think that's for the best, sir,* she said with her back to me as she lifted a pan onto a high shelf.

It wasn't the response I had hoped for. I said, perhaps rather impatiently: *Why are all you females so anxious to make me go? Is there some sort of conspiracy amongst you to get rid of me?*

Now she did turn to me. She looked discomfited. Her mouth was slightly open and her eyes seemed huge in the shadows. In spite of my irritation at her remark, I felt a strong desire to lean forward and kiss her.

Have just written to Bartlemew. Shameful to be asking him for a favour.

*2 o'clock.*

Set off for church. As we approached the village Mother told me to run on quickly and take my letter to the post and then catch them up. There was nobody in the dark little shop apart from Mrs Darnton who scowled as she took the letter from me.

*Memorandum:* OPENING BAL: 9s. 9½d. EXP: Stamp: 1d. FINAL BAL: *9s. 8½d.*

It suddenly occurred to me to ask her the postal direction of Davenant Burgoyne. She glared at me with open contempt and said: *Why? Do you intend to send* him *a letter?*

What business is it of hers if I do? And why the emphasis on *him* as if I've been handing in other letters?

As I left the shop Old Hannah, the letter-carrier, came out behind me and I suddenly heard: *Young fellow!* I stopped and she caught up. *Don't let Madame Sourpuss know I've told you, but the earl's nevy lodges in the rear premises of his uncle's house.*

*Castle Parade?* I asked.

*It's round the back. It's the same building but it's called Hill Street.*

I thanked her and ran on and caught up with Mother and Euphemia and we reached the church with some time in hand.

. . .

Was Mother misleading me deliberately or did she not realise the two addresses refer to the same building?

. . .

We found General Quance mounted on the steps of the porch and reviewing her forces. In response to our bows and smiles we received only the curtest salute.

At that moment Mrs Paytress appeared at the lych-gate and hurried towards us with a smile, raising her veil. Mother looked straight at her and when she was only a few yards away, showed the poor woman her back. While this was happening, Euphemia fiddled with a ribbon on her dress and then turned without raising her eyes and followed Mother into the church. I saw a look of dismay appear on Mrs Paytress's face and then she lowered her veil and slowed her pace. I tried to catch her eye but I don't think she noticed me.

Mrs Quance's pebbly little eyes lurking in their folds of flesh had watched the whole episode unfold and I saw an expression of gratification pucker her mouth with anticipation. At the end of the service as we came out she rewarded Mother with a smile that was more unnerving than any grimace and then engaged her and Effie in conversation: *How were we settling in? Did we need any advice or information to make our lives more agreeable?*

We have crossed the lines and are now marching under the Quances' colours! I'm ashamed of Mother.

*½ past midnight.*

Warm only in bed. The air like a blunt knife scraping against my skin. We all have chilblains and cold-sores though we wear mittens indoors. Our hands are chapped as if gnawed by the frost.

[A page is left blank here in the Journal. *Note by CP.*]

*Monday 21ˢᵗ of December, 9 o'clock in the evening.*

Everything has changed. Euphemia wants me to stay! And to accompany her to the ball!

And to cap it all, Mrs Yass is leaving.

Yet today began badly. After Effie went off to Lady Terrewest's, Old Hannah brought Mother another letter from Uncle Thomas. As we sat over the remains of breakfast, she read it with a frown.

Then she said: *I don't understand. Why does someone called Webster demand seventy-four pounds from Thomas?*

So it has come to that. I had to explain that he is the father of the friend who lent me that sum.

She frowned and said: *I don't think your uncle will be very pleased.*

. . .

Shortly before luncheon there was a commanding rap at the front door. Mother and Betsy stared at each other in terror and it fell to me to venture into the hall and open the door. There stood a tall man-servant in livery holding out an envelope addressed to Euphemia from Mrs Quance. Mother and I were frantic with curiosity. Could it be about the famous tickets, we wondered.

I spent an hour packing and making ready to leave in the morning.

. . .

As soon as Effie got back this afternoon I saw that her mood was transformed and she behaved to me in a perfectly friendly manner for the first time. That's what makes me think it wasn't just the tickets. Because of course that is what the letter was about. A pair was available for her and Mother. And that news was conveyed in a charming note from Mrs Quance in which she invited Effie and mother to tea on the Sunday after Christmas.

I was not named. Am I being snubbed or am I too unimportant to be remembered? To be snubbed is at least a form of recognition.

I said something about being sorry not to be going to the ball.

*Of course you must come*, Effie said graciously.

*You're forgetting that I will have gone long before the 9<sup>th</sup>.*

*Why should you go?* Effie exclaimed. *Mother, Richard may stay, mayn't he?*

Here was a reversal indeed! I couldn't decipher Mother's expression. She studied Effie's features. *If you so wish*, she said.

*I do wish it*, Effie said. Then she turned to me: *I will ask Mrs Quance for a half-ticket.*

*Darling girl*, Mother exclaimed. *Can we afford it? It's half a guinea. Let Richard take mine.*

*No, Mother. I'll pay for all the tickets.*

*But there's also the cost of the rooms and hire of a carriage.*

*I have an idea about that*, Effie said mysteriously.

How could Effie find a guinea and a half?

*Anyway*, she said, *think what we'll save by dismissing Mrs Yass.*

*Are we dismissing her?* Mother asked and her voice trembled.

*Of course. She can't cook.* Then she looked at Mother meaningfully and said: *And we don't need her.*

*Dearest girl*, Mother cried and jumped up and ran round and embraced her and kissed her. She sat down again almost in tears. *What a relief it will be to have that woman out of the house.*

Mother got excited at the prospect of a ball and put her hands over her head and executed a few mincing steps in what I suppose was the style of twenty or thirty years ago. Effie ran to the pianoforte and began to play an old-fashioned polka and Mother danced around the room. It was strange. I suddenly saw her as a girl in her teens. I turned away.

I caught Effie smiling at me. As she played she tossed her head and the hair fell against her cheek while all the time she kept her gaze on me.

. . .

During dinner Effie offered to play duets with me since I now had my flute and so we played some little pieces together. Mother listened and said to Euphemia: *I'm so glad that at least one of you has inherited my musical talent. When I was young I had a lovely voice. Everyone said so. I gave it up for you children, as I gave up so many of my pleasures.*

I realised she was sobbing.

. . .

When I reached out for my music earlier this evening, Effie's hand touched mine and stayed there for a moment.

*11 o'clock.*

The reason for Euphemia's changed mood must be that Davenant Burgoyne has proposed marriage. Mother knows and that is why she wept.

*A ¼ past midnight.*

Just now I heard raised voices. I crept down the stairs and found that Mrs Yass and Mother were arguing in the front parlour. I couldn't make out the words.

Then Mrs Yass stormed into the passage followed by Mother. Just at the door of the kitchen, she turned and said: *You've treated me bad and I've lost money by it, Mrs Shenstone. It's not you I blame. But I will say this: I've niver heard of nobody changin' her mind. Not as late as this, leastways.*

She went into the kitchen banging the door behind her.

. . .

Miss Fourdrinier is a real beauty and such a face promises other virtues that are hidden—so unlike the brazen vacancy of an Enid. And the fact that she keeps her counsel makes her all the more fascinating and mysterious.

*Until I saw you I looked on womankind with a bitter smile. Distracted by your beauty, I have missed my footing on the path of life and fallen into the waters of love where I am drowning in the deep blue of your eyes.*

. . .

[A passage in Greek letters begins here. *Note by CP.*]

It is a hot day in July. We meet on the Battlefield. We lie concealed by a bush. She helps me to unbutton her bodice. Her golden hair is down now in the confusion of our haste and falls unregarded across her naked breasts. I brush it aside, my fingers just touching her . . .

Δ

[The passage in Greek letters ends here. *Note by CP.*]

*Tuesday 22<sup>nd</sup> of December, 11 o'clock in the morning.*

C̶ame down late and missed all the pother over Mrs Yass. She had not made breakfast and when Mother went up to her room she found it had been cleared and there was no clue to where she has gone.

The letter-carrier had brought a letter for me and it lay reproachfully on my place at the table. Mother was annoyed with me and I soon found out why. Bartlemew's mother had written on the envelope: *Return to sender. My son has left home and I have no communication with him.*

Luckily, Effie had gone to spend the day with Lady Terrewest.

*I could not think of anyone else to go to,* I said.

*Even his own parent has disavowed him,* Mother said.

*He's not my friend,* I said. *I never liked him. I've told you.*

*But you met him during the holidays.*

*I only ever ran into him in the street by chance.*

*You seem to be forgetting, Richard, that you brought him to the house. You introduced him into the family.*

She said it as if she were charging me with some capital offence. I said: *You must be confusing him with someone else.*


**Noon.**


Have just remembered that I once ran into him in the street during the Easter vacation. We were almost outside our house and he made it plain he wanted to be invited in.

Father came home earlier than usual and the three of us talked in the drawing-room and Bartlemew mentioned that he had sung at Harrow and Father encouraged him to join the Cathedral choir. By that stage the malevolence of the Precentor had barred Father from involvement with the choristers.

*5 o'clock.*

Walked to Thrubwell with the idea of meeting Euphemia. I was approaching the village when a big wagon came lumbering towards me. It halted about thirty yards away and the carter got down to look at the hoof of one of his team.

There was a man lying in the back among the bales and he was struggling with something. I came closer and realised that he had a dog—a bull-terrier—under his coat. It was trying to escape and managed to get out from under the coat and I saw that it was wearing chains—iron links looped around its body whose purpose I could not imagine. The beast jumped out of the vehicle while the man shouted at it and then tugged on the thick leather lead fastened to its collar whose other end was shackled to the stranger's belt with iron fetters.

The man, still in the wagon, had yanked the lead so viciously that the animal was pulled off its feet. Then he knelt over the edge of the vehicle, took a whip from his belt and began to give it a prolonged and brutal flogging while the creature growled and whimpered and bowed its head in submission. He stopped the beating and shouted: *Get back, sirrah. Damn you!*

The dog tried to jump up but the weight of the chains was preventing it.

I had been standing a few feet from the wagon and now the man noticed me and said: *What the devil are you doing? Walk on or you'll get the same treatment.*

To my astonishment he spoke, despite his labourer's dress, in the tones of an educated man though his speech was roughened as if he were accustomed to the society of working men.

I said: *Your dog can't get up with that weight he's carrying.*

For answer the man leant further out raising his whip and then he brought it down so that it missed me by a few inches. He said: *I told you once. You won't get another warning. If you don't walk away I'll tear your arm off and beat you with it till you piss blood.*

I don't know what I would have said or done if at that moment the dog had not managed to scrabble up the wheel and get back into the wagon. The man began hitting it with the handle of the whip. I was going to protest but the carter had got back on his seat and the wagon lurched into motion.

I walked home without seeing Euphemia.

*9 o'clock.*

At dinner Mother told us that she had received a letter from Boddington containing bad news about the Chancery suit: Her father's will has been set aside. She will have to pay the costs so far incurred not only by herself but also by Cousin Sybille. Almost frightened to utter the words I asked how much that would be.

In a tiny voice she muttered: *About two hundred pounds.*

We are ruined. I cannot imagine where that sum of money will come from. Effie and I stared at each other. Mother will be in a debtors' prison for the rest of her days.

*So that's the end of it,* I said. *There is no hope of regaining your rights.*

*On the contrary,* Mother said. *I am confident of winning. Now that my father's will has been annulled, it is as if he had died intestate.*

I said: *There is a set of rules for sharing out an estate among the relatives in such a case, but I'm not sure what they are.*

Mother smiled. *They are very simple. As his only child I will inherit everything.*

Effie asked: *But if that is so, why has Cousin Sybille gone to all this expense?*

Despite our efforts, Mother would not say any more.

### 10 o'clock.

Got Betsy alone ten minutes ago and asked her to bring up hot water tonight.

Effie was charming after dinner. We played some duets for a while and she did not lose her temper when I got out of time.

### Midnight.

She's so much younger than me—three years—I don't want to do anything to frighten her.

.   .   .

[A passage in Greek letters begins here. *Note by CP.*]

She came up with the bucket of hot water ten minutes ago. I stood beside the bath in nothing but my gown. In the candle-light her pale skin and large eyes made her seem very desirable. I believe my rising cock lifted the gown a little but she didn't look at me so she couldn't have seen that.

I heard my voice trembling with anxiety and desire when I said: *I was afraid you wouldn't come once again, Betsy. I'm so glad you're here. You look very pretty tonight.*

She said: *None of that nonsense, Master Richard.*

She had to come and stand beside me to pour the water into the bath and I didn't move away. I wanted to touch her but I merely said: *Would you wait until I get in and then wash my back?*

She looked down at what she was doing and made no response.

I said: *Are you shy of seeing a man? Have you ever seen a man's thing?*

She bent over to feel the temperature of the water in the bath and I slipped the gown off so that I stood naked with a stiff cockstand beside her but she kept her head turned away. I moved forward slightly so that when she straightened up and backed towards me my cock poked at her thick skirt at the waist and we both stood for an instant like that. She didn't seem to have noticed. I leaned towards her, my teeth almost chattering with the cold and with nervousness, and whispered: *Betsy, give me your hand. Let me put it on me.*

She seemed to be hesitating. Had she noticed it? Did she like to feel it prodding her in desperate supplication?

After a moment she turned away and went out of the room without speaking or looking round.

I should have put my arms around her from behind and nuzzled her ear and said nonsensical things about how she was driving me wild while my cock jabbed at her rump and my hands get under her collar and stroke her breasts and she starts to breathe faster and says: *Oh, sir, don't make a poor girl do anything bad and . . .*

Δ

[The passage in Greek letters ends here. *Note by CP.*]

*3 o'clock in the morning.*

*Idiot idiot idiot!*

About two hours ago I was trying to sleep when I heard a sound I could not identify. I put my greatcoat on over my nightgown and crept downstairs. In the dark scullery I found a stub of candle standing burning on a sideboard. The noise was coming from outside and so I pushed open the door which was unbolted and went out into the yard.

It was bone-chillingly cold. I saw Mother working the pump-handle beside the well-head and filling a bucket. As I watched she suffered a fit of coughing and was doubled up by it, her thin shoulders jerking awkwardly. I could see how much pain her coughing was causing her. She was holding her hands over her mouth.

When I spoke to her she started guiltily and said: *Whatever are you doing out here at this hour?*

*I might say the same to you,* I answered. *It's freezing now. The cold air is making you cough.*

I took the bucket from her and we went into the scullery. I closed and locked the door.

When I turned back she had plunged her hands into the sink and was rubbing pieces of cloth between her fingers. I said: *What in heaven's name are you doing, Mother?*

*Do you remember how Mrs Green used to starch the trimmings to Father's vestments and his bands and cambric ruffs? I often watched her and that is how I learned how to do it.*

*Can't Betsy do it?*

She smiled. *No, Richard. Betsy can't do it.* She explained patiently as if to a child that good linen of this kind—the few articles of value still in our possession—had to be washed very carefully and then parts of the garment starched and that it was a delicate and painstaking operation requiring skill and patience.

I saw that her hands were red and raw. I seized one of them and it was cold as ice and chapped.

I said: *Those are Effie's collars, aren't they?* She nodded. *Does she know you're doing this?*

Mother said almost indignantly: *She is a beautiful girl and deserves the best that I can do for her.*

So that's what Euphemia meant when she told Mrs Paytress there is *someone in the house who is very adept at that kind of work.* A classic instance of Euphemia's fine-ladyism! She knows Mother performs this arduous task for her but chooses not to think about it.

*You mustn't do this,* I said.

*Richard, people make sacrifices for those they love.*

I said: *I hate to see you doing this. Why are we so poor now? Why did you have to sell Father's pension?*

She stopped what she was doing and said: *I didn't tell you I sold it. The pension was never granted.*

*Whyever not?*

*Because of the circumstances in which your father resigned.* She looked down at her work. *While he was Canon Treasurer he made some mistakes in his accounting. The Dean—who as you know hated your father—demanded full repayment. So everything we had was seized by bailiffs and a sale was held.*

*That was the shock that brought on Father's death?*

She paused and then nodded.

I asked: *That was the revelation you threatened me with if I didn't go away?*

She scrabbled nervously at the wet linen. Then she said brightly: *Yes, that was it.* She turned away and for a minute or two concentrated on wringing out the wet cloth.

Then she said: *So you can see why I was so upset to learn that you've been getting into debt. Uncle Thomas said he has learned something he doesn't want to tell me. Something the College is upset about.*

I hope the darkness hid my face.

*I'm not a complete innocent, Richard. I've heard that young men at the Varsity behave really quite . . . That some of them . . .*

I said quickly: *Mother, you can set your mind at rest on that score. No woman was involved.*

She gave me such a strange look. Why wasn't she reassured?

Then she suddenly said: *Richard, promise me you'll have nothing to do with him. That dreadful creature, Bartlemew.*

I said I had no intention of seeing him ever again.

*4 o'clock.*

Why did Father need money? Why did such a proud and upright man do what he did?

I wanted so much to ask her more questions and yet I dared not press her. She looked so frail and gazed at me timidly even as she asserted her maternal authority.

. . .

*Not defiled with women.* Unfortunately not.

. . .

I must be careful. The girl is young and easily frightened. I don't want to frighten her into complaining to Mother about me—though I believe she would not dare to make trouble for fear of losing her place.

*Wednesday 23rd of December, 11 o'clock.*

The post came so late that we had had breakfast and Euphemia had left for Lady Terrewest—yet again!—by the time Old Hannah arrived. She handed me two letters—one for Mother and one for myself. Both were from Uncle Thomas and I took mine up here to open.

He wants to ship me abroad like a convict transported to the colonies! And with the threat to reveal everything to Mother! How dare he try to blackmail me! *Unthinkable that I should employ you in a position of trust.*

I have plans for my life and they don't involve being despatched to some stinking den in the stews of Canton or a log cabin on the shore of a frozen lake in Ontario.

*By return of post.* He can whistle for it.


*2 o'clock.*


I had to read the letter to Mother because he told her he had made me a proposal she should discuss with me.

*This is beyond my hopes*, Mother said. *A clerkship in one of the trading-companies with which he corresponds! How generous.*

*Generous! It has cost him nothing but the time he took to write a couple of letters and in return he gets rid of me for ever. Canton or Hudson Bay! Both of them on the other side of the world.*

*I'm sure he has your best interests at heart.*

*Does he? I think he wants to avoid any prospect of having to pay my debts—which I don't for a minute expect him to do.*

Mother shook her head. *What nonsense! And besides, you have to earn your living in some way now that you won't be resuming your studies.*

*Won't I? Why do you say that?*

She shrugged. *Even if the College will have you back, I doubt if Uncle Thomas will continue to support you.*

*I'm not even sure I wish to return.*

*Then if you won't go back and won't go abroad, how do you imagine you will earn your living?*

So I took a deep breath and told her. *I intend to write for the literary pages of the newspapers.*

She stared at me in dismay and said: *I had a suspicion that something like that was in your mind.*

I told her that I was perfectly realistic about the difficulties. I will go to London and make my way by dint of hard work and talent.

At last she said: *Well, I know you can work very hard on something as long as it holds your interest.*

*So we may ignore Uncle Thomas's offer?*

*You must write very courteously declining it and tell him you will visit him when you arrive in London.*

Thank heavens for the improvement in the weather. It will be a fine afternoon for a walk.


*6 o'clock.*


The world has gone mad.

I was in the middle of the Battlefield when I spotted that old lunatic Fourdrinier standing in a patch of wild grass that came above his knee. He was bent over and using a long-handled tool to cut the roots of the undergrowth. It resembled a large dibber or a pruning-hook with a curved blade at the end.

When I spoke his name he turned to me such an unfriendly face that I almost thought I had the wrong man. He looked like nothing so much as a parrot scrabbling in the sand of his cage who had been surprised in mid-scratch—beak at an angle, one leg slightly raised, head turned so that only a single eye was visible, large and unwinking through the thick lens of his pince-nez. I can't imagine how I ever thought of his features as cherubic and innocent when they are so manifestly corrupt with that small mouth and the round eyes with drooping lids.

It's not just his nose that is pinched: it's his whole moral being.

I said: *Mr Fourdrinier, I have not forgotten your gracious invitation to tea.*

He made no remark but began packing away his implements in the huge bag I had seen him with before. Then he suddenly swung round and gazed at me intently and asked: *Do you know anything about a letter?*

*A letter? From whom?*

*From whom?* he repeated indignantly. *That's just the point. A letter from someone I don't know.*

I looked at him without trying to hide my astonishment. I asked: *If it's from someone you are not acquainted with, then how could I have any information about it?*

He rudely showed his back to me without answering and carried on packing up.

I asked: *Where is the young lady?*

He turned and glared at me and delivered the breathtaking words: *What damned business is that of yours? Any more than it was your business to find out where I live?*

He glanced—I assume involuntarily—towards the north-east and there, about a hundred yards away, was the girl and she was coming towards us. She stopped and then turned her back and began to walk very fast the way she had come.

Then the most extraordinary thing: He said: *Do you hope to stir my pot? Is that what you're thinking, young fellow? You take me for a limp brush?*

I must have stared at him like a madman myself. I felt that the obligations of social intercourse were suspended and so, without another word to the old booby, I turned and ran after the girl. He called out furiously: *Sirrah!*

She glanced back and saw me and quickened her pace. By now I had become excited by the chase and, furious at the old rascal's discourtesy, I threw propriety to the four winds.

After twenty or thirty paces I came alongside her. *Please don't be alarmed,* I said. *There appears to have been some misunderstanding.* She walked on quickly, looking behind her. The old man had dropped the tool and was scurrying towards us on his fat old legs.

Then she spoke: *Wut the ell djoo want wiv me?*

It was the accent and language of the London streets—the lowest and meanest of its most abject rookeries. The contrast between the delicacy of her features and the coarseness of her voice was so striking that I stopped dead.

She turned back and began to hurry towards the old man. I let her go. The scales had fallen from my eyes. The girl is certainly not the old scoundrel's niece. But what does puzzle me is what has occasioned this sudden change in his attitude towards me. And what the devil he meant by that letter he was talking about.

*10 o'clock.*

After dinner Mother said that we had to have a serious talk. She began by addressing Euphemia: *Richard and I have discussed his intentions for the future. He intends to start earning his living by . . .*

She interrupted: *That's all very well, but what is going to happen about his debts? Who is going to pay them?*

I said: *I will. If you will have the courtesy to allow Mother to speak, she will explain how.*

Mother went on uneasily: *Once my claim to my father's estate has succeeded, there will be no difficulty in paying all our creditors.*

*So I'm to see a part of my inheritance given up to pay his debts? My birthright sold like Esau's for a mess of pottage.* She paused and then with an angry smile asked: *Did Uncle Thomas say anything in his letters about settling with Richard's creditors?*

Mother and I exchanged a look and Euphemia said: *Oh, weren't you going to tell me? You see, I met Old Hannah on her way here this morning and asked if there were any letters and while she was rummaging in her box, I saw them.*

There was no escape. Mother showed her the letter Uncle Thomas had sent her and she read it several times and then asked Mother to explain what his proposal was. When she had heard it she turned to me: *This is a magnificent offer. It means you can leave all your mistakes behind you and start a new life.*

No regret that her brother would be on the other side of the world! (And how dare she refer to *all my mistakes!*)

*It's not much of an offer,* I pointed out. *I'd be away from England for many years and I'd be nothing more than a mere clerk.*

*But with wonderful opportunities. You must know how many young men went out as penniless clerks and came back as millionaires.*

*Well you go and spend the rest of your life in some remote colony,* I said.

*I would if I were a man! But why do you say "the rest of your life"? When you've earned enough to pay off your creditors, you can return.*

*I could never return. Not after fleeing abroad to escape my creditors. No gentleman could face the shame.*

*You should forget all those notions. Nobody cares now who someone's father was. Only what talents he has and how hard he works.*

Who has she been talking to? That note of *sansculottism* is a striking change of tune. This is the girl who grovels and curtsies to a title at every chance! The girl who is risking everything to catch herself an earl! Is there something I have failed to understand?

Then she said: *Mother, Richard must accept immediately.* She turned to me: *When are the sailing dates?*

I said: *A few weeks.*

*Well, when?* she demanded. *Before or after the ball?*

What an extraordinary remark! *What does it matter?* I said.

*It matters a great deal,* she said. *You can't leave before then.*

*Go and fetch the letter,* Mother ordered.

I hurried up here to get it and then read out to them: "*On Thursday 14th January* The Hibernian Maid *departs from Southampton bound for Newfoundland.* The Caledonian Maid *sails from Rye, after being refitted, on Saturday 16th January for Hong Kong.*"

*Then there's no difficulty,* Euphemia pronounced. *The ball is on the 9th.*

Mother seemed as surprised as I did at the idea that the course of my entire life should depend on the date of a ball.

*But I'm not going to accept Uncle Thomas's offer,* I said. *Mother and I have agreed that I will follow another course.*

*And what is that?* Euphemia asked sarcastically.

*I will become a literary journalist!*

Her eyes widened in amazement. (Quite the actress!) I explained what I had said to Mother while she listened impatiently.

*You're deluding yourself,* she said, interrupting me before I had finished. *To earn your living by your pen at seventeen! Without even a degree! Do you have any conception of how difficult that would be?*

I said: *Mother agreed that I could do it.*

*What does she know about it?* She turned to Mother: *You know nothing about the world outside the cloisters of Thurchester Cathedral.*

She spoke with such unveiled contempt that Mother started as if she had been struck. *How dare you take that tone with me.*

*Well it's true. All you've ever thought about is running a house and looking after us. Father could never talk to you about anything serious. Anything that he really cared about.*

*That's a wicked thing to say.*

*He admitted it himself. You never understood him properly. You never helped him when he was persecuted by the mediocrities who hated him because they could never match him.*

*I think you're exaggerating,* Mother said.

*Are you saying he imagined it?* Euphemia demanded. *You know that Father made enemies—as he used to say himself, "effortlessly"—because people envied him, and if you'd understood that better you could have saved him from what happened.*

*That wasn't my fault. It wasn't I who did those things. He chose to do them.*

*I'm not going to deny that he didn't make mistakes but he only made them because you failed him when he needed you.*

Mother stared at her and then rose and walked stiffly out of the room.

When the door had closed behind her, Euphemia said: *You're like Mother. You delude yourself about what is really happening. You're not going to make me suffer for your stupidity.*

I said: *What mistakes? Are you referring to his accounts? How could any of that have been Mother's fault?*

She crossed to the pianoforte and began to play vengefully.


*½ past 11 o'clock.*


She must have felt it. She must have known what it was. She cannot be so innocent. It must have felt like a finger prodding her even through her thick dress. The thought that she knew what it was is gratifying. If she hadn't known she would have looked round to see what it was. She is interested!

. . .

Mother and Betsy have been busy in the kitchen much of the day preparing for Christmas. It's like a pale ghost of the old times with all the servants scurrying around and the holly and mistletoe everywhere and the comings and goings and the making up of the Christmas boxes.

*Midnight.*

From my room I can just see Euphemia's window and, I think, Betsy's above it. I have just noticed the candle being extinguished behind the curtains in Effie's room. Then exactly four minutes later the candle went out in Betsy's room.

Mother caught me on my own after breakfast and told me that she now believes that my hopes of starting a literary career are "absurd".

Between hacking coughs that shook her thin shoulders in their threadbare covering, she said: *Your sister is right. You would starve in London. You must take up Uncle Thomas's offer. Otherwise, what will become of Euphemia and me? I want to live long enough to see my children comfortably settled. I don't want to be a contemptible dependant like Miss Bittlestone—patronised by people like Mrs Quance.*

I said: *Uncle Thomas's proposal is a sentence of transportation.*

*There is no argument about it, Richard. You must accept. And he requires a reply within the next couple of days.*

*And what if I won't?*

*You're my child, Richard. I bore you and raised you and have loved you and it would be tearing you out of my heart by the roots if I had to sacrifice you, but I warn you that under certain circumstances I would do it.* Then she left the room.

*2 o'clock.*

At luncheon Mother calmly announced to Effie and me that she had taken an important decision without consulting us. Boddington had written this morning to say that since she was determined to go ahead with the Chancery suit, she should sell part of the claim for a share of the costs. I had no idea such a thing was possible but it seems there is a market for actions at law as there seems to be for every-thing else. She now told us that she had written immediately giving him instructions to do that and had posted the letter in the village this morning.

Effie just shrugged. I said nothing.

*½ past 6 o'clock in the evening.*

I can hardly write for anger.

I had passed the end of our lane and got some way towards Strat-ton Herriard when I saw a tall man approaching me walking with a limp. It was clear from his handsome surtout and beaver hat that he was a gentleman of means. I recognised him from his height and when he had passed me I turned round and, keeping about twenty yards to his rear, I tagged him along the road wondering how to approach him. Since I was behind him I could not come up to him face-to-face. I had followed him for only about two hundred yards when he suddenly swung round and lunged at me. Before I knew what was happening he had gripped me by the shoulders and spun me around so that he was behind me. He twisted my arms so that I cried out in pain.

*You damned cur! Why are you following me? Who paid you?* To my astonishment he started searching my pockets with one hand. *Are you carrying a firearm?*

I said: *Certainly not!*

He wrenched me round to face him and shouted in my face: *I have one and I warn you, I will use it if I need to.* Then he said: *I won't be taken for a sitting duck a second time.*

When he had satisfied himself that I was not armed he thrust me from him.

With as much dignity as I could muster, I said: *I believe you are Mr Davenant Burgoyne.*

He said: *You know damn well I am but who in the name of the devil are you, sirrah?*

I told him he had mistaken me for someone else. I said *My name is Shenstone. Richard Shenstone.*

*What's that to me?*

I'm sure he was pretending not to know the name. He must have recognised it. Damnable coxcomb.

I said: *I'm the brother of Miss Euphemia Shenstone.*

*Effie, eh?* he said with a sneer. *Are you, by God? What do you want to make of it?* He studied me for a few seconds and then turned away.

This was not at all what I had expected—or had the right to expect. I said: *Sir, I am a gentleman and entitled to courtesy from another. And moreover, you might have recognised from my name that you and I are related, albeit very distantly.*

*The devil we are*, was all the courtesy that speech elicited.

I persevered: *My mother is the daughter of the late Nicholas Herriard, Esquire.*

Then he halted and turned to me with a thin-lipped smile: *Well, Master Shenstone, I took you for some low sneaking fellow. But now that I understand you are the grandson of Nicholas Herriard, Esquire, I realise that I have not done you justice.*

We began to march along the lane together in the most absurd manner quite as if we were partaking of a companionable stroll. I was wondering what to say. I must be wrong about him and Euphemia for surely even the most arrogant aristocrat could not be so offensive to his prospective brother-in-law. In that case, how do relations between him and Effie stand?

Then he said—almost as if he meant his condolences to be taken at face-value: *I heard of the sudden death of your much-respected father and regret that I never had the honour of meeting him, but then I don't remember ever finding myself in The Dolphin Tavern.*

The name meant nothing to me at the time. But when I thought about it afterwards, I remembered that I have heard Bartlemew mention it as a place he frequents.

Davenant Burgoyne and I proceeded in silence for a few yards while I wondered how to respond, and then he said boorishly: *Are you following me?*

*I have no desire to impose my company upon you, sir,* I said with dignity.

I slowed my pace. He strode on ahead of me and after a few minutes turned up the path towards Upton Dene. I looked at his gait as he walked away and I was struck by how much more marked his limp was now than it was a few days ago.

I can't imagine why he was in such a funk. Could he really have believed that a complete stranger—met by chance—meant to take his life?

I was marching along in a complete daze when, as if waking from a dream, I found myself suddenly a few feet from the Quance girls.

Guinevere said: *What a surprise!*

She smiled pertly and I know the sly little miss was implying that I had contrived to meet them. Her sister stared at me coldly.

I don't know why I didn't pass them by without speaking except that I am drawn to them as to something that both hurts and gives pleasure.

*Are you on patrol?* Guinevere asked, glancing at my walking-stick.

*Why should I be?* I asked.

She studied my face with an intensity that was insolent and yet rather gratifying. *You haven't heard what has happened to set the whole neighbourhood by the ears?*

I shook my head.

*You truly know nothing of what some wicked person is doing to poor harmless beasts?*

*On my honour. Are you saying that animals are being killed?*

*No, not killed.* (A quiver of excitement in her face.)

*What then? Harmed?*

*Yes and in a special way,* Guinevere said and then laughed.

Was she laughing from fear or pleasure? And what could she possibly mean by "a special way"? I wanted to ask, but when I saw Enid giggling with spiteful glee I remembered that I had promised myself to have no more to do with them. I quickly took leave of them with the barest minimum of formality and walked on.

They seemed not to know that Davenant Burgoyne was in the district. Odd. Is Enid out of the running?

As I walked through the village in the twilight with the girl's words ringing in my head, the world I had thought I knew began to metamorphose: the slumbering hills, clumps of trees, and dark shapes of houses that had seemed so safe and familiar, became the hidden lairs of some unknown and evil passion. Where the houses ended, the undifferentiated fields lay on either side of me under their coverlet of snow. By now the sun had slipped out of sight and the wind whistled through the hawthorn bushes like a sigh from the end of the world.

I was almost at Stratton Herriard when I saw two figures ahead of me in the near-darkness. I caught up with them before I realised they were Mother and Miss Bittlestone and because Mother was carrying some packages, I was about to signal my presence and take them from her when I heard her say something which made me fall back and walk behind them:

*Like his father he falls into black depressions in which he spends time by himself and does not answer when spoken to.*

Miss Bittlestone said something I didn't catch and then Mother went on: *He's never made friends easily—and when he does, he chooses them badly.*

At that moment we arrived at the turning to our house and they both stopped. I hailed them as if I had just reached them. Mother asked the old hen to come and celebrate the season with a glass of punch but Miss Bittlestone happily explained that she was on an errand for the Quances in Upton Dene. She then chattered boastfully about how she was spending Christmas with the Rector's family as usual. I took Mother's parcels from her and when we arrived home she laid out their contents on the table in the parlour together with the results of a day of baking. So there were all the things she used to prepare in the drawing room at Prebendary Street: mince-pies, mulled wine and punch for the men and fruit cordial for the choir-boys, candied fruit, and so on.

*This is very lavish. Are we expecting the waits?* I asked.

*Of course*, she said with a tired smile. *It's Christmas Eve.*


*9 o'clock.*


At about seven o'clock while we were eating our supper we heard the distant sound of the band approaching down the road from Stratton Herriard. I looked at Mother's face. This meant so much to her: recognition that we were back in the clerical fold. The thought that she cared so much that a mere rural Rector and his swinish wife should consider us to be worthy of their attention is upsetting. But it was not to be. After a few minutes it became clear that the sounds were getting fainter and I saw on her face her growing dismay at the humiliation and the waste of money that could ill be spared. The church-band and choristers had taken the fork that led to Netherton.

*Don't they know that this house is now inhabited?* Mother said.

I was sure I detected the hand of Mrs Quance in this. It was a signal that we were not yet wholly accepted. More penance would be required. I was angry with Mother for caring so much.

After supper I got Betsy alone in the passageway to the kitchen and asked: *Have you heard talk of anything strange going on? To do with animals? Something nasty?*

*You mean cutting off their ballocks, sir?* she said boldly looking straight at me. Was she smiling?

I hope I didn't blush. To hear that word on her lips was strangely exciting. *Is someone doing that?*

*So they say. Going out at night with a knife or summat and stuffing their ballocks down their throats and slashing open their wames.*

She told me that everyone had been talking about it at the shop. Someone had gone out last night and not only maimed animals but also written lewd messages in red paint on walls in the village.

I said: *That's frightening. Are you frightened, Betsy?*

*Why should I be afeart, sir?*

*Well, of that or anything else. Ghosts. They say this old place is haunted.* Then more softly I said: *If you're ever frightened by a ghost or anything else during the night, come to my room.*

She didn't say anything but as she turned away she pressed her mouth into that sly, pleasure-hinting smile, half-secretive, half-inviting.

. . .

How can Mother say I don't have friends? It's true that I have always had fewer than Effie, but that is because I choose them more carefully.

*10 o'clock.*

I've just found out that a goose has been purchased from a nearby farmer. Betsy and Mother intend to pluck it tomorrow. Back at Prebendary Street she left that to the cook so I don't know how she will manage it herself. She has been putting up holly and mistletoe around the house in an attempt to recreate the old Christmases. But it's absurd. This year nobody has sent a single card. All of that is over and done with. I tried to tell her that but she became very upset.

This evening we opened our presents to each other as we always used to do on Christmas Eve.

Euphemia said: *My gift for you, Richard, is the ticket I bought.*

What generosity! I don't even want to go to the damned ball.

Mother gave Euphemia a miniature of Father as a young man that used to hang by the mantelpiece at Prebendary Street, and she received in return a silver thimble Effie had owned for years and never used. What a contrast with last year! My gift from Father was a silver shaving set and Mother's was my very handsome knapsack. This time she handed me an old shirt that I thought she had thrown away but she had secretly repaired it and embroidered the neck and cuffs into a kind of embossed lace. She asked me if I was pleased with it. How did she imagine I would respond? I shrugged and said it would do. How could she expect me to be cheerful when she was saying such cruel things about me to virtual strangers?

Euphemia said: *Don't take any notice of him. He's just a sulky little boy.*

That was it. I got up and left them sitting there with their sad little presents around them.

. . .

*½ past 10 o'clock.*

A moment ago Betsy tapped at the door and came in with a plate of mince-pies! It was her own idea, as she admitted when I asked. I begged her to sit down for a minute while I ate so that she could take the plate back and she shyly seated herself in a chair facing me.

I was afraid I had frightened her last time so I decided not to say or do anything but all the time I was thinking how under that rough woollen skirt is a soft warm girl's body that I longed to touch. I said: *I hope Christmas away from your own family isn't too dreary a time for you.*

She pressed her lips together as if to discourage me from that topic. Perhaps it is too painful for her to think of her family now.

It was hard to think of any new subject after that and yet there was no awkwardness and we sat in companionable silence while I ate.

I said: *I hope I don't frighten you, Betsy?*

*Frighten me, sir? Whyever should you say that?* And then she gave that enigmatic half-smile as if I wouldn't understand her amusement. And now she was looking directly at me in a way that she has rarely done before. It was oddly disconcerting and yet it was what I had been trying to get her to do ever since I had arrived.

I said: *Because I'm a man and so much older than you.* She kept on smiling at me as if she were enjoying a joke I had made. I was a little irritated and I said: *And because I know so many more things than you do.*

Then she stood up and took the empty plate from me saying: *But perhaps I know things you don't know.*

She walked out. I don't know what to make of that.

. . .

*½ past 11 o'clock.*

Astonishing! Just two minutes ago I passed Betsy in the hall and she came close and whispered: *I can milk your udder for you if you like.* She moved away before I could answer. So she did notice my cockstand. And didn't mind it!

*If I like!*

. . .

A day or two ago Mother complained about the smell from my smoking. (I thought I was far enough away for it not to be detected.) She said there was an odd odour emanating from my part of the house. Effie said: *Just what are you smoking up there?* Mother pricked up her ears at that. I must be more careful.

I've noticed a smell, too. But it's not anything I'm doing. It seems to be coming from somewhere near the front parlour or the hall. Something corrupted and decaying.

*A ¼ to 1 o'clock in the morning.*

[A passage in Greek letters begins here. *Note by CP.*]

She glides into the room carrying a candle and comes towards my bed. She says: *I'm dreadful skeert, sir.* I say: *Sit on the bed, my girl.* She does so. I lean forward and blow out her candle. My hand slides under her rounded haunch, soft and smooth and warm. I say: *You'd be warmer under the covers.* She gets in. I say: *You must be hot with that thick nightdress.*

Δ

[The passage in Greek letters ends here. *Note by CP.*]

A lowering sky and clouds like a dark hand closing over the countryside. I had no desire to write this morning. I am bored and wretched.

Just after breakfast the farmer's boy from up the way brought the goose to the door holding it upside down by the feet. To our horror it was alive. We told him we had expected it to have been killed but he just thrust it into Mother's hands and then hurried away.

None of us—Betsy included—had ever seen a goose put to death but Mother said she had watched it being done to chickens and knew the method.

We all went into the kitchen-yard at the back. Mother gripped the head of the poor creature with one hand and the body with the other and then began to twist the head.

*It should break*, she said. The miserable bird flapped its wings and scrabbled desperately with its feet. After several failed attempts, Mother said: *I'm not strong enough. You try, Richard.*

I felt an overwhelming reluctance to do what she had asked and I said: *This is your fault, Mother. I didn't ask for a goose.*

She cried: *At least hold the wretched thing and I'll try again.*

Euphemia offered to do it but I felt humiliated by that and so, much against my will, I gripped the poor frightened creature while Mother tried to snap its neck. We must have been doing something wrong for it stubbornly failed to break.

Betsy had vanished and now came back with a broom and said we should try something she had heard about: You put the fowl on the ground and lay the broom across it and then stand on both ends of the handle and yank the neck up sharply to break it.

I tried to do that. Somehow it escaped us and ran round the yard flapping its wings. I chased after it and Betsy laughed so much she was unable to speak so that Mother lost her temper and snapped at her.

*Oh this is ridiculous,* Euphemia said. She hurried away and I thought she was abandoning us. But a few moments later she came back with the axe that is used for chopping wood.

Mother cried out: *Don't do that! There'll be blood all over you.*

*You can't do it on the ground,* I said. *I'll get the chopping-block.*

When I had placed it in position Euphemia and I chased round the yard until we had caught the damned bird. Then I held it while Effie hit it on the head with the flat of the axe-blade and it went still. She then laid its neck across the block and swung the axe. She severed its neck with her first blow and sprang back but not fast enough because blood spurted out in short bursts for about five seconds and the first spattering caught her on the arm. She gave a sudden laugh in exultation. Horribly the wings continued to flap for half a minute until the bird finally lay still.

Seeing a creature blindly fighting for its life—resisting death by the same instinct that possesses us—awakened so many images in my mind. I saw Father falling to the ground helpless, gasping for breath, terrified of the approaching darkness. And then involuntarily I saw Edmund not fighting for his life but choosing to give it up.

Effie was smiling at her handiwork but I couldn't help saying that the whole thing had turned my stomach.

She said: *You're a hypocrite and a sentimentalist. You're going to eat it, aren't you? In that case, it has to be killed.*

Mother and Betsy plucked the goose and have just put it in the oven. They had some difficulty because of its size.

Time for church.

*3 o'clock.*

When the service ended the Lloyds happened to be leaving the church behind us and with them was a young woman whom I did not recognise. Then it struck me that it was their daughter Lucy. She has grown up since I last saw her. That red-golden hair is now darker and is decorously concealed, of course, beneath a bonnet from which a few locks peeked.

She saw me staring at her and gave a slow half-smile, her eyes sliding away from mine so that I could not decide if she was pleased to see me or merely amused. She kept her eyes demurely lowered while her parents moved off towards the gate while she lagged behind. At my prompting, Mother spoke to her, telling her our name and reminding her of how we had all known each other in the old days in Thurchester. (Effie walked on ahead of us as if she had not seen her.) She seemed pleased by our overture and explained that she had been away at school in France for several years.

She said: *I attended the convent-school in Toulouse where Mother was sent as a girl. And it turns out that Mrs Paytress was a pupil there—years after Mother, of course. And so we speak French when we are together.* She smiled and turned to me: *I know who you are. You're the little boy we all used to pinch.*

*I don't recall that,* I said.

*Yes, we used to tease you mercilessly, we girls. And we would make you cry. What little monsters we were.*

Mother laughed and said: *I remember what monkeys you three girls were—you and Euphemia and Maud Whitaker-Smith.*

Lucy said: *Oh yes, Maud. I have something to tell you about her.*

She glanced at Euphemia's back and, lowering her voice, began: *The clever creature has . . .*

We were destined not to hear it because at that moment Mrs Lloyd turned towards us and looking straight at her daughter frowned in a way that clearly meant: *Stop talking to those people and come here.*

With an apologetic smile at Mother and me and a defiant toss of her head, Lucy took leave of us. But instead of rejoining her parents, she skipped pertly across to the Quance sisters who were waiting a few yards from their mother and father. With a charming little bow and a dimpled smile she said something to them. Whatever it was horrified them. Enid seemed to totter and was caught by her sister and her mother. They supported her as they made their slow way towards the Rectory with Miss Bittlestone fussing along in the rear.

As we walked home I speculated on the meaning of that little drama. Could it be connected with Davenant Burgoyne's presence in the district yesterday?

*A ¼ to 9 o'clock.*

Disaster! A few minutes after we got home, I was alerted by raised voices in the kitchen—audible all the way from the parlour. I hurried out and found Mother and Betsy having a furious argument. The goose was barely half-cooked and Mother was saying that the girl had failed to keep the oven hot enough while Betsy was protesting that the bird was simply too big.

Eventually Mother decided that it should be cooked over the open fire. That meant that poor Betsy had to stand in the heat and keep turning the spit while she ladled hot fat over the bird.

The three of us sat in the parlour getting hungrier and hungrier and drinking the one bottle of sherry that had survived from Prebendary Street. Mother would hurry out at intervals to see how the goose was coming on and to prepare the vegetables.

While she was out there for about the fifth time Effie and I heard a scream and we both ran to the kitchen.

The fowl was ablaze! The hot fat had caught fire. Betsy seized a pan and began to fill it with water from the cistern but Mother shouted: *No! Don't do that! You'll ruin it!* She seized a cloth and threw it over the bird and then wrapped it around it and the flames died out.

When Mother removed the cloth—now singed and full of holes—we all looked at the goose and then Mother prodded it: It was burnt on the outside and still raw inside.

She reproached Betsy bitterly for having allowed too much fat to build up in the pan.

To see her bullying a servant like that! It was so unlike the old days. I looked at her thin shoulders under her worn and patched Sunday best and thought how she had come down in the world. How we all have. So much has slipped away from us that we—I at least—had always assumed was permanent: civility, graciousness, and generosity. Now the wood is showing through the varnish. We are all as likely to detonate as a loaded spring-gun.

Euphemia had one of her sudden fits of rage and cried: *Oh damn the wretched thing!* She seized it and was going to throw it into the waste-bucket but it was so hot that she dropped it.

Mother was furious with her and picked it up with the burnt cloth while Effie stormed out. I withdrew while Mother was giving Betsy instructions on how she should wait until the goose had cooled a little and then wipe it down and carry on cooking it.

It all happened because Mother was determined that we should eat a proper Christmas dinner like the ones we enjoyed in the past. Foolish, foolish Mother! How I hate it when she does something like that and then becomes frightened and angry when it turns out badly.

We went back into the parlour and sat in a simmering silence to wait for the goose. Mother brought out what she said was the single good tablecloth she still had—one made of "damasked linen" with lace edging. Nobody had bid for it at the auction, she said, because it had a tear that had been repaired but which didn't show when the table was small enough. I thought it looked rather absurd with the cheap old cutlery laid on it.

I had finished the last bottle of Father's good claret the day before but to my astonishment Mother announced that she still had one. I asked where it had come from and she said she had put it aside because *I did not trust you with all that wine!* She asked me to decant it. I pointed out that it should have been opened a couple of hours before but when I saw the bottle I realised she had chosen poorly and the wine was hardly worth decanting. Mother, however, insisted on my doing so.

We sat and drank without speaking. We had nothing to say to each other. Then unfortunately Mother—just to break the silence—asked me if I had yet replied to Uncle T. I said I hadn't and she became very indignant. It's my life, my decision. I think I should be allowed to take my time over it. I tried to say that but Mother told me I was throwing away the best opportunity I would ever be offered and that if I stayed in England my debts and lack of a degree meant that I would be a burden on her and my sister!

The best opportunity! Banishment for life! With perils on the way there and further dangers once I arrived.

Euphemia backed Mother up. How dare she interfere! She wants me to go to the other side of the world just to please her—but only when I've escorted her to a damned ball! Frankly, I don't see why I should humour her when she cares so little for my interests and my wishes.

We were almost shouting at each other when Mother said: *We'll drop the subject. I want to hear no more about it. This is Christmas and we're together as a family.*

. . .

When at last we began dinner, we had all drunk too much sherry and claret. Though burnt on the outside, the goose was still bloody in places but some of it was eatable.

We hardly spoke as we chopped and chewed. Mother and Effie talked about what they would wear to the ball and I hardly listened as Mother said she had an old dress that she had worn many years ago and that she believed could be given new life.

I said: *You do both realise that while we're in here celebrating the chief Christian festival of the year like a loving and affectionate family, poor little Betsy is out in the scullery cleaning pots on her own.*

*Of course I'm aware of that,* Effie began.

*What are you suggesting?* Mother demanded, interrupting her as she rarely does. (The wine!) *That we invite her to share our dinner? Have you forgotten that at Prebendary Street the servants had their own meal downstairs at Christmas?*

*Yes,* I said, *but here there's only Betsy.*

*Don't you preach to me about Betsy's virtues,* Effie cried. *I know all about them and you can't deny that she doesn't contribute ten times what you do for this family.* Before I had a chance to point out that she had said the opposite of what she had intended, she went on: *Look, I'm carving some of the meat to take out to her now.* She began placing slices of breast on a plate.

A moment later she jumped up and hurried out with it.

Mother and I sat for a long time in silence. At last I said I'd go and see what had become of my sister. As I approached the kitchen Effie and Betsy must not have heard me because they were standing together holding each other. Betsy, so much smaller, had her head against Effie's bosom and from the movements of her head seemed to be weeping quietly. Then I realised that it was Effie who was crying and the girl was comforting her.

I sneaked away without letting them know I had seen them and told Mother that Effie would be along in a minute.

She took her time. Eventually she joined us again and we started our dessert. Then, as I'd guessed she would, Mother began reminiscing about past Christmases in a voice that trembled on the edge of tears. Euphemia joined in and it became a threnody of self-pity. I kept mum even when Effie began to talk about Father and said it would be remiss not to pay our respects to his memory on this day. What is strange is that Mother did not endorse that sentiment. I've noticed that she has been more and more reluctant to defend Father and less and less hostile to Uncle Thomas.

Effie talked, her voice almost breaking, of how she had longed to lighten Father's periods of darkness. And then she said: *Father would have been a much happier man if he had gained his bishopric.*

I could not stop myself saying: *Would he?*

That threw her for a moment. Then she said: *What do you mean, Richard? Do you mean that the Church could never have found a proper use for a man of his abilities?*

*If you want to put it that way.*

She objected to what she called my "tone". We grew heated. Strangely, Mother sat in silence without making any attempt to defend Father. And then disaster! I don't know how it happened but I knocked my wine-glass over and the tablecloth was soaked. Mother gave a cry as if she had been physically hurt. She said: *That was stupid of you.* She accused me of having taken too much wine. (Hypocrite! She'd drunk at least as much as I.)

I told her it was just a tablecloth. She said: *That's typically selfish of you. There's so little left of my life and now you've taken one more thing from me.*

Euphemia told me to apologise and I said you can't apologise for an accident.

I think that what was really annoying me was that Mother was making me think the less of her for being so obsessed with material things. I said: *Can't you let your mind rise above tablecloths and bed-linen?*

She said: *How dare you. Your father would be horrified to hear you speak to me like that.*

I said: *I've heard him say worse things to you.*

*You are being impertinent and unkind! Go to your room this instant.*

I said: *I don't see why I should. I'm not twelve years old any more.*

Euphemia said: *Then stop behaving as if you were.*

I said: *Since you feel like that, you won't want my company at the ball. I've decided I'm not going.*

Instantly she got that look like a snarling cat with its ears flat-
tened against its head and its eyes wide and she said: *In that case,
you're of no use here. You're in the way. Just go. I don't care where. Just
leave the house tomorrow. And then take ship for anywhere in the world as
long as it's far away from here.*

I got up and said: *I won't inflict my company on you for a minute longer.*
Came up here. Left them to their bickering and spite.

*½ past 11 o'clock.*

They don't care what happens to me. Very well. In that case, I don't
care either. I won't struggle against temptation any longer. It will be
my Christmas gift to myself.

*3 o'clock.*

Σ

Walked to the village. The stars were like a million sharp eyes blink-
ing down at the earth where nothing moved. The moon, hidden by
transparent veils of cloud, suddenly sailed out from behind a gauzy
net of mist and the cattle looked ghostly in the silver glow she cast.
Bats flickered in the milky light like cinders swirling up in a fireplace. One of them flew at my head—a tiny monster with a cruel little face—and I thought I saw jowls and small round spectacles and
heard it squeaking out its venomous proprieties.

As I walked among the silent unlit houses I felt I could jump into
the air and hover there like a falcon, slowly raising and lowering my
arms to skim above the houses and fields.

Woke up dry-mouthed, head aching, fingers and toes prickling. Managed to stagger down to breakfast very late. As I came into the room Euphemia stared at me malevolently.

Mother went into the village to do her marketing and since Effie had gone back upstairs, I lay on the sopha in the parlour with a book and I must have drifted off for I was suddenly wakened by my sister saying: *Perhaps you might think of dozing during the hours of darkness? Or do you have more interesting pursuits while decent people are asleep?*

Then she said she would have to warn Mother what I was doing if I did not stop. It explained so much of my "eccentric and disruptive" behaviour—and for example my ridiculous refusal to accompany my own mother and sister to the ball. But she would spare Mother that if my conduct improved.

I replied that she could tell Mother what she liked. The truth was that I have given it up and will never take the stuff again.

She told me I was deluding myself and she was certain I had indulged as recently as last night and with that she walked out.

*1 o'clock in the afternoon.*

Old Hannah brought a letter late this morning and I took it from her and seeing that it was addressed to Effie—in oddly illiterate handwriting—I carried it to her in the parlour. She opened it and gasped and flung it down and then stared at it as if she were terrified of it. Mother jumped up from the table and cried out: *What is it?* Effie hurried out of the room and I heard her running up the stairs. Mother picked up the letter, glanced at it, and hastened after her.

The cry, dropping the thing, running out. That's not like Effie. It looked like the first-act climax to some lurid melodrama.

When Mother came back I asked her who the letter was from. She said: *I don't know.*

I said: *How is that possible? You must know who wrote it?*

She sat down heavily and said: *What I mean is that what matters is what was in it. Mr Davenant Burgoyne has become affianced to Miss Whitaker-Smith.*

Extraordinary news given that he and my sister have been meeting regularly! What puzzles me is how Effie was able to talk so calmly of Davenant Burgoyne being engaged to Enid as she did when Miss Bittlestone came to tea, and yet she is so upset by this news? I suppose she must have been confident that he had no intention of proposing to the Quance girl. The blackguard! All the time he was planning to marry Maud.

I feel sorry for Effie. Her dearest, oldest friend is marrying the man she loves. Her father's wealth has secured her the prize.

This revelation throws a new light on Lucy. That piece of news must have been what she told Enid yesterday and she must have known how much pain it would cause.

I wonder who sent the letter that came this morning. Maud herself crowing in triumph? Surely not. More probably some "friend" in town anxious to pass on the news.

No wonder that arrogant brute was so offensive on Thursday. He knew very well who I was: the brother of the girl whom he was planning to jilt.

If someone once tried to harm him, I hope they try again.

*5 o'clock in the afternoon.*

Euphemia did not appear at luncheon. Mother was tight-lipped about her and just said she had a headache.

.  .  .

Can't stop thinking of that smile of anticipation on Lucy's face as she tripped over to Enid.

*Beautiful creature, I have fallen into the waters of love and drowned in the deep brown of your eyes.*

*7 o'clock.*

Out on the Battlefield this afternoon I ran straight into that surly fellow with the red neckcloth I had seen with the tall stranger. I greeted him and quickly put a sixpence into his hand and now that I had his attention, asked him about the oaf in the wagon with the chained dog.

*That's Tom the Swell,* he said, *damn his eyes.* I asked if he was the man I had seen talking to him ten days ago and he confirmed it. He told me that nobody knows much about him or where he lives but he is thought to be a "swell" by which is meant "gentleman".

I asked him why the animal had been in chains and he explained that the man is involved in dog-fighting and the chains were attached to the poor beast in order to build up its neck and shoulder muscles so that it would be stronger for the fray.

*He's gone to cover, curse him,* he said. The man had cheated him and others in "the Fancy" and had not been seen in the district since then. He became more and more enraged at the memory and finally turned and strode off.

*Memorandum:* OPENING BAL: *9s. 8½d.* EXP: To informant: *6d.* FINAL BAL: *9s. 2½d.*

· · ·

I was approaching Stratton Herriard when I saw a large group of people clustering at the side of the path against the wall that marked the boundary of the adjacent field. As I approached they revealed themselves to be the Greenacres' brattery and their governess whom I had seen in church. The two older girls—Juliet and Emma—were clutching each other and in tears. The governess was holding the hand of the youngest child, a little boy of about six, who was also weeping.

The older boy—Frederick who is about ten or eleven—was behind the wall so that all but his upper body was hidden. He appeared to be hitting something. The youngest girl was standing on the track and watching in fascination.

I greeted the governess and went to look over the wall which was just low enough to allow me to see over it. To my horror I saw a sheep lying on its side with blood spattered across its body and over the grass around it. It was feebly kicking its legs in what looked like a mild protest at what was happening. I now realised that the boy was not just hitting it but stabbing it with a knife—raising his arm and thrusting it down into its belly with all his strength. There was a long slash from its neck down its front from which unimaginable things were bulging. I felt dizzy with the horror of it.

As in a nightmare the boy's arm rose and fell like a piston.

I thought: *Gracious heavens, I've found the madman who is doing these dreadful things. And he's not much more than ten years old.*

I hurried over and seized the child's arm. *For God's sake*, I said. *What in heaven's name are you doing?*

He said: *I'm putting it out of its pain.*

*Then cut the poor creature's throat and make a quick end of it.*

The boy raised his arm and I looked away. I heard a sound I can't describe. When I turned back a few seconds later the animal lay mercifully still.

Frederick was smiling and wiping his knife on the grass. There was now fresh wet blood all the way up his right arm.

*What on earth has been going on?* I asked.

Frederick took no notice of me. He seemed excited and proud at what he had done.

The governess said sharply: *Frederick, answer the gentleman. And I too wish to know what you were doing.*

She began to walk towards us as if she intended to look over the hedge. I held up my hand and said: *Don't come any closer. There's something here I think the other children shouldn't see.*

She stopped and looked at the boy expectantly. He explained that he and Amelia had heard the animal whimpering and looked over the wall and spotted it several minutes before the rest of the party had caught up. Seeing that its belly—*Stomach, Frederick!* the governess interrupted—had been slashed, he had used his knife to bring its suffering to an end.

Amelia is about twelve years old and has a sharp little face. She will be pretty once she has learned to hide that scowl. She made me think of Effie at that age. Now the spiteful little minx cut in and said: *You're lying. It was you hurt the sheep. You saw it in the field and you went and stabbed it. You wanted to try out the knife Father gave you for Christmas.*

Frederick shouted at her: *You're a horrid liar!*

He advanced towards her still holding the knife, but the governess interposed herself.

To my amazement those decorous young ladies in embryo, Juliet and Emma, started shouting at their younger sister that she was a deceitful fibber and a malicious trouble-maker. One of them exclaimed: *You're always trying to make trouble for Freddie. You're just jealous.*

Amelia, undaunted by this attack, screamed: *I'm telling you, I saw him. He was cutting the poor sheep. There was nothing wrong with it before that.*

*I was putting it out of its misery,* he shouted. *My knife couldn't have made that slash down its body,* he said. He appealed to me as the only competent male present: *Look. My blade is not long enough to go so deep.*

He bent over the animal and I assume was prising apart the wound but I couldn't watch. I heard him say: *I'm shoving it in. See? The blade doesn't go to the bottom of the cut.*

Amelia came closer and peered at it. She said: *You did it twice. You slashed once and then went back and slashed again.* She called on me to play the arbiter: *Look. Here's the first cut and here's the second.*

I said: *I can't believe Frederick would do such a thing.*

Amelia said: *What do you know about it? He does horrible things all the time.*

The governess said: *Amelia, be silent. You're being very discourteous.*

But the girl shouted at her brother: *Look what you've done to your coat! Mama will be furious.*

*Yes,* he cried. *And now I'll get it all over you, too. And serve you right for telling such lies.*

He moved towards her and both she and the governess scurried aside, not wanting to be touched by this blood-soaked apparition. With gore smeared over his coat and spots of it on his face he looked like some figure from a Gothic melodrama. I stepped forward and held out my arm to bar his path. *That's not a gentlemanly way to behave,* I said.

That seemed to have an effect. He stopped and replaced the knife in its sheath.

The little governess thanked me as if I had performed some heroic action. Then she knelt and kissed the youngest child who was sobbing and said: *Now, children, look how you've frightened poor Sammy.*

I watched in amazement as all the children hurried over to comfort their little brother—hugging him and ruffling his hair and digging into their pockets to find small gifts. Stricken with remorse for what they had said and done, they started sobbing and embracing one another. Amelia gave Frederick a cautious kiss, holding herself away from his blood-smeared sleeve, and they seemed to have forgotten and forgiven the cruel insults they had just thrown at each other. What a contrast with my own family!

We strolled on and it seemed natural that the governess and I should walk together with the children going before us.

She told me her name is Helen Carstairs and said that she knew who I was. I asked her if she liked her present employment. She hesitated and said: *I am very fond of the children.*

She must have seen my surprise because she smiled and said: *They are not always as troublesome as this.* Then she talked of the difficulty of a governess's position caught between the family and the servants. She admitted that she had had little choice in taking up such a post and said: *I have a widowed mother and two younger siblings who depend on me.*

What is a governess paid? Fifteen pounds a year? Certainly, it is very little since she is given lodging and sustenance. If her relatives are so much in need of that, their circumstances must be desperate indeed.

We found that we both love the poetry of Keats and the novels of Jane Austen and the Brontë sisters. She is teaching herself German and has begun to read Goethe. She loves music, too, and told me how she would creep down the stairs at night and listen when anyone was playing in the drawing-room.

I asked: *And are they kind to you?*

She said: *Mr Greenacre and I have long conversations about books and ideas.* She paused and then said: *Mrs Greenacre used to be very considerate but she has been influenced by the Rector's wife. I fear that Mrs Quance dislikes me for some reason.* (You're young and clever and not positively ugly. That's reason enough, I thought.)

I told her I hated Mrs Quance for her sanctimonious self-righteousness and her wicked mischief-making. Helen was silent for a while and then she said a strange thing: *Such people are their own punishment.*

We talked of the isolation of the district and she asked: *Aren't you lonely out here so far from everything?*

I said without reflecting: *Only when I'm with other people.*

She laughed and said: *Then it's fortunate we have come to the parting of our ways.*

I hadn't noticed but we had reached the turning down our lane and so we made our farewells.

Now that I have had the chance to look at her closely, I see that she is not really pretty: the poor girl squints. But she is thoughtful and clever.

. . .

Such an open display of emotion! Such volatility! Another family is a foreign country. Why were we so inhibited? Was it because we had always to calculate: *Will this revelation of my feelings anger Father?* If I replied to him in a sulky tone Father would shout: *I will not allow these moods.* Strikes me now that he was the only one of us who showed his feelings without restraint.

When I entered the parlour they were so engrossed that they did not notice me. Mother was standing smiling and clapping her hands while Effie walked round and round in front of her showing off a rather magnificent red dress that I hadn't seen before. Mother's eyes were hungrily devouring her daughter. I spoke and as they turned and looked at me her smile faded.

*Euphemia is trying on the dress that we're making for the ball*, she said in a tone that implied that I would not find it of any interest.

Effie, however, smiled at me and made an elaborate curtsey in my direction.

Mother said: *It looks almost as good on you as it did on me. I was a fine-looking girl once myself.*

I heard a catch in her voice and she put her head down and hurried out of the room.

Effie twirled round to show me the garment. The dress left her arms and shoulders bare and because it was unfinished it was open far down her back. I must have blushed because Effie laughed and said: *Are you embarrassed? It wasn't many years ago that you and I used to share a bath-tub.*

With a mocking smile she sailed out of the room.

*9 o'clock.*

Just before dinner I was in the kitchen and saw Mother trying to reach a canister down from a high shelf. I did it for her. She had been standing on tiptoe and scrabbling for it. Those quick, nervous movements. I wonder why she cannot take things more slowly but she does everything in that rapidly scrabbling manner as if she needs to clutch at everything she desires before it disappears. She looked so thin in her worn and patched garments. I wanted to put my arms around her and hug her but she wouldn't have cared for that.

*½ past 9 o'clock.*

I've been thinking. I let Mother down. I should have lent her better assistance with the goose. And I don't know why I said that about the shirt last night. It wounded her as it was meant to, but why did I want to do that? Why do I feel a desire to cause her pain, and often at exactly the moment when she is showing that she loves me? What I heard her saying to Miss Bittlestone, it wasn't unkind. The intention wasn't to denigrate me. She was sharing her concern.

So after dinner I waited until Euphemia had left the room and said: *The shirt is beautiful. I'm sorry I didn't thank you properly. I'm very grateful.*

She smiled and said: *That's better, Richard. And now I hope you'll make it up with your sister and drop this silly refusal to accompany us to the ball.*

That is a concession I don't feel ready to make.

Later on, heroic Mother, bloodied but unbowed after the goose, began to talk of her intention to cook a fine dinner on New Year's Eve.


*11 o'clock.*


Effie came back into the room and gave me what seemed to be a warning look and then started talking about the stories she had heard from friends and their brothers about the decline in morals of undergraduates.

While Mother was preoccupied with her knitting, Effie was signalling to me her intention to approach closer and closer to the subject she had raised with me this morning.

She said: *There have grown up a number of very self-indulgent and dangerous habits amongst the young men at both the Universities.*

Mother nodded absent-mindedly.

Effie went on: *The excessive drinking has, of course, been traditional for many years and can hardly now be regarded as a vice. But there are new dangers that have arisen in recent years.*

Like any blackmailer, her power ends at the point where the truth is revealed and so she adroitly held back. She had fired a warning-shot. The next broadside would be aimed below my waterline.

After half an hour Mother went into the kitchen to give Betsy some instructions. Effie asked me to help her move the pianoforte a few inches to avoid a loose floorboard. As I bent to push the instrument, her shoulder brushed against me and then she turned and her bosom was against my chest.

*I'm so sorry,* she said and when we had completed the task she said: *It hasn't made you dusty, has it?* She ran her hand down my chest and then down to the top of my leg, brushing gently. She gazed up at me with eyes sparkling. Then she flung herself onto the stool and burst into a fast waltz.

Mother came back and resumed her knitting. Effie was now playing very softly and I went closer. In a low voice she said, while her fingers still danced over the keys: *I often see your candle burning till late when I look out of my window. I wonder when you intend to sleep tonight?*

I muttered: *Late.* I felt my voice croaking as I said it.

She made no response but continued to play. Why did she ask me that?

*Midnight.*

I will never smoke again. Tomorrow I will destroy everything: the pipe, the stuff itself. I will not let it have power over me.

Am still haunted by the agony of that wretched animal. Who is carrying out these deranged attacks? (I can't believe it is Frederick, though he was clearly enjoying using his knife.) Whoever cut open the animal's belly must have been very near us. Could it have been that angry young countryman I talked to?

. . .

Pleasure in inflicting pain. An interesting phenomenon. Frederick stabbing the sheep. Amelia enjoying it as much as he. Mrs Quance at any opportunity. That man beating the chained dog. Effie now and then, I'm afraid.

*½ past midnight.*

I was writing that when there was a gentle tap at the door and Effie glided in! She smiled and said: *I'm not disturbing you, I hope?*

I said she was not and asked her to sit. There was only the bed and she seated herself on that so I turned my chair full-circle and sat facing her.

She looked round: *It's very cosy. I can see why you spend so much time up here.*

I found it hard to speak. She was wearing a robe that she was clutching around herself as if it might fall open at any moment. I was trying to keep my eyes on her face. She was perfumed with the scent of soap and had the rosy glow that showed she had just come from her bath.

We talked for a few minutes and I hardly recall what was said. We expressed our concern for Mother and the strain she was under. Then she brought the subject round to the ball and talked of the pleasure she was sure I would derive from it. As she was speaking her gown began to open and I found it hard to attend to her words.

I hardly knew what I was saying and was not surprised to hear myself agreeing to attend the ball. She rose and came towards me and I stood up and she thanked me and then kissed me on the cheek, her hand pressing on the back of my neck to bring my head closer and lingering there as she said goodnight. I put my arms around her briefly and felt her warm body and my hands touched her back low down and it felt almost naked under the thin material.

Then she was gone.

· · ·

Δ

*Sunday 27th of December, noon.*

I was spared church today because we are going to Stratton Peverel this afternoon. My strategy for the tea-party: Say as little as possible and listen for any fragments of information that I can make sense of. Both we and the Quances now have an animus against Davenant Burgoyne for the same reason: Each has a daughter who has been humiliatingly rejected by him. A strong alliance might well be constructed on such a foundation.

.   .   .

Managed to get Effie alone for a few minutes. I said I wasn't going back on what I had agreed last night but that in return for consenting to go to the ball, I required her to make a promise: She must stop threatening to tell Mother about various imagined offences of mine and prying into whatever it was that I was rusticated for.

She accepted those terms.

.   .   .

*Drowned in the deep brown.* I don't feel happy with that.

*6 o'clock.*

As we neared the village, I spotted Miss Bittlestone ahead and increased my pace. I went straight to the point and mentioned that I had encountered Mr Davenant Burgoyne on Christmas Eve.

She needed no further prompting: *He came to tell the Lloyds about his betrothal to that brazen creature in Thurchester but he did not have the decency to come and tell us.*

(*Us!*)

I reminded her that when she came to tea we had discussed what would happen if he died without an heir. Now I asked bluntly: *Who is the "connection of the earl's late brother" who would inherit the money at his death?*

She shuddered at that last word and looked at me in dismay. *Why, Mr Davenant Burgoyne's brother.*

*His brother!*

*Well, his half-brother.*

I've never heard that he had any kind of brother!

At that moment, unfortunately, Mother and Euphemia caught up with us and Mother asked the old trout: *Are you going to tea at the Rectory?*

She jumped as if she'd been accused of some discreditable act. *I'm going there but I'm to sit with Miss Quance. She's not very well, poor lamb.*

It was strange to find ourselves ushered into the Rectory and to be greeted warmly by Mrs Quance and Guinevere. (Warmly except that Mrs Quance stared at me as if in surprise at my presence.)

While we were unhatting and uncoating in the hall, Miss Bittlestone scurried up the stairs and Mother said: *I'm very sorry to hear that your elder daughter is unwell.*

The chatelaine of Castle Quance shook her head as she directed us into the drawing-room saying: *The poor child has suffered a shock to her delicate sensibilities.*

Yes, her most sensitive parts: her vanity and ambition!

The room was light and airy and there was a cheerful fire blazing in the hearth. We all sat on one or other of the sophas disposed about the room and Guinevere came and placed herself beside me.

Mother began to babble: *It's very kind of you to invite us, Mrs Quance, and I'm embarrassed that we are unable to return your hospitality with our own house still in a dreadful state.*

*Please don't apologise*, Mrs Quance said magnificently. *I understand completely. This house was in an appalling condition when we moved from Bath two years ago.*

Bath! Confirmation—not that I needed it—that Miss Bittlestone's story was about the Quances.

Without warning Mrs Quance swung her heavy artillery in my direction. *I am flattered, Master Shenstone, that you have bestowed some of your valuable time upon my daughter and myself.*

I took cover behind a convenient banality: *Our stroll here this afternoon has been a pleasure, Mrs Quance. I love to walk.*

*At night?* she demanded.

Odd question! Why the devil should she care? I didn't feel I owed her the truth.

*I never leave the house after dark, Mrs Quance. In the evenings I stay at home and lucubrate.*

Her eyes came out on stalks. *You do what? You lubricate?*

Ignorant old bitch. Failing to hide my smile at her stupidity, I said: *I lucubrate. It is from the Latin and means "to work by artificial light". I mean that I read and think.*

She received with complete impassivity this piece of information. What she did not already know could not be worth knowing. Then she fixed me with her stony gaze and demanded: *How long is it since you came to the neighbourhood?*

*Just over two weeks.*

*And would you have the goodness to remind me of the name of the school you attended?*

*Harrow*, I said.

She nodded as if I had confirmed some dark suspicion of hers. Then she turned from me abruptly like a bird dropping a worm from its beak and addressed my mother.

From this point onwards she did not speak another word to me but several times I found her looking at me with an expression of deep malevolence mixed with speculation.

I wanted to hear what she was saying but unfortunately Guinevere began to prattle about some trivial matter.

I heard Mrs Quance say something about "farm-animals" and "paint".

Guinevere noticed that I was distracted and began to frown. She said: *Who do you believe is doing these dreadful things?*

I shrugged. A moment later she raised her voice and, ignoring the fact that her mother was speaking, said: *Mama, be sure not to forget about the tickets.*

*You're quite right, my dearest,* her mother said with remarkable amiability.

What a paradox that the bullying Mrs Quance is as soft as warm beeswax in the hands of her daughters. I suppose they are versions of herself, colonies of her imperial ego.

Euphemia began to talk of how much she was looking forward to the ball. She discovered that the four Quances were going in their carriage and was delighted to find that they would be perfectly comfortable in a vehicle that was, as her hostess was only too pleased to point out, designed to carry six in comfort. It was clear to me what my sister was driving at and eventually the slow-witted Mrs Quance saw the danger that was approaching. However, by her boasting she had left herself open to attack. Effie mentioned how worried she was at having to entrust herself and her mother to an unknown coachman hired from Thurchester.

Mrs Quance fought hand-to-hand at the end: *While you and your mother would be most welcome to ride with us, a difficulty arises from the fact that our horses would be too fatigued to go all the way to Herriard House.*

Euphemia routed that attack: *The walk from the village would be very welcome after the excitement of the ball.*

Mrs Quance raised the white flag of surrender and Euphemia and Mother thanked her. So that saves the expense of both a carriage and the rooms. Clever Effie! Though it was embarrassing to see her do it. Mrs Quance produced the tickets and Euphemia her money.

Then Effie, bless her, said: *My brother is unexpectedly here on the night of the ball and so I would very much like a half-ticket for him as well.*

Mrs Quance shot me a glance of undisguised loathing and handed over the three tickets saying: *I'm afraid there is no question of the carriage being able to accommodate Master Shenstone.*

.  .  .

*Drowned in the deep hazel of your eyes.*

.  .  .

Guinevere Guinevere Guinevere! I can't stop seeing her sitting with her long golden hair flowing down her back. How old is she? Too young for me to care about her.

[This is the first of the anonymous letters which, at some point in the past, have been pasted into the Journal at the relevant place. This one is addressed to Enid Quance. *Note by CP.*]

You hore you thouht you were too good for any of us didnt you—preening and primping with your lowcut dresses to catch his eye with your fat udders like you done in bath when you tried to ketch your half-wit lord.

Your bitch mam thinks your to good for anyone but an earls nevew.

You wanted to trap him into wholy matrimoney. He didn't want to put his cok into you you cow but into another bitch. You made him fuk you you dirty sluttan. You took his cock in your dirty hands and you put it in you

Well see whare it is got you. Youre not showing yet you hore but everybody knows the truth about you.

hah hah hah

The Haroer

The damned Feast of the Holy Innocents so we have to go to church this evening.

I asked Euphemia at breakfast what she was going to do today and she said in a very strange manner that she was going to Thrubwell *as normal*. But there's nothing normal about the way she battles through any sort of weather to sit beside a dying old woman. I'm convinced there is more to it than she has revealed. I suspect she's up to something and I'm going to follow her.

*5 o'clock.*

When she left the house I tracked her from a couple of hundred yards back. As I guessed she had barely reached the end of our lane when a tall man appeared from the direction of the village. From his height I'm sure it was Davenant Burgoyne though I could not get close enough to see his face and he did not seem to be limping. They turned up the lane onto the Battlefield and walked slowly towards Monument Hill and I suddenly lost sight of them in the spinney there.

She always got away with things as a child. If we were both in disgrace, she only had to smile at Father and he would let her off and beat me all the harder. It's not fair.

I'm beginning to wonder about that tower. Can't get out of my mind what that old fool, Fourdrinier, told me about it: that it was built for the most immoral purposes. Does it have an entrance? I'm going to have to take a closer look.

*10 o'clock.*

Another strange scene at the evening service. We had all taken our places when Mrs Paytress arrived late. She walked down the aisle averting her gaze from everyone until she reached Mr and Mrs Lloyd and Lucy when she raised her veil and smiled. As one they turned away or dropped their gaze to their prayerbooks. She flinched and lowered the veil and walked on.

After the service I noticed Mother talking to an old lady who had arrived with the Lloyds. On the way home I asked if she had learned why they had snubbed Mrs Paytress. She shook her head distractedly and said they had been talking of another topic but that the Lloyds had "received evidence" that Mrs Paytress was not what she seemed.

．　．　．

Mother seemed restless and distracted this evening. To my surprise she asked at dinner: *Are you going out tonight?*

Was that prompted by Mrs Quance's questions? Does she know that I have sallied forth a few times after dark? I blurted out: *No, certainly not.*

*11 o'clock.*

We were sitting in the parlour less than an hour ago when Betsy suddenly came running in without a warning knock and, white-faced and with her eyes starting from her head, cried out: *There's someone out at the back! I heard them!*

Mother rose to her feet. *What do you mean? A visitor? At this hour? At the back-door?*

She and Effie exchanged a look and my sister shrugged as if to disclaim any knowledge of the matter.

*No,* Betsy shrieked. *It's not a living being. It's a dead child!*

Effie stood up at that. She gasped: *What are you talking about?*

Betsy, shaking with fright, stammered: *I heard it weeping! It's come out from the mere! It's at the back-door.*

It was immediately obvious to me that the girl had been out there on her own in the dark kitchen scaring herself with stories of apparitions on the night of Holy Innocents when the dead—especially children—return to haunt the living.

Her fear had infected Mother and Effie.

I said briskly: *Come along, Betsy. I'll open the door and show you there's nothing there.*

She was petrified and dumbly shook her head. I said: *I need you to hold the lamp.*

I took her warm hand and led her along the dark passage to the kitchen. I handed the lamp to her and unbolted the back-door and we stood listening. It was a cold starless night. I was struck by how indifferent—even inimical—to humankind the dark landscape seemed: the flat expanse of marshland and the dark shapes of the slopes rising from the mere. A thought that had nothing to do with reason and daylight came to me: when we die do we wander at night across a cold expanse of desolate land wailing for attention from the living? Betsy was standing behind me and I could hear terror in her shortness of breath.

I must have caught something of the contagion of fear for although I knew they were creatures of my imagination, I could almost believe I saw figures in the misty darkness dancing around the house in antic shapes.

Then there came a strange sound—high, unearthly and apparently very close to us. I felt the hair rise on the back of my neck. A bird or a fox? Immediately Betsy gave a shriek and retreated into the kitchen. I closed and bolted the door.

In that instant I felt the most powerful conviction that whatever it was that was causing me unease wasn't outside—that was a fox or a bird—but inside the house. There was some evil creature locked in with us, something that had suffered unendurable pain and was trying to inflict it on others.

The girl had put the lamp on the floor and was cowering in the opposite corner. I went over to her saying: *It's just the cry of some wild creature, Betsy.*

I put my hand on her arm and tried to pull her to her feet. To my astonishment she tore my grasp from her and screamed: *You keep away from me, you dirty thing. I'm not having any more of that.*

Any more? What did she mean? I have hardly touched her.

I hurried back to the parlour. Mother and Effie were sitting on the sopha, Mother holding a handkerchief to her face and weeping into it while my sister tried to comfort her. Mother hadn't heard me and as I entered, she said: *That poor boy.*

*It's just an animal,* I said in bewilderment.

*I'm all right now,* Mother said, dabbing at her eyes with the handkerchief. *I became frightened because there isn't a man here now.*

Because she was still upset, I didn't say: *Of course there's a man here.*


*A ¼ to midnight.*


*There isn't a man here now.* That's what Mother said and I'm struck by the oddness of that "now". There has been no man in the house since they moved out here.

Or has there? Did Davenant Burgoyne come here before I arrived? And now they meet at the tower?

His hands on her waist, on her bare skin, on the smooth roundedness of her breasts. His mouth on hers, on her neck. She gasping out pants of pleasure at his fingers on her most intimate parts. Is my sister sneaking out to meet her lover like a bitch in heat?

[This is the next of the anonymous letters relating to the case and it is addressed to Mrs Lloyd. *Note by CP.*]

*I know how much you like french coks and as many of them as you can get you filthy hore. you fuked and fuked in france when you were young. then you sent your dauter there to lern to fuk.*

*That bitch Lusy with her conceeted french ways she thinks she's so much better than every one else—well the erls nevue didn't think so did he*

*did you send her to France to lern tongue frigging from the nunns in Tooloose like you did?*

*Tuesday 29<sup>th</sup> of December, noon.*

Euphemia went off to Lady Terrewest at about eight. That makes two days in succession!

Old Hannah arrived with a letter for Mother shortly after that. I brought it into the parlour and was at the table when she opened it. She gasped and sat down quickly. I tried to get her to tell me what it said but she clasped it against herself and stared at me shaking her head. Then she read it again.

I suddenly realised what it was. What a dunce I have been!

I begged Mother to let me read the filthy thing but she refused and was about to throw it into the fire but I said: *Don't do that, Mother. Please. If you destroy it, we lose any possibility of identifying the sender.*

She asked me how I knew what it was and I told her. I said: *I assume it was a letter of that kind that upset Effie the other day?*

She nodded. Still she refused to let me read it. However, I guess she is hiding it wherever she hides the cash.


*3 o'clock.*


When Effie came back Mother told her she had had "another horrible letter" and that I had found out about them.

We speculated on who the author could be and I pointed out that the attacks on farm animals must be connected. To my amazement Mother accused Mrs Paytress of being the author. She was taking her revenge against those who had ostracised her and had tried to disguise her rank and her gender by writing in a way that no respectable woman could.

Mother said: *The Lloyds are convinced that she is the author. Mrs Lloyd received a letter which alludes to her and Mrs Paytress having been educated in France. That's why they cut her at church yesterday.*

I was so angry that I had to walk out or I would have said something. Why on earth would Mrs Paytress do such a thing?

*5 o'clock.*

Have just told Mother I was going into the village and asked if she wanted anything from the shop. She gave me ninepence for some cotton-thread. She took it from her pocket so I still don't know where she hides things.

*7 o'clock.*

Walked to the village. Bought the thread and then asked Mrs Darnton about people posting letters and buying stamps. Had anyone started posting more letters than usual in the last week or two? She was surly and would tell me nothing.

Went to the tower: There is one grimy window about halfway up and a small door about four feet off the ground. It looks as if it might have been opened recently.

Coming back I ran into the bewhiskered old party I had talked to when I was trying to find Mrs Bittlestone's cottage. It occurred to me that he might know Tom the Swell so I put that question. I was in luck and he was anxious to tell me. So while I accompanied him to the door of his cottage I learned the following: This egregious individual used to come down for dog-fights in the district and for about half a year he brought a dog that defeated all challengers.

I said: *So he made money from his dog?*

*He did at first but of course that didn't last.* He explained that after the dog had won a number of fights, nobody would bet against him. He said: *He dursen't show his face around here. Not after the last match when he done the Fancy brown.*

He would say no more than that.

When I mentioned the attacks on animals, however, he became positively loquacious. Horses and sheep have had their eyes gouged out and there have been several assaults on pregnant cows involving the ripping of their bellies with what is believed to be a slaughterman's or a thatcher's tool. He said that several guard-dogs have been poisoned which has led to speculation that the perpetrator is planning to break into houses.


*9 o'clock.*


Over dinner Mother and Euphemia talked about the letters each had received and Effie, insisting that Mrs Paytress had nothing to do with them, said that hers seems to be the work of a deranged young man who has some knowledge of the area. I asked her if she had any particular person in mind and if so, whom she meant. She declined to say.

Mother said: *I don't believe it's a man. It has too much insight into how to wound a woman.*

*Well*, I said, *I know a young lady who is more than capable of writing malicious letters.*

I was thinking of Lucy's face when she was telling Enid of the betrothal.

Mother instantly said: *It's not the work of a young lady.*

*10 o'clock.*

*Not the work of a young lady.* What makes Mother believe that? Does she mean that Mrs Paytress is not young or not a lady?

How frustrating to know that I could glean so much from a sight of just one of the letters!

·   ·   ·

*He done the Fancy brown.* He cheated the dog-fighting fraternity? Hence that surly young labourer's resentment?

*½ past midnight.*

Came up here and gave in to temptation. Now that I've started again it seems that I can't stop. But it helps. It helps so much.

*½ past 8 in the morning.*

Σ

A little before midnight I stole from the house and walked east along the shore of the mere. Saw a flickering light moving a few hundred yards from me on my right. Had no idea if it was a marsh-light or someone carrying a lantern but I hurried towards it. I thought of the old stories of how the evil spirits that haunt the wetlands try to lure victims into the boggy ground where they drown. Following it as best I could while it vanished and reappeared hundreds of yards away, I rounded the headland. Far out beyond the mudflats I saw the lights of ships that winked as they rocked with the waves. After that the light turned inland where the land begins to rise.

Somewhere around there I lost sight of it—if it had ever existed and was anything more than the fiery emanation of the marshes.

Now light was seeping into the darkness of the eastern sky like cream being poured into a bowl of puréed blackberries. I stood entranced as a great orange sun edged above the horizon with a vivid luminescence spreading from it like a bruise while bare trees on a hill before me raised their branches like a chorus of witches with their arms up to invoke a curse.

Felt terrible when I woke up. I must stop. I must take all of the things from the trunk and hurl them into the ocean. I will do that. I will do it very soon.

*5 o'clock.*

Just read all morning. Since it was a fine cold day Mother and I decided to walk out to meet Euphemia coming back from Lady Ter-rewest. Just as we were at the end of the lane we encountered Old Hannah. She said she didn't have anything for us today but there was something she clearly wanted to impart. *Have you heard what happened at Farmer Edwards's place?* she asked. *He found one of his billy-goats this morning with a sharpened stick fastened in it.* Mother asked: *Where?* Before the old woman could answer in—I am sure—anatomical detail, I said: *In a paddock, I assume.* Mother is so embarrassing sometimes.

Then the old creature said that a certain person was recognised near there about the time the deed was done. Who could she mean? Edwards's farm is not far from where I was last night. Could the light I saw have been carried by the offender?

We had gone some way past the village before we met Effie. Coming back we were at the top of Brankston Hill when we saw a carriage some distance away coming to a halt beside a figure in the road. Someone got out. As we drew nearer we saw that it was Mrs Quance who had descended to speak to Miss Bittlestone.

The Rector's wife greeted us without enthusiasm but Mrs Greenacre poked her head out of the window and in the most friendly manner introduced herself to Mother and they talked of having known each other slightly in Thurchester. Mrs Quance seemed surprised and even dismayed that we knew her. Mrs Greenacre reminded her of the dinner to which they had invited her on New Year's Day.

At that moment, Mr Greenacre leaned out of the carriage to doff his hat and say to Mother: *You must come and dine with us on that day. Your son and daughter as well, of course.* He smiled benignly at Effie and me.

Mother accepted, though she was evidently as disconcerted as Mrs Quance and Mrs Greenacre were.

The carriage moved away.

There was an awkward silence in which we heard the creaking of the ice as the waters of sociability froze. Mother began to talk rapidly about the Greenacres: how charming they were, what beautiful children they had, and so on. That, with mutters of agreement from Mrs Quance, got us to the bottom of the hill.

It seemed absurd to me that nobody had raised the topic that was on everyone's mind. When Mother paused to draw breath, I said: *My mother has received one of those letters.*

As if doubting me, Mrs Quance swung her massive head towards her with an interrogative expression.

Mother nodded meekly.

My remark had drawn the enemy's fire: *Master Shenstone, you walk about the countryside a great deal.* She paused meaningfully and then said: *It is obvious that whoever is sending the letters is also responsible for these outrages against dumb animals. I wonder if you can throw any light on the matter?*

*None at all,* I said. *As I mentioned a few days ago, I never leave the house at night.*

She stared at me as if silently accusing me of lying. And what a pleasure it was to know that I was telling her a flagrant untruth. I caught Mother's eye and she gave me an anguished look.

*How is poor Miss Quance?* she asked in desperation.

Mrs Quance sighed heavily and began a reply.

I fell back and talked to Miss Bittlestone. I reminded her of our previous conversations about who would benefit from Davenant Burgoyne's death.

*Who,* I asked, *is this mysterious younger half-brother.*

*In fact, he is older.*

*In that case,* I said, *why is he not the heir?*

She lowered her eyes and a pinkish tinge flushed her cheeks. *He is the acknowledged son of the earl's brother.*

All was clear. The man is in plain English a bastard. I asked what was known about him.

She has never heard his name and knows only that he has no money and, since he is estranged from his uncle, will inherit nothing.

*Unless,* I said, *Davenant Burgoyne dies.*

*Before his twenty-fifth birthday,* she returned. *Those are the terms of the trust their father established.*

*When is that date?*

*A few months from now.*

I mentioned the defamatory letters and the flood-gates opened. She had received one herself! It was such a recognition of her importance that I believe a love-letter from Mr Disraeli could not have occasioned more joy. However, she would not say what was in it except that it made "the most unspeakable allegation" against Lucy.

So much for my theory that Lucy is writing the letters. She would hardly attack herself to a third party.

.   .   .

Those women in the shop were talking about a man being disinherited by his younger brother. Were they discussing the earl's nephews?

*7 o'clock.*

This afternoon I was on Bransbury Lane when whom should I see in the distance but Lucy herself! She was with a younger sister. I wondered if she would deign to stop and speak to me. I strode on keeping my eyes ahead as if I had not noticed her.

She marched right past.

I turned back and half-ran towards her but she must have heard my footsteps because she glanced round and then she and the girl began to walk very fast. I stopped and resumed my way.

*10 o'clock.*

I think Old Hannah believes I am the madman who was at the Edwards farm that night. Was it a mere coincidence or does the perpetrator lurk along the lane at night and follow me?

. . .

During dinner I had such a strange fancy. I looked at my mother and sister and thought: *These people are strangers. If I had met them for the first time today I would not wish to know them.*

*A ¼ past 11 o'clock.*

I can't throw off the feeling that something malign is coming nearer and nearer. And in this house at the end of a promontory, I'm trapped. There is only that single lane back to the road. Unless there is a way to cross the marshes to the south-west.

If I were to attempt it, it would have to be at low-tide. If that story of the mad bride is true, however, to venture into that marsh is to embrace a muddy death.

*A ¼ to midnight.*

I think I've worked out Mother's hiding-place: her ever-present work-basket.

. . .

*you foolis old bitch when your husband*
*was a rich cannen you thoht you wer better*
*than everiboddy. Everiboddy laffin at you*
*now Your hor darter is getten fucked every*
*day and everyboddy know it They all know it*
*xcep you*
*    dont be proud the erls nevys grinding her.*
*he sticks his dick werever he can men boys*
*women girls cows sheep goats monkies. Even*
*that wite corps Eenid. Damn his eyes. Hes*
*done wrong to me and mine and I wont deny*
*that I arent the man to give him a good*
*thrashing.*

*The Harroer*

*2 o'clock in the morning.*

Wicked ugly foul perverted filth! I wanted to tear it up and burn the pieces and take the ashes out of the house and throw them into the mud where such foulness belongs. I almost wept to think of poor Mother reading such words.

Is that what is being said? *Every day!*

When everyone was asleep I crept downstairs and found the work-basket on the sopha. At first I could discover nothing but then I noticed a hidden pocket containing some coins and the letter.

The Harrow allusion explains Mrs Quance's interest. And why Effie believes Bartlemew is the author. But I think the name implies "one who harrows" or "harries". Bartlemew could not be so well informed about Mrs Paytress and the Quances. And besides, he would certainly not have written such an illiterate letter.

Is it a man or a woman?

The letters are sent to women and defame and abuse that sex which implies female authorship, although the language and attitudes are unwomanly.

(I wonder, however: Did old Fourdrinier receive one? He asked me if I had had *A letter from someone I don't know.*)

What I might call the "strategy" the writer is using is to defame one person to another because while people will conceal allegations against themselves, they will pass on charges against their neighbours.

. . .

I've just managed to make out that the postmark is Thurchester. I need to know if letters handed in locally are franked here or there. Who are the possible authors?

Nr 1.) Betsy. Yet Mother said she is unable to read or write.

Nr 2.) Mrs Yass. She departed in fury and the first letter arrived not long after that. But she has left the district so she would have no way of knowing what is going on here.

Nr 3.) Old Hannah. She hears everything and is a bloodhound for scandal.

Nr 4.) Mrs Darnton or her miserable slave at the shop, Sukey.

But the assaults on animals and the slogans—they must be part of the same wicked campaign, and a woman out in the fields at night would attract too much notice.

So is it after all a man?

[This is the next of the anonymous letters relating to the case and it is addressed to Mrs Quance. *Note by CP.*]

mrs qwunts youre the wors boredyhouse keeper in the county so you got no rite to call out another womun. It's true she run a horehouse in Soresbury but now she fucks for nothing. The old earl fucks her every week but she likes a young man better and she knows how to give a fellow his lickerbrations good

But you are no better. You turned your own daugter into a hore. She tried to trap the earls nephue Well he got away from her but he wont get away from me. Wen I ketch him I will tear his arm of and thrash him with it till he pisses blood.

Every man and boy in the village has rogered Enid. She cant get enough of a man's cock. If her dad had anything dangling between his legs he would have fucked her too by now. He's supposed to be the Erector ha ha

I will fuck Enid but ony wen I am sick of fucking Lousey loyd. She do it well. She has had lots of praktiss. Her dad started her wen she was ten year old and she liked it and gone on liking it.

*I am starting to putt my nife to work. I stuk my nife in and ripped open that sheep's belly just before the greenakkers came along and they didnt gess it was me. How I lauffed afterwards. ha ha ha there is more werk for me and my nife to do. I like ripping bellys and I like it even more when I can cut out a living babby from the woom.*

*The Harroer*

*Thursday 31<sup>st</sup> of December, 11 o'clock.*

Found an opportunity to test Betsy. I left a volume of Gibbon's *Decline and Fall* on the table and sat down. When she came into the room I said: *I think there's a book I want there.*

She picked it up and began to walk towards me but I said: *No, tell me its title.*

She stopped dead and looked at me strangely and then said: *I have not learned my letters, sir.*

Of course, that might not be the truth. If she is writing those letters, pretending to be illiterate is the best disguise.

*1 o'clock.*

Have just done the most reckless thing of my life and nearly died in the attempt: I tried to find a way across the marsh.

The weather was perfect for it—an icy sunlit day with a bright hard light. I could see the road to Upton Dene a few hundred yards away. I found no stepping-stones but could place my feet on the tussocks. The stench of decaying seaweed and brackish water was overpowering. The ice in the puddles cracked under my feet like a glazed cake and only in some places was thick enough to bear my weight. But for that I would have slipped deep into the slough. As it was my legs kept sinking and finding no *terra firma*, and then I was forced to go back and try another route.

At the furthest point I reached I could see firm ground only twenty or thirty yards away but the marsh that lay between us offered nothing that would bear my weight. So I turned back. I thought I was retracing my steps precisely but I must have made a mistake for suddenly my left leg sank up to the knee and kept on sinking. I moved my right leg forward to keep my balance and that, too, began to descend and the mud reached the top of my boot before I managed to lean sideways and grab a clump of vegetation from a tussock. Luckily it held and for some time—ten seconds? a minute?—I hung there feeling the tug of the quagmire and wondering if I would be dragged into it. Then I slowly began to pull my right leg free of the tenacious loam and eventually I succeeded in manoeuvring my foot onto the tussock so that as I straightened up, I was able to lever my trapped leg up from the grip of the marsh.

. . .

*2 o'clock.*

After cleaning my boots I went to the shop. Mrs Darnton grew distinctly cool when I asked her some questions: What happened to a letter that was handed in? Did she frank them herself? Stared at me as if she thought my wits were distracted. Of course not. They are taken back by the chaise that brings the mail and are franked in Thurchester.

I had had my quota. She is a tall woman with black eyes and looked rather terrifying when she said: *That's enough questions, Master Shenstone. Is there anything you wish to buy?*

*6 o'clock.*

Every receiving-house in the district must be on the watch and so it's virtually certain that the letters are posted in Thurchester and probably into the box outside the main office.

But who has the means to do that? Not Betsy or anyone else I can think of!

*A ¼ past midnight.*

I joined Mother and Euphemia in the parlour for our special dinner with the bleakest of expectations. Betsy was taking charge of the meal with occasional assistance from Mother who had purchased a small capon—already killed and plucked, thank heavens!

Mother started talking about the New Year's Eves of her child-hood. She was more loquacious on the subject than I had ever heard her. (She had mysteriously found another bottle of wine despite hav-ing assured me at Christmas that we were drinking the last one.) She recounted how she and her mother would put on their very smartest clothes and set out from their little cottage on the outskirts of the town. I had never heard her speak of it before and asked her where it was.

She said *Trafalgar Row* and then seemed to regret the words. She hurried on: *I was given such a beautiful silk gown and I wore it for my visits.*

She and her mother would call on her aunts and uncle at their big old place in Trinity Square: *It was called Mulberry House and was the townhouse of the Herriard family and had been in their possession for more than a hundred years.* They would be led up to the dining-room and Mother would go round and curtsy and kiss each of the old creatures and then be sat at the table and fed nuts and sweetmeats.

This annual ritual ended when she was twelve. The old peo-ple were dying one by one and Cousin Sybille did not keep up the tradition.

She talked of how her ancestors had been among the biggest land-owners in the district and, fixing me with her (slightly unsteady) gaze, said: *Richard, never forget that you are a Herriard.*

Euphemia said angrily: *Why is it of any importance who our forefathers were? What matters is what we make of our own lives.*

Mother looked really frightened and said no more on the topic. Euphemia has always cared about rank. Why is she saying these things now?

The dinner turned out to be dreadful: the capon over-cooked and the carrots and potatoes underdone. When the girl came to take things away Mother followed her into the passage and I heard her giving her a savage telling off for her carelessness. The next time Betsy brought dishes to us she had her head down and when she raised it I saw her sullen expression. It looked to me as if she had been crying. When the others weren't looking I caught her eye and smiled at her and she seemed to brighten.

We somehow got through a long ill-tempered evening and then, just as we've always done, we went into the hall to listen for the old clock striking midnight. It was cold and draughty. On the twelfth stroke we all kissed each other.

I wonder if Mother and Effie were thinking of the contrast with last year. God alone knows if the new year will be better than the old one. I don't imagine that it could be worse. A shame to have to begin it with dinner at the Greenacres. I will not waste my breath trying to talk intelligently to Quance: Fine words butter no parsons.


*1 o'clock.*


Of course, Mrs Darnton herself could add a letter to the post-bag before it went to Thurchester without anyone knowing. And she hears everything in that shop. There was that fat woman I saw her gossiping with who was obviously a rich source of scurrility and slander. The one who seems to know things about Davenant Burgoyne and his half-brother.

*Friday 1ˢᵗ of January, 4 o'clock in the morning.*

That little glimpse of a smile that Betsy gave me. That woebe-gone little face. Thought I'd go and cheer her up.

I tapped at the door and asked if I could come in and she called out in an unsteady voice: *Give me a moment, sir.*

I waited a minute and heard her light a candle and then I advanced into the room. She was sitting up in bed and pulling her nightgown around her.

*I heard you weeping,* I said.

*No,* she said boldly, her eyes red and moist. *I wasn't.*

*I'm sure the dinner wasn't your fault.*

She nodded.

Seeing that she did not seem frightened and since there was nowhere else to sit, I sat on the little bed.

I said: *I've come to apologise. When we stood in front of the clock to mark the New Year, we should have invited you to join us.*

*I'm not kin to you, sir,* she said.

I asked her if she had any family in the neighbourhood and she seemed surprised that I did not know that she was what she called "an outcountry gal". Mother had taken her from a parish workhouse some miles to the east. (Why had she gone so far to find a girl, I won-der? There must be armfuls of destitute girls all around us.)

Her mother had died when she was very young and she had kept house for her father and brothers. The parish took her in when she was eleven and hired her out by the week to local families as a petty-servant.

[A passage in Greek letters begins here. *Note by CP.*]

I was touched by her story and told her so. It was the last thing on my mind but she suddenly reached her hand up my leg under my nightgown and ran it up my cock and squeezed it. She gave me a sweet quizzical look and murmured: *Master Peg's asleep.*

She gently stroked it. Master Peg woke up.

Then she yanked up her own nightgown exposing the whole of her belly and her pudenda with its thin wispy cluster of hair and indicated that I should lie across her so that my cock was on her belly and when I did that, she rubbed it against her soft stomach with one hand while her other hand was running over my chest and shoulders. I pulled her nightdress down and lowered my head and licked one of her little bubbies. She kept up a stream of whispers: *Do you like that? Is that nice? Does that feel good?*

She gripped my hand and moved it down her body and showed me how she wanted me to rub her. I did so but was shocked by this eagerness for her own gratification. She began to pant and gasp and I felt irritation and even envy that I was giving her so much more pleasure than I was gaining—as well as dismay that the sounds she was making might be heard on the floor below. Now we seemed to be addressing the point and I tried to shift myself down but she said: *You can't come in. I don't want to be one of those gals that get caught. You'll have to spend on my belly.*

Almost as she said the words—so matter of fact about it, so happy to accept it—I became so excited that I spent. She gave me a quick smile and then mopped it up with her handkerchief.

Δ

[The passage in Greek letters ends here. *Note by CP.*]

We lay together for a while not speaking, half-dozing. Then she started talking drowsily about my being nice to her next time and hinting that she would do more to give me pleasure and that I only had to be "kind" to her in return.

I was horrified. She was asking for money. I had thought she was doing this because she felt some affection for me. I had given her presents but that was different from hard cash. She curled up beside me and within a minute she was snoring. I was cold though it seemed that the bitter chill had lifted a little. I crossed to the window and pulled back the curtain and saw heavy snow falling steadily. It seemed unkind to leave while she was asleep so I lay beside her and tried to keep warm and stayed there for a ½ hour or so.

*6 o'clock.*

[A passage in Greek letters begins here. *Note by CP.*]

Shameful. I was thinking about Guinevere while she was doing it—imagining her delicate little white hand on my swollen cock, her mischievous face with that slightly turned up nose, looking up—eyes dancing at me. It's her and not her lemon-faced sister that I love. How could I have failed to see that?

[The passage in Greek letters ends here. *Note by CP.*]

*½ past 8 o'clock.*

Hardly slept at all. I can hardly believe what I've done. How could I have lured a girl as young as that into disgusting and bestial activities which she performed solely in the hope of a gift. I must be depraved. I will not give her cash if that is what she was asking for. That would

demean both of us. I will buy her something as a recompense. Something handsome.

*11 o'clock.*

Just back from the shop. As soon as I entered, Mrs Darnton started
harassing me with questions: What was I looking for? A gift was it?
Was it for my mother or my sister? Or did I have a sweetheart? I said
it was for my sister and I bought a packet of ribbons. (I hope the prying tittle-tattle does not ask Effie how she liked them!)

*Memorandum:* OPENING BAL: *9s. 2½d.* EXP: Gift for B: *1s. 1d.* FINAL BAL:
*8s. 1½d.*

. . .

How I'm dreading dinner at the Greenacres'.

*Midnight.*

What an utterly abject and humiliating disaster. We had strolled
across the Battlefield in the golden light of a beautiful late afternoon
to dine with one of the most respected families in the neighbourhood.
We dragged ourselves home, nursing our wounds, cold and dejected.

We were the only guests apart from Mr and Mrs Quance. The
latter glared at me and then decided to pretend I didn't exist. As we
went in to dinner Mrs Quance lumbered majestically ahead of me and
I recognised her suddenly as a barbaric figure of the kind I've seen in
engravings of African monarchs. I almost saw the shrunken heads of
her victims swinging from her belt.

Unfortunately, even before we had finished the soup Mrs Greenacre, casting about for a topic, brought up Davenant Burgoyne's engagement. Presumably she had no idea of its significance for both Euphemia and Enid.

I glanced surreptitiously at my sister. She was impassive.

Mrs Quance volunteered that the earl's nephew had behaved disgracefully by playing on *the hopes of other young ladies*. Whether deliberately or not her eye fell at that moment on Euphemia.

My sister took the bait: *Maud has told me of the attempts made by other girls to ensnare her fiancé. Some of the mothers were a thousand times more shameless than their daughters.*

Here she smiled charmingly at Mrs Quance.

In pursuit of revenge, that lady brought the conversation round to the isolation of the district and the need for a carriage and then pretended to sympathise with us for not having one and yet moving to a neighbourhood where we knew nobody.

I blurted out: *Oh but we do have some connections here. Our cousin, Lady Terrewest, lives a mile or two beyond Stratton Peverel.*

Mother shot me a glance of disapproval.

*I know a great deal about Lady Terrewest,* Mrs Quance said threateningly. She turned to Euphemia and smilingly asked: *Are you enjoying working for her?*

I felt my cheeks burning with shame. Of course: Effie was paid to visit the poor old creature.

I could feel the Greenacres wondering why they had invited us. People who came to dinner on foot in mid-winter and whose daughter worked for her living.

Effie parried well: *Lady Terrewest has a sweet nature and presses gifts on those whom she loves.*

In a desperate attempt to change the subject, Mr Greenacre asked in a bluff manly tone: *Has anyone heard any more of these wicked hoaxing letters?*

All the women present had received one and so had others not there: Enid, Miss Bittlestone, Mrs Lloyd and her daughter Lucy.

*All the letters have been addressed to ladies,* Mrs Greenacre remarked thoughtfully.

*Apart from that strange man, Fourdrinier,* her husband objected.

Quance nodded sagely and indicated that we were about to benefit from his superior insight.

The man carries his dignity before him like an Oriental potentate with an umbrella-bearer walking in front of him. And yet, with his small frightened eyes and those papery jowls that hang straight down like the hindquarters of a pig, there is nothing impressive about him. If his nose were a tail he would be the perfect image of a sow's rear end.

When we had acknowledged his importance with a respectful silence, he said: *That fact suggests to me that the author is a woman. A deranged person would want to inflict pain on his or her own gender.*

*And yet much of the content is masculine,* Mother said with a shudder. *Grossly so.*

*Quite,* said Mrs Quance. She glanced sharply at me. *I'm convinced that there are elements in those letters that can only have been imagined by a man. Or more likely, a youth.*

So has she dropped her absurd idea that the writer is Mrs Paytress? Or is she simply torn between wanting it to be her and hoping that it will turn out to be me? I suppose a collaboration between us would be most gratifying to her.

*But the concerns of the author are feminine,* Mrs Greenacre said. *I can hardly be more specific without indelicacy, but the author seems to be preoccupied with what one might call the defining function of the female gender.*

*And yet a woman could not be responsible for the other atrocities,* Mr Greenacre pointed out. *The attacks on animals.*

*Then we should be looking for a man who is out in the fields at night,* Mrs Quance interrupted, staring at me.

*My point is,* Mr Greenacre persisted, *that a woman would be noticed. Certain articles would need to be carried. Paint and brushes for the obscene slogans. The fetishes.*

*The fetishes?* Mother asked.

Since it was a shocking revelation, they were all delighted to explain. Objects representing human beings—either a child's doll or a crude mannikin made of wood and straw—have been left outside houses at night or fastened to gates. In several cases the fetish was clearly intended to represent one of the occupants of the house. They had often been savagely damaged: a wooden knife stuck through the heart or the neck broken so that the doll's head lay at an unnatural angle to the body.

*What I suspect,* Mrs Quance announced gravely, *is that the letters are written by a man and a woman in collaboration and the acts are carried out by the male person alone. The woman is educated but the man is not.*

*I beg to differ, Mrs Quance,* Mr Greenacre said. *I believe the letters are wholly the work of an uneducated person.*

*The letters certainly appear illiterate,* Mr Quance said. *But there are a few anomalies that struck me. Perhaps my training in Biblical scholarship has given me an advantage. For example, in one of them the writer makes an accusation of mercenariness as a motive for marriage and writes of "wholy matrimoney".* He spelled the words out and then said: *In my view that piece of wordplay betrays a much higher level of education than is being pretended. And there are others, some of which are too coarse to be mentioned—a play on my own title and a disgusting allusion to Salisbury.*

Quance, pompous old fool though he is, has hit upon the truth. I recalled the sentence *he sticks his dick werever he can men boys women girls cows sheep goats monkies.* I had only half-noticed its strangeness. The phrase *goats and monkeys* is of course Othello's when he is thinking of his wife's suspected adultery.

In that case, is the author an educated person? If so, could it be Lucy after all? I believe she is malicious enough but is she capable of such obscenity?

Interestingly, Mrs Quance began talking about Lucy. Not by name, of course. She was saying that the letter she had recently received made reference to a young lady known to us all. She was the daughter of a gentleman of means living quietly in retirement near Upton Dene.

Mrs Greenacre asked what the nature of the allusion was.

Mrs Quance paused importantly and then said: *It made the grossest charge imaginable against the young woman and . . . a close relative of hers. A male relative.*

There was a shocked silence as we all pretended not to know what was meant and then, whether in order to divert us from that topic or fuel our outrage with further horrors, Mrs Greenacre volunteered: *In the letter we received our governess was attacked in the most vicious terms.*

*What was said?* Mrs Quance asked, almost slavering.

Mrs Greenacre hesitated. *There were dreadful charges against her character and her chastity. We felt that we had to put the allegations to her and she broke down in tears.*

Mrs Quance looked at her shrewdly and said: *Very probably a sign of guilt. I've always disliked that young woman. A sly creature who never looks you straight in the face. Were you sure of the references when you employed her?* She moved on to her next target: *One of the letters addressed to myself reveals facts about a certain individual who has attracted notice since she arrived in the neighbourhood.*

The Rector looked alarmed and said: *We can't be certain they are facts.*

His wife held up a hand to silence him and went on: *Although some of the details are luridly exaggerated, I know that the central allegation is true because I have heard other reports that confirm it.*

Like a rather stupid terrier with its teeth stuck in a bone and growling at anyone who tries to remove it, she was back on her favourite victim. Her husband had tried to prise the bone from her but she was too stubborn to let him. Only a brisk kick to the jaw would have any effect.

Effie rose to the defence of Mrs Paytress: *At least she cannot be guilty of both of those things. She cannot be writing the letters and besmirching her own character.*

Mrs Quance stared at her stonily. Her bluff had been called and she did not know how to respond.

It suddenly came to me: That is precisely what Lucy is doing. Without thinking, I said: *Why not? Whoever is writing these letters might have a good reason for doing precisely that.*

Mrs Quance stared at me: *Can you explain that extraordinary remark, Master Shenstone?*

I said: *The writer might try to throw off suspicion by defaming himself or herself in such exaggerated terms that the allegations cannot be believed.* For once I was listened to.

To my dismay, however, Mrs Quance then said triumphantly: *That answers your objection, Miss Shenstone. The person we are speaking of has exaggerated the facts to the point where nobody will believe even the truth.*

I was already regretting having given Mrs Quance this weapon against Mrs Paytress. My sister turned towards our common enemy: *Are you now saying, that the allegations are too grotesque to be believed?*

*In their most extreme form, yes. But the underlying substance is true.*

*So you're simply choosing which of the lurid charges against that lady to believe?*

*My dear girl,* Mother said warningly.

Seeing the way things were going, Mrs Greenacre stood up as the signal for the ladies to withdraw. As she rose from the table, Euphemia shot me a glare which was my reward for having suggested the idea.

As soon as the ladies had left there was a general relaxing of manners, language and even dress as buttons were undone while the port began to circulate. Greenacre said: *I believe that odd little man Fourdrinier was one of the first to receive an abusive letter.*

Quance said: *Yes, he showed it to me. It was about his trollop. That little chit he calls at different times his god-daughter or his ward because he forgets which lie he has told about her. He deceives nobody. She's clearly a young strumpet he picked up from the streets.*

*Is it known what was alleged in the letter?* I ventured to ask.

Quance smiled at the recollection and said: *"You should watch out for your whore, old man. A strapping young wench like that needs a stiff rod to stir her paint-pot and not a limp brush."*

(So that explains the old fellow's crazy speech to me!)

*I wonder, Greenacre,* Quance went on, *whether my wife has hit on the truth about these letters. That there is a combination of an educated woman and an illiterate man at work here and it is that strange mixture of elements that has thrown us off the scent.*

*What can you mean?* Greenacre demanded.

*That the lady at issue—if we will bestow that term upon her—is writing the letters in collaboration with a cloddish male. Perhaps her servant.*

Greenacre laughed. *I know who you mean. My wife has mentioned that ripe morsel of gossip to me.* He shook his head and said: *If only man-traps and spring-guns had not been made illegal the blackguard wouldn't dare to wander about in the dark.*

*You're right,* the Rector said. *A broken leg was a very effective deterrent to poaching.*

Greenacre said: *Have I ever told you the story of the poacher who was caught in a mantrap on my father's land? He was gripped fast by the ankle. He knew he faced transportation if he was taken, so I'll be damned if he didn't cut his own foot off!*

Quance laughed.

When we rejoined the ladies in the drawing-room we found our hostess and Mrs Quance discussing governesses once again—the deficiencies thereof, weaknesses of character, unreliability. Then, having damned the whole miserable tribe, Mrs Quance turned to Euphemia and said very sweetly: *I understand you are seeking a position of that kind?* (Heaven knows how she had learned that!) *I might be able to recommend you to a family of my acquaintance.*

Euphemia thanked her as if that were a well-meant offer. The evil old dragon began to quiz her about her skills as if she were interviewing her for a post herself. Mother looked on anxiously. We both know that Euphemia's patience has limits.

When Effie admitted to playing the pianoforte, Mrs Quance invited her to perform now and that request (command?) was backed up by our hosts.

She went to the pianoforte and played a short piece by Mendelssohn.

When she had finished Mrs Quance clapped briefly and then said: *That was charming. Of course, my own daughters have had the advantage of the best tutors and consequently play to the West-end standard. And speaking of Mayfair,* she went on, *as it happens there is a family of my acquaintance in Grosvenor-square who are looking for a governess.* She turned to Mrs Greenacre as if to convene an *ad hoc* committee of public-spirited mothers: *However, to make such a recommendation would be a serious responsibility.*

*Indeed,* said our hostess. *I have always made the most searching enquiries into the character of the young women I have hired.*

*Yet that is not always enough,* Mrs Quance said gleefully. *I heard the most dreadful story the other week about a young woman whose character one might have expected to be above reproach. And yet her conduct had become notorious in the neighbourhood.* She paused and gazed round at each of her listeners. Then she enunciated slowly and in a dramatically lowered voice: *She had been seen late at night coming from the lodgings of a single gentleman.*

That old *canard* again.

With complete disregard for the consequences, Effie galloped, banners waving, into the Valley of Death and "charged for the Russian guns". She said: *I too have heard a most shocking story of that kind about a young lady belonging to a most respectable family then living in Bath. The family of a clergyman.* She smiled at Mrs Quance.

They talk of someone's face hardening. In fact, hers softened. It collapsed, the folds of flesh dropping. Her breathing quickened. She reminded me of a rusty little shunting-engine standing in a station and quietly getting up steam.

*One of the parishioners was a family whose only son was not merely wealthy but in line to inherit a title. The young man had every advantage except one. He was, to be blunt, mentally incompetent. Because of that his guardians were wary of fortune-hunters and they soon became suspicious of the vicar and his family. With the help of her parents, however, the young lady contrived to entrap the poor gull into an engagement.*

Any duel—boxers, fencers—is not merely a competition in skill and determination but in the ability to stay calm. Mrs Quance and my sister might have been equally matched in the first two respects, but in the last one Euphemia had the clear advantage. What was so clever was that any attempt by the Quances to stop her narrating the story would only point the finger at them. I saw the Rector keep his eyes warningly on his wife, trying to restrain her from interrupting.

*His mother and sisters managed to spirit him away to Brighton but the girl's family pursued them and eventually organised what was in effect an abduction. The young lady collected him late one night and took him to a church where her father was waiting to perform the marriage. Luckily the man's family found out what was happening and managed to thwart this unscrupulous scheme and rescue the unfortunate heir.*

I saw for the first time in my experience that Mrs Quance was speechless.

*What an appalling story,* Mrs Greenacre exclaimed.

Euphemia said coolly: *I assure you it is true. I had it on the very best authority.*

(*The story is extant, and written in very choice Italian.*)

*This has been quite fascinating,* Mrs Quance declared with a bright smile. She turned to Euphemia. *I'm sure we could entertain each other by trading lurid stories until late into the night. Especially—alas!—tales of the misdeeds of clergymen which appears to be the theme of the evening. There is one in circulation in this very diocese about a man in a very elevated office who was accused of the most unspeakable offences. Would you care to hear it?*

Euphemia said: *I'm sure you've told it too often to want to do so again.*

*Oh, a good story is always worth telling. And I believe our hosts, who left Thurchester several years ago, are not familiar with it.*

*I think it's late enough,* her husband interrupted, placing his hand on her arm.

*It will keep to another day,* Mrs Quance said to Mrs Greenacre. She turned to Mother. *Mrs Shenstone,* she said with a smile of the deepest insincerity, *meeting you this evening has allowed me to give you in person some bad news that I was afraid I would have to express in a note. I very much regret that my husband and I are unable after all to convey you and your daughter to the ball in our carriage.*

Mother looked anxiously at Effie whose face remained impassive.

I admire our enemy's skill in one respect at least. It would have been wounding to have given no reason at all, but what was even more hurtful and insulting was to give one that was transparently absurd. This she now did: *My daughters have informed me that the boxes they will need to take to dress at the inn where we have engaged rooms will unfortunately occupy the seats that I had anticipated would be free.*

*I understand,* Mother muttered. *It was kind of you to have made the offer.*

We decided to leave as well. We were thanking our hosts at the door as Mrs Quance and her husband got into their carriage. She lowered the window and said: *I do so regret that we are unable to give you a lift and you will have such a cold walk home, but if we tried to take you so far out of our way the coachman would give notice. His principal concern is for his horses.*

She slammed the window shut. Her words had the more force since we all knew that for at least the first mile we would be taking the same route as they.

As soon as we were clear of the house I said to Euphemia: *You provoked that dreadful woman and now that she has withdrawn her offer of a ride, we can't use those expensive tickets so I hope you're pleased with yourself.*

*Yes we can,* Euphemia said. *I have money.*

*From your employment,* I said bitterly. *Why didn't you tell me the old woman is paying you?*

*Paying!* she repeated with contempt. *She gives me a little now and then. She can't afford to pay me. She can barely feed herself and her servants and keep warm in that great ruin of a house.*

We walked on in silence, tramping in the cold and dark along a muddy lane and stumbling on frozen ruts. A few minutes later the Quances' carriage came rumbling along with its dim lights flickering and we had to crush ourselves against a snow-covered wall to avoid its great metal-clad wheels as they clanked past a few inches from our feet.

When it had clattered out of earshot Mother said: *It's not just a carriage we'd have to pay for. We'd need rooms at an inn to dress in and stay the night.*

Euphemia insisted she would pay for everything and so, very unwillingly, Mother said she would write tomorrow to make the arrangements.

*Mother*, I said. *Let me go into Thurchester and do that. I can look at the rooms and the carriage and make sure everything is as it should be.*

At first Mother insisted it was too far to go there and back in one day but at last she agreed reluctantly and it was settled that I will make the trip on Monday.

That suits me perfectly. Several birds with one stone!

.   .   .

When we got back I found Betsy in the kitchen. I held my hands behind my back and told her to close her eyes. She did so and, oddly, she raised herself on her toes. I put the ribbons into her hand and told her to open her eyes and she looked at my gift in surprise. I said: *I've done something nice for you. If I come to you tonight, will you be especially nice to me?*

She gazed at me so strangely that I asked her if she was pleased. She said: *This ain't what I meant.*

I said: *Well then what do you want?*

She seemed upset and didn't speak for a moment. Then she said: *What do you think I want?* I didn't reply and she said: *I want money.*

I was shocked. So I hadn't misunderstood her last night. I said: *I thought you liked me.*

She said: *And I thought* you *liked* me. Then she turned and hurried out of the room.

Odd little episode.

*2 o'clock.*

I think Quance is right about *"wholy matrimoney"*. So if the author of those letters is not only pretending to be illiterate but is also defaming himself—or more probably herself—it could be any literate person. Lucy is the most likely suspect.

. . .

This expedition to the ball is becoming more and more bizarre. We will lay out in one night what we spend on the household in two or three months! What lunacy is this?

[This is the next of the anonymous letters relating to the case and it is addressed to Maud Whitaker-Smith. It is the only one that has survived that was received by someone living outside the district. *Note by CP.*]

You bitch. You wanted to be a cuntess and you got it bicause he could not get enough of your cunt. But he better enjy it wile he can bicause I am getting reddy to use my big sharp tool. I can cut off a bulls balicks in the dark now and when I am good and reddy I will slash open his belly and cut off his ballicks and hang them round his neck strung on his guts.

Effie went off to Thrubwell despite the heavy fall of snow over-night and the low sky threatening more. Old Hannah came struggling through the drifts very late and gave Mother a letter. It was from Boddington and informed her that he has sold the claim on her father's estate on these terms: A cash payment of two hundred pounds—which exactly clears the outstanding bill for the costs—and a third share of the proceeds if the suit is successful. And the purchaser will bear the future costs of the suit.

I was horrified and pointed out that the property in dispute is worth thousands of pounds.

I suspect that Boddington himself has secured it at a knockdown price. I will tackle him about that on Monday.

Then Mother started talking to me about our precarious social and financial position. She said: *I just want to see your sister settled while I'm still able to. And that will be hard because we are tainted by association with your father.*

I said: *Tainted! That's so unfair. It was wrong of Father to have borrowed money without authority, but since he intended to repay it, it can't be called embezzlement.*

Mother was silent for a moment and then said: *I should warn you, Richard, that you might hear worse allegations against him than that.*

Worse than fraud and theft?

*3 o'clock.*

Been thinking about Betsy's attitude last night. The fact that she wanted cash and not a gift is actually reassuring. She simply sees what we did as a transaction—nothing more than that. There will be no awkwardness as long as I pay her. No nonsense about *liking* or *not liking* or *getting sweet* or anything like that. I will offer her enough money this very night to give me the gratification I desire. I almost began to think that I was becoming fond of her. That would be absurd. She is an instrument of pleasure and if I do her no harm and even bring her some solace and delight, there is nothing to reproach myself over.

*6 o'clock.*

Spent the afternoon working on a poem for Guinevere. Those dancing eyes fizzing at me. That naughty little face—half painted doll, half wicked scallywag.

It started snowing heavily again and Mother ordered me to go and meet Euphemia. I didn't object because it occurred to me that I might encounter the Quance girls and find the opportunity to give my poem to G without her stiff-necked sister noticing. I set out half an hour earlier than I needed to and waited near the Rectory. After about twenty minutes I saw them approaching. I hurried towards them and without saying anything I pressed the paper into her hand and began to walk on. I heard footsteps hurrying behind me and when I turned found Enid approaching me scowling with rage. I had not thought she had so much passion in her. I'm sure she was angry that I had preferred her sister but what she said was: *How dare you attempt to compromise a member of my family in that way.*

*Compromise,* I said. *You're the last person in the village to object. If these letters have any credence, you've committed the act of darkness with that debauched rake.*

I turned my back on her and hurried on. I met Effie just the other side of Stratton Peverel and she didn't seem at all grateful at the sight of me. We'd only gone a few paces when she started telling me she had been into the shop earlier that day on her way to Lady Terrewest and heard people gossiping about the letters. She said that someone there had parroted my "foolish idea" that Mrs Paytress had written obscene letters about herself as a way of diverting suspicion. I said I had not meant that and did not believe it for a minute but she became angrier and angrier and at last she told me to walk on and leave her alone. Mother had given me a lantern so I thrust it into her hands and strode on ahead. The snow was quite deep by now and was being blown into my face.

I had got to this side of the village when away to my right I caught a glimpse of a light moving. There were no farmhouses or cottages just there and it was odd that someone should be out in the woods and meadows in that weather.

Was it the perpetrator of the outrages? In the hope of catching him in the act, I struck into the fields and was soon lost in the darkness with all physical features blanketed by snow. I blundered about and at last saw the lantern. It seemed to be heading back toward the village but where had it come from? I saw the shape of a barn several hundred yards away. Had the bearer of the light been coming from there? There seemed nothing else in that direction. I followed the glow over fields and across fences and climbed gates in an attempt to catch up with it.

My pursuit led me back into the village through lanes that ran behind the houses. As my quarry drew near the church I managed to get closer. The man went round to the back of Mrs Paytress's house and passed in through a side-door. I was almost certain it was the jockey-like man-servant of hers whom I had seen a couple of times.

I suppose there could be an entirely innocent explanation for what I saw and yet I cannot dismiss from my mind that idea of a man-servant carrying out the offences on the orders of his mistress. In that case, what was the *ripe morsel of gossip?*

I need to go back tomorrow and find out more.

### *11 o'clock.*

I have little more than eight shillings in the world. I hope one will be enough to persuade Betsy tonight.

### *½ past 1 o'clock.*

[A passage in Greek letters begins here. *Note by CP.*]

A little after midnight I went to her room and woke her up. She smiled when she saw me. I held out my hand and raised the candle over it so that she saw the shilling. She looked at it and then stared up at me. I thought she was going to make some protest. Was she now going to say she *didn't* want money?

No, because she reached out for it saying: *Is that how you want it to be, sir?*

I don't know what she meant by that but I snatched my hand away and dropped the money in the pocket of my nightgown and said: *You'll get that only if you're a good girl.*

She looked up with her hair falling over her forehead, quizzical, timid. Then she moved over to make a little space beside her and I managed to squeeze into her tiny bed. Our heads were touching. I wasn't sure what to do or say next.

She said: *What would you like for your shilling, sir?*

My voice croaking a little, I said: *I'll leave that to you, Betsy.*

She rolled up the sleeve of her nightgown and spat into her hand as if she was going to do some heavy job in the kitchen.

Then she pulled up my nightgown and began to rub my cock very gently. It was already halfway stiff and in an instant it was like a rod of iron.

I leaned forward to kiss her but she drew back and frowned and said: *Kissing is for my best boy and he's the one I'll wed.*

So be it.

Then to my surprise she knelt on the bed and bent over me and took my cock in her mouth and worked on it with her tongue and it was the most wonderful feeling and after just a few moments of bliss, I spent.

Δ

She wouldn't put her lips on mine but she would do that other thing! How did she know that trick?

I gave her the shilling and came back here.

[The passage in Greek letters ends here. *Note by CP.*]

. . .

*Memorandum:* OPENING BAL: *8s. 1½d.* EXP: To B: *1s.* FINAL BAL: *7s. 1½d.*

*4 o'clock.*

Have hardly slept. Was so upset that I broke my promise to myself and smoked again. Something about her manner made me feel foolish and in the wrong.

Rose and went out very early. About 5 or 6. Had to know about that man I followed last night to Mrs Paytress's house. I started from the place where I had picked up his trail and tried to find the footprints he must have left before I had encountered him. Unfortunately, so much snow had fallen overnight that there were no tracks at all except those of birds and rabbits and mice and *such small deer.*

I headed towards the barn I had seen last night and found it was ruined—roofless and open to the elements. However, there were some small outhouses beside it. They seemed to be derelict and abandoned but one of them had a padlocked door. I kicked away some of the snow that had fallen overnight and found dark streaks of blood.

I looked around and spotted something strange on a gate about eighty yards away. I went closer. It was a grotesque doll some eighteen inches high that had been nailed to the gate.

As I walked away I looked back and saw a man dressed as a farmer examining the object. I hope he didn't spot me.

I was on the road home when I saw Lucy Lloyd coming towards me. She was alone. I decided to walk on staring at her all the time to give her a chance to acknowledge me. When she was about forty or fifty paces away she glanced at me quickly and then gazed straight ahead and walked past me. I could not bear to be snubbed again so I turned and ran back and called out: *This is too bad! You're cutting me again!*

She looked furious and walked on.

I said: *I know what is going on. Someone is spreading the vilest untruths about me.*

She said—and her voice was trembling though whether with anger or fear I could not tell: *I have no idea what you're talking about.*

I said: *Don't try and play the innocent.*

She looked over my shoulder and said: *My father and mother are behind me in the carriage. I only descended to take exercise. Please let go of me.*

I had not even realised that I had taken her hand in mine. I released it. I said: *Have people told you things? What have you heard?*

*I've heard nothing.*

I said: *You're surely aware that disgusting libels are being published about young women in the neighbourhood—including my sister.* She feigned a smirk of perfect innocence that goaded me beyond endurance. I said: *The letters make allegations against you as well.*

She stepped back as if I had raised my hand to her. What a look of outraged purity came over her face.

I said: *Mrs Quance repeated one of them at the Greenacres' two nights ago and all but named you.*

She put her hands over her face and turned away.

I said: *You're pretending to be shocked. You're writing those letters yourself, aren't you?*

Now at last she gazed at me in astonishment—or a good simulacrum of it. She said: *It's your friend Mrs Paytress who is writing them. With that man-servant. Everyone knows that.*

*Her man-servant?*

*That ugly bent little man who is employed in her stables.* She smiled in an unpleasant manner and said: *They say he is her paramour. They say . . .*

I cannot write the filthy words. Now I understood the hints those old men had been making during dessert. That was why that sinister dwarf was out last night planting the fetish. He writes the letters with her and takes them to the post.

I must have stood there like a lummox.

*How do you like your own medicine, Master Shenstone?* she asked with a smile.

At that moment I became aware of the sound of hooves and wheels and turned to see an open carriage come to a halt a few dozen yards away. In it were her father and mother.

Lucy ran towards the vehicle calling out for help and her father gave the reins to a man-servant beside him and jumped down holding his whip.

Lucy clung onto him and cried out: *Master Shenstone has insulted me and laid hands on me. He has accused me of being the defamator.*

Lloyd raised his whip and advanced towards me. I stood my ground and he lashed the whip at me so that it kicked up the pebbles at my toes. He said: *If you ever come near my daughter again I will swear out a warrant against you.*

I told him calmly that his daughter was a liar and a mischief-maker and it was she who stood in need of a good whipping and not I.

He flushed and said: *I won't take that from a member of your family—a family that has displayed such degraded behaviour that it has earned them notoriety over the entire county.*

I was so stung that I said: *Do you know that the whole district believes you have debauched your daughter?*

He lowered the whip in surprise. Then, defying him to attack my undefended back, I turned quickly and walked away while he shouted insults after me.

. . .

So all the evidence points to that grotesque charge being true: She and her servant are lovers. She must be one of those women who are drawn to the uncouth, the savage, in a man.

I can hear Mother calling me to get ready for Morning Service. Damn. Damn. Damn.

*½ past 1 o'clock.*

We had almost reached the church when, as we passed Mrs Paytress's house, the hideous goblin who I now believe is her lover stepped forward from where he had been waiting by the gate. I stared at him and the image came into my mind of his gnarled hands on her body, his pitted cheeks pressed against her soft skin. He put into Mother's hands a note which she opened and then showed us:

> *Dear Mrs Shenstone,*
>     *I beg you to forgive the unconventionality of my request and spare me a few minutes of your time.*
>     *Most respectfully yours,*
>     *Jane Paytress*

Mother hesitated but Euphemia pointed out that after the open conflict with Mrs Quance, we had nothing to lose by going into the house in the full sight of all the district's churchgoers.

Mrs Paytress received us in her drawing-room. I could hardly bring myself to meet her gaze in the light of what I now know. She said she was desirous of giving us an explanation of her character and her conduct because we were the only persons in the neighbourhood whose good opinion she valued. She realised that she had in some way forfeited it and lost the opportunity to count us as friends and she believed that that had happened because we had been led to believe false stories about her that were in circulation. She wished to lay before us the facts.

For a moment I believed she was going to confess to her *amour* with the man-servant. However, this is the story she told us:

*I suffered the double misfortune of being an heiress and of seeing my parents die while I was still young. They left me with material riches but without the protection of competent guardians. My wealth made me prey to a much older man—worldly and charming—who was looking for a rich wife. I married without provision being made for my independence. All too soon I understood the truth about my husband and I became extremely unhappy. He turned out to be a violent drunken gambler and worse than that. Eventually I managed to flee taking my jewels which, in the eyes of the law, now belonged to him. I lived under a new name because I had to hide from my husband. There was another factor which is too painful to talk about. I will merely say that it vastly increased the difficulties of my situation.*

What did she mean? That she became the earl's mistress? That she had fled with her lover, the servant?

*I sought refuge with an old friend in Salisbury. I raised money from the sale of the jewels and together we founded a school. Recently my husband's mental faculties so far deteriorated that he was made a ward in Chancery and I was able to salvage some money from the wreckage of his estate. I sold my share of the school and moved here. In the last couple of weeks I have learned that my husband has died. I can now call myself a widow and return to my legal name—Mrs Guilfoyle.*

I said: *Why did you come to this neighbourhood?*

She looked surprised: *Because of the sea which I have loved all my life. I grew up on the coast of Suffolk.*

I said: *You knew nobody here?*

I heard Mother muttering reproachfully.

*No. I had an acquaintance in Thurchester but nobody closer than that.*

Was that an allusion to the earl?

I asked: *What do you know about the anonymous letters that someone has been sending?*

Both Mother and Euphemia cried out in protest at my words. Mrs Paytress said: *I've received two myself. I destroyed them immediately.*

How very convenient!

Then she fastened her gaze on me and started saying that whoever was writing them was deeply unhappy. The letters were intended to inflict pain and that was a sign of the agony that their author must be feeling.

I decided to spare her nothing. I said: *The servant who brought us here just now, I happened to see him out in the fields late last night. Do you know what he was doing?*

She looked at me with feigned surprise. *I haven't the least idea. My servants' free time is their own. Are you accusing him of something?*

I said: *Are you trying to protect him? Do you know what is being said by your neighbours? About your relations with that man?*

*I apologise for my son's conduct*, Mother said rising to her feet.

When we were outside she and Euphemia turned on me and said the harshest things. I swung round on my heel and walked home.

I think she came here to be fucked by the earl and when he's not fucking her she settles for her servant.

. . .

*Harry—or Richard if that is what you now prefer*

*What a surprise to hear that you wrote to me. I can't say it was a pleasant one. You were always happy to toady after me at school, but back home you pretended you didn't know me. Why should you when your dad was a Canon of the Cathedral and mine was a poor bousy schoolmaster?*

*Well, how do you like it now your governor's dead and your mam's as poor as mine? I suppose you blame me for all of that. I wish I could take the credit for the fall of the House of Shenstone. You were always laughing up your sleeve at everyone else. You thought you were so superior. See how high-minded you can be now that you're a friendless beggar.*

*And don't pester my mother again.*

*B*

Spiteful, vicious, carping sneak. This is his response to a perfectly amiable overture from myself.

If I'm going to be sure that Mrs Paytress and not Lucy is the writer, I need to see more of the letters. I must get the one old Bittlestone talked about. Assuming it exists. If she offers some excuse for not being able to produce it, that will be evidence that *she* is the author.

. . .

*I suppose you blame me for that.* What does he mean? Mother and Effie certainly blame him for something.

. . .

*You pisernouse old witch. You spread the lies wot that evil quants bitch makes up. You lik the arss of that bloted bag of wind—Do you eat her shit too.*

*You spread lyes about young wimman because noman would want to fuck you you dried up old kipper. I fuck anything but even I woodnot fuck you. One thing you say is right thogh. Loosy Leud is a whore. She fucks her dad and likes it.*

*Why dont you tell the truth about the lyes that dirty little Pursniffle tole. wen I ketch him I will cut of his little dick and stuff it up his wellfukd arssholl.*

*If you do not give over spreading lyes, I shull come and visit you one nigth and you wunt like it if I do.*

*The Harrower*

*4 o'clock.*

I obtained it from the old woman easily enough. I knocked on the door of her little hovel and walked straight in. She was horrified to see me. I found I could hardly breathe. The smoke blowing back from the fireplace stifled me and I choked. I can't imagine how she can endure to live like that.

I just told her bluntly what I wanted. She looked at me in such terror that I thought she was going to admit that it never existed. But she turned and opened a drawer. She brought out a wooden box and it seemed to be full of her treasures. A miniature on a chain. What looked like a legal document. A dried flower. A faded visiting-card. A large yellowed invitation with a dance-card tied to it with a piece of ribbon on which three names only had been written out of a dozen dances. Several letters tied up in ribbon. She removed one of them and handed it to me. All the while she was nodding her head at me like a demented hen.

. . .

What can I learn from this hate-filled eruption?

That monstrous calumny against Lucy. I now think it rules her out as the author. She could not write such a thing unless she were completely depraved. But then whoever is writing these letters must be depraved. And yet there is nobody in the district who shows signs of the seething inferno of hatred that must be bubbling beneath the surface.

I can make no sense of the reference to "Pursniffle".

There is so much about "fucking" that I think the author is a female who is trying too hard to sound like a man. If it's not Lucy it must be Mrs Paytress. And her servant-beau!

But why write such libels? And attack animals?

*½ past 6 o'clock.*

I have wronged her, thank heavens. She is as innocent as the new-fallen snow. I have found out the truth! The foolish old crone has exposed herself. And only to save the price of a stamp.

Mother insisted we attend Evensong since we had missed the morning service. As we reached the gate into the churchyard, the Quances were converging on it slightly ahead of us on their way from the Rectory. Though they must have seen us, they walked straight past without turning their heads in our direction like a line of soldiers on parade. Once inside the gate we saw the Bittlestone creature standing forlornly as if waiting for them on the path to the church, but they ignored her and marched past without breaking step. The old thing, as if pushed aside by the wake of the Quances' passing, washed up beside us like a dead leaf against the river-bank.

*Mrs Quance won't speak to me*, she wailed to Mother and without prompting told us how her patroness had come back from the dinner at the Greenacres' and instantly ordered her out of the house.

Then the old coot started whining to Mother about how I came to her cottage that morning and took the letter.

Mother ordered me to return it immediately. Seeing a look of alarm on the old woman's face she said: *But you must never go to Miss Bittlestone's cottage again alone.*

She invited the old creature to tea on Tuesday. She could have the letter back then.

I had a flash of inspiration. I said: *One thing, Miss Bittlestone. Would you be good enough to bring the envelope that it came in?*

She looked dismayed and said: *I've probably thrown it away.*

Then it came to me in an instant: There is no envelope because she did not post the letter! She wanted to save the money for the stamp. She wrote out the letter to show around but she had not spent the tuppence to post it to herself! I have her!

In the earlier letters she attacked Mrs Paytress in order to please her patroness. Then she libelled Lucy because she was a rival of Enid's. She lives her life on the droppings from the tables of others and must resent her treatment—for all her appearance of unassuming humility. Now that the Quances have rejected her, she turns on them.

How could I have been so foolish as to think Mrs Paytress was behind the letters?

The old woman hurried on ahead. As soon as we were out of her hearing Mother said: *I am very annoyed with you for what you did to that poor harmless creature. You must have terrified her.*

I said: *Has it occurred to you that Miss Bittlestone might be responsible for these letters?*

She stared at me in astonishment. Did she think I might be right?

As we entered the church, heads turned and I distinctly heard a voice I did not recognise say in a loud whisper: *Rotten fruit falls from a rotting tree.* Why did they all look at me like that? As if they knew a terrible thing about me? I heard muttering on all sides. I noticed among the congregation the farmer I had seen watching me when I found the fetish. He was pointing me out to his neighbours and I guessed what he was saying.

Mrs Paytress entered a moment or two after the service had started. She glanced around and I tried to catch her eye to send an apology and it seemed to me that our gazes locked together for an instant but she quickly turned and took her place in her pew. What a fool I had been to suspect her. Virtually to accuse her to her face. I burn with shame at the memory.

While the congregation was singing, I stared at the mouths opening and shutting around me and they seemed to me to be so many dead bodies, yawning pits for mouths, worm-mouths drawing in food at one end and expelling excrement from the other, corpses in their Sunday best.

Then a dramatic interruption. Halfway through the service a female in servant's costume entered the church and slipped up to Mrs Paytress's pew and said something to her. She turned and I saw an expression of alarm on her face before she lowered the veil and hurried out with the woman behind her.

*½ past 8 o'clock.*

Up here absolute silence. I stare out and the window is black like the back of a looking-glass. If I cover the candle with my hand a weirdly distorted face appears on the pane: my own. I could fancy that the rest of the world has died mysteriously and there is nobody on the planet except myself in this ancient house sinking into the marsh.

. . .

*Rotten fruit from a rotting tree.* I am the fruit. Father the tree. Why are they saying those things?

. . .

I have been cruel and stupid and yet I believe she forgives me. There was that moment during Evensong when she turned and gazed straight at me. She was saying: *Come to me.* She needs me. I should have gone to her by now. She must be wondering why I have not come.

*½ past 11 o'clock.*

I do not understand why she spoke to me like that.

At the door I knew the maid-servant was disobeying her mistress's orders so I pushed past her but she clung onto me and screamed. That dwarfish man-servant came hurrying from the back of the house and seized me. Hearing our voices Mrs Paytress came down the stairs. For some reason she asked me to leave her house. I said I had to speak to her alone. I had something urgent that was for her ears only. She indicated that I should go into the drawing-room and told the man to wait at the door. We stood just inside the room. I tried to tell her how sorry I was for the things I had thought about her and I told her I had been deceived into believing lies and I saw in her face that she was upset to think that I had mistrusted her. I said: *I must have been insane to have given any credence to that rumour about your man-servant. And even though everyone thinks it, I was mad to have believed that allegation about the earl.*

For some reason she failed to understand me. Or she pretended not to. She said: *You are being very impertinent.*

I said I would die to defend her honour. I was ready to go anywhere with her at any time of the day or night. We could go now, this very minute. She moved towards the door. I stood in her way and said I felt about her as I knew she did about me. I don't remember the things I went on to tell her for I found myself speaking without choosing to do so and without thinking of what the consequences might be or even knowing what I was going to say until I heard the words. I don't recall what I said but I know my language was passionate and heart-felt.

She put her hand on the door-handle and when I moved to prevent her leaving she asked me to stand aside. I did so and she went into the hall and told the man-servant to make sure I left the house immediately.

There is only one explanation: She has been told wicked lies about me. She has been made to believe that I am the person responsible for those letters!

Who has turned her against me? Who has poisoned her mind with lies about me? It must be Lucy and her damned parents.


*4 o'clock in the morning.*

I have just seven shillings and three ha'pence. Half a crown should be enough. If it's just cash she wants, that suits me very well.

*A ¼ past 5 o'clock.*

Went to her room. Showed her the half-crown. She nodded and tried to snatch it. I said: *When I've had what I want.*

She said: *You can't come into me for that. It ain't enough to be worth the risk.*

Like the other time she got me to straddle her and she pulled up her own nightshift.

She started stroking me and touching herself and she put her hand on mine and directed me to where to place it in order to pleasure her.

After a minute or two she began breathing heavily. Then she said: *You can come in but you shan't spend in me, sir. Do you promise?*

I nodded. I thought this was the moment and started to try to insert myself.

She said: *Not yet.* She put her hand on my neck and brought my head down so that I could nuzzle at her nipple. Then she grabbed one of my hands and placed it over her most private part and started rubbing. I continued that motion. Now she began to gasp.

She shoved my hand away and began to frig herself, greedily slurping shamelessly in front of me. There was the smell of her sweat and other uncleanlinesses. She was panting for breath as fiercely as if she had been running and now she clutched me almost roughly and at last she pulled me into her.

I stayed hard and I thrust but I didn't feel any pleasure. She was gasping and crying out. Screaming as if I were murdering her. I was afraid she would wake the house. I spent suddenly and joylessly.

Ω

She nudged me away and vigorously rubbed at herself with her head thrown back and then gasped and moaned and cried out and shook and then fell back against the pillow.

We lay in silence for a while. Then in a heavy, sleepy voice she said: *I didn't ought to have let you do that. What if I'm caught again?*

It was her fault. She had pushed me into her. I hadn't even enjoyed it. She had become carried away by her own gross appetites. Gorged on pleasure she drifted into sleep, slumbering like some piglet at the sow's teat.

Was that what it was supposed to be like? I had derived no gratification from it.

After a while she started shaking and crying in her sleep. A few minutes later she woke herself up with her movements and I said: *What were you dreaming about?*

She said: *I dreamed I was back at my dad's.*

*You mean home?*

She said: *No, my dad's. This is my home. All the home I've ever known.*

I asked her why she did not think of her father's house as her home.

She looked at me in amazement and said: *I got took away on account of what they was doing to me there, my dad and my brothers.*

*They slept with you!* I exclaimed.

*Bless you,* she said. *I dunno about sleeping but they fucked me from as soon as I can remember. They stopped when I got old enough to get into trouble. But my dad was drunk one night and he did it again and I got caught. That was when the parish found out and took me in.*

*And the baby?*

*Didn't have it. Died when I was four months gone.*

I had been deceived. I had taken her for an innocent girl and now I found she had committed incest. I felt I had done something wicked. I had allowed myself to be contaminated by impurity.

She must have seen the disgust on my face. She looked at me in alarm and then made the strangest remark: *We can't help what our dads do. None of us.*

*What do you mean?* I asked.

She looked frightened and refused to say any more.

What can she possibly have been hinting at? Has she heard some story about Father?

I stood up and began to leave the room. At the door I remembered something and said: *You haven't asked for the money.*

She said: *I don't care about it.*

I threw the coin onto the bed.

I was disgusted. She wasn't doing it for the money. She had come to like it so much that she was allowing me to do it for nothing. It was her own pleasure she was thinking of rather than mine! And she had acquired the taste for it by the most degraded and unnatural means.

Because I was distracted, I walked past Mother and Effie's rooms instead of taking the back stairs. At the end of the passage, I looked back and there seemed to be a figure at Effie's door—though it might have been a shadow.

*Memorandum:* OPENING BAL: *7s. 1½d.* EXP: TO B: *2s. 6d.* FINAL BAL: *4s. 7½d.*

*6 o'clock.*

No time to sleep since I have to set off for Thurchester. Mother has given me three shillings for it.

*Monday 4<sup>th</sup> of January, after midnight.*

Σ

When I saw that loathsome creature I wanted to smite him to the ground and spit on him. I understand now why Mother and Effie hate him. He dragged my father down into the mire with him. And it was I who first brought him to our house.

The town was like a dark pit, a miasma of foulness, streets strewn with ashes. The uncleanliness. I feel contaminated merely by having been there.

When I grappled with my tormentor in the mist and we wrestled thigh to thigh, I was fighting not a man but a demon. He was delivered into my hands for me to punish according to his deserts. The rushing of the waters sounded in my ears and I wish I had had the strength to hurl him into the racing torrent.

I've slept for a few hours. I must write down everything that happened yesterday while it is vivid in my memory.

I left the house long before it was light. Just beyond Stratton Peverel I was passed by a carriage going very fast. It was hard to tell but I thought it looked like Mrs Paytress's landau.

Reached Thurchester late in the morning. Went first to The George and Dragon and booked rooms for the night of the ball. Then I went to a livery-stable nearby and ordered a post-chaise.

Then to Boddington's office. Gave my name. Cocky little pen-pushing clerk went into the inner sanctum and came back and told me with a saucy grin that the old man was out. Sure he was lying and Boddington was cowering behind his desk. Hiding from me like a frightened rat squatting in its filthy drain.

Looked at the posting-box in front of the post-office. It's the only one in the county. But who is putting the letters in there on behalf of the old trout? She certainly can't be getting into town every few days any more than she can be sneaking around the fields at night with a knife and pot of paint.

After a quick dinner in a tavern I made my way to Trinity Square and found Mulberry House: a big cheerless old place that looks as if nobody has lived there for years, with tall, blind windows that have bars on the top floor that give it the air of a prison.

I walked up the hill to look at the earl's townhouse on Castle Parade. The street is built only on one side and Burgoyne House is the largest of the houses and slightly at an angle to the others so that it looks out over the town with an arrogant squint. Its back is on Hill

Street. I walked down that street and I was sure I had identified the house where the cur lodges: It has a torch-snuffer above the entrance in the form of a boar's head—the Burgoyne crest. It should be a boor!

The Dolphin is up a dark alley off Angel Street. I had to find out why Davenant Burgoyne mentioned it when he spoke of Father. I went into the taproom and at the bar the landlord looked at me in surprise and then smiled and asked: *Are you here to meet someone?*

I should have told him to mind his business but I blurted out: *That's what I'm hoping.*

He said: *I'm sure that can be arranged.*

While he was speaking he was pulling a pint of ale and he now handed it to me. When I made to pay he shook his head and said: *Take a seat, young fellow.*

I picked up a newspaper and positioned myself on a bench by the door.

After about fifteen minutes a boy came in. He was about fourteen. I had a feeling I recognised him. I think he is in the Cathedral choir. He didn't go up to the bar but the landlord nodded him over to a seat by the chimney.

A few minutes later a man entered. He looked at the landlord who turned his head briefly towards the fireplace. The newcomer did the same and then nodded and went to the back of the taproom and passed through a door. After a few minutes the boy got up and went through the door at the back.

I understood everything. All the hints and half-confirmations I had heard. I was about to leave when the street-door opened and Bartlemew came in. I raised the newspaper to hide my face.

I looked at him around the corner of the paper. That wide thin mouth with the slippery smile. Those bright guileless-seeming eyes that miss nothing. He was far from a dunce at school but he is not interested in anything abstract, anything not of immediate use to himself. He is cunning, crafty, manipulative, intuitive—all the characteristics that make someone successful, if that's the appropriate term, at exploiting other people. There is not a thoughtful, introspective, altruistic bone in his body. I wonder what turned him into such a creature, an abject slug that feeds off other's weaknesses without a trace of self-respect. The only honesty in him is that he knows you can see what he is, and yet even so he manages to surprise you by further betrayals.

I was paralysed as I sat there. I wanted to hurt him. It horrified me to realise how strong the desire was to inflict pain on him. He had done so much harm to us. And yet it was my fault. Mother was right about that. It was I who introduced him into the family circle last summer. He had been poverty-stricken then but now he was prosper-ously dressed in a good surcoat and jacket while an expensive watch hung from his fob-chain. I knew precisely where the money had come from to buy him his finery.

I was afraid that at any moment the landlord would point me out to him. But after a whispered conversation, he went out through the back-door. I decided it was cowardly to do nothing and that I would challenge him when he returned.

I went up to the bar and ordered a double measure of brandy. The man waved away my money but I insisted on paying for it and for the ale and that seemed to make him angry.

I drank it quickly and demanded another. This time the man made no attempt to stop me paying. When I went back for a third brandy he must have seen how enraged I was for he said: *I don't want trouble here. I'm not serving you no more.*

I said: *Damn your eyes for a low sneaking rogue.*

He gestured at the door with his thumb. I walked out. I had for-gotten my resolution to wait for Bartlemew but my head was spin-ning by now and I wasn't thinking clearly. A thick mist had formed while I was in the public-house and I was lost for a while and wan-dered blindly, not caring where my feet were taking me.

Suddenly I found myself outside Boddington's office. I don't know how long I lingered, leaning against a doorpost nearby.

He came out at last and I stood in his way and spoke his name. He looked green when he saw me. I said: *I have to speak to you. You can't keep hiding behind your clerk.* He smiled—smiled!—and said he had no idea what I meant and he had heard I had called while he was out and it would suit him better if I could come back another day. I said I was sure it would but it suited *me* to see him now and he said *Very well* and turned and led me upstairs. There was nobody in the house but the two of us. We went into his office. The fire had been smothered and the room was cold.

He started asking about the health of my mother and sister and I could see that he was making every effort to disarm me. I told him bluntly that I wanted to talk about my mother's affairs. How was it that everything had vanished: the furniture, the investments, the pension? He said in his lawyerly fashion that without my mother's permission he could tell me only what was publicly known: That my father's estate had been declared bankrupt on the motion of his creditors, of whom the principal one was the Dean and Chapter of the Cathedral. All his assets had been seized.

I said I could not understand how everything could have gone and I wanted to see full accounts. Instead of becoming indignant as an honest man surely would have, he smiled and told me he would have a copy posted to my mother the very next day and it would be for her to show it to me if she chose to.

Then he starting trotting out homilies about how he knew how hard it was to be my age—how could he remember that far back! He talked of his own son Tobias and compared him with me: Tobias had lost his mother just as I had my father. How dare he make any comparison between us! Tobias is a bousy wastrel and good-for-nothing.

I was not going to let him off so lightly. I told him I wanted to know about the Chancery suit that he had sold. Why had he obtained so little for it?

He gave the same answer: *Only your mother can tell you about it.*

I said: *It was your fault. You encouraged her to make her doomed claim. You just wanted her to run up expenses and fatten your fees.*

He didn't like that. He flushed and said: *We will discuss it no longer.*
With those words he rose and unceremoniously ushered me out to
the stairs.

When we reached the front-door I passed into the street without
a farewell.

The fog had thickened and it was now dark and I had great difficulty finding my way even though I know the streets so well. I
followed the rising ground since I knew where it would lead me.
As I went up and up my footsteps rang on the rounded cobbles that
were wet and slippery with dew. Somehow I found myself near the
Castle. The town lay at my feet but I could see nothing but a wall
of grey mist.

I decided to go down Hill Street. By now I could make progress
only by feeling my way along the walls or scraping my foot along the
kerbstone to find the edge of the pavement. Like a blind man I used
my hands and followed the railings and as I descended the street I
became aware that there were footsteps behind me. I could not tell
how close. When I stopped they seemed to stop. The person was tag-
ging me, was staying behind me and not passing me. I became sure
he meant harm to me. I turned and called out *Ho there!*

Silence. I continued and I came to an entrance with steps where
the railings rose into an arch. I reached up. I felt the snuffer—that
damned boar's head.

I waited there. I could detect nothing above the hiss and tumble
of the water passing under the bridge at the bottom of the street.

I don't know how much time had passed—a couple of minutes,
half an hour—when I heard the footsteps again—at least, they
seemed the same. I called out and there was no response but I saw
a movement and assumed the man was attacking me and I hit out
where I believed him to be but my fist struck empty air.

A sound came from another direction and I ran at it and I hit
someone or something with my shoulder. It seemed harder than a
body should have been. The pain made me mad with rage. I heard

steps some yards away and rushed at the source of the sound and this time I encountered a person—we buffeted into each other striking shoulder to shoulder—and I swung my fist and it met something and there was a choked exclamation.

I was sure it was my enemy and I gripped him and held onto him by the coat and hit him again and then again though we were so close that my blows were ineffectual. I thrust him from me intending to aim my fist at him but he vanished into the mist. I heard a sound of metal hitting stone and I thought he had dropped a knife or a gun. I was determined to stand my ground and I remained listening for at least three or four minutes. There was nothing. I wondered if he were crouching a few yards from me waiting for me to go. Or to turn my back and then he would retrieve the weapon and strike at me or shoot. There was complete silence. Nothing but the rustling of the water.

After a while I began to walk slowly and quietly towards the High Street. I was sure there were footsteps behind me. Someone was following me once again. Every time I stopped, he stopped. Whenever I looked round, he halted and pressed himself into the shadows. I joined the crowded streets in the centre and wove my way through the throng and must have thrown him off.

I passed through the town. Once I was away from those streets and out in the hollow of the valley, the mist thinned and I was able to quicken my pace.

I don't regret it. I hope I hurt him. It is an outrage that he walks the same earth as I, that I have to breathe air polluted by him. Such creatures should not live: He was born to wealth and privilege and he has thrown aside the obligations that went with them and squanders his money on gambling and whoring.

Yet it is not *his* wickedness that disturbs me. Nor even the vile pandaring of Bartlemew. What shocks me is to learn of something evil in one who has been so near to me all my life. My father was always secretive. Now I'm starting to uncover his nakedness. I understand now why the Precentor made such efforts to keep him from the choristers. Has everyone in the diocese known these things about my father but I? Is that why Mother and Effie and I have been shunned or have received pitying looks or at best been patronised by those kind enough to overlook the sins of the father? And once the Precentor had closed the door to him, Bartlemew's role was to introduce him to The Dolphin and supply him with fresh meat from the Choir.

It was a long weary walk home though I accepted a ride on a cart for some of the way. I reached the house late at night. I could see from the darkness of the windows that nobody had waited up for me. I came into the parlour where there was a fire still alight though it was dying and I started writing in this journal while the wind sighed restlessly and moaned down the chimney-flue. From somewhere came strange noises that seemed to be human voices wailing in the distance. In broad daylight I would not have been concerned but sitting alone at night, the only person awake in the house and perhaps for half a mile around, I felt very uneasy.

Suddenly there was a scrabbling noise and a whirring sound. I was really scared now. I thought of all the wicked things that had happened in that house—the murdered lover and the burning of the baby—and wondered if the restless spirits of those who had suffered were still haunting the place.

And then I even found myself wondering if the maimings of beasts were not being carried out by any human but were supernatural manifestations of anger—perhaps directed against me for what I had done to Edmund or had failed to do.

Then I realised that what had frightened me was merely the wind, for the chimney was acting like a vast stone flute. The sound of scratching was perhaps caused by something that had blown down it and become lodged.

But no sooner had I comforted myself with that thought than I heard from somewhere inside the house a slow shuffling noise. The strangest ideas passed through my mind.

Suddenly an apparition came round the door: a haggard ashen face with grey hair. I did not recognise it for a moment. It was Mother. In that instant I had a vision of her as she will look when she is dead: her face collapsed, cheeks sunken, eyes hollowed out.

So strong was this impression that I started when she spoke: *Richard, why are your clothes torn and blood-stained?*

I hadn't realised they were. I told her I had lost my way in a dense fog on the road back from town and had fallen into a ditch beside the carriageway.

She kept her unsteady gaze on me as if she did not believe me. Then she said: *Is that the truth? People tell me they've seen you late at night in places you had no business to be. Heaven only knows what you were doing.* She put her hand on the sopha to guide herself and then almost fell into it. She stared at me and blinked several times. She said: *There is something very serious that I have to talk to you about. It has been reported to me that you have been making a nuisance of yourself. In relation to young women.*

*Who told you that?*

*Everyone is talking about you. You chased Miss Fourdrinier and terrified her. You've frightened the Quance girls. And just yesterday you were grossly offensive to Lucy Lloyd and then in the evening you forced your way into Mrs Paytress's house.*

*Mother, you can't believe these grotesque stories.*

*You prowl around at night getting up to heaven alone knows what kind of nastiness. Now you come home covered in blood. What should I believe?*

I tried to speak but she held up her hand.

*I had a letter from Thomas this morning. He's told me the most dreadful thing about what happened to make the College dismiss you. That a young man died. A friend of yours. And you were in some way involved.*

Here it came. I just nodded.

She said: *How did he die? Who was he?*

I said: *Didn't Uncle Thomas tell you?*

*Don't be impertinent. I asked you a question.*

*Two questions, Mother. But I think we should talk about it in the morning.*

She said: *You've been deceiving me, Richard. Thomas has informed me that your offence is so grave that the College would never have taken you back even if he were prepared to go on paying for you.*

When I made no response she leaned forward and said: *You don't know what you've done to me. When I saw the Quances and the Lloyds looking down their noses at me I was able to say to myself, at least I have a son at Cambridge who will soon have his degree and be making his way in the world. Now I learn that you've been lying about that.* She began sobbing and coughing at the same time. *You're a broken reed, Richard.* She rose to her feet and then had to hold out her hands and grip the back of a chair to keep herself from falling. *All the hopes I had—that I would be able to hold my head up again and your sister take her rightful place in the world—became impossible as soon as the College rusticated you. Well, I wash my hands of you. I no longer care what you do.*

Yet she said that with tears running down her cheeks.

*Your sister and I must look elsewhere for support whatever the consequences. And you will leave this house as soon as possible.*

She then shuffled out of the room.

---

*Memorandum:* OPENING BAL: *4s. 7½d.* RECT: (from Mother) *3s.* EXP: Dinner (*1s. 2d.*) and what I drank at The Dolphin (*9d.*) TOTAL EXP: *1s. 11d.* FINAL GROSS BAL: *5s. 8½d.* (of which I owe Mother: *1s. 1d.*). FINAL NET BAL: *4s. 7½d.*

. . .

you dirty horish bitch the men you fuck
arent enough to satisfy you are they You go
out to find more. And you still get fucked
by that ariggant brute who thinks he has

*rights over every woman in the district just bicause his uncel owns most of the land. I've seen you going to your meeting-place on the batelfeeld. You didn't know I was following you, did you.*

*I will make him wish he had never been born. I will make him blubber for what he has done. I will hurt him bad with my tool.*

## The Harrower

*11 o'clock.*

I came down for breakfast very late and Mother hardly spoke to me. She looked wan and haggard. I wonder how much of last night she remembers. Effie had gone to the village early and Mother and I were sitting in silence in the parlour (sewing and reading respectively) when she came back. She came bounding in, full of some gossip she had heard in the shop. This is what she told us: That oppressed little being, Sukey, who helps Mrs Darnton in that evil den of spitefulness, was passing the house of Mrs Paytress very early yesterday morning when she noticed a carriage pulled up at the door. She stopped to look and in the light from the lamps saw the mistress of the house emerge carrying a child in her arms. It was about five or six years of age and she was unable to see if it was a boy or a girl.

The vehicle overtook her a few minutes later going at a great rate towards Thurchester. (So that was the carriage that passed me yesterday morning!) It was now being given out that Mrs Paytress was not intending ever to return. She has left most of her servants in the house and they are packing up and will reveal nothing in response to questions.

I thought Mother was going to accuse me of having driven her out of the village by my misconduct the other day but in fact just the opposite: her sudden departure is, according to gossip at Mrs Darnton's, being interpreted as an admission of guilt. I'm sure Mrs Quance and her Myrmidons are encouraging that lie.

Mother spoke of her amazement that Mrs Paytress had successfully hidden the presence of a child in the house. And there could be only one reason for concealing the fact that she was a mother.

We were still talking about that when the old letter-carrier brought a letter addressed to Effie. The postmark was Thurchester and the handwriting was crudely formed.

I handed it to my sister saying that I believed it was one of *those* letters. She opened it and after a few seconds threw it from her with a scream. I picked it up but she rallied and snatched it from me, snapping at me for wanting to read "such nasty stuff". I said I only wanted to see if I could work out who had written it.

I watched her studying it. It rattled her badly. It's not like Effie to be bowled out by something in that manner. The letter is a horror. But is she upset because it's cruel or because what it alleges is true? She gave it to Mother but wouldn't let me see it.

Then after a while she started saying that what was in the letter was so completely deranged that it could have no more effect on a sane person than the ravings of a lunatic in Bedlam. She was now angry and determined to track down the author. She said: *I've had certain suspicions for a while and this letter virtually confirms them.*

I guessed which way the wind was blowing. I asked: *Does this person live within three miles of Stratton Peverel? If not, he could not possibly know as much as he does.*

She ignored that and said to Mother: *It's someone who has pursued our family ever since he was introduced to us.* (Here a glare in my direction.)

I said: *Since you haven't allowed me to see the letter, I can hardly agree or disagree.*

She handed it to me. *See what you make of it.*

. . .

That's when I hurried up here and copied it.

The author obviously hates Mother and Effie. Should I be relieved that I am neither addressed nor even named? He hates my sister's lover even more.

But whoever wrote it, it's confirmation that Effie is still meeting Davenant Burgoyne at the tower. The writer must have followed them, and if I can catch him doing that again, I can unmask him.

The letter itself offers few clues to its authorship. The pretence of illiterateness, however, has been virtually abandoned. The writer has forgotten to misspell a number of words, has used mainly correct grammar, and has neglected to omit the apostrophe. In fact, I now realise that the writer was only pretending in the most superficial and transparent way to be illiterate.

I can see why Effie thinks that the "Harrow" reference points to Bartlemew. But she's wrong. He is too distant to know what is happening here. I see no reason to change my mind: The writer is that spiteful old Bittlestone cat. Yet she must have a male collaborator who is posting the letters in town and savaging livestock. I'll confront the evil old witch this afternoon when she comes to tea.

### 2 o'clock.

I have made a conquest! I saw it in her face. If only she were prettier.

I went up to the Battlefield to see if I could spot either Effie's inamorato or some skulker spying on them. I saw nobody and was almost at the tower when I noticed the little governess with her gaggle of children. I hurried after them and when I caught them up, she looked round at the sound of my running feet. All the children except that damned Amelia were walking ahead of her and had not heard me.

I had to warn Helen of what I had learned at that dreadful dinner-party. Without wasting time I asked her if that meddling shrew, the Rector's wife, had tried to turn Mrs Greenacre against her. Clearly she found Amelia's presence inhibiting and told her to run on ahead. The wretched girl disobeyed her. I repeated the instruction and the child just stared at me insolently. So I ignored her. I said to Helen: *The old Quance witch has told Mrs Greenacre that there is a secret attachment between you and her husband.*

She started at my words and I saw a play of emotions on her face. She cares for me, that is clear.

Amelia said: *Should you be talking to a strange gentleman, Miss Carstairs?*

To my amazement Helen said: *You are perfectly correct, Amelia. It would be improper for us to continue to enjoy the advantage of Mr Shenstone's company.*

I could see that she was forcing herself to end the conversation because of that tiresome child. She hurried on, pulling Amelia with her. The little minx turned and gave me a look of triumphant malice.

I came home and then remembered that I had meant to visit the tower.


*6 o'clock.*


Old Miss Bittlestone had barely removed her topcoat and shawl before she delivered an astonishing piece of news. *Do you know why Mrs Paytress drove into Thurchester yesterday morning?* she asked Mother. She hurried on without waiting for an answer: *She went straight to a doctor with her child in her arms.* She stopped and gulped and then went on falteringly: *The most dreadful thing. Quite, quite dreadful.* She paused again and then almost in a whisper she said: *He pronounced it to be . . . to be no longer alive.*

Mother glanced at Effie who had turned her head away. Then she said: *The death of a child is the most terrible thing. And I cannot help feeling sorry for that woman. She must have felt a mother's grief. Even for a child conceived in sin and whose existence she was ashamed to acknowledge.*

Miss Bittlestone said with uncharacteristic sharpness: *That is not correct. If you'll pardon me, Mrs Shenstone, I believe we were all wrong. And Mrs Quance most of all.*

What a change of tune! The child, she said, was born to Mrs Paytress and her husband while they lived together and there was not the slightest reason to assume any irregularity. Mrs Paytress had fled the marital home with her child because of the conduct of her husband. She had taken refuge in Salisbury. There was no substance in the idea of a liaison with the earl and that misapprehension was based simply on the fact that he had once owned a house in that city. The truth was that he had sold it some years ago. She went on to explain that the child, a boy of about ten or eleven, had suffered seizures all his life. His mother had taken measures to protect him from being seen by strangers whose reaction caused him distress, and that was why he never left the house. The mysterious woman-servant was his constant nurse.

There was silence when she had finished.

(*Sacrifices for someone I love.* I hope Mother was ashamed.)

I got up and crossed the room and shook the old lady by the hand. She blushed and said: *Why, bless my soul, Master Shenstone. I have done no more than tell the truth.*

I said: *Telling the truth about that lady requires courage in this neighbourhood where she has such a powerful enemy.*

She smiled ruefully and said: *I have already been cast into utter darkness though I have no notion why.* She sighed: *Whenever my eyes fall on the chair Mrs Quance used to occupy, I am reminded of our lost friendship.*

*I don't want to see it ever again. Yet it's a fine piece of furniture. Would you like to have it, Mrs Shenstone?*

Mother said she would be glad to and suggested that I could borrow a hand-cart and fetch it one day. What have we come to that I should find myself carrying old chairs around the countryside!

After a few minutes, at an unignorable signal from Mother, I rose and handed old Bittlestone the letter I had borrowed from her with my expression of regret for ever having caused her unease.

She said: *Oh yes, of course. I meant to tell you that I did manage to find the envelope after all.* She reached into her battered reticule and handed it to me. I was astonished. It is genuine since the hand is unmistakable and the date clearly legible and it was posted in Thurchester. Would she have bothered to pay for the postage if she had no need to? Perhaps she is not, after all, the author of those letters?

If it is not she, then who is it? Who could get to Thurchester so often and rely on being able to post a letter unobserved? The Lloyds do not go into town frequently enough and Lucy would surely not entrust such a letter to anyone else.

I stood up and took my leave. I had to get to Monument Hill. I had to find out about the tower.


*7 o'clock.*


There is a single window and it is on the western side but is about fifteen or twenty feet up. I have no way of reaching it unless I can I climb an oak-tree that stands nearby. I could not do it today because I was wearing my boots and would not have been able to get a foothold.

As I walked home I was thinking about the puzzle of how the letters are posted and I suddenly saw how the trick might be done and who might be doing it. All that is needed is a friend in Thurchester and Lucy has plenty of those.

*10 o'clock.*

I went down for dinner. As soon as I walked into the room I knew that Mother and Euphemia had been talking about me. I'm sure my sister knows what is in that letter Mother has received from Uncle T. It's so unfair that she knows and I still don't.

I asked Mother: *What has Uncle Thomas told you?*

*He said the authorities in Cambridge are still looking into the circumstances of your friend's death.*

*Since I'm not going back, it doesn't matter what the College—or even the University—might have to say.*

*It's neither of those, Richard. It's out of their hands now. It's the police and magistrates who are investigating. There is some document they have been shown that casts a new light on the matter. It bears on the motive.*

I hope they couldn't see how alarmed that made me.

Euphemia asked: *Your friend, Edmund Webster, how did he die?*

*He swallowed poison,* I said.

*Deliberately,* Euphemia said with only the slightest interrogatory intonation. I said nothing. Then she looked meaningfully at Mother and asked: *Was he alone when he swallowed it?*

I was saved having to answer because an extraordinary thing happened. The house shook suddenly as if thumped by a giant's fist and in a moment the room was filled with a loud drumming—steady and inexorable—which seemed to be growing in intensity. We all gazed at each other in horror. It was impossible to know where the sound was coming from. It became deafening. At that moment the strangest thought came to me: that we have tried to lock danger out but in doing so have sealed ourselves in with something that is mad and dangerous and filled with hatred. And then it became clear that the noise emanated from the great chimney, for a rapid thudding reverberated from deep in the wall.

Suddenly some creature was spewed out of the mouth of the chimney and the foul thing—whatever it was—hit the carpet with a thud and lay twitching and jerking on the floor. It had a tiny head with staring eyes and a blackened body with shrivelled legs. What seemed to be arms were spread out with skeletal webs hanging from them. It was still twitching and juddering as it lay there scattering ash and heaven knew what else on the carpet.

Mother stood frozen staring at it but Euphemia stepped back and then screamed and hid her face. My calm, rational sister was having a fit of hysterics.

*Get it out of here! Get it away from me!* she cried. It lay on the floor between her and the door of the room jerking spasmodically and it was clear that she was too terrified to step past it.

It was a complex structure of tiny bones, white as teeth in a barrel of pitch, with a scattering of black specks and trailing filaments of something leathery and unclean.

Betsy came running in, drawn by the noise. She pulled off her pinafore and flung it over the thing saying: *It's just a bird, ma'am. Just a dead crow.*

And she was right. It was a great crow that must have become trapped in the chimney. How long it had stuck there flapping its wings and causing the noises we had heard it was impossible to guess. Then it had been dislodged by the sudden gust of wind and the movement of its wings had been in response to the change in temperature when it fell into the room.

Betsy cleared up while Mother took Effie up to bed.


*A ¼ to midnight.*


Did the crow fall into the chimney tonight while it was perching on the rim and was blown in by the sudden gust? Or was it there much longer? Did it become trapped in the flue that day the smoke blew back down the chimney?

On this occasion Effie's horror seemed completely authentic and made me more suspicious of some of the earlier scenes of outrage or shock.

. . .

*Herriard House,*
*by Stratton Herriard,*
*near Thurchester.*
*January the 5ᵗʰ, 1864.*

*Dear Uncle Thomas,*

*I am most grateful for your generous offer of free passage abroad. However, to accept it would be to run away from my obligations. Instead, I beg you to be so generous as to settle with my creditor. I give you my most solemn and binding promise that I will repay you if it takes the remainder of my life. I ask this for the sake of my mother and sister rather than for myself. If Mr Webster seeks vengeance by pressing the authorities into bringing charges against me, the consequences could be dire for all of us.*

*Your affectionate nephew,*
*Richard Shenstone*

. . .

Have been trying to avoid Betsy and have had to walk past her a couple of times without looking at her. Don't know what I feel about her. Angry with her. Disgusted with myself.

*Wednesday 6<sup>th</sup> of January, 10 o'clock.*

After an early breakfast I went straight out wearing walking-shoes. Climbed the tree and looked through the window and though the light was very dim, I thought I could make out shapes and shadows and believed I saw rugs on the floor and the silhouette of what might have been a divan or sopha. It is as I feared! The disgusting dissolute filthy rake! He has furnished a place to take her. And she. The shameless brazen creature. What does she hope to gain from this? How dare she take that tone of moral superiority towards me!

*3 o'clock.*

A real facer from the old biddy!

I showed Mother my letter to Uncle T—sealed so that she could not read it—and she was delighted. I took it to the shop and while I was consigning it to the care of Mrs Darnton, I took the opportunity to try out my theory. I asked: *Is anyone regularly handing in a bulky letter? One that is addressed to someone in Thurchester?*

She glared at me and said: *I don't believe you should be posing such a question, Master Shenstone. A body can have no honest reason for asking that.*

I had heard the shop-door open but had not turned around so I was astonished to hear Miss Bittlestone say behind me: *That's quite unfair, Mrs Darnton. The young man is anxious to find out who is sending these horrible letters. As anxious as any of us.*

It made no difference to the Gorgon and I nodded my thanks to the old creature as I began to leave but she asked me to delay a moment until she had made her purchases. I waited outside and when she came out we began to walk slowly along the street.

I began to say: *I asked that question only because . . .*

She held up a hand and said: *You don't have to explain anything. I don't believe you are writing these wicked letters, Master Shenstone. It's not in your character. You had the insight to see that Mrs Paytress was being wronged by our little society when many of us older heads were wrong.*

I thanked her and said that I had a theory about how the letters are contrived. I explained that I thought that someone living locally could write a hateful letter and then put it inside an envelope and send it to an acquaintance living in or near Thurchester to be posted there. And that second individual might not even have any idea that such letters were being received in this district.

She considered this in silence and then agreed with me that it seemed a possible explanation.

It seemed unfair that she had no idea why Mrs Quance had dropped her. And so in a few words I informed her of what Effie had done that had alienated Mrs Quance: She had recounted at the Greenacres' dinner-party the story about the Quances told us by Miss Bittlestone. I stressed that she had done it quite without any malicious intention towards Miss Bittlestone. I suppose that is true in the sense that she was thinking only of the harm it would inflict on Mrs Quance.

She stopped walking to consider this piece of information. Then she turned to me and thanked me very graciously for having enlightened her. She heaved a great sigh and strode on saying: *How strange it is that I risked the anger of Mrs Quance by being neighbourly to your mother and sister when they came here, and now your sister's actions have, quite innocently, exiled me from that lady's favour.*

*Why was Mrs Quance so ill-disposed toward them?*

She turned to me in surprise: *Because of what had happened with Miss Whitaker-Smith.*

*Maud? I don't understand. I know that she and my sister and Enid Quance were all rivals for the hand of Mr Davenant Burgoyne. There was bad feeling between the families as a result.*

*It was more than that. There was the business with that poor boy. And it has had such dreadful consequences.*

*What boy?*

She blushed. *I've said too much. I thought you must know and it's not my place to talk about it if you don't.*

I pressed her but she was adamant.

Rather clumsily changing the subject, she said she would like to do me a good turn as thanks for mine. To my surprise she asked if I was going to the ball on Saturday and when I gloomily confirmed it she smiled and said: *Most young persons find the prospect of a ball very exciting. When I was a girl I went to one once. My Mama's cousin lent me the most beautiful dress of yellow taffeta and I danced with the same young man three times!*

I saw a plain frumpy girl twenty-five years ago standing shyly in the corner of a ball-room wearing her best dress. *I was adored once too.*

Then she frowned and put her hand on my arm: *But I have an ominous feeling about this one. Some of the obscene letters have alluded to it and it strikes me that everyone addressed or mentioned in them is going to be present. I have a presentiment that I can't justify logically that it is going to be the culminating point of this wicked campaign. There have been so many strange and menacing events and they seem in some inexplicable manner to be weaving you and Mr Davenant Burgoyne together in partic-ular. You will both be at the ball and—call me a superstitious old fool if you like—I can't help wondering if something is intended to happen that night.*

I laughed and asked: *Intended by whom?*

She gazed into my face without speaking and at last she just said: *Be careful.*

We had reached the bottom of Brankston Hill and so we parted and I came home.

. . .

I don't see why I should tell Mother anything about Edmund. There are times when she seems like a stranger to me. Someone who might come up to me in the street and make some fearful demand. Why should I care what she thinks? And Euphemia has no claim on me at all after the way she has been behaving.

*10 o'clock in the evening.*

During dinner Euphemia suddenly asked: *What can this Mr Webster do if the money is not paid back? Is he angry because he blames you for his son's death? Is it revenge he wants?*

How did she know so much? Has she some unknown informant? She is right about his desire for revenge. Hateful, hateful man. He made his son's life a misery and is now using his death to hound others. It was because Edmund loathed him that he suggested we take from him the only thing he cares about: money.

I kept silent and she said: *Since Edmund Webster was your friend, why didn't he cancel your debt before he took his own life?* I just shook my head. Then she asked: *What was the poison?*

*Laudanum,* I had to say at last.

*Opium and alcohol,* she murmured.

Seeing that I was going to say no more, she turned to Mother: *I don't think Richard has told us the whole story.*

How dare she! What a hypocrite!

I said: *I don't see what right you have to say that. What have you been getting up to? There's an allegation in that letter. What truth is there in it?*

She gasped.

(*You still get fucked by that ariggant brute.*)

Mother said: *That's unforgivable, Richard.*

*Thursday 7<sup>th</sup> of January, 11 o'clock.*

I can't imagine how I failed to see what a handsome creature that little governess is. It is no common "prettiness" that she has but a rare inner beauty that shines from her face.

Euphemia said at breakfast that she was going to Lady Terrewest this morning. Mother suggested that she and I accompany her some of the way. I agreed, just to show I don't bear a grudge about last night.

At the top of Brankston Hill we ran straight into the entire Greenacre family—the parents striding along in front and behind them the little governess and all the children. We slowed down and prepared our social faces but Mr and Mrs Greenacre marched straight past as if they had not noticed us.

While the rest of the party walked on, the governess turned and let go the hand of the smallest child and ran back and grabbed me by the arm pulling me away from Mother and Effie who were ahead of me. In a hoarse whisper she said: *I don't believe what is being said about you, Mr Shenstone.*

*What is being said?* I demanded.

I saw that the little baggage—Amelia—had turned to watch us. She tugged her mother's arm and Mrs Greenacre also looked round.

Helen gazed at me in surprise. *Everyone believes that you are writing those hateful letters and doing those terrible things at night.*

I must have stared at her like an idiot. Does *everyone* believe that? Not just Mrs Quance and Lucy's parents?

*Mrs Quance has received another letter and believes it was written by you because it makes the most dreadful threats against Mr Davenant Burgoyne. And the boy.*

I said: *What boy?*

She did not answer and before I could ask her any more questions, she ran back to her party. Mrs Greenacre was still watching us.

Mother had at first strode on without noticing but Euphemia had turned round and looked at us and then touched Mother's arm. She too stopped to watch my brief conversation with the girl.

So the whole district is convinced that I am a deranged monster! Everyone believes it: Enid and Guinevere, Mrs Darnton, Old Hannah. But not Miss Bittlestone! And not Lucy if she is the guilty person herself!

How can I clear my name? Only, I believe, by exposing the true perpetrator of these outrages and I believe I am close to that.

If Lucy is writing those foul letters and sending them to a friend in Thurchester to put in the post, that still leaves the question: Who is going around at night blinding cattle and stabbing pregnant horses? There is one obvious answer: Her father. I glimpsed the anger and cruelty of the man in that display of violence with the whip. I can't imagine what their motive for doing these things can be, but I now believe that the allegation of a wicked relationship between them must be at the heart of it.

But what on earth could that charming girl have meant? What boy have I been accused of threatening and for what imaginable reason? Both Mother and Miss Bittlestone have mentioned some boy so are they all talking of the same one?

The little governess risked the wrath of her employers to warn me and that can only be because she loves me. How deeply, how profoundly gratifying it is that that little being, that pale-faced little creature, has faith in me. I value that a thousand times more than if some potentate of the hamlets like Mr Greenacre had assured me that he knows me to be innocent. I can't imagine how I failed to see the girl's beauty. Those lovely greyish-green eyes with their beguiling obliqueness of vision. That sweetly curved little mouth and the small chin. Very different from the brassy allure of a hussy like Lucy.

*6 o'clock in the evening.*

Mother came back full of the news from the village that Mrs Paytress's house is being shut down and everything inside it removed. She said there were wagons and closed vans outside and men carrying carpets and furniture into them. The rumour is that Mrs Paytress's creditors have sent in bailiffs and that her ostensible prosperity was a sham based on fraudulent credit. Euphemia failed to rise to her defence and I said nothing. But I don't believe it.

*10 o'clock in the evening.*

At dinner Euphemia asked me: *What did that girl, that governess, have to say to you that was so secret? What have you been doing to her, Richard?*

I said: *She had the decency to warn me that people think I am writing these filthy letters.*

Instead of expressing outrage at that, Mother said calmly: *I've heard that Mrs Quance has received another.*

I said: *And she is accusing me of having written it. Aren't you indignant that people believe that, Mother?*

She didn't reply, but Euphemia said: *You haven't explained why Mr Webster blames you for his son's self-destruction.*

I was caught by surprise and foolishly I said: *It was your fault, Mother. You should have written to me to say that Father had died. I was shown it in a newspaper. I was furious with Edmund about something and I was so upset that I didn't think properly. I sent him a letter that I shouldn't have.*

Euphemia said: *It drove him to take his own life?*

*I don't know if he died on purpose or by accident. But the Dean found my letter lying beside him.*

Euphemia asked: *And what was in it that was so reprehensible that the College rusticated you?*

I just told her it was the sort of letter you write to a friend when you think you've been badly treated. I suppose that's more or less the truth.

. . .

Mother went up to bed early and so I found myself alone with Effie. I said: *By questioning me about Cambridge you've broken your promise and so I am not bound by my undertaking and therefore I will not go to the ball.*

She said very calmly: *Richard, I'm not asking you to do it to please me but for Mother's sake. She has set her heart on seeing me there. She wants to relive her own youth while she can.*

I said: *She doesn't want to go to the ball. It's you who are forcing her.*

She replied: *How little you understand Mother. How completely self-absorbed you are. I suppose you think her constant coughing is just because of a winter chill?*

*What do you mean?* I demanded.

*Letting Mother see me at the ball is one of the few things left for you and me to do for her.*

I said: *I don't know what you're implying, but I've made up my mind. I'm not going.*

*½ past midnight.*

Extraordinary. Until about 11 o'clock I was reading in front of the dying fire after Mother and Effie had gone up. I was on my way to bed when I saw Betsy carrying a jug of hot water upstairs and remembered that Effie had asked her to make ready her bath. So I was astonished when, about five minutes later, Betsy tapped at my door and said my sister wanted to see me immediately.

I knocked at Effie's door and heard her say come in. I thought at first she must have taken me for Betsy for, although the room was dark and the only light came from a small fire in the grate, I could see that the tin bath was before the hearth and that Effie was sitting in it. I began to back away closing the door but she called out: *Don't be shy, Richard. Come on in.*

I kept my eyes cast down and she ordered me to sit on a sopha nearby which was made up as a bed. The door of the inner room was open and I saw a large bed in there. The room was very warm—there was a fire blazing in the hearth—and the air was heavily scented with some exotic fragrance—attar of roses? sandalwood?—and my head swam with it. As we spoke I looked up and she was silhouetted against the fire. I could almost make out her breasts. I could hardly pay attention to what she was saying. Seeing my embarrassment she laughed and said: *You're my brother, Richard. And it's almost pitch dark. There's no impropriety.*

I looked up and she splashed water over her neck and bosom. She started talking about the ball and how much she and Mother were looking forward to it and how it would break Mother's heart not to go. I hardly know what we said but I gave way and said that I had not intended to be taken seriously when I said I would not go.

I left and came back here.

Δ

[This is the next of the anonymous letters relating to the case and it is again addressed to Mrs Quance. *Note by CP.*]

Damn him just because he is the nevue of an erl he thinks he can do what he likes. He has harmed the name of a good girl he has jilted Effi and let himself be trapped by a gileful hussy like Mawd who is not worth ten of her.

I hate him as much as you do. Woudnt you like to see him dead?

He takes my own girl to the place he has made on the hill for fucking girls and he fucks her there because she is still sweet on him even though he threw her over. Poor Effi. She is too trusting. He will ruin her all over again.

He does not deserve to live. I will use my nice sharp hooked blade. It will slide into his belly and slice his guts. He will spill out his lites like the cows and I will laugh.

That will poke that bitch Mawd wittiker smith in the eye. And serve her right. She got that littel brat Pursiffle to spew his lyes against an inosent man. I will make him cry out for that. I will strangel him with his own gutstrings.

Harry the Harrower

*Friday 8th of January, 11 o'clock.*

Mother went out very early this morning before I was even down for breakfast. And Euphemia had already set off to walk to Thrubwell.

When Mother came back she told me she had been into the village to ask Mrs Quance to show her the letter the governess had told me about!

I asked: *Why did you do that?*

She didn't look at me. She muttered: *It was vile. Unimaginably vile. It said things about your sister that . . .*

She suddenly said: *Weren't you known as Harry at school?*

*Yes. I preferred my second name at that time. What of it?*

She stared at me without speaking. And then I understood. I said: *Mother, please tell me you don't believe that I am responsible for those deranged letters?*

She didn't answer and continued to evade my gaze. There was nothing to say. If she could believe that about me, I was not going to defend myself. I got up and walked out.

.  .  .

Can Mother really believe that I have been spewing out that filth? Can she think that I have sat up here day after day scrawling those letters that could only have come from some mad hell of rage and cruelty?

*3 o'clock.*

Utter, utter madness! I was walking through the village on my way to try to find Euphemia and see if I could catch Lloyd skulking after her, when I was suddenly accosted outside the shop by that lunatic Fourdrinier, red in the face and shouting. He started accusing me of having stolen some tool of his.

I asked him: *What in heaven's name would I want with it?*

He said: *Sirrah, the whole district knows what you wanted with it.*

I said: *What on earth are you implying?*

He said: *You walk about at all hours of the night. You were strangely anxious to learn my address when we first met. Then only a few days later I received one of those vile letters.*

I shouted: *How dare you!*

He began to walk away but I wasn't going to let the scoundrel insult me with impunity. I grabbed him by the coat and hauled him back and demanded an apology. He started bellowing as if he was in danger of his life. Several of the onlookers stepped forward as if to support him. I saw that evil witch Mrs Darnton staring at me. I let go of the old fool and gave him a push.

I said: *You're a depraved old lecher. A whoremonger. Everyone knows that.*

I turned my back on him and left him standing there.

*½ past 5 o'clock.*

Effie wasn't back when I got home and Mother told me she wanted to have a serious talk. She began by saying that although Euphemia had tried to protect me for a long time, she herself had noticed the odd smell coming from my chamber and remarked my eccentric behaviour at times and realised that I was indulging in a very dangerous habit up in my room and that was what was making me behave so erratically. She had asked Euphemia if her suspicions were correct and after prevaricating for a while, my sister had admitted it.

I told her it wasn't true. (I don't want her to worry about me.) What she had smelled was merely an exotic variety of tobacco. I wasn't sure if she believed me.

*½ past 6 o'clock.*

Dreadful. I don't know what's going to happen to us. We can't go on living together like this.

Euphemia got back this afternoon and burst into the parlour. She said to Mother: *Have you heard of this new shame he has brought upon us?* She gave Mother a grotesquely distorted narrative of my encounter with Fourdrinier and ended by saying: *Everyone in the shop was talking about how Richard assaulted the poor old gentleman.*

*Poor old gentleman!* I exclaimed. *Repulsive old sensualist, rather.*

*And it's worse even than that, Mother. People are saying that Mr Fourdrinier's stolen tool is the one that is being used to harm animals.*

Mother turned to me and said: *Your conduct is becoming more and more disgraceful. You seem to have cast off all restraints. Even after my warning, you behaved shamefully towards the Greenacres' governess only yesterday.*

I tried to defend myself but Mother held up her hand and went on: *There is a graver charge against you, Richard. I understand from your sister that you have dishonoured this very house. Euphemia has told me that Betsy has complained of you.*

I stared at Effie. She said: *She has told me that you have given her presents. And cajoled her into committing various acts.*

I seized her by the arm and said: *What do you mean?*

She squirmed and said: *Richard, you're hurting me. Let go of me. You're frightening me. But I'm telling the truth. Betsy has told me of the disgusting way you've been pestering her. The filthy things you want her to do.*

I was so surprised I released her.

She sprang away rubbing her arm and said: *Can you deny that you've indulged in unrestrained grossness with the poor child?*

*How dare you!* I said. *And what a hypocrite you are! You're the one who's gross. Everyone knows what you've been doing in the tower with that man.*

She stared at me sullenly.

*I won't have this,* Mother said. *Richard, go to your room.*

*No,* I said. *You need to hear this, Mother. What those foul letters accuse her of, it's true. She has been meeting that man. On the Battlefield. And then he takes her to the tower on the hill and . . . Well, he has it fitted out for entertaining women. I won't say any more.*

They both stared at me: Euphemia in horror that I knew so much and Mother in dismay at learning the truth.

Then to my astonishment Mother seemed to lose control of herself completely. She almost screamed at me: *That proves it! You're the one. Nobody in the world believes that nonsense apart from the madman who's been writing those foul letters.* She paused and said more calmly: *I've decided. You leave the house tomorrow morning.*

I stared at her in amazement.

Then something even more extraordinary. Effie spoke up for me! She said: *Mother, you're quite wrong. I know Richard has been behaving strangely but I don't believe for a moment that he has anything to do with those letters.*

I don't know whether Mother or I was the more surprised.

*You're mistaken, Euphemia. The last letter Mrs Quance has received, the one she showed me this morning, it makes exactly that allegation—that absurd allegation—against you. In the coarsest terms. And not only that. It displays a vicious—a quite deranged—hatred of Maud Whitaker-Smith and her family for the harm they've done to us.*

*That proves I can't be the author,* I protested. *I don't know what they did.*

*Don't you?* Mother said. *Hasn't your friend told you the whole story?*

*Bartlemew? How could he? I haven't seen him since I've been back.* I corrected myself: *I haven't spoken to him.* Mother gazed at me with such open disbelief that I faltered not because I was lying but because I couldn't bear to see her look at me like that.

*You've been in correspondence with him*, Mother said coldly. *But one thing above all convinced me though, God knows, I didn't want to be convinced. When we went to tea with Mrs Quance you teased her with the word "lucubrations." A little later a disgusting version of that word appeared in one of the letters she showed me this morning.*

*I don't know what you are referring to, Mother. So I can't defend myself.*

*There is no defence. The evidence is overwhelming—the parallels with the letters, the actions I've seen and heard you commit, what you've been doing with Betsy, and Mr Fourdrinier's claim that you stole the implement being used in the attacks. I've made a decision, Richard, and it's irrevocable. Tomorrow morning you leave here. I have a few sovereigns I can spare you. You depart this house and this district. You go to Thurchester and you get on a train to somewhere. I don't know where and frankly I hardly care. But you leave here for your sister's sake and, if it comes to that, for mine.*

Before I could say anything Euphemia exclaimed: *No, Mother! Let him stay a little longer.*

Mother remained obdurate.

Then Effie turned to me: *Leave us, Richard.*

I obeyed.

*11 o'clock at night.*

So my own mother thinks I'm a night-prowling madman! Isn't your mother supposed to be the last person to give up on you?

And I've been betrayed even by Betsy. *I thought you liked me.* And I didn't force her to do anything she didn't want to.

They've been shut up in that room for ½ an hour. I must try to find out what they are talking about.

*½ past 11 o'clock.*

Shamefully I lurked outside the parlour door but nothing was audible except the murmur of voices. Then I heard a quick step and hastened into the hall. Mother came out walking fast. As she passed she started at the sight of me and shot me such a haggard, careworn look that I almost forgave her for the cruel things she had said. I turned to follow her but Euphemia hurried out and seized my arm: *Let her go, Richard. I want to talk to you.*

She almost pulled me back into the parlour. We sat down and she said: *You don't have to go away. I've convinced Mother that you didn't write those letters or do any of those other things.*

I hardly knew where to begin. If that was so, why did Mother look as if she had aged ten years?

*What did you tell her?* I asked.

*Never you mind and I don't want you to ask her. Anyway, she won't tell you.*

I'm going to wait until Effie has gone to bed and then try to talk to Mother.

*A ¼ past midnight.*

I sneaked along the passage and knocked very quietly at Mother's door and went in. The sitting-room was deserted. I tapped at the door of the bedroom and cautiously pushed it open. Mother was lying fully dressed on her bed holding an open bottle of wine. It was nearly empty and there was no drinking-glass. She looked up at me in terror, frowning and squinting. I had never seen her like this—apart from the night I returned from town, but this was much worse.

She said: *I don't want to talk to you, Richard.*

I said: *I have to know what Euphemia told you. If she persuaded you I'm innocent, why aren't you pleased?*

*She did persuade me,* she muttered. *I don't believe you did any of those things.*

Why was she saying it like that, in that cowed and beaten manner? *What did Effie say?* I persisted.

She looked terrified and didn't answer.

I said: *Then there's nothing to worry about.*

*Yes there is,* she said, glancing fearfully towards the door. She said in a low voice: *Come closer.* I advanced and she clutched my arm and whispered: *Willoughby means you harm. I went along with them. I didn't know what they intended.*

I said: *Willoughby? What does he have to do with it? Why should he wish to hurt me?*

She said: *I can't tell you any more. I shouldn't have said so much.*

*What have you "gone along with"?* I demanded.

*I don't want to be old and poor and lonely. I don't want to die here on my own in this cold damp old barn. Is that so wrong of me?*

I don't know why she said that. I asked: *What makes you think I won't look after you? And Effie, too?*

As if she had not heard she said: *You must leave right away.*

I said: *Do you mean this minute? It's very late.*

She look confused and said: *No, not this minute. But the first thing tomorrow morning you must pack and go. Don't let your sister know I told you.*

I said: *But, Mother, Euphemia is determined that I should escort you both to the ball. That's tomorrow evening.*

She started: *The ball! That's the point. You must not go to the ball.*

Without my having heard her approach, Euphemia glided into the room. She hissed: *I told you to leave Mother alone. Now get out.*

. . .

Why should Willoughby Davenant Burgoyne want to harm me? It makes no sense. It is I who have reason to harm him.

The little governess, Helen, seems to be the only person who trusts and believes in me. But what was she saying about a boy? A child I am believed to have threatened? I've racked my brains but cannot imagine who is meant. I need to ask her. If I wait near the gate to the Greenacres' place tomorrow morning I'm sure I will see her come out with the children for their daily walk.

[This is the next of the anonymous letters relating to the case and it is addressed to Mrs Greenacre. *Note by CP.*]

*That girl that you hired to look after your kids, I was fucking her until he came along with his smart carrige and horses and fancy clothes and she went with him and now she is with child and whether its his basterd or mine or your husbands noboddy knows not even she herself.*

*He will not get any more poor girls into trubble I will take my knife and cut off his ugly cok.*

*He thinks he is safe now. He thinks he is safe in the town but I hurt him there once and I will hurt him again. He is a cripple and he cannot run fast enough to get away from me. He will danse his last danse at his uncels ball.*

*The Harroer*

**B**reakfasted on a hunk of bread before Mother and Effie came down. Ran much of the way to the Greenacres'. Then waited behind the hedge for nearly two hours. The wind was freezing. At last she came down the drive but she was alone and carrying a leather bag that looked heavy. She turned to the north.

I walked behind her for some distance and she must have heard me because she glanced around and then quickened her pace. She could not go very fast because of the bag.

We were now almost at the top of Brankston Hill. I caught up with her and asked if I could take her bag. When I spoke she started and looked at me with such dismay that I almost wondered if she had failed to recognise me. Then she shook her head. I asked her where she was going. She didn't answer. Then at last, without turning towards me, she said: *I've been dismissed.*

I said: *Was it because you spoke to me the other day?*

She said: *Mrs Greenacre has had another letter. She let me read it. It was foul.*

Now she looked at me for a moment. Such a cold regard. Not just cold but frightened. Who was she frightened of?

She said: *My employers have refused to give me a character. I don't know what will become of me.*

I said: *That bag looks heavy. Can I help you?*

She increased her pace and said: *If you want to do me a kindness, turn round and walk away from me.*

I said nothing but swung on my heel and walked quickly back the way we had come.

Realised I had forgotten to ask her about the boy.

*½ past 2 o'clock.*

Got back to find Mother and Effie fussing about the clothes they are to wear this evening. I had the impression that Mother had been cowed and whipped back into line after her brief attempt to break out last night. Without looking me in the face she silently placed an unopened letter in my hand.

Damned Uncle T. The self-righteous old curmudgeon. *No question of bailing you out ... You incurred those debts and must take responsibility for them one way or another ... The shame you have brought on your mother and sister ... The chance of a passage on those two vessels remains open, but they sail within the week and my generous offer will not be renewed.*

To hell with him and his *generosity*.

*A ¼ past 3 o'clock.*

I was wrong about Mother having been beaten. At the last moment she raised another doomed mutiny and suddenly suggested that we abandon the ball. Euphemia was furious. She ordered her into the dining-room and closed the door and I heard her voice going on and on.

When they came out Mother's spirit was broken. I believe she fears that Effie is planning to make a scene with Maud and her fiancé. I half want her to do something like that. Create a scandal that would destroy any chance we have of ever being accepted in this part of the country.

I can see no purpose in our going all that distance in our finery, bumping over frozen roads simply in order for Euphemia to watch her rival triumphing in front of her—rich, about to become a countess, surrounded by friends and admirers—while we endure the humiliation of being ignored and snubbed by families that toadied to us when my father had position and influence.

Never did any family prepare to set off for a ball in worse spirits or on worse terms with each other.

Mother is calling me and I know she wants me to go up the lane and meet the carriage. God alone knows what this ball will bring. I have an ominous feeling about it.

*Saturday night or rather Sunday morning at about ½ past 5.*

So much to try to cling onto and hold down. The swirling of the dancers, the heat of the ballroom, the dazzle of the lights, the odour of rich perfumes and then Tobias's pig-face, burping and leering and making those insulting insinuations. Damn his squinting eyes.

My own sister was running down the stairs flushed and in tears. What was I supposed to do? And then that arrogant boorish oaf, his big ugly jaw moving up and down. Bastardy! How dare he!

If I can just manage to get it all down then I can make some sort of sense of it.

Carriage came. Got to town. Changed at the inn. Reached the Assembly Rooms by eight.

I was sure that our poverty was blazoned in the patches and stitchings of our threadworn clothes. The footmen sneered as they took our greatcoats and capes and then held them as cautiously as if their inadequacy gave off a palpable stink.

The heat and the press of bodies and the smell of the candles and the lamps. I saw the earl. Old man of about fifty or sixty. Just stood in the same place smiling as people came up to him. Could have replaced him with a mechanical dummy. Squeeze the hand and the mouth opens. All the arrogance of those thousands of acres and hundreds of years is in that black-toothed smile.

And of course there in the centre of a busy throng were the Lloyds—pointedly ignoring us. Lucy was staring venomously at Maud who had carried away the richest prize in the county.

She came in on the arm of that man. People smiled and called out good wishes. Primped and preened and smirked at each other. Cooing doves. As if she had him on a string. They went over to the earl and I watched them talking and smiling. The happy couple. The most hated and envied people in the whole assembly. Those two little Quance vipers could not take their eyes off them. Enid's vacant face like the back of a saucer and her dead eyes staring.

And then the dancing. The screeching and scratching of the fiddles and the wailing skirl of the flutes and horns. The dazzling lights overhead and around us, stinking of burnt oil, mingling with the perfumes and sweat of the crowd.

It was the bridal pair—of course—who opened the ball with the first dance. He was barely able to make the movements because of his injured leg. Grinning with delight at his own pluck as he hobbled through the quadrille. I'd cripple him properly if I could. I'd make sure he never dances again. I watched to see if Maud and Euphemia looked at each other. Or if he looked at Effie. I saw no sign that my sister and those two had ever known each other. Cunning and devious but not sharp enough to deceive me.

It wasn't my fault. I just meant to get wine for Mother and Effie. But when I reached the table with the champagne cup I found myself standing beside that oaf Tobias Boddington. He greeted me as if we were intimate friends. And yet I've hardly spoken to him. An ignorant stupid tosspot. He kept filling my glass. I guessed he wanted to tell me something that would cause pain. Why would he have spoken to me otherwise?

Then it came: He was sorry to hear about *my governor and everything*. His pretended sympathy was worse than open insults would have been. Am I now to be pitied by a wastrel like that? A man with all those opportunities which he has thrown away?

Would not let me escape. He kept grabbing me by the arm and saying: *I say, old fellow, I heard an awfully good yarn the other day.* They were all stories of men as stupid and feckless as himself. Then he told me a long complicated anecdote about how he himself had recently been cheated at a dogfight. It was something about *rigging the odds for a game dog and it was done by a fellow who's half a gentleman and half a low scrub.*

The drivelling drink-sodden fool. What do I care about fighting dogs? Then he started to whinge about the *short commons* his father keeps him on so he *never has any tin.* How he won't give him *an allowance fit for a gentleman* and yet he's ready to empty his pockets for some of his clients. He gave me such a stupid sly look that I realised he meant Mother. I asked him what the devil he was getting at and he said I must know how kind his father had been to my family.

I could hardly believe what I was hearing. That Boddington should not only rob and cheat us but have the brazen effrontery to boast that he has helped us! I had to put the poor nincompoop right. I told him his father had chiselled my mother out of everything she should have inherited and he almost alone had brought us to the straits we were in.

He shouted: *You're a damned liar. My governor's a tightfisted old skinflint but he's straight as a die.* I laughed in his stupid face. He said: *Why do you think he bought your mother's ridiculous claim?*

Just what I'd guessed! He was the secret purchaser! The lying cheat!

I said: *Why? In order to defraud her and get it at a knockdown price, that's why. That's why he did it in a sneaking underhand manner and you've let the cat out of the bag now.*

He stuck his ugly phiz in front of me and laughed, spitting in my face and reeking of wine, and then he shouted: *You dunce. He paid well over the odds for it. He did it to stop your damned mother beggaring herself.*

Must have raised my voice a little myself and I think I may have seized him by the lapels because some of the stewards came over and told us to take our argument outside. I said that it wasn't an argument worth pursuing and turned my back on the drink-sozzled jackanapes. Went to find Effie but couldn't see her. Had to ply my elbows to force my way through the press of damned idiots getting in my way.

I didn't notice Mother until she suddenly seized me by the arm and, saying she was worried about where Euphemia was, hurried me into the hall—a huge lofty vault with a cupola and a grandiose flight of stairs. Mother looked upwards and there was Effie standing at the top and at that moment she began to run down the stairs.

She was in tears, her dress and hair disarranged, holding her hands over her face. Everyone was looking at her as she descended. I rushed towards her and we met halfway up with everyone watching and I seized her by the arms and asked what had happened but she wouldn't answer me and just shook her head and broke from my grasp saying she was going to Mother.

I ran up the rest of the stairs and went into the main room. The billiard room. Only men were present. And there he was, the low cur. Willoughby Gerald Davenant Burgoyne himself. Lounging by the fireplace with a gang of his cronies: arrogant young bucks by the look of them who hunt and shoot and lounge around spending their fathers' money.

I went straight up to him and said: *You've insulted my sister.*

He smiled insolently and said, looking round at his friends as if he were about to deliver a witty riposte: *I have no idea who your sister is.*

I spoke her name.

He peered at me and asked languidly: *Have you and I met?*

*Yes and you conducted yourself like a boor on that occasion as well.*

Some of his henchmen muttered threateningly but he raised a hand to calm them and drawled: *I remember now.* He turned to his companions: *This strange fellow accosted me out in the wilds and seemed to think we were relatives. He claimed kinship with me on some tenuous grounds.*

I said: *My grandfather was the last of the name of Herriard. You and I are related though I wish it were otherwise. You may be the nephew of an earl, but you are no gentleman.*

One or two of his chums shouted at me when I said that.

*Well, Master Last-of-a-Family-of-Bastards,* the boor said. *Remind me, will you? When did I insult the young woman?*

*Just now,* I said.

*My good fellow, there has been no lady*—he lingered meaningfully over the word—*in this room in the last half an hour.* He grinned round at his toadying friends.

*You have insulted my sister and you have insulted me,* I said. *I demand that you fight me.*

He said: *Fight?* He turned to his cronies and exclaimed: *I've been challenged to a duel by a young whippersnapper in a patched up coat that my valet would refuse to wear!* He addressed me again: *But perhaps that's not what you mean by "fight"? Do you intend to jump out at me in the dark again?*

That took me unawares. I said: *I don't know what you mean.*

*You tried it at Smithfield a few weeks ago. And then again at my lodgings on Monday night. Do you deny being hired by that blackguard Lidiard?*

*I've never heard that name in my life,* I said.

He looked round at his companions with a theatrical grimace of disbelief and said: *I don't think we can take his word for it. After all, he's the boy whose father was shown to be an embezzler even before he was disgraced and sacked because he was drummed out of the Church for . . .*

I can't write it.

I saw a red curtain descend and I must have tried to throw myself at him because I found myself caught by two of his friends. They dragged me to the door and there was Euphemia! She must have come back and heard what had passed between us.

I was propelled down the steps with as little dignity as if I had been a drunk being thrown out of a beer-shop.

Mother was at the foot of the stairs in a crowd of people drawn by the noise and Euphemia came hurrying down after me. I saw Mother frowning at me. She's never looked at me like that. As if I weren't her son. As if she didn't know me.

I was dragged to the door and then flung out into the street.

As we walked back to the inn I started to explain what had happened but Euphemia interrupted and said I had behaved disgracefully. She insisted she would not share the carriage with me. I was drunk and she feared that I might do something outrageous. She said I could walk home and I might be sober by the time I got back. I pointed out that it would take me five hours on foot and appealed to Mother. To my surprise she was adamant that I could not ride back with them. I had conducted myself in a scandalous manner and shamed the family in public.

I said I had seen Euphemia running down the stairs in tears and I believed Davenant Burgoyne had insulted her. Euphemia said I was talking nonsense. She had come down the stairs quickly and cheerfully and if her eyes were glistening it was with excitement at the prospect of the dancing, nothing else. I had destroyed her reputation by making such a public accusation. She had not been in the billiard-room but in the adjoining card-room and had not even seen him.

When I tried to explain what had occurred between that man and myself, Euphemia almost shouted: *I can't endure to be in your company.* She suddenly broke into what was almost a run and took off down the dark street.

I began to go after her but Mother clutched my arm and said: *Let her go, Richard. We'll find her at the inn. And in view of how she feels, there's no question about it: You'll have to walk home.*

We returned to The George and Dragon and went to the rooms we had hired and waited. About fifteen minutes later Euphemia arrived. She ignored me entirely.

It was a relief when the night-porter knocked on the door and told us the carriage was ready. I saw them into it and watched it trundle out of the inn-yard but instead of following on foot, I came back to the room and started writing this on sheets of paper that I will paste into the Journal when I get home.

. . .

He's a low scrub for all his dandyish airs and his aristocratic blood and his enviable expectations. He has insulted an honest and upright man who's worth a dozen of the likes of him and I'll be revenged on him if it's the last thing I do. I'll make him sorry he ever met a Shenstone. I'll make him grovel for forgiveness at my feet.

[A page is left blank here in the Journal. *Note by CP.*]

*Sunday 10<sup>th</sup> of January, 4 o'clock in the afternoon.*

I've just pasted those last ten pages into this book though I almost threw them away since they now seem to me wild and almost frantic. How little I understood just eight or twelve hours ago. Everything has been turned on its head since then so that I hardly know where to begin.

After Mother and Euphemia went off in the carriage I continued writing for an hour or two and left the inn at about half-past seven and set out to walk home. I was going along Market Street when a carriage that was approaching from behind me stopped. The window was lowered and I was hailed by old Mr Boddington. He very civilly asked me where I was headed at that hour and offered me a lift, but instead of answering him I said: *Why did you buy my mother's claim? Don't try to deny it. Tobias told me.*

He looked astonished and said we couldn't discuss it in the street and, opening the door, invited me to get into the vehicle.

When I was seated beside him I said (and I blush at the memory): *Did you cheat my mother?*

He shook his head and said: *The claim was baseless. Nobody else would have bought it.*

Then in a few eloquent sentences he justified that remark. The world seemed to spin about me as everything I had been led to believe about my mother and her inheritance was turned on its head. *Oh Mother, Mother. Poor foolish self-deceiving Mother.*

When I could speak, I said: *You've bought out Mother's claim to prevent her wasting any more money?*

Mr Boddington nodded and said: *I tried from the beginning to dissuade your mother from embarking on the suit. I knew that she had no case.*

I sat with my head in my hands, too ashamed to look at him. At last I was able to say: *Mr Boddington, I have done you an injustice and I apologise.*

He said briskly: *We'll say no more about it.*

He explained that he was on his way to the Assembly Rooms to fetch Tobias since the man-servant who had accompanied him had reported that he was the worse for drink.

Then he fixed his gaze on me and said: *I'd hoped my boy would do well, but in the last few years he has fallen in with a bad set. He's only a year or two your elder, isn't he? Do you think I expect too much of him? He never was much of a scholar. Was it unfair of me to hope for more?*

I said I didn't know. He looked so kind and so unhappy that I wished I could have said something to help him.

Then he said: *I fear he might have started to indulge a taste worse than wine or brandy.* He looked at me sharply and I blushed. *I know it has become fashionable now among young men.*

Mother must have told him enough for him to have guessed. I vowed to free myself once and forever from that vile habit.

He began talking about how Tobias had befriended some of the "young bloods" in Davenant Burgoyne's set—all of them high-spending and loose-living men from wealthy families who indulged every appetite without restraint.

That reminded me of what I had just heard. I asked if he could reveal anything about an assault on the earl's nephew in London a few weeks ago. He looked surprised but told me what I wanted to know: One night Davenant Burgoyne was in the disreputable district of Smithfield—for what purpose heaven alone knew!—when he was attacked by an assailant who seemed to have no interest in robbing him but had simply fired at him from close quarters with a handgun.

I interrupted to ask: *You mean, it was an attempt to kill him?*

He nodded and said: *Assuredly.* The intended victim had hit the man's arm with his walking-stick as he pulled the trigger and so the bullet struck him in the leg. The attacker smashed him in the arm with the butt of the gun and then ran off.

*Is it known who was behind the assault?*

He drew down the edges of his mouth to indicate an affirmative and I asked if it was a man called "Lyddiard"—however you spell it—and he looked surprised that I knew so much. I asked him to spell the name and he did so.

I said I understood that this man was the illegitimate half-brother of Davenant Burgoyne. I had primed the pump with this and now the waters gushed forth. The old fellow told me the man was a rogue and reprobate who has always been on bad terms with his uncle and his half-brother because of his demands for money and his debts and disgraceful scrapes. His uncle sent him to Cambridge but he behaved so badly that he was rusticated before the end of his first year. The earl then purchased a commission for him in the Guards, but he was cashiered following the disappearance of mess funds. Since that shameful episode he has been shunned by all his relatives except an eccentric old creature called Lady Terrewest who had long nursed a grievance against the earl over some long-forgotten squabble.

I asked Mr Boddington if he had ever met Lyddiard and he said he had merely seen him at a distance. He was a loutish individual— exceptionally tall and with a swaggering ruffianly manner. Yet he felt some sympathy for the man. He had been abandoned by his father and left an orphan by his mother's early death. He had grown up shunned by his own relatives in the knowledge that his younger half-brother would inherit both the title and the fortune of which his own illegitimacy had deprived him.

*So he had nothing to hope for from his father's family?* I asked.

*Nothing, except that under the provisions of the trust his father created, he will inherit the fortune if his half-brother dies before reaching the age of twenty-five.*

*And he would have done so if that attack in Smithfield had succeeded,*
I commented.

The old lawyer's features remained as enigmatic as a painting. I
knew he was anxious to find his son so I thanked him and we parted.
I descended and the coach rumbled on ahead of me.

I walked on and as I passed into a damp, low-lying district on the
edge of the town I saw a sign telling me this was Trafalgar Place. I
remembered my mother's reference to it and I found the Row of the
same name easily enough. It's a squalid terrace of ill-constructed cottages running along a ditch that feeds into the river and is exactly where
a drunken wastrel might keep his mistress and her unwanted child.

I had gained the outskirts of the town when I saw a figure in the
barely-lit road ahead of me lurching drunkenly along. I recognised
him and hurried to overtake him. It was Tobias. He greeted me affa-
bly, clearly having forgotten that we had had an argument a few hours
earlier. He revealed that he was executing the insane idea of walking to
his father's house at Upton Dene. When I told him Mr Boddington had
come to find him and was at the Assembly Rooms, he turned uncer-
tainly and started stumbling back towards the town. I wanted to find
out something and so I walked with him. I reminded him of the story
he had told me about being cheated over a dog-fight and he started
muttering imprecations. I asked him if the man who had defrauded him
was called "Tom the Swell". He shook his head and said he did not recognise the name but knew him as "Lyddiard".

I said: *Yes, I thought so. Davenant Burgoyne's bastard half-brother.*

*That's the fellow,* Tobias mumbled. *Willoughby Lyddiard, damn his eyes.*

I was so astonished I stopped dead while he staggered on ahead
so that I had to run to catch up with him.

I grabbed his arm and demanded: *Do he and his half-brother both
have the name "Willoughby"?*

*Yes,* he threw over his shoulder and blundered into the darkness.

I stood there for a minute or two in the middle of the carriageway. What he had blurted out is extraordinary. It changes every-

thing. It was not Davenant Burgoyne who came to the house on my first evening home. Whatever had occurred between him and my sister was over by then. Her visitor was Lyddiard—her new admirer, lover, or whatever word is appropriate. And worst of all: My mother knew that! In the next few days I had confused two tall men seen at a distance and Euphemia had allowed—indeed, encouraged—me to persist in that mistake. But what I could not understand was why Mother—so bent on Euphemia making a "good marriage"—wished her daughter to marry an impecunious and illegitimate good-for-nothing. Or had she wanted that? Had that been the subject of the arguments I had overheard?

The lawyer's allusion to Lady Terrewest set me thinking. Euphemia's insistence on going to the old lady so often had puzzled me and now I thought I had guessed her motive. I decided to make a diversion as I walked home.

I reached Thrubwell while it was still dark and the house was shut up. But there was a light burning on the ground-floor. I climbed over the wall that separated the house from the road and approached it. I peered through the window where the light came from. I saw a fat old lady seated in a high-backed armchair in a sitting-room. I remembered Euphemia saying that Lady Terrewest spends all her time downstairs because of her incapacity. She was talking to someone whom I could not see. Tears were running down the old creature's cheeks and her face was convulsed. I thought she must be in great pain. Then the other figure passed into view and I saw that it was a second obese woman dressed in the plain gown and apron of a housekeeper or a cook. She put her head back and shook with unheard laughter. I recognised her as the woman I had seen talking to Mrs Darnton in the shop—the one I'd called "Blubber". I looked again at Lady Terrewest and saw that what I had taken for a grimace of agony was amusement. Her tears were being shed in delight at some joke or story the two old parties were sharing.

This was not a house of grief and pain as I had imagined. This was no ailing invalid living in quiet retirement as I had been led to believe. I had thought of Euphemia as sitting in sombre silence or playing mournful threnodies on the pianoforte. Now I realised that every time she went there she was taking part in a vast joyous feast of scandal-mongering. The house is a veritable laundry of gossip in which every scrap of information is beaten until it yields its dirt.

The servant disappeared for a minute or two and then returned with a tray which she laid before the old lady. At the sight of her devouring the most copious and delicious breakfast, I felt a pang of hunger. I had taken nothing since the night before.

A dog's paws suddenly appeared on the old lady's lap. A mastiff. It tried to shove its nose into a plate of buttered muffins she was eating. She pushed it away saying something to the servant who seized its collar. She disappeared. After a moment I heard an outside door open at the back of the house and, guessing that the dog was being released, I began to make my retreat but I wasn't quite fast enough and as I was scrambling up the wall the brute came up to me and started barking and growling. I landed on the road and hid behind the tree I had used to conceal myself on an earlier occasion. I waited to see if the dog had alerted the occupants of the house to the presence of an intruder. It fell silent and nobody came out.

I stayed hidden, hoping that I might be able to return if the dog went back inside. After about twenty minutes something happened that I had not anticipated: a man approached from the direction of Stratton Peverel. He was walking swiftly and yet furtively. When he reached the opening in the wall surrounding the house, he produced a huge key from his pocket and unlocked the outer gate and the dog ran up to him barking loudly. The man reached towards his belt to which I saw there was secured a short whip and the dog stopped barking and growled, stretching out its paws ingratiatingly.

I had recognised him. He was the stranger I had seen sitting in a wagon with the chained dog. Because he had been lying down, I had not realised on that occasion something that was evident now:

He was extremely tall. I knew exactly who he was. He was the man referred to as "Tom the Swell"—the very tall man I saw with Euphemia and took for Davenant Burgoyne. Now I was pretty certain I knew his real name: *Willoughby Lyddiard*. I could imagine his mother giving him that absurd aristocratic name to try to buttress his claim on the Burgoynes.

He walked past the door from which the dog had been ejected and used another key to let himself into a different part of the old house.

There was nothing more to be gained from staying there. I continued on my way. On the road between Stratton Peverel and Stratton Herriard, I encountered the carriage which had conveyed Mother and Euphemia home—or at least, to the end of our muddy lane—and it rattled past me without the driver noticing my salute.

I reached the house at about one o'clock and entered as silently as I could, squeezing the front-door shut behind me. I stole through the hall to the door of the parlour and peered through the gap between it and the doorframe. My mother was sitting on the sopha and looking up at Euphemia who had her back to me and was saying something in a voice that was too low for me to catch.

I entered the room. My mother started and looked up at me guiltily. Euphemia turned and presented me with a defiant face.

As soon as I saw her I felt a wave of hatred. I could hardly bring myself to meet her gaze. She stared back at me boldly.

My mother asked me why I had taken so long and said they had been expecting me for an hour and a half.

I said: *Have you been worried about me? I do apologise.*

Then I walked out and came up here.

I need to understand. Not what my sister and her minion have done, for that is clear enough. It is they who have been writing those wicked letters. (How close Mrs Quance came when she suggested they were concocted by a woman in collaboration with a man.) They used gossip that Euphemia had gleaned from Lady Terrewest and her housekeeper. Then he took the letters into Thurchester and posted them there.

And it was he who crept out at night from his lair at Lady Terrewest's house and practised his savage knife-work on farm-animals. All that is apparent to me now but what still eludes me is the point of it all. Why, after my mistaking one tall man for another, did they set out to make me think that my sister was still meeting Davenant Burgoyne and to inflame my jealousy against him? What were they hoping to gain? Why send those letters making savage threats against him as if coming from me? And why was it so important that I attend the ball? Above all, how much did Mother know?

Having had no sleep since yesterday morning, I must stop now and rest.

*7 o'clock.*

I had lain down on my bed fully dressed and had been sleeping for several hours when I was awakened by a distant banging. I hurried along the passage and watched as Betsy opened the door. On the step loomed a magnificent man-servant in livery who announced in a booming voice that he came from Mr and Mrs Tomkinson. Betsy stood in paralysed dismay in front of this impressive figure and I hurried down. The man handed me a sealed envelope addressed to my mother.

I took it into the parlour. My mother was alone there. The name meant nothing to either of us but the note explained in the most courteous terms that they were the brother-in-law and sister of Mrs Paytress. They had come to Stratton Peverel at her request to close the house, retrieve her possessions, and pay off the servants. (So much for the cruel slander about bailiffs!) Mrs Paytress had asked them to convey a certain object to us as a gift and if it were convenient, they would like to bring it within the next couple of hours and have the pleasure of meeting us—if only very briefly.

My mother sent Betsy to fetch Euphemia down, and after discussing it with her, she scrawled a reply pressing the Tomkinsons to join us for tea and the footman hurried away with it.

Of course all Mother and Euphemia could talk about was the strangeness of it and then they threw themselves into frantic efforts to make the house look less dilapidated and the rooms less threadbare. Betsy was soon running around mopping and polishing.

I had cleansing of my own to carry out. I came up here and broke the pipe and put everything connected with it into a little wooden box. I went out and walked along the path to the beach and opened the box and scattered its contents in the sea. It had brought about the worst thing that I had ever done and had helped to put me in the power of those who wished me ill.

On my way back in I passed Euphemia in the hall and, allowing myself a sarcastic sneer, said to her: *Not going to Lady Terrewest today?*

She walked on without replying. I believe the attraction that took her to Thrubwell is no longer present. Moreover, I don't think there will be any more threatening letters. Whatever purpose they served has either been achieved or has failed.

I called out to her: *Can you delay your departure for a few minutes? I have something I want to say to our mother and you.*

She halted and turned and slowly followed me into the parlour.

Mother was sitting at her embroidery and looked startled as we came in. I asked Euphemia to sit down and then I said: *I'm going to tell you what happened at Cambridge. I don't want to hide anything from you any longer. Things are too far gone for that. Here's the truth. I became a friend of Edmund Webster before I understood how dangerous to me he was. I had never known anyone I liked so much. But what I only gradually discovered was that because of his wealth, he had been recruited into a dissolute circle. He and his rich friends drank and gambled and did worse things. But there was one other thing that Edmund introduced me to and it led to all the bad consequences. It was opium.*

There. I had said it and I knew that Euphemia had no power over me now. She and Mother exchanged a look.

I went on: *We didn't realise how dangerous it was. Edmund's uncle had made his fortune as a China merchant and taught him to smoke the drug as they do in the East. It's even harder to break the habit if you've been doing that. But I have wonderful news to tell you. I've given it up. I've just thrown away all my opium and the pipe.*

Neither of them seemed impressed or pleased by my news.

Euphemia asked: *Was it because of opium that your friend took his own life?*

I just shook my head as if puzzled rather than denying it. Euphemia knows more than I had realised. I suppose I will have to tell Mother the rest of it.

. . .

After what Mr Boddington said, it is clear that when the lease on this house runs out at the end of this year, Cousin Sybille will demand rent and when Mother is unable to pay it, will evict her and Euphemia.

*½ past 8 o'clock.*

I stayed in my room until I heard the Tomkinsons arrive. (They had had to leave their carriage some way up the lane and walk from there.) I joined them but I spoke not a word the whole time we were in the parlour together. They were very charming and seated themselves on the dirty old sopha as if they were in the most elegant drawing-room in Marylebone.

The man-servant who had brought the letter followed them into the house carrying a large square object wrapped in a thick hessian cloth. Mr Tomkinson told him to prop it against the wall.

When the usual civilities had been gone through, my mother asked about the closure of the house and dismissal of the staff. Mr Tomkinson said all had gone well except that he had had to deal with a very abusive servant who had become involved in some criminal enterprise in the district.

Mrs Tomkinson opened proceedings by saying that her sister had wanted us to hear the truth because we were the only people who were kind to her during her brief residence in the district. I looked at my mother to see how she took that.

They confirmed what Miss Bittlestone had told us about the child. His condition had been deteriorating for several weeks and on Sunday night his mother had rushed into Thurchester with him, but he had died in her arms in the carriage.

The proper things were said in the proper tone. Then Mr Tomkinson unwrapped the picture with some help from me. Of course it turned out to be the painting of Salisbury Cathedral that Euphemia had admired.

Mrs Tomkinson began to talk of how her sister had been ostracised in the district because of an incident shortly after her arrival. She was dining with the earl to whom she had a recommendation through a shared acquaintance: *Unfortunately she unintentionally offended the wife of the local Rector. The company were talking of Mr Dickens and his travels in Europe when Mrs Quance said: "He is most assuredly in the Parthenon." Nobody understood what she meant. The earl asked: "Do you mean at this very moment?" Mrs Quance said: "Certainly. Now and for all time. He is in the Parthenon with Byron and Shakespeare." People looked at each other in puzzlement and my sister, just to retrieve the situation, most unfortunately exclaimed: "Oh, you mean the pantheon! The pantheon of great writers."*

I could imagine how Mrs Quance must have brooded about this slight—all the more offensive for being unintended.

Our guests rose to leave and then Mrs Tomkinson exclaimed that they had almost forgotten that her sister had expressly asked her to invite Euphemia to come and choose for herself as much of her music as she wished. I could see how pleased my sister was at this. So it was settled that she would go back with them now in their carriage.

Euphemia went to put on her bonnet and I walked with the old couple a little way up the lane to their coach. I took the opportunity to ask if the servant they had mentioned had been the one who looked like a jockey. It was indeed he and Mr Tomkinson explained that he had been keeping a fighting-dog in an abandoned outbuilding. He had been cheated in some fraud involving the animal and had killed the dog in a paroxysm of rage. To restore his losses he had stolen and sold one of his employer's saddles.

So that explained what he had been doing that night when I followed him across the fields in the snow. And I'm sure he was a victim of the fraud that Tobias told me about in which Tom the Swell *alias* Lyddiard had deceitfully improved the odds against his winning dog by disguising it.

Euphemia came hurrying up and got into the carriage without looking at me. As soon as it began to move I turned and ran back to the house.

Now was my chance to talk to my mother alone. I rushed into the parlour and she looked up in astonishment. I wasted no time on preliminaries: *The evening I arrived you addressed me as "Willoughby" and I know now that the man you took me for was Willoughby Lyddiard—the earl's illegitimate nephew—and that he used to come regularly to the house before I came home. You were expecting him when I arrived. That was why Euphemia went out into the rain: To warn him not to come into the house. Later I saw Euphemia out walking with him. Because both men are very tall, I assumed he was Davenant Burgoyne. Euphemia realised that I had made this mistake and she took advantage of it. She saw that she could make me hate Davenant Burgoyne by making me believe he was compromising her character in the most flagrant manner. Mother, you must have understood all of that. Why did you allow her to deceive me?*

Her hands moved restlessly and she avoided my gaze as she answered: *I have no idea what you're talking about. You've been behaving more and more strangely, Richard. I don't think you always know what is true and what is invented.*

She must be lying. She used that name to me. She must have known about Lyddiard and Euphemia meeting on the Battlefield and at Lady Terrewest's house. In that case, why is she denying it?

*Mother*, I said. *I know what has been going on and I want you to explain to me what the point of it is. Why were you and Euphemia so anxious to get me to go away? That revelation you threatened me with, it was about my father and what he and Bartlemew had been doing, wasn't it? I now know about all that.*

She simply shook her head from side to side in bafflement.

*What were my sister and her lover hoping to gain by misleading me?* I asked. *And why was the ball so important?* Mother kept her eyes cast down. I said: *Are you really saying that you know nothing about this?*

*Nothing*, she said.

I said: *I met Mr Boddington last night and he told me everything about the Chancery suit.*

She turned to me a wavering look: *Is he hopeful?*

*Hopeful! On the contrary. He explained why it is without foundation. The court set your father's will aside because he was not mentally competent when he wrote it.*

Mother flinched and said: *That was Sybille's lie! My father was not insane. He became confused in his later years but he always knew what he was doing. But even if that had been so, I am his only child and therefore his heir.*

I said: *I'm afraid not, Mother. Mr Boddington explained to me that the distribution of the estate follows the rules of intestacy. Cousin Sybille is your father's heir.*

*I just need more time and I know I will be able to find the proof I need.*

I said: *Mr Boddington says it's a waste of money to continue.*

She twisted her hands together and said: *My mother always told me she had married my father and I don't believe she would lie to me.*

*Of course she would lie to you*, I said more brusquely than I had intended. *She wanted to hide the unpalatable truth from you just as you wished to conceal it from me. And while we're talking of lies, Mr Bodding-*

*ton told me the facts about your marriage to my father. You weren't lowering yourself. It was the other way around. The reality is that my father risked his career. He was a rising clergyman who was marrying the illegitimate daughter of a wastrel and a drunk.*

*Not that,* she protested. *Not illegitimate. My father always treated my mother like his wife.*

I said: *You mean he beat her when he was drunk and then abandoned her to poverty and shame.*

### 9 o'clock.

I can understand why Mother turned the circumstances of her early life into a fairy-tale. Growing up in a shabby little cottage in a row of ill-built houses, visiting her raging-mad father once a year, enduring the patronising contempt and miserable charity of his starched brothers and sisters. To be so close to wealth and rank and yet to be on the wrong side of an invisible barrier. What a wound it must have been for my mother to feel shut out of that big house. To walk past it with her scandalous mother—an illiterate servant seduced by her addle-pated master. Her drooling, pitiful, worthless father—she had to transform him into a parent worthy of her, of her illusions at least. A generous, admirable figure—the cynosure of the town, the county. A Trimalchio of legendary hospitality. Not a lunatic scattering his inheritance on gaudy trifles. A madman spending his last years in a barred room at the top of his siblings' house. And I've done something as stupid and self-destructive as she. I've taken upon myself guilt for my father's offences. What a fool I've been. Why should I feel any shame on behalf of another? My father did those things, not I. All my life I felt an obligation to please him even though my truest nature caused him displeasure: my refusal to take seriously the things he believed to be important. Above all, a religion which seemed to scorn the idea of earthly happiness and yet over-value social status. When he died I felt relief and then I felt overwhelming guilt for that. I look back now at what I wrote and see it so differently. Now I realise that I didn't just fail to love him. I feared him. I knew he threatened my deepest being. He wanted in effect to kill me in the sense that he struggled to force me to become the cleric he wanted me to be.

Our father made us love him because he was weak—not because he was strong. We all collaborated in the pretence that he was a good parent and a worthy cleric because none of us could face the truth: that he was a bully and a lazy drunken incompetent dishonest man driven by bestial desires who neglected the modest talents he possessed. He condemned others for small moral lapses in order to divert suspicion from himself. A man who judges others so harshly must be judged as harshly himself. I always hated him and I felt guilty about that. Well, I feel guilty no longer.

. . .

The pains have begun. I have no means of alleviating them and no desire to do so if I were able. The worse the agonies—the sleeplessness, the headaches, the stomach cramps—that I suffer now, the less likely I am to relapse, knowing that I would have to go through this again.

*Monday 11<sup>th</sup> of January, 11 o'clock.*

I came down late for breakfast to avoid the others and just went to the kitchen to beg some bread and coffee. Betsy was curt and simply thrust the loaf and a knife into my hands. I tried to find out how she feels about me, but she said: *I've to go to the village to buy provisions. I don't have time to waste.*

I thought *I* was avoiding *her* but it seems *she* has been avoiding *me.*

*3 o'clock.*

Everything is now clear!

I was upstairs at about noon when I heard someone running up the path and then the slamming of the front-door and I hurried down just in time to see Betsy come into the hall with a flushed face and an air of excitement. She glanced at me and then rushed into the parlour without knocking. I entered right behind her. My mother was sitting at her embroidery and Euphemia was playing the pianoforte.

Betsy cried: *He's dead. The earl's nevy is dead.*

Euphemia rose to her feet in horror and then staggered and nearly fainted, sinking back into her chair pale and shaking. The performance was so accomplished that I almost clapped.

Mother's response was hard to interpret. She seemed shocked rather than surprised.

Betsy poured it all out. She had heard the news in the shop and according to Mrs Darnton, Davenant Burgoyne's body had been found in a ditch beside the road to the earl's country-house late yesterday.

In an unsteady voice Mother asked if he had fallen from his horse and Betsy said she didn't know. Nobody had seen him since he left his uncle's house in town a few hours after the ball to ride to Handleton Castle.

I came up here to ponder this turn of events. In the instant that Betsy spoke, I saw the point of it all. The deed has been done and the trap has snapped shut upon me. It is more than just the letters that I am to be incriminated for. I am overcome with admiration for their ingenuity.

Davenant Burgoyne did not fall from his horse. He was murdered. I am certain of it. And it has all been done so cleverly. Suppose that I want to kill someone. Suppose further that I am the obvious suspect because his death benefits me. And I am all the more likely to be suspected because it is thought that I have already tried to murder him and failed. Under those circumstances I would select a plausible culprit—someone who is believed to have a grudge against my quarry. I would goad and deceive him so that he appeared to be violent and even unstable and if possible I would try to make it seem that he was the author of a series of deranged letters filled with threats of violence against the intended victim and that he was wandering the fields at night venting his rage on dumb beasts. If he could be induced to threaten my "mark" in front of witnesses, that would be perfect. And it would be ideal if I could arrange for him to have no alibi at the moment I committed the murder. If I managed all that successfully, the police would not even bother to investigate me.

Looking back through these pages I can see things so clearly now: They met at Lady Terrewest's house—perhaps Lyddiard sought Euphemia out after hearing that Davenant Burgoyne had jilted her—and made common cause since both had good reason to hate Davenant Burgoyne. I imagine that the bargain they struck was that once he was dead, they would marry. So although Euphemia would not be a countess, she would be the wife of a wealthy man at least. He visited her often and that is why, the evening I returned, Mother mistook me for him and why Euphemia was wearing her best clothes. Davenant Burgoyne had to die—and, as Mr Boddington explained, that had to happen before his next birthday—and the difficulty was that Lyddiard was the obvious suspect and was already widely believed to have made an attempt on his half-brother's life. So they needed a scapegoat. When did the conspirators conceive the idea of making me their dupe? I believe I know that. It was the moment I revealed my erroneous belief that Euphemia was still meeting Davenant Burgoyne out on the Battlefield. She and her lover realised that they could take advantage of my mistake to whip me into a fever of rage against the man they wanted dead. That's why Euphemia unexpectedly changed her mind about me. Instead of being hounded out of the house I was urged to stay and then charmed into agreeing to attend the ball. (The Yass woman—the so-called cook—was sent away the same day and I must admit that I don't yet understand the significance of that.) And then the letters and the attacks on animals. They wanted to arouse fear that some deranged person was on the loose and then gradually incriminate me. That is why Euphemia was so determined that I be present at the ball: I had to have a public confrontation with the victim a few hours before he was murdered.

I have been reading and re-reading what I wrote in this Journal about the ball, trying to find some clue that might help me. Some things I understand and others I don't. That moment when I saw Euphemia running down the stairs in tears was the bait that led me into the argument with Davenant Burgoyne.

Yet I had seen her again as I was being pushed out of the billiard room a few minutes later. Had she come up to listen at the door? And then there was that mysterious business of her hurrying off while we were going back to the inn. At least I now understood her insistence that she would not share a carriage with me: I had to be made to walk home to ensure that I had no alibi. But I'm sure there is something I have failed to grasp.

However much I disliked Davenant Burgoyne, I take no joy in his premature death. I can't help thinking of the grief of the old earl. This is a blow for him. Although he has two good-for-nothing nephews, he is said to be a decent and honourable person. And as for Maud—I am truly sorry to think how devastated she must be. Just a day ago I saw them smiling and laughing. She and the earl are the really innocent victims in this imbroglio. I, in contrast, have contributed to my destruction: I have at the very least been guilty of wilful stupidity.

*5 o'clock.*

Events are unfolding with the strange logic of a dream where what should appear astonishing seems inevitable and normal.

A couple of hours after luncheon we heard the sound of a chaise in the lane and then there was a hammering at the door. I went out and found a police-officer in uniform with a man in civilian dress. The latter introduced himself as Sergeant Wilson of the Detective Force. He asked if he might talk to my family and myself about a grave matter and I led him into the parlour where my mother and sister were.

He explained that he was from Scotland Yard and had been commissioned to investigate the circumstances in which Mr Davenant Burgoyne had died.

Mother asked in a trembling voice: *Why have you come to this house?*

Wilson said: *I'll deal with that in a moment, ma'am. First I have to inform you of something that you may or may not know.* Here he turned and looked at me: *Mr Davenant Burgoyne was murdered.*

Mother gasped and Euphemia turned away.

Wilson said to me: *You don't seem very surprised, Mr Shenstone?*

I shrugged. *It didn't sound like an accident.*

*Now that's an interesting remark,* he said.

At my invitation he seated himself and told us this story: Davenant Burgoyne left the ball an hour or two later than us and in the company of his uncle. They went back to the earl's townhouse and had breakfast together and then he set out on horseback along the Handleton road to ride to his uncle's country-house. Nobody saw him alive again. His horse was found wandering back towards the town. Late in the day his body, lightly covered in leaves, was discovered in a ditch at the side of the road about ten miles from the town.

I asked how he was killed.

The officer turned to me: *We believe his assailant was waiting for him.*

*On foot or horseback?*

*On foot. A horseman is always going to announce his presence and will leave traces that might enable detection, but a man on foot at night can move as silently and invisibly as a cat.*

*So the attacker had not followed him from Thurchester?*

*We think not. We believe he was lying in ambush at a place previously selected where there were trees at the side of the road. That allowed him to jump out on his victim with all the advantages of surprise.*

*Then did he shoot him?*

*Mr Davenant Burgoyne had not been shot,* he said sadly like a disappointed schoolmaster receiving a wrong answer from a favourite pupil. *Can you make a guess as to the means used?*

I smiled. *No, Sergeant Wilson, I cannot.*

*He brought him down with a most unusual weapon. It had a sharp blade and a long enough handle to let him swing it up at him and deliver a hard blow that would have knocked him from his seat.*

My mother gave a cry of horror.

Wilson turned and bowed. *I apologise for these distressing details, Mrs Shenstone.*

I said: *That sounds like a very extraordinary weapon, Sergeant Wilson. Have you any idea what it was?*

*We know exactly what it was, Mr Shenstone. It was found in the ditch beside the corpse. I am not at liberty to particularise its nature. I can say that it is highly distinctive and is of considerable significance in our investigation.* He paused weightily and then said: *There is a matter that seems to be connected to this dreadful business. A number of menacing letters have been received in recent weeks by several individuals in the district.*

*Yes,* Mother said in apparent surprise. *Both my daughter and I have received such letters.*

*I would like to have sight of them, Mrs Shenstone, in order to further my investigation.*

*I will be glad to have them out of the house,* Mother said. She began to rummage in her work-basket saying: *One of them has been destroyed. It was the first that my daughter received. But there are two others that we kept. And I don't want them returned.*

She handed them to the detective. He looked down at them. *The author of these is of great interest to me. For one thing, he made numerous threats against Mr Davenant Burgoyne. Threats of a very disgusting nature which I wouldn't for a thousand pounds say any more about in the presence of ladies. And it seems reasonable to suppose that he is the individual who has been maiming animals in the locality since some of the same indescribable acts were performed against them. Against the stallions and rams. And the implement he used for that is most probably the one used in the murder.*

At that instant I guessed what the weapon was and another piece of the design fell into place. It was Fourdrinier's stolen tool! I said: *But to repeat my mother's question, why have you come to this house?*

He smiled appreciatively as if I had made a witticism that required no reply. He addressed himself to my mother: *I understand that after the ball you and your daughter returned from Thurchester by carriage on Sunday morning leaving Mr Shenstone at the inn?* She nodded. *At what time did you part from your son?*

*The vehicle was ordered for ½ past 5,* she said. *We must have left the inn a few minutes after that.*

The detective took a note-book from his pocket and wrote something in it. He turned to me: *And you walked back?*

I nodded.

*Was there any reason for that?*

*None,* I said quickly. *I just needed some fresh air after all that time in a stuffy room.*

*A long walk,* he commented. *It must have taken you about four hours. Perhaps longer. At what hour did you set off?*

*I didn't leave immediately. I stayed for a while at The George and Dragon. I left at about a quarter past seven.*

*Did you speak to anyone?* the detective asked.

*I met my mother's lawyer, Mr Boddington, near the Assembly Rooms.*

*What time did you part from him?*

*A little before eight. And a few minutes later I had a brief conversation with his son, Mr Tobias Boddington.*

*And from that moment until you reached here, can anybody confirm your presence on that road?*

*Nobody, as far as I am aware.*

He looked at Mother: *What time did the young gentleman arrive here?*

Mother hesitated. Before she could speak, Euphemia said: *It was about one o'clock.*

Wilson turned to me and said lugubriously: *Then from eight until one o'clock there is only your own word for it that you were on a walk that should have taken you about four hours?*

I could see exactly what was going through his mind. During that period I could have taken the road towards Handleton and arrived at the fatal spot before Davenant Burgoyne, done the deed, and then cut across country along lanes and by-ways and got back to the route from Thurchester to Herriard House without being seen. Telling the truth would gain me nothing since nobody had seen me make the detour to the house of Lady Terrewest which had lengthened my journey home.

*My sister is mistaken about the time I reached here,* I said. *It was an hour or two earlier but I came in quietly and went straight to bed so she didn't hear me. She is thinking of the time she saw me which was when I came down for luncheon.*

Wilson made a note. Then he smiled and turning to my mother, said: *I love to walk in the evening air, ma'am, when the bustle and noise of the day have died away.* He turned back to me: *I understand that like myself you enjoy taking a stroll after sunset?*

*Now and then,* I agreed.

*Often till quite late?*

*Occasionally.*

*It has been alleged that on some of these occasions you have been seen peering through the windows of various houses at night.*

I smiled and said: *You've been speaking to Mrs Darnton, I suspect. Has she also told you that I have harassed several young ladies?*

*Since you mention it,* he said good-naturedly. *It seems the whole neighbourhood has been talking about you. Mrs Darnton has also told me that you have been very curious about how the post is collected and franked and delivered.*

*I was trying to discover who was writing those letters.*

*Mrs Darnton says that on one occasion you asked her for the address of Mr Davenant Burgoyne.*

I shrugged. I could think of no explanation for that which did not enfold me still more securely in the coils of the plot against me.

He gazed at me speculatively for several seconds and then said in the most avuncular manner: *Of course, you understand why I've come to have a little chinwag with you?*

*My conversation with Mr Davenant Burgoyne at the ball, I assume.*

*Rather more than a conversation, by all the accounts I've heard,* he said cheerfully.

*An altercation, then.*

He smiled. *If that word means that you shouted at him and threatened him, then it's the right one.*

*I think his friends may have exaggerated what occurred,* I said.

*He accused you of having made an attempt on his life?*

*Yes, he made the absurd allegation that I attacked him outside his lodgings about a week ago.*

He looked surprised and stared at me for a moment still smiling: *The assault in Hill Street?*

I nodded. What else were we talking about?

He said: *That's enough for now, Mrs Shenstone.* He turned back to me as he stood up: *Would you see me to the door, young fellow?*

When we were out in the passage and the door was shut behind us, he said: *That's very interesting. You misunderstood me a moment ago. When I brought up the accusation that Mr Davenant Burgoyne made at the ball I was referring to the incident in London back in November and I know you were not involved in that because I've already telegraphed my colleagues in Cambridge and established that you were there at the time. Incidentally, they told me about a little bit of trouble involving you and a chum of yours who died in somewhat mysterious circumstances. A young man to whom you owed a great deal of money.*

I tried to dissimulate the dismay his words caused me.

He went on: *But when I mentioned an assault on Mr Davenant Burgoyne you thought I was talking about the more recent incident in Hill Street. Now I wonder why.*

Foolishly I blurted out: *I wasn't in Thurchester on that day.*

*Which day?* he asked quietly.

*The day that Mr Davenant Burgoyne was attacked.*

*What date was that?*

*I don't know,* I had to admit.

*It was Monday the 4ᵗʰ of January,* he said.

I said: *That wasn't the day I went to Thurchester. It was about that time but I believe it was a Tuesday. I went to book rooms and a carriage.*

Even as I uttered the words it seemed to me highly probable that Wilson would establish the true date from the people at the inn or the livery-stable and if not from them, then certainly from Mr Boddington.

The officer looked at me pityingly. Then he put his arm on my shoulder and said softly: *Now, is there anything you wish to tell me that you didn't want to say in front of the ladies?*

*Nothing,* I said.

He looked offended and withdrew his arm. *As you wish.*

*Just one thing,* I said. *How can you be sure the murder was not just a commonplace highway robbery?*

*Without going into the details which are highly distasteful, I would refer you to the point I made about the threats in the letters and the things done to animals.*

*Do you mean that things of that nature were done to the body of Mr Davenant Burgoyne?*

He just smiled at me and opened the door. The uniformed policeman was standing by the horse's head. Wilson nodded at him cheerfully and then turned back to me. *I'll just stroll around talking to people for the next day or two. I love this part of the world, though I don't know it well. This is a chance to become acquainted with it. And the people are so friendly. I've talked to Mr and Mrs Lloyd and, as you guessed, to Mrs Darnton—all charming, quite, quite charming. And I've made a friend of that good soul Miss Bittlestone who was in Mrs Darnton's shop when I looked in and I'm planning to pay her a little visit. They've all had so much to tell me. There's a gentleman with a strange name who is anxious to speak to me. Has the odd pastime of poking about in the dust looking for dead Romans, as far as I can gather. And there's more for me to learn from these good people, I'm sure of it.*

As he and his subordinate climbed into the trap he said: *So as I say, I'll be here for a while and I'm sure I shall have the pleasure of speaking to you again very soon, Mr Shenstone.*

*I look forward to that,* I responded with a slight bow.

When the men had gone I hurried up here to write it all down.

I'm surprised Wilson did not arrest and charge me. He knows that I threatened Davenant Burgoyne in public and that I have no alibi for the time he was killed. He probably believes that I wrote the letters and committed those disgusting acts against animals. If he doesn't think that yet, he will after listening to my neighbours on the subject. He hardly needs any more evidence against me.

. . .

However, when my mother tells Wilson that I arrived home at eleven o'clock yesterday and therefore could not have been on the Handleton road at the time of the murder, that will go some way towards clearing me.

*9 o'clock.*

I did not utter a syllable to my mother or sister from the moment of the officer's departure until I seated myself at the table for dinner. Would either of them ask me about Wilson's suspicions?

Apparently not. We began to eat in silence. It seemed absurd for us not to talk about what had happened. I said to Mother: *It's unfortunate that nobody saw me between eight and one yesterday since it has led that detective into wasting his time investigating me. You could help everybody if you were to tell him that I got home at eleven.*

Before she could respond Euphemia said: *It's outrageous that you expect Mother to lie. If she said that in court she would be committing perjury.*

I told her that I found her respect for the truth deeply moving. Nobody spoke again.

Striking that Mother never looked me in the face.

I see nothing to be gained by challenging Euphemia. She knows I have no evidence to prove what she and Lyddiard have done. And I would lose the one advantage I have which is that they don't know that I have guessed everything.

If it comes to a trial then I'm pretty sure that . . .

### *A ¼ to 11.*

I was interrupted twenty minutes ago by a loud hammering at the door. I went down and found a uniformed police-officer standing there. He told me he had a message from Sergeant Wilson requesting that I be at home at eleven tomorrow because he is coming again to discuss "a new piece of evidence".

I assume that Fourdrinier has claimed ownership of that implement and made his grotesque allegation against me. I now know who misappropriated that tool. We weren't the only people on the hill that afternoon—Fourdrinier and the girl and I. The implement was snatched while I was running after the little jade and the old dolt was chasing us. I am sure of that and yet I have no way of convincing anyone else of the truth. Will Wilson bring a warrant and arrest me tomorrow?

### *Midnight.*

Found Betsy drying pans in the scullery and asked if she had heard anything new in the village today. She said in a tremulous little voice: *His cock and ballocks was cut off and stuffed into his mouth.* She turned away and said: *As every man's would be if I had my way.*

Very queer!

anaged to get Mother alone after breakfast. She sat looking towards the fire all the while as it slowly burned itself out. As I talked, I felt as if I were inching forward over the frozen surface of something that—if it gives way—will suck me down and drown me.

I appealed to her again to say that I was home by eleven o'clock.

She said nothing and didn't look at me but just sat gazing ahead and twisting her hands together.

Why is she so reluctant to tell that small lie on my behalf?

*½ past 1 o'clock.*

The detective came as promised. We received him weirdly like an old friend of the family or a distant relative with a claim of kinship—a wealthy cousin, perhaps, whom none of us liked—ushering him into the parlour, plumping up his cushions, and plying him with offers of tea and cakes.

He launched into a good-natured complaint about the amount of work he was having to do. *You've no conception,* he said, *of the number of helpful members of the public who come forward with information they are convinced is the key to the case. And ninety-nine times in a hundred, all they turn out to be is bits of gossip, misunderstandings or grudges against neighbours. Take the business of the weapon. Rumours about it have got into circulation and a certain gentleman—the interesting customer I mentioned before who spends his time poking about in the dust for things the*

*Romans dropped hundreds of years ago—has come to tell me about an item of his that was stolen that he believes sounds very like it. He claims he knows who stole it.*

His gaze rested on me benignly as he uttered those words.

*And then there's a delightful family—a couple in their middle years with a young son and daughter, well when I say young I don't mean children but young persons of ball age if I might be permitted that expression— who live in a charming house. Do you know that quiet little street between the Cathedral and the bridge—The Parade? No, really? It's a lovely spot. That's where their house is and it's so handy for the centre of town that they were able to stroll home after the ball. (They all attended it. Did I mention that?) Anyway, they were walking along in the early hours of Sunday morning when they found themselves behind three people who had also just left the ball. A lady and her son and daughter, as they thought. And what they could not help noticing was that they were engaged in a bitter dispute. The two ladies were reproaching the young man and he seemed to be in a highly excitable state. It sounded as if it might have been your good selves?* He turned his mild gaze to Mother: *Was Mr Shenstone angry and upset?*

*Yes*, she said.

*And was peace made at The George and Dragon?* he asked as if hoping the answer would be in the affirmative.

*I'm afraid not*, Mother admitted. *When my daughter and I left in the carriage, my son was still very overwrought.*

*Is that why he walked back from the ball? Because he was irate and, if I may put it like this, flown with wine?*

Mother nodded. *I'm afraid he had had more to drink than was wise.*

Then came the question I had been fearing.

*And what time was it that he arrived home, Mrs Shenstone?*

*I expected you to ask me that, Mr Wilson, and the truth is that I simply cannot remember. I had so many things to do that morning after the ball that I hardly noticed the moment at which he appeared.*

Wilson listened sympathetically, his head on one side. Then he leaned back in the sopha. *The post is an odd affair, isn't it ma'am? One day you mail a letter and it arrives almost before you've handed it in or put it in the box. (We have a great number of those new boxes now in London.) Another time it takes an eternity to travel just a few miles. And in a case like this, there is another complication. If an unopened letter is found addressed to a person who is, unfortunately, not in a position to open it by virtue of being deceased, then it can be very awkward for us. The letter might be a vital piece of evidence but can we simply open and read it? No indeed. The next of kin have to be consulted and give their permission.*

I couldn't bear the way he was torturing me. I asked: *Was such a letter found?*

*Odd that you should ask, Mr Shenstone. Yes, it was as a matter of fact. At the poor deceased gentleman's lodgings in Hill Street. It was not discovered until this morning and then it had to be conveyed to his lordship, the earl, as the sole person who had authority to open it. And that letter has contributed something very specific to the case. It is one of those distasteful ones that people have been receiving in recent weeks.*

*May we know what the letter contained?* Euphemia asked.

Her curiosity seemed genuine. What an actress! Though, now that I think about it, her lover must have written it himself and so she won't know its precise wording. I wonder if she doesn't quite trust him to have done it properly.

Wilson said: *It made some very disagreeable threats in which the writer undertook to do to the poor young man pretty much what was done a few hours later.*

*A few hours later?* I repeated.

*Yes, Mr Shenstone. The letter was mailed before Mr Davenant Burgoyne was attacked. Placed in the posting-box in front of the main office, in fact. The individual who wrote it must have done so after the ball but before the first collection at 7 o'clock because it was franked within an hour of that.*

I asked: *Might we be permitted to learn its contents?*

Maddeningly he crossed one leg over his knee, leaned back, and said: *This is such a charming old house. So much character. I love these old places. Mrs Wilson and I have a semi-detached villa in Clapham. (Do you know it, ma'am?) Run-of-the-mill little house. Built barely ten years back. Well, not so little, I admit. But nothing like as spacious and historical as this building.* He turned to me: *I imagine you have a funny old room up in the top with a floor that slopes in one direction and a ceiling that goes off in another? Am I right?*

I nodded.

*Would you do me the honour of showing it to me?*

*If you wish*, I said.

*Capital!* he exclaimed, rising from his chair with more alacrity than might be expected of a man of his age and girth.

So I led him up to this room and all the while he kept up a stream of small talk—very small. When he came in here he looked around with his head slightly on one side like a great sparrow. I saw his eyes resting on the trunk and then on this Journal. I suddenly realised that the law allows him to seize it if—say rather, when—he comes to arrest me. Once he had made himself comfortable in a chair he began in his rambling way: *I don't know about you, young man, but I find that when I've done something that I feel I really shouldn't have, I have an oppressive sort of sensation. I have to tell whoever it is that I'm keeping it from. I'm afraid I'd make the most incompetent secret agent if the Home Office were ever ill-advised enough to ask me to undertake such work. I say this because I'm wondering if there's something you might want to get off your chest.*

He paused.

When I said nothing he went on: *I thought we could have a frank chat man-to-man about how you might have taken the wrong way walking home early on Sunday morning and found yourself on the road to Upton Dene and then along came a horse and rider and something happened. I once knew a case where a young chap was heated and—to be absolutely frank—a little the worse for drink and in some way or other there was a contretemps with another young fellow and our man believed the other was attacking him and defended himself.* He sighed. *A wretched case. But it's perfectly understandable how such misunderstandings arise. And in a situation like yours, when you were on foot and a rider came galloping towards you and perhaps recognised you and stopped and said things. Well?*

*I was not on that road, Mr Wilson,* I said. *Why should I have been? I came by the shortest way—through Whitminster.*

He smiled as if encouraging me to continue. I went on: *And that brings me to another point. The weapon used to kill Mr Davenant Burgoyne was, by your account, a large object that it would have been difficult to conceal. Where could I have hidden it? Nobody saw me with it at the ball or at the inn. Could I have had it with me all that time without its being noticed?*

*That would be an excellent objection, Mr Shenstone, if it were not that we assume that the killer had already hidden it at the spot chosen for the murder.*

*Then the idea that the murder occurred as the result of an accidental encounter must be wrong,* I pointed out.

He smiled ruefully.

I followed up my advantage: *And since the murderer must have known that Mr Davenant Burgoyne would be taking that road alone at that hour, that in itself exonerates me. How could I possibly have known that?*

*Unfortunately for that argument, Mr Shenstone, it was no secret that Mr Davenant Burgoyne planned to ride to the Castle that morning because he had arranged to go out with the Handleton hounds. He talked about it at the ball and explained to several people that it was why he would be leaving the company early. In fact, he was first missed when he failed to attend the meet.*

*Well, I didn't know his intentions,* I said feebly. *How could I have?*

He went on as if I had not spoken: *I can comprehend completely how anxious you are not to cause distress to your mother and sister. What I suggest is that we slip away now and you come into Thurchester with me in the trap and we can talk comfortably at the station-house and clear this up to everybody's satisfaction.*

*Are you arresting me?*

He looked hurt: *No, Mr Shenstone. I need a warrant to do that. And to be absolutely frank, I was hoping you would save all of us a great deal of pother and quill-work and avoid the necessity for that by telling me the whole unfortunate story chap-to-chap. Otherwise I would have to go and bother some poor old magistrate for a warrant.*

*I'm sorry that my innocence is causing so much inconvenience.*

He appeared to be wounded by my sarcasm: *Oh you're enjoying your laugh, Mr Shenstone. And you're so much cleverer and better-educated than myself, that I'm not surprised at that. And yet for all your sharpness, you made a bad slip when you virtually admitted to the attack on the late Mr Davenant Burgoyne in Hill Street on the 4th of January.*

*As I told you, it was the following day I went to Thurchester.*

He shook his head reprovingly. *Let us be frank with each other, Mr Shenstone. Why not confess that you fought with Mr Davenant Burgoyne that evening? It was an honest mistake. You believed you were being attacked. It does not prove that you killed him six days later.*

I was tempted to grant the point. But on reflection, I decided that that would be to concede too much. I said nothing.

He shrugged and then pulled a sheet of paper from a cavernous pocket and put on a pair of half-moon spectacles. *This is the letter I was talking about downstairs. At least, this is part of it since his lordship did not permit me to read the whole. It's an important new piece of evidence. I won't bore you with the whole of what his lordship allowed me to copy, but here are some of the more interesting passages:*

*"If you lay hands on a decent girl you must pay for it. I don't mean money. I am going to make you pay with your blood. You think you have got away with it. But you are wrong. You won't be able to hide behind your friends the next time we meet. I am going to kill you but before I do that I am going to hurt you so badly you will scream for mercy. You are so proud of your cock. See if it will get you an heir when it's stuffed down your lying throat!"* Wilson paused in order to give the next words special emphasis: *"You may be the heir to an earldom, but you are no gentleman."*

He looked at me sadly over the top of his spectacles.

In that instant I understood why Euphemia was listening at the door when I quarrelled with Davenant Burgoyne and why she had run off by herself as we were walking back to the inn. I had already guessed by whom that letter had been written and put in the posting-box and now I saw how Euphemia had supplied Lyddiard with its contents.

I said: *I understand completely. You have a dozen witnesses who can attest that they heard me address more or less those precise words to Mr Davenant Burgoyne a few hours before he was killed.*

He nodded with a melancholy expression. A loving uncle whose hopes have been betrayed by a promising nephew.

I said: *But there is an absurdity involved. Why would anyone put such a letter in the post knowing it would not arrive until at least the afternoon, and then set off to kill the person to whom it is addressed?*

*You're very sharp, sir. You've given it some thought. It's true that there is an apparent anomaly and it had struck me in my own ponderous labouring manner though it took me a great deal longer to see it. But one possibility is that the individual decided to do what he did only after posting that letter.*

*But had already taken the precaution of hiding the weapon several miles away!* I exclaimed. *It must be clear to you that that letter was written and posted for another purpose entirely: to incriminate me further.*

He shrugged. *In every investigation there are always a few tangled threads that we never unravel.*

I said: *Then here's a reef knot for you. From what you've read out, the author seems not to have bothered to feign illiteracy.*

He looked at me with interest. I explained that the letters I had seen were pretending to be the work of an unlettered person.

He waited until I'd finished and then said: *What do you conclude from that?*

I said: *As you will find out when you look at the letters you've collected in their order of sending, the writer began by impersonating someone who was barely literate and then successive letters gradually revealed more and more education. The intention was to draw out the process of speculation in the neighbourhood before narrowing the pool of possible authors. The letters were designed to make it look as if the libeller was pretending to be unlettered but failed to keep up the illusion as he became carried away by his hatred of his victims. This last letter threw off the pretence—or, I should say, pretended to throw off the pretence—because it was written in order to inculpate me more unequivocally than all its predecessors by quoting words that a number of witnesses had heard me utter.*

He made no response and seemed to be considering my point. Then he said: *The individual who wrote that letter must have been present at the confrontation between you and Mr Davenant Burgoyne.*

*Many people were present,* I pointed out. *And in fact the writer need only have spoken to someone who heard—or overheard—what I said.*

I thought of Euphemia listening at the door and then hastening to tell her fellow-conspirator what I had said.

He was silent for a while and then said: *You've given me something to chew over. I won't deny that. Frankly, you don't strike me as someone who would commit such an act. I need to read through all the letters I've collected. I've got a couple from Mrs Quance and one from poor Miss Whitaker-Smith and a number of others. I'll tell you what I'll do, Mr Shenstone. I'll talk to a few more people tomorrow. One of them will be the old gentleman who is so sure that the weapon that was used against Mr Davenant Burgoyne is the tool that was stolen from him. It's Mr Fourdrinier, as you must know. He hasn't seen it yet but he says he knows it from the description. And he's convinced it was you who took it because there was nobody else in sight at the time—apart from that young lady of his who is his niece on Mondays and his ward on Tuesdays. Now if Mr Fourdrinier is wrong about his precious hoe or dibber or whatever it is, then I'll pay more attention to the possibility that the crime was committed by some passing rogue or vagabond and has no connection with the letters despite all the apparent links. But if he recognises that thing, then I'll have no choice but to get a warrant. Is that reasonable?*

What could I say? I said nothing.

He stood up and I followed him out. As we went along the passage and then down the stairs he asked conversationally: *Do you have any plans for leaving the district today or tomorrow?*

*None at all.*

*Just as well. Would you oblige me by staying within a mile of this house? I'd be quite anxious if you went any further than that.*

I indicated my agreement. He knows as well as I do that since the house stands on a peninsula, there is no way out except by the single path to the mainland and I imagine he will have it watched.

We went back into the parlour and found Mother and Euphemia sitting as we had left them.

Wilson smiled and said: *Your son and I have had a delightful little tate-a-tate, Mrs Shenstone. But there is something you might be able to assist us in. That recent trip he made to Thurchester to book the rooms and arrange the hire of the carriage and to visit Mr Boddington—there is some uncertainty about the date. Your son is convinced it was Tuesday the 5th. Neither mine host at The George and Dragon nor the ostler at the livery-stable has the slightest idea of which day it was. Rather surprisingly, Mr Boddington says he can't remember and that he made no note of it in his daybook.*

(Good for the old man!)

Wilson went on: *Fortunately his clerk—a smart fellow who should go far—remembers distinctly that it was the 4th. So there we have it. Evens on both sides. Do you happen to remember, Mrs Shenstone?*

The most extraordinary thing. Trembling and speaking in a small voice, Mother said: *It was Monday the 4th of January and I recall it distinctly because it was the night my son came home with his clothes ripped and stained with blood.*

Wilson turned to me in surprise.

I stood paralysed in a state of complete shock. My mother could only have said that if she believed I had murdered Davenant Burgoyne. And that I had written the letters and maimed the beasts. In a desperate attempt to save myself, I said: *No, Mother. You've confused that occasion with an earlier one. It was another time that I lost my way in the mist and fell into a ditch beside the road.*

Almost whispering, Mother said: *I'm quite sure of my dates, Mr Wilson.*

I grabbed Wilson by the arm and muttering that I would see him out, I led him into the hall. When I was sure we were far enough from the parlour not to be heard I said: *I admit it, Sergeant Wilson. I've been lying to you. It was very foolish of me but I simply assumed you would not believe the truth. You are right. It was I who attacked Mr Davenant Burgoyne a week ago. We blundered into each other in the fog and mist and I did not know it was he and thought that whoever I had collided with intended to harm me and merely defended myself.*

He raised a sceptical eyebrow. *You had no idea it was he?*

He must have guessed that I was holding something back. Did I expect him to believe that it was by chance that I had run into the one man of all the inhabitants of Thurchester whom I was now suspected of murdering?

I had to say: *I knew I was in the street where Mr Davenant Burgoyne lodged but I could not know whom I was fighting. I have frankly admitted that I lied to you about that incident but that is the only lie I have told you.* I stopped. With a kind of recklessness, I clutched at the truth to save me from drowning: *No, there was one other lie. The fact is that I arrived here at one o'clock on Sunday and not earlier. I tried to lie about that because I was frightened when I came to understand the whole case against me and see how strong it is. And yet I am entirely guiltless. I did not write those foul letters nor maim cattle and I did not kill Mr Davenant Burgoyne.*

His face conveyed neither acceptance nor disbelief.

With an increasing sense of my predicament I went on: *The evidence has been constructed to incriminate me. Let me give you an example that you are not yet aware of. When you see him tomorrow Mr Fourdrinier will certainly identify the murder weapon as the tool that was stolen from him. But I did not steal it. I can explain all of that just as I can explain every shred of evidence against me. The trouble is that I'm not sure if any-one will believe me.*

Wilson had listened attentively. Now he said: *I'm a just man, Mr Shenstone. I'll tell you what I'll do. I won't apply for a warrant merely because Mr Fourdrinier confirms that his tool was used to commit the mur-der and that he is sure you stole it. Though that would be* prima facie *evi-dence for any justice of the peace. No, what I'll do is I'll look into another matter, one that I haven't mentioned so far. Some of the revolting commu-nications received in the district seem to have been written by a man who felt that a young woman—apparently a close relative—had been seduced and abandoned by Mr Davenant Burgoyne. Now I know you accused him of having behaved discourteously to your sister during your confrontation with him at the ball, but of course the letters started a couple of weeks before that. So I'll ask my new friends and see if you had any reason to think that the murdered man had impugned the virtue of your sister in the weeks or months before the ball. Is that fair?*

*It's very fair, Sergeant Wilson,* I said with feigned cheerfulness.

*I'm going back to Thurchester now and I'll drive out to Mr Fourdrin-ier's house first thing tomorrow and show him the weapon. I need to estab-lish the truth about that. Then I'll talk to some of the kind neighbours like Mrs Quance and Mrs Greenacre who have asked to speak to me and give me some more of the letters and I'll get to the bottom of this business of who wrote them and who had a grudge against the deceased. If I decide I need a warrant, I'll have it in my hand by the evening.*

I managed a smile and Wilson shook my hand and I saw him out. This time there was no constable waiting for him and he walked up the lane alone. He had mentioned a pony-trap but I could not see one.

I went back into the parlour and found Euphemia and Mother sit-ting where I had left them—the former holding a book and the latter bent over her embroidery-frame. I said: *Mother, I want to speak to you in private.*

Still looking at her work she said quietly: *Anything you have to say to me can be said in front of your sister.*

I said: *I just want to ask you, how could you have told the detective about the blood-stains?*

She wouldn't look at me.

I said: *I am innocent. How can I make you believe that?*

She just shook her head.

Suddenly Euphemia said: *Stop bullying Mother, Richard.*

I looked at her and she stared back impassively and after a long while during which we held each other's gaze, she dropped her eyes to her book.


*½ past 2 o'clock.*

Why did Mother say that? Even if she thinks I am guilty—which is an astonishing reflection anyway—why did she volunteer that damaging piece of information?

The trap is closing around me. Now more than ever in my life I need to keep calm and think this through rationally.

Could I put pressure on Euphemia by threatening to reveal to our mother the iniquity of her actions? Would she be swayed by that? No, of course not. How ridiculous to think she could be shamed into condemning herself! If she were capable of feeling shame she would not have embarked on this undertaking.

Could I frighten her into betraying Lyddiard? What argument or strategy could I use? She would impeach Lyddiard only if she were sure that I could prove that they conspired to commit murder and that her only chance of escaping a guilty verdict would be to turn Queen's Evidence against him and plead that he had forced and tricked her into it. Yet I cannot prove that Lyddiard was anywhere near the scene of the murder at that time. He has crept about at night and hidden at the house of Lady Terrewest so that nobody can testify to his presence in the neighbourhood. That time I saw him hiding in the cart as he went back to Thurchester, he was in the guise of Tom the Swell and I cannot even be sure of proving that they are one and the same man.

Apart from Euphemia, only Lady Terrewest and her servants know that he hides at her house. And perhaps even they did not realise he was there on the night of the ball since he has a key to his own part of it.

I can imagine how enthusiastically the Quances and the Greenacres and other wagging tongues will provide all the evidence against me that Wilson needs: Davenant Burgoyne publicly compromised my sister and then abruptly threw her over when the scandal of our father's wrong-doings threatened to erupt. Everything points to me as the defamer and the murderer: the abusive letters, the tool stolen from Mr Fourdrinier, my foolish threats against Davenant Burgoyne at the ball that were echoed in the last letter.

The one chink in the armour of the conspirators might be Betsy. She knew that Lyddiard was here—even slept here. And if she knew that, then Euphemia might have told her things that could be used in evidence against her. But would Betsy tell me anything? She is as offended and upset with me as I am with her.

Odd how concerned I am to think that she is unhappy because of me. Can't forget her miserable little face when she said *This is my home*.

I suppose I treated her badly. She is only fourteen. But I can't apologise to an illiterate servant-girl. And yet I keep thinking of the way she took a handkerchief and mopped up what I had spilt on her belly with such intense concentration and then when she had done that, she smiled at me as if to reassure me that she was not annoyed. And it's not her fault that her father and brothers did those things to her.

Even if I could find a way to prove Euphemia's guilt, I don't want to send my sister to the gallows in my place.

. . .

It's as if I were sitting in a darkened theatre waiting for the curtain to rise on a play whose script I have already read: I will be arrested and tried and convicted and hanged and I can do nothing about it. Everything I will say in my defence will be seen as the rantings of a lunatic or a man desperate to save himself from death. Euphemia will brush aside my allegations against her. Why will she care if I impugn her reputation? She will be married to a wealthy man.

What witnesses will I have to speak in my defence? Old Mr Boddington? But he can say nothing to overturn the evidence against me. It will be claimed that Bartlemew posted on my behalf the defamatory letters that I was writing and although he will deny it, once his character has been established, he will not be believed.

.   .   .

Idle thought: I wonder what was in the part of the letter that the earl did not let Wilson read. Was there some hideous allegation against the murdered man that would have brought shame on his memory?

.   .   .

Mother believes that I am guilty of the murder and that is why she has refused me an alibi and even volunteered to Wilson that damning piece of evidence against me. That is the high Roman style: My son has done wrong and I will not defend him. But does she not understand what will happen? Does she not see the inevitable consequence of her decision? As to why she would not tell a lie to protect me, is there something that I don't yet know about? Is it to do with what happened in the autumn? And that terrible secret she threatened to reveal to me?

I must talk to her alone.

*3 o'clock.*

I found her in the parlour. I said: *Mother, I'm in dreadful danger. I need to know everything. And I'll be equally frank and tell you all that occurred in Cambridge.*

Without giving her a chance to respond, I went on: *I borrowed money from Edmund but then I needed more than he could give me and we conceived the idea of my taking a loan from his father using my own father as security. That's how I obtained the seventy pounds.*

She looked at me in surprise.

*No, you're right. My father didn't consent to that. He knew nothing of it. Edmund's father's bankers, of course, required his signature guaranteeing repayment. I knew he would never sign it and since the loan was between friends and Edmund promised to pay it back when he reached his majority, we didn't think it mattered.*

I thought it would be hard to confess but she seemed to be paying little attention to my words. I went on: *So I forged my father's signature. But then Edmund and I quarrelled. At that moment my father died and the news of his death upset me so much that I wrote a cruel letter to Edmund accusing him of having made me an opium-smoker and then seduced me into forging the signature in order to put me in his power. Edmund saw me as his only friend in the world and if he chose to die—and I don't know if he did— then my letter might have tipped him over the edge. It was found beside his body. Edmund's father used it to press the authorities to make trouble for me. He convinced himself of the absurd idea that I had a hand in Edmund's death because he was my creditor. That was why the Dean and Master rusticated me and reported me to the police for fraud. And perhaps worse.*

She said: *I don't know why you're telling me this now.*

I said: *Because I want you to tell me the truth with equal frankness.*

When she didn't speak I said: *Mother, I had nothing to do with the death of Mr Davenant Burgoyne.*

She did not even look at me.

I said: *I suspect that this terrible event has something to do with whatever happened between Euphemia and him while I was in Cambridge. I'm surely entitled to know about it now?*

Still she kept silent.

I said: *They'll say I killed him because he publicly humiliated my sister in the sight of Thurchester society.*

She put her hands up as if to shield herself from my words.

I asked: *What happened, Mother?*

She just shook her head.

I said: *Mother, I beg you. You know me. You can't think I wrote those filthy letters? That I killed a man?*

She made no response. How could I persuade her that I had nothing to do with those crimes without pointing towards Euphemia? I had no choice. I had to tell her. I warned her that I was going to tell her something that would shock her terribly.

I said: *This involves Willoughby Lyddiard.*

And then I told her what I had seen at Thrubwell on Sunday morning. I said: *He was sneaking into the house like a criminal and I know he had just killed Mr Davenant Burgoyne.*

She remained impassive. I concluded: *I implore you to tell me everything you know. My one chance is to find something that I can produce as irrefutable evidence.*

She said: *This is all nonsense. You've taken leave of your senses. It's because of what you've been smoking in your room that your conduct has been so irrational since you returned from Cambridge. That wicked practice has addled your wits.*

I said: *Please listen to me. Lyddiard is the man who has done the things that I'm being accused of.*

I went over the evidence that will surely convict me if I am put on trial: my threats at the ball; the letters attributed to me—especially the one sent to Davenant Burgoyne; and finally Mr Fourdrinier's famous dibber.

All the while she stared at me, shaking her head as if mourning my insanity.

I said: *There is something much worse, much more painful that I have to break to you. It's going to distress you terribly. I fear that my sister knew at least something of what Lyddiard was planning.*

She turned her head away and did not answer me. I suppose she was hiding her shock.

Then I said that Euphemia had been somehow persuaded or intimidated into helping him write the defamatory letters at the house of Lady Terrewest which he then posted in Thurchester. He had plotted the murder of Davenant Burgoyne in order to inherit the fortune that would come to him on his death and it is possible that Euphemia at least had some inkling that he was planning that. I put it that way to soften the blow for her.

Now for the first time Mother turned to look at me. In a harsh voice I had never heard before, she said: *Leave Euphemia out of this.*

I said: *I can't. It was she who first involved me!*

Mother hissed at me: *You will not interfere with your sister's plans. You will not ruin her life as you have ruined your own.*


½ *past 3 o'clock.*


Even if Mother thinks I am guilty, why would she not tell a small lie to protect me? She must believe that to exonerate me is to endanger Euphemia.

Is there something that I don't yet know about? If so, Miss Bittlestone might have the answers. I must pay her another visit.


*4 o'clock.*


Up the lane and just before the turning to Netherton there was a horse and trap with a postboy on the seat and a man sitting beside him who was in civilian dress but was very obviously a policeman. He had a shotgun propped beside him. When I had gone a hundred yards up the lane I looked back and of course he was following me. He tagged me through the afternoon and I'd stake my life that he or his relief will be there all night guarding the only path from here. This house has become my prison.

When I pushed open the door in response to her call, Miss Bittlestone greeted me without any surprise: *Oh, Mr Shenstone, this terrible news about poor Mr Davenant Burgoyne!*

She showed no fear or even unease at the sight of me. It was very cold and there was no light in the cottage except from the glowing embers of the fire. She cannot read in that gloom and I wonder what she does hour by hour alone in the near-dark with no living creature save her cat.

I said: *We both know, don't we, Miss Bittlestone, who will inherit his fortune now?*

She nodded slowly. Then she pointed to the battered but heroic old chair once reserved for her most illustrious visitor and said: *Please be seated.*

As I did so she said: *I wish never to see that chair again. When I saw your mother on Saturday I asked if you could come and take it after the service on Sunday morning but she said you would not be able to.*

With great ceremony she reached into the scuttle and put another lump of coal on the fire in my honour.

The cat emerged from a corner and began to weave a pattern around his mistress' feet. Miss Bittlestone said: *I've got such a treat for you, Tiddles.*

She bent down and offered him a small piece of meat. I suspect she gets more pleasure from feeding her cat than herself.

The old lady saw my eyes fall on a newspaper lying on a dresser, *The Thurchester Intelligencer. Kind Mr Lloyd gives it to me when he's finished with it*, she said.

So the Quances' enemy has become her ally—like a rival empire taking on a vassal state from which the opposing troops have been withdrawn.

I looked at the shipping pages. *The Hibernian Maid* of the Black Ball Line sails with the first tide from Southampton on Thursday the 14th bound for Newfoundland. I still have Uncle T's mandate to her captain.

Miss Bittlestone was anxious to tell me her news: the detective, Sergeant Wilson, had visited her earlier today. She said: *He is a very charming person, extremely courteous. Only he does have a strange manner of conducting a conversation. I even wondered at one moment if he were intoxicated.*

I asked: *And what did he want to know?*

*I'm afraid he was dreadfully inquisitive about you and what he called your "nocturnal perambulations" which made them sound very sinister. I assured him that there was nothing in the least reprehensible about them. He asked if you had "bothered" the Quance girls with unwanted attentions. I said the contrary was more probably the case.*

(Now there's a surprise!)

I told her that for all his affability Mr Wilson believes me to be the author of the abusive letters and a murderer.

She gasped and covered her mouth.

I said: *There's something I need to understand. Just before I went up to Cambridge, Miss Whitaker-Smith and Mr Davenant Burgoyne were close to announcing their intention to marry. Then the engagement was broken off. Can you tell me what happened?*

She was quite pink with embarrassment. Eventually I extracted the story from her. Euphemia met Davenant Burgoyne at Maud's house and set out to steal him from her best friend. In the middle of October she was seen coming out of his lodgings in Hill Street at ten in the evening in a risky attempt to force him to marry her by creating a scandal. It seemed as if the ploy had worked and he had proposed.

The old lady came to a halt and I had great difficulty coaxing her into going on. *Mr and Mrs Whitaker-Smith approached your mother and warned her that unless your sister withdrew, there would be a worse scandal.*

*I don't understand.*

*It involved Miss Whitaker-Smith's brother. Perceval.*

Maud's tearful younger brother. As soon as she uttered those words, it all fell into place: His singing lessons with my father. His membership of the Cathedral choir. Bartlemew's joining it at my father's behest. Everything that I had seen and understood at The Dolphin.

The old lady stared at me, unable to go on. I helped her out: *I understand. They threatened to expose my father unless my sister ended her attachment to Mr Davenant Burgoyne?*

She nodded, eyes averted. *But your mother must not have believed they would do such a thing.*

*She called their bluff? She defied them to denounce my father?*

She nodded timidly.

I heard the blood dinning in my ears. Miss Bittlestone's revelation turned everything upside down. Far from her misfortunes having fallen upon her head from a clear blue sky, it was my mother who had herself precipitated the scandal that destroyed my father and ruined all of us. And she had done it because she had taken a cold ruthless decision: that the parents of a child of twelve would choose not to put him through the experience of having to give evidence about the wrong that had been done to him.

A phrase from one of those foul letters sprang to mind: *the lyes that dirty little Pursniffle tole.* The person who wrote those words hated Perceval because he had revealed the truth.

Now I understood the obsession with Bartlemew. He had played a role in putting Perceval in the power of my father and then extorted money in return for his silence.

My mother had risked everything for the chance of Euphemia marrying her future earl and millionaire. Well, the earldom had gone now but if the plan succeeded, her daughter would be the wife of a rich man. Whom would she not sacrifice to achieve that goal?

I didn't listen as the old lady wittered on about her diet and her cat.

After a minute or two I asked her to continue with her account. She said: *The Whitaker-Smiths took their son to the Dean to tell his story.*

*My father was dismissed*, I said. *And it came out that he had been embezzling to pay off a blackmailer. The strain of all that brought on his fatal heart-attack. And my mother's gamble failed since Mr Davenant Bur-goyne threw Euphemia over as soon as the scandal broke.*

Then Miss Bittlestone said: *There has been the saddest news in the last couple of weeks. Perceval was at home for the holiday and it seems he was very unhappy at his public school where he had been cruelly bullied once the other boys found out what had happened to him in Thurchester. On the morning of Christmas Day he was found to have vanished from the house and he has not been seen since.*

What a dreadful story. My mother must have heard it at church and that is why she was so upset when Betsy came in that evening to say she had heard a child crying out on the marshes.

I rose and thanked the old lady. Just as I reached the door she stopped me and, looking very embarrassed, she said: *There is one other thing. I've heard something that might be of interest to you. It's about your servant. The older one who briefly worked for your mother.*

*Mrs Yass?*

She nodded. *Since she left your mother's service, she has been working for a family near Southampton. Very sadly, one of the young daughters has recently died. Very horribly.* She hesitated. *A girl who wasn't married. Mrs Yass has been arrested and charged with . . . with . . .*

I touched her arm to show that she need not continue.

At the door I glanced back and when my eyes fell on the famous chair with its elegantly curved back and faded red satin seat, I remembered something.

*Miss Bittlestone, what did you mean about my mother saying I would not be able to fetch the chair last Sunday?*

*Your mother said you would not be back from Thurchester before lunch-eon because you would walk home.*

She must have seen from my face that she had said something more significant than she realised.

I was so surprised that I actually sank onto that once-sacred piece of furniture. After a moment I managed to say: *I know you hate the sight of it so I'll take the wretched thing now.*

We parted affectionately and I am sure she knew she would not see me again.

The policeman was attempting to hide behind a tree nearby as I left the cottage and must have been sorely puzzled to see me half dragging, half bearing a battered old chair. I did not carry it any great distance but flung it into the nearby marsh. It tilted over as it settled into the mud and then it began to sink. As if invisible arms were pulling it down, it twisted slowly as it disappeared beneath the surface.

I walked back by way of Monument Hill and climbed the tree again. With the light shining from the west, I was able to see nothing inside but bare brick walls and naked floorboards. The divan and carpets had been the creation of my fevered imagination.

How much I had failed to understand.

Mrs Yass: Now I understood why it was so urgent that Euphemia secure a husband soon. What the purpose was of the towels and the metal dishes I had seen when I arrived unexpectedly. What the revelation was that my mother had threatened me with and that I was too cowardly to hear.

By now I had made a circuit of the Battlefield. An idea had come floating up towards the surface of my mind. Flight. But if I were going to attempt it, I had to throw Wilson off the scent. Miss Bittlestone's newspaper had suggested a means.

As I passed through the village I called in at the shop. Mrs Darnton glared at me from behind the counter. I asked her what newspapers she offered. *You know very well*, she said and indicated copies of *The Thurchester Intelligencer* lying nearby.

*No*, I said. *That's not what I want. Have you a paper that serves towns to the east of here?*

She jerked her chin towards a pile of copies of *The Rye and Romney Mercury* and I seized one and turned to the shipping pages, holding the paper so that she would see what I was looking at. It confirmed that *The Caledonian Maid* would sail from Rye for Hong Kong on Saturday the 16th.

Mrs Darnton had been peering over my shoulder and now asked sarcastically: *Are you planning a sea-voyage?*

I turned and, looking as guilty and furtive as I could, replaced the paper.

*Aren't you going to buy it?* she demanded.

*Certainly not,* I said. *It's a dreadful newspaper.* I left the shop and as I walked away I glanced back. The policeman was going in and I knew he would find Mrs Darnton eager to complain about what I had just said and done.

.   .   .

Poor old tabby. I imagined her in that lonely cottage listening for a step outside after receiving that letter: *I shull come and visit you one nigth.*

*½ past 5 o'clock.*

As I entered the house I met Betsy in the hall and asked her to tell my mother that I was not hungry and would not dine with them. She looked at me in surprise.

I came up here.

I now see that it wasn't in order to *spare my feelings* that my mother kept me away from Thurchester until she had moved out here. It wasn't my father's misdeeds that she wanted to hide from me but her own and my sister's: the attempt to ensnare Davenant Burgoyne by even the most reckless means and then the calling of the Whitaker-Smiths' bluff and the consequent sacrifice of Perceval.

I'm still reeling from Miss Bittlestone's remark that my mother knew I would not be back from the ball in Thurchester until late in the day. That I would not be riding back in the carriage. She knew what Euphemia and Lyddiard were planning. So many other things that I had not wanted to notice fell only too neatly into place.

I know now when it was that my mother learned about the plot. It was the night before the ball when she made a feeble attempt to warn me—*Willoughby means you harm*—and I misunderstood her.

*6 o'clock.*

Betsy just knocked at the door and came in with a heel of bread and a piece of cheese. Even she deceived me and betrayed me to Euphemia. I ordered her to put the plate down and get out. She scuttled towards the door like a scared rabbit.

I could not stop myself. I said: *Why didn't you tell me what was going on? That my sister's lover had been coming here?*

She turned. She said nothing but just stared at the ground in front of my feet with sulky resentfulness.

*And why did you tell my sister what you and I did?*

Then she muttered: *You've been avoiding me. Once you'd had your way, that's all you wanted from me.*

I said: *It's you who have been avoiding me. Well, pretty soon you won't be seeing me at all and that should make you happy.*

To my astonishment she burst into tears and ran out of the room. Puzzling, but I haven't the time to think about a little skivvy.

I understand what has been done to me but that helps me not at all. Nobody will believe my account of events. No jury, as Wilson made clear.

I almost wish I had not thrown away my lovely little friends—my only friends. That is the only sure means of escape that is open to me—illusory and temporary though it is.

Except that there is one other way to get myself out of this trap but it is fraught with peril and I don't believe I have the courage to attempt it.

*A ¼ past 6 o'clock.*

A few minutes ago I heard a sound outside and peered out of my window. I saw Euphemia walking up the path and I assumed she was going to Lady Terrewest's. I'm sure Lyddiard will not be at the house. After lying low on Sunday, he would have made his escape when darkness fell.

Now was my chance. I went into the parlour and I can't forget my mother's voice asking sharply: *What do you want, Richard? Are you going to try to get me to commit perjury again?*

I said: *Your alibi won't help me now. But don't play the outraged innocent. Your lies have got me into this situation.*

*How dare you address me in that tone,* she said with querulous dignity.

*You told Miss Bittlestone that I would walk home on Sunday morning and you could only have said that if you knew that Euphemia would provoke an argument after the ball and then refuse to ride with me. What I wonder is this: When did you first begin to understand what she was plotting? You must have realised that she had some secret intention once she had abandoned the project for which Mrs Yass had been hired.*

She turned away. I said: *Yes, I know that the revelation you would have made to me if I hadn't agreed to go away was that that woman was going to induce a miscarriage or something worse. That day Euphemia came back from Lady Terrewest's house and had secured the tickets, when she said Mrs Yass was to be dismissed, I remember how you danced around the room. You knew she wouldn't be risking Mrs Yass's dangerous ministrations but you must have known that she was planning some sort of resolution to her situation. What did you think she was going to do? Did you think Euphemia had decided to marry a man like Lyddiard—penniless and illegitimate? You must have realised that they had worked out something that would rescue them from penury. But you convinced yourself that all would turn out as you hoped, as you always do.*

She kept her face turned away and said: *I've only ever tried to do what's for the best.*

I said: *Did that include the business with Maud and her parents?*

She flinched and I said: *Yes, I know about that now. I know that you sacrificed Perceval in order to preserve Euphemia's chance of marrying Davenant Burgoyne. You didn't believe his family would make use of him to bring shame on my father and force Davenant Burgoyne to throw Euphemia over. But they did and the poor boy suffered the consequences.*

She almost hissed: *That creature you brought into the family, that was his doing.*

I said: *You're right that Bartlemew pandered to my father's illicit appetite and then started to blackmail him. But he didn't tempt him into anything he hadn't been doing for years and I'm sure you knew about it.*

She was muttering my name as if in despair at my insanity.

*When the letters began, I believe you didn't know that they were writing them. Your shock at the first letter was authentic. And then eventually you began to suspect me. That night I came back from Thurchester you virtually charged me with being a deranged harasser of young women. And then the day before the ball you got up very early and went to Mrs Quance and read the letter that had a play on the word "lucubrations". That confirmed your suspicions of me. That evening you accused me of having written those filthy letters and you insisted that I leave here the next day. Euphemia was horrified because that would have ruined her plan. So she talked to you in private and persuaded you that I was not responsible for those letters. And the only way she could have convinced you was by telling you who had written them. So she did, didn't she? She told you everything.*

*This is all fantasy, Richard.*

*That must have been a shock. But there was a worse one coming. She told you that they intended to murder Davenant Burgoyne and incriminate me.*

She said: *You're talking nonsense.* She turned away abruptly.

*And you were so horrified that you drank some of the wine you kept hidden in your rooms and then you tried to warn me to run away. You said that Willoughby wanted to do me harm. The only Willoughby I knew of was Davenant Burgoyne. Euphemia interrupted us before you could explain. That was the moment when you had to make a choice between Euphemia and me. And you chose her. That's why you sought me out at the ball and led me to where I would see her coming down the stairs in tears.*

*There was no plot.* She sat covering her face with her hands and gently shaking her head.

I said: *I'm going to be charged with murder. If you don't tell the authorities the truth you will be responsible.*

She was crying now and said: *How can you say these wicked things?*

Euphemia suddenly entered the room. I was so intent upon what I was saying that I hadn't heard the front-door. She was flushed and upset and I noticed a letter in her hand. My mother glanced at it and then exchanged a look with her daughter.

Euphemia said: *You've been bullying Mother.*

*I've been asking her to admit to some things.*

*How dare you!* she said. *You're the one who has serious charges to answer.*

I said: *We don't have to pretend any longer. There are only the three of us here and we all know the truth. I know how you and your paramour plotted to kill the man you both hated and incriminate me.*

My sister gazed at me impassively while she said: *Has he been raving like this to you, Mother?*

Our mother didn't look round.

I said: *What drove you to it? Did you really hate Davenant Burgoyne so much? Or did your new lover refuse to marry you unless you helped him to inherit? Even when you had the most pressing reason to enter the married state?*

She frowned and I said: *Oh yes, I know what you planned with Mrs Yass. But then my telling you I had mistaken your new lover for your old one gave you an idea. You could make me the dupe for your crime. Your plan seems to have succeeded. But how can you be sure your lover will keep his side of the bargain?*

Euphemia glanced down at the letter.

*Is that what's happened?* I asked. *Has he thrown you over already?*

*And you can't do anything. If you denounce him he will be executed but you will hang too.*

There was nothing to be gained by staying. I walked out.

. . .

*A ¼ to 8 o'clock.*

My mother knows I'm innocent but is condemning me to death.

I am caught in a trap. Literally. There is a police-officer guarding my one way out. I am as good as dead. *I'll have the warrant in my hand by the evening.*

Occurs to me that Betsy might be able to tell me about that letter Euphemia was holding. It just might offer me some hope. If the two plotters have fallen out, that can only benefit me. I want to talk to the girl anyway. She knows more than she has admitted. If I have to, I will force the truth out of her.

*8 o'clock.*

I crept up to her room and without knocking, pushed open the door. She was in bed with just one candle beside her lighting the room and she was holding something in her hands.

At the sight of me she jumped out in her nightshirt and stood nervously beside the bed.

I said: *Why did you tell my sister about us?*

She said: *Miss Effie saw you leaving my room. That time you gave me a half-crown. She made me tell her what we'd been doing.*

I was furious and said: *Since you've told her everything about me, you can tell me everything you know. There is a man—a very tall man—who came to visit her until I returned. What happened when she told him she was in trouble?*

*He said he wouldn't marry her. He said he had no money. He would only marry her if she helped him to get what was his due. I don't know what that meant.*

*It means my death.*

She cried out: *I didn't mean any harm to you. I don't want anything bad to happen to you.*

*It's too late for that,* I said. In a rage I advanced towards her and she pressed herself against the wall and I seized her and shook her. Then the strangest thing happened. As I was staring into her face a few inches from mine in the flickering candlelight, I saw her eyes glistening with tears and realised that I too was weeping. This little creature, this illiterate drab who had been a mere object of pleasure to her own father and brothers, has believed in me when my own mother and sister have been plotting against me. How could I have spoken so harshly to her? The most innocent person in the house. And if I accused my sister of having made use of me, I had used Betsy as if she were an insentient object. An ignorant defenceless girl who was hardly more than a child.

I took her hand and drew her towards the bed and we seated ourselves on its edge. I kept my arm round her. I said: *Forgive me. I shouldn't have been so angry with you. I know you had no choice.* Her eyes seemed to be enormous and they were filling with tears. I said: *Betsy, I'm sorry I caused you grief. I thought you just wanted money.*

She said indignantly: *I never wanted money! I only wanted you to be kind to me.*

*But you asked me for money! You wanted something nice, you said.*

*I didn't mean money!* She blushed. *It wasn't money I was talking about. Not at first anyway. But you thought that was what I was after and I was so upset that I said it just to get back at you. That time when you told me to close my eyes and you gave me those ribbons, I thought you were going to kiss me.*

I took her in my arms and said: *Oh Betsy, Betsy, how silly I've been.*

She bent and picked up something from the floor. It was a child's reading-book. *Look*, she said. *I was conning my letters when you came in. You made me feel so stupid that time you asked me to read something and I couldn't. Miss Effie used to come up here at night to teach me or I'd go down to her. But we spent most of the time talking and crying. She was dreadfully upset when that man that's dead, the earl's nephew, threw her over.*

I tried to imagine. Was it a broken heart or wounded vanity or thwarted greed that had driven her into her murderous alliance? Or a mixture of all of those?

Betsy said: *And now it's happened again.*

*What do you mean?*

*She's just had a letter from the other fellow. There's a big fat woman-servant that brings letters from Thrubwell. Miss Effie went to the shop today and found one. She was very upset by it.*

*He's refusing to marry her?*

*Yes. He says he can't be sure that the child she is carrying is his and not the poor dead man's.*

It was grotesque, almost funny. But what had my sister expected? The man was a professional sharper who earned his living by fraud. What arrogance and vanity had led her to think she could outwit such a person?

Betsy was close to tears and I said: *You mustn't ask me to feel any sympathy for her.* I told her as briefly as I could about the plot that my sister and her lover had carried out.

She hid her face and wept. Then she said: *That's the most dreadful thing. It makes me even sorrier for her.*

I couldn't understand that. I said: *Don't you hate her for what she's done?*

She said: *I hate what she's done but I still love her.*

*You can say that even though she's sending me to my death?*

*What do you mean?* she exclaimed.

*You don't know that the police think it was I who wrote those letters and killed the earl's nephew?*

She said: *That's crazy.*

*Crazy or not, they're going to hang me.* I explained how I had been duped into incriminating myself.

She gripped my arm and said: *They mustn't catch you. You must run away.*

I said: *How? There's a policeman guarding the lane.*

*Then run at him and knock him down.*

I managed a choked laugh: *I'm afraid he has a gun.*

*Do something! Don't just sit here waiting until they come for you. At least try to get away. Isn't there anything you can do?*

*There is just one possible way out.*

*Then take it!* she hissed.

She reached over to a little battered side-table and seized a small box. She opened it and poured out its contents on the bed. It contained the ribbons I had given her and some cash. She gathered up the coins and tried to put them into my hands saying: *Take this, you'll need it.*

It came to about four shillings—all that I had given her and a few pence more.

I refused it and she wept and clung to me and said I had to go, even though she would miss me. I hushed her because I did not want Euphemia to hear us but I found I was in tears myself.

I left her at last.

. . .

Although I pretended to myself that I didn't, I knew that Edmund felt about me in a way that I could not reciprocate and I took advantage of that to accept money from him without thinking what the consequences might be. And now I've done something similar to Betsy.

*½ past 10 o'clock.*

I feel as if I'm no longer afraid of anything. All my life I've been scared. Now I realise that what I was frightened of was the truth.

And when my mother threatened to make her devastating revelation, I was terrified not because I did not know it but because in some sense I did. I knew how my father's ruthless selfishness had twisted and warped our family. That we all crept about in stockinged feet to avoid waking some slumbering monster. I knew my father was capable of any act to gratify his appetites even if I had not guessed the exact nature of his predispositions. All three of us suffered by having to adapt. My mother's spirit was crushed by his demands and my sister and I were forced to learn how to defend ourselves by guile and flattery. Euphemia paid a higher price than I.

There is anger towards Euphemia in my heart and yet I can't find hatred. I don't know what power my father exercised over her but something occurred—some twisted exploitative love—that made it impossible for her to acknowledge to herself, as I have managed to do, that she hated him. And perhaps that hold our father had over her—whatever it was—drew her towards Lyddiard because his ruthless pursuit of his own interests reminded her of him. When I saw him as a cowardly bully brutally beating his dog, she was imagining him as her masterly and determined saviour from poverty.

*11 o'clock.*

Betsy is right. Better to die trying to escape than to wait here and let them hang me.

The idea that came to me this afternoon as I walked around with that policeman behind me—it would be foolhardy, crazy, dangerous. In the daylight it seemed possible and that's why I went to the shop and laid a false trail. I made Mrs Darnton think my goal would be Rye but, in fact, if I were to risk the attempt, I would go west so that when my disappearance was discovered, the police would chase off in the wrong direction.

I cannot imagine what my mother must be feeling. She has sacrificed her son—for whom she must feel something however hard she has tried to stifle it—and now she realises that she has done it for nothing. Euphemia and she will be left with no resources and in a few months will be evicted from this house by Cousin Sybille.

I will give her one last chance.

### A ¼ past 11 o'clock.

I have only four shillings and sevenpence ha'penny. That will not carry me far.

Once I was sure my mother and sister were upstairs, I went into the parlour and felt in the dark for the work-basket which I found lying on the sopha as usual. In the hidden pocket there were a number of sovereigns and some silver and coppers. I counted it: fourteen pounds, thirteen shillings and tenpence.

I left the money there and crept up the stairs to my mother's rooms.

I tapped very softly on the door of her sitting-room and pushed it open. Empty. I did the same on the inner door and she called out to enter. She was sitting at her dressing-table brushing her hair and started when she saw me.

I put my finger to my lips to indicate that we should keep our voices low so that Euphemia would not hear.

I said: *I will be arrested tomorrow and if you don't help me, you know what will happen to me, don't you?*

She kept her head turned away.

I said: *I will be hanged.*

She turned slowly to look at me, still holding her hairbrush. In a small voice she said: *That's not true, Richard. It won't come to that.*

I said: *Of course it will come to that. You've always managed to persuade yourself of the truth of what you wish were the case but you won't be able to do it this time. The earl will not rest until the murderer of his beloved nephew is executed. All the evidence points to me.*

*They're not going to do anything to you. You've got these ideas in your head . . . You've been behaving so strangely. You've . . .*

*If you want to help me you have to tell that policeman the truth. I don't mean the whole truth. You can keep Euphemia out of it. But you must tell him everything you know about Lyddiard. He did all these things and Euphemia had no knowledge of them.*

She didn't look at me. I suppose she knows she could not incriminate Lyddiard without endangering her darling daughter. He would drag her down with him out of spite.

I said: *Mr Wilson will be here to arrest me tomorrow.*

No response.

*Very well,* I said. *In that case I have no choice but to try to cross the marsh.*

*Cross the marsh? You can't do that.* Now at last I had her attention and it gave me a sweet pain to see her so concerned. *Richard, you'll be swallowed up if you try. Have you forgotten that story of the mad bride?*

*It will bear my weight if it's frozen hard enough.*

She shook her head but did not speak. The foolish, foolish old woman. She puts me on a course that must end in my being hanged but tries to stop me drowning myself. However things turn out tonight, she will regret what she has done.

I said: *Then I must risk the marshes.*

She put her hands over her face. *I don't know how it's come to this.*

*If I reach dry land, I have a chance of evading the authorities.*

She asked in a low trembling voice: *If you do, where will you go?*

I hesitated. *I will circle round to the east and walk along the coast towards Rye and take the train from there up to London. I need money.*

*I have none to give you. A few shillings. That's all.*

*I need at least two or three pounds. Do you really not have it?*

She said: *Let me go and fetch what I can spare—ten or twelve shillings. No more than that.*

I wasn't sure I could speak. I had to swallow a few times and then I managed to say: *Don't put yourself to so much trouble, I beg you. If that's all you can offer me, then there is no more to say. We will have to see what the morning brings.*

I walked out of the room without another word or a backward look.

I was so upset that I forgot to take the long way round by the back-stairs and I passed Euphemia's door. It was open—which was rare—and I saw the dark shape of my sister's head on the pillow and I hesitated just for an instant and as I did so it seemed that she half-opened her eyes and that I saw them glittering, but the moment was too brief to be sure.


*Midnight.*

It is as I said to her. I have no choice. That anecdote I heard at the Greenacres'—the poacher caught in a trap who severed his own leg. It haunts me. The man chose unimaginable pain, possible death, and a life of incapacity in preference to waiting there like a dumb beast to be caught, charged and transported. Perhaps I'll die in the attempt, but if I do, that is better than submitting passively to my fate and dying for sure.

I will be walking out on my debts but I now see those values of honour and gentlemanliness for what they are: delusions. I blush to recall how proud I was of being a Herriard. Of having a "Lady" for a connection.

A severance. Whether I succeed or fail, I will never again see the people and places I love. What people do I love? Who loves me? Edmund who is dead and whose love was not of the kind I wanted. Betsy who believes she loves me but is not much more than a child. Can I say that my mother loves me even as she is arranging the noose about my neck? I suppose, strangely, she does. But though I am hacking her off as if she were one of my own limbs, it was she who made the first cut. She has made her choice. I can also make a choice.

They've committed a murder and now I am going to kill them. The two people whom I most love. Whom I have loved, I should say. They killed a man—Euphemia by proxy and my mother by her silence. And they have tried to kill me. I'm going to cut them out of my love and my life and that is a kind of murder. They will cease to exist as far as I am concerned.

· · ·

*1 o'clock.*

Was stuffing some bread into my knapsack—Mother's gift to me only a year ago—in the kitchen just now when Betsy loomed up out of the shadows. (I had just a candle with me.)

She saw what I was doing and said: *You're going to cross the marsh?*

I nodded: *It should bear my weight now that it's frozen.*

Her face lit up and she said: *Let me come with you.*

I said: *Out of the question. It's too dangerous.* I could see what she was going to say so I quickly added: *I can do it alone but not if I have to help another person.*

She looked so unhappy that I said: *When I am settled where I am going, I will write to you.* I saw in her face that she feared I was teasing her again. I said: *Visit Miss Bittlestone. She would like that. And I will send the letter to her to read to you. In fact, I'm sure she will teach you to read.*

Even as I spoke those words, I wondered how long it would be before this household was broken up. I'm haunted by the fear that I might have brought on Betsy the trouble that has come to Euphemia. If so, what would become of her? My mother and sister would not help her. Miss Bittlestone does not have the resources.

I said: *Betsy, the things we did. The nice things.*

She nodded with a secretive smile.

*Tell Miss Bittlestone if it turns out that there are any consequences and if I do manage to get away to somewhere safe, she can write to me and I'll send money.*

She indicated her assent. Then she said: *Look up at my window as you go and I'll leave the light burning to give you your bearings.*

She stood on tiptoe and raised her face to me and we kissed for the first time. Then she scurried into the dark.

*½ past 1 o'clock.*

By the morning I will be far from here or I will be dead. The false trail I have laid should lure my pursuers in the opposite direction and give me time to reach my destination. The two or three sovereigns my mother begrudged me but that I will take from her hiding-place, will get me to Southampton. Once there, Uncle T's letter will convey me across the Atlantic.

There is no moon tonight which means I will not be seen—though I'm sure that nobody but Betsy will be watching—but which will make it hard to pick out the safest footings. I dare not take a lantern since it might alert the policeman if he happens to look in that direction.

The tide is at half-flood now and will be at its lowest at about two hours after midnight. The crucial questions are these: Is it cold enough for the marsh to have frozen and bear my weight? And can I find my way? Apart from Betsy's dim glow, there will be no light by which to direct my course. As I found when I attempted the crossing ten days ago, there are no houses on the shore and if there are more distant ones, they will not have lights in the middle of the night. I will be like a mariner at sea with no features on the horizon or in the heavens to steer by, knowing that hidden reefs are all around me and that a false move will not be retrievable. If the marsh swallows me, so be it. Better to drown than to swing.

If all goes well I should reach Mr Boddington's house at three or four o'clock and there I will place this Journal in the hands of the sole person whose judgement and honesty I can trust and I will impress on him that it should be made public only if I am captured or an innocent person is charged. If I die this book will be lost with me and the truth will never be known. Whether I live or perish, I will be remembered as a vicious and cowardly murderer—but I do not care what others believe about me.

Whatever happens to me, I believe the guilty will escape punishment. I should say, judicial punishment, for the impulse that has driven them to this piece of wickedness will not cease to inflict pain on them.

If I make it that far, will I stand at the stern of *The Hibernian Maid* and watch England disappear? I think not. I will look into the darkness ahead of me rather than the darkness behind.

*Richard Shenstone,*
*Wednesday 13<sup>th</sup> of January, 2 o'clock in the morning.*

## ⌐ *Afterword* ⌐

Richard must have crossed the frozen marsh and left the Journal at Boddington's house or it would not have survived. After that he vanishes from the historical record. Whether he made it to Canada is unknown. If he did, he must have changed his name for I have not been able to find any trace of a "Richard Shenstone" there during the relevant period. What I have established is that nobody was ever arrested or charged with the murder of Willoughby Davenant Burgoyne. Mrs Shenstone died less than a year after these events. There is no record that Euphemia ever married and she certainly did not wed Lyddiard, who died destitute and still a bachelor only eight years later.

The last sighting I have traced of Euphemia finds her living in London at an address in Clerkenwell—then a poor district—in 1873. After that, she disappears—possibly because she married and changed her name—though I have discovered no record of that.

At some point Boddington must have collected the letters from Wilson and pasted them—except for the final one that was in the earl's possession—into the Journal. When, many years later, his firm was taken over by another, the Journal was deposited in the County

Records Office where it lay—apparently undisturbed—until I opened it two years ago.

One of the mysteries that remain is why Lyddiard did not claim the money he was entitled to under the terms of the trust set up by his father's will. If the whole point of the conspiracy was to gain the inheritance, then he must have had a strong motive.

I had been struck by something that Richard recorded the detective, Wilson, as having said. When he read out the final anonymous letter, he mentioned that he had been permitted by the earl to make a copy of only part of it and that he was not allowed to read the whole. The earl himself was the only person to have seen the full text. I wondered what there was in the letter that the earl wanted to conceal. It occurred to me that if I could find the deed of trust executed by the father of Davenant Burgoyne and Lyddiard, it might lead me to the missing letter.

After an extensive search I found the deed in the national archives at Kew, London, called the Public Records Office. As Richard had been told, under the terms of the trust, Lyddiard inherited the fortune if his half-brother died before the age of twenty-five and without an heir. But I also learned that Lyddiard had to make his claim within twelve months or the entire sum went to the earl.

The name of the solicitor who had drawn up the deed led me back to the County Records Office where, as I had hoped, the archives of his firm had been deposited. And there, carefully preserved in an envelope inside a leather portfolio, lay the taunting letter sent to Davenant Burgoyne a few hours before he was killed.

Just above the passage which Wilson had copied and read out to Richard, there was a crease. The most interesting part of the letter had been folded over—presumably by the earl when he showed it to Wilson—so that the detective could not see it. The words that his lordship had kept hidden were these in which the writer, goaded by hearing from Euphemia that Davenant Burgoyne had sneered at bastardy in his confrontation with Richard at the ball, forgot, in his anger at the slur on himself, that Richard himself was not being accused of being illegitimate:

*You throw the word bastard in my face but just because your mother was married and mine wasn't, doesn't make you any better than me. My mother entered a love-match not a contract of sale negotiated by lawyers. It was your mother that was the bought and paid for whore and not mine.*

Writing in the early hours of the morning after the ball, Lyddiard, possibly drunk and certainly excited at the imminence of the murder of his hated half-brother, had made a stupid mistake. This was the sole letter that he had written alone and, without Euphemia to rein in his anger, he had blundered into pointing the finger at himself instead of Richard. The earl must have understood that. He therefore showed Wilson enough of the letter to incriminate Richard but not the part that inculpated his nephew. He then used that piece of evidence to force Lyddiard into dropping his claim on the trust. Far from being the "decent and honourable person" Richard had taken him for, his lordship conspired to let him hang for a murder he knew he did not commit since that both averted the scandal of a nephew being tried for murder and brought him a fortune.

Other mysteries remain. Was Betsy pregnant? Did Richard send her money and even pay her passage out to join him in Canada? It seems unlikely that the answers to those questions will ever be known.

CP.

*London, 14ᵗʰ October, 2012.*

# ⊰ *Acknowledgments* ⊱

A number of people read and commented on this book at various stages of its composition and I am enormously grateful to the following: Helen Ash, Karin Badt, Linda Buckley-Archer, Emma Dixon, Chris Ellis, Lorna Gibb, John Glusman, Bill Hamilton, Jane Harris, Liz Jensen, Jacqui Lofthouse, Shira Nayman and Joanna Pocock.

# ⊰ *About the Author* ⊱

Charles Palliser has published four works of fiction, including the historical novels *The Quincunx* (1989) and *The Unburied* (1999), and has written plays for BBC Radio and the stage. Before becoming a full-time writer in 1990, he taught literature and creative writing in universities in the UK and the US. His fiction has been translated into a dozen languages. *The Quincunx* was awarded the Sue Kaufman Prize by the American Academy of Arts and Letters. With Irish and US citizenship, Palliser has lived mostly in the UK.